THE BITE THAT BINDS
The Deep In Your Veins Series

Suzanne Wright

The characters and events portrayed in this book are fictitious. Any similarity to real persons, living or dead, is coincidental and not intended by the author.

Copyright © 2012 Suzanne Wright

All rights reserved. This book or any portion thereof may not be reproduced or used in any manner whatsoever without the express written permission of the publisher except for the use of brief quotations in a book review.

ISBN-13: 978-1482515237
ISBN-10: 1482515237

For a person who always makes me smile – my brother, Steven

CHAPTER ONE

(Sam)

She was there again. She came nearly every night. I still wasn't sure whether she was a dream or a hallucination. But I knew that as soon as she crooked her finger, I'd follow her like she wanted me to. It was always the same.

It was like being in a trance, and yet not. I knew the choice to follow her was mine, but it was like there was some kind of pull that overrode my reservations. So, like I always did, I slipped out of bed and walked behind the tall, slim vampire who was clothed in only a torn emerald-green dress that matched the colour of her eyes. Her coal-black hair was so thick and long that it covered most of the pale skin of her arms. Just like always.

I followed her into the living area of my apartment where a large oval-shaped mirror stood, totally out of place. The vampire turned and smiled; it was reassuring and friendly, but I wasn't reassured at all. Then she lifted her arm and pointed at the mirror. It wasn't my own reflection staring back at me. Instead, it was like I was looking through a large doorway. There was a derelict one-floored house that seemed to be in the middle of no-man's land.

The vampire stepped through the doorway and gestured for me to follow her. Not bloody likely. Every instinct I had in this dream or hallucination or whatever it was screamed, 'No!'

So I did the same thing I always did; I shook my head and mouthed 'no'. Again the vampire indicated for me to follow her, but again I shook my head. Her smile fell as anxiety and dejection filled her eyes. The doorway closed behind her, and that was when it ended.

"Sam," a familiar voice murmured as fingers combed through my hair. His spicy, masculine scent swirled around me, stirring my senses. But, then, everything about Jared had each of my senses on high alert. And the cocky sod knew it. "Sam, baby, wake up."

Nah. Although the mattress felt a little harder than usual, I was too tired to care. I shoved at the firm, hard chest I could sense hovering over me, but Jared only chuckled.

"You did it again."

"Did what?" I mumbled.

"You went for a stroll in your sleep and ended up on your living room carpet."

Peeking through one eye, I saw that he was right. Groaning, I allowed my eyelid to drift shut again. Apparently tired of waiting for me to move, he scooped me up and arranged me so that I was straddling his lap on the floor. "I dreamed about her again," I explained drowsily as I rested my head on his shoulder.

He sighed. "You know, I think we should arrange a meeting with Antonio so we can talk to him about this."

"It was just a dream. I don't think that warrants a visit to the Grand High Master Vampire." In truth, I wasn't as unworried as I sounded.

"Almost every night over the past two weeks, I've woken up to find that I'm alone in bed. What if it wasn't a dream and you weren't sleepwalking at all? What if it would have been possible for you to follow her through that door, or whatever it was?"

I'd wondered about those things as well.

"I don't want to take the chance that one night you do as she asks, and I wake up to find that you're gone. You need to talk to Antonio." He lifted my head to seize my gaze with those hazel eyes that had more of an effect on me than I cared to admit. It was like they were designed to snatch and trap a person's attention – they certainly seemed to have that effect on the females around here. The effect wasn't lessened by the red tinges to his irises that marked him as a Pagori vampire and glowed whenever he was thirsty, angry, or horny.

I didn't envy Jared being a Pagori, despite that that breed of vampire was the most powerful of the three and had incredible strength and speed as that strength came with a price – their bloodlust was just as strong.

The bloodlust wasn't so bad for the hypnotically beautiful Keja vampires. All vampires had a preternatural allure, but a Keja's allure was enchanting and bewitching. The breed was identifiable by the fact that they had fangs and also amber tinges to the irises. Like with Pagoris, the tinges glowed if the Keja was angry, thirsty, or horny.

Sventé vampires, like myself, didn't have this characteristic, which I was quite happy about – I liked my irises just as they were thank you very much. But although Sventés were stronger and faster than humans, we were weaker than the other two breeds of vampire. We did have some strong points; not only did we have the agility of jungle cats, but our bloodlust wasn't overpowering – enabling us to walk among humans without losing control and leaping on one. Having a manageable bloodlust, however, meant that the other two breeds considered Sventés to be very tame and human-like and, therefore, inferior. Snort.

Unfortunately, Jared had once been one of those prejudiced vampires. When I'd first arrived at The Hollow from London to partake in the try-outs for a place in the legion – Antonio's personal army – Jared had thought the idea was absolutely ridiculous. It hadn't mattered that I was unique in being a Feeder: a vampire gifted with the ability to absorb and manipulate the energy around them. Nor had he been impressed by my perfect control of this overwhelming gift that should technically only be a Pagori power. He, like many others, had been too hung up on the fact that I was not only a Sventé, but female.

As such, it hadn't helped my cause that Jared was one of the assessors during the try-outs. He had denied me a place in the new squad, despite that I'd earned one. But that attitude had kind of backfired when Antonio then made me Jared's co-commander. Ha. It had been a while before Jared accepted me as his co-commander, but now the arrogance and narrow-mindedness that had created his prejudices was gone.

Not that Jared had had a personality transplant or had switched from alpha to beta. No, he was still assertive, imposing, and demanding – and could even be cocky and irritating, for that matter.

But the narrow-mindedness that had once acted as a huge barrier between us was no longer there.

He wasn't a chocolate and flowers person, wasn't the type to spout pretty words or shower a girl with compliments. In fact, he could probably be described as a little emotionally awkward. He very rarely shared those three important little words, but he was also attentive on the most intense level. When I needed him, he was there. When I wanted his attention, he gave it. When I had a problem, he tried to fix it – even when I didn't want him to.

It was strange to have someone who I knew I could totally rely on. I'd never had that before, didn't want to lose it; didn't want to lose this person who I had come to love and had every intention of Binding with in just nine evenings' time.

Imagine my surprise when I discovered that a Binding was a week-long event that culminated in a wedding-type ceremony. The guests would all arrive in two evenings' time, and entertainment would be provided each and every night as part of the celebrations.

Taking me from my thoughts, Jared gently mashed his mouth with mine. "Want me to help you pack your stuff so we can move it all into my apartment after the meeting?" He narrowed his eyes when I didn't speak, scrutinising my face in a way that made me squirm. It would be fair to say that I'd been seriously procrastinating taking this big step. "If you expect me to live apart from you, Sam, get that idea right out of your head. Is it that you're having second thoughts about the Binding? You have to be honest with me. How am I supposed to tie you to the bed and make you come until you change your mind if I don't even know you're having second thoughts?"

I smiled – he wasn't kidding. Lightly running my fingers through his short, chestnut hair, I told him, "It's not that."

"Then, what?"

Finding it hard to explain, I released a frustrated sigh. "For so long, I was under the control of Victor" – my deceased Sire and a prick of epic proportions – "and had my every move watched. The weird bastard even chose my clothes; it was part of the control. I didn't have anything that was mine. So getting a position in the legion…it was the most amazing feeling. Suddenly I had a title, a job, an apartment – things that were mine, and mine alone. So this place is more than just a home to me, and I guess I feel a bit possessive of it since I only got it a few months ago."

A short pause. "That's it?"

"Yes." Even if it didn't make an awful lot of sense.

He shrugged carelessly. "Fine. I'll move in here."

I gaped rather unattractively. "You're blowing smoke up my arse, right?"

He nipped my lip before sucking it into his mouth. "No."

"You'd really give up your big, swanky apartment?"

"If you don't want to move in there with me, yes."

"But you love your apartment."

"I love you more, dumb ass."

Although he didn't say the words often, there was no doubting that he meant them. It was in his eyes, his tone, his expression. "Thank you for understanding."

He snorted. "Baby, I'm not that selfless. Maybe you haven't considered that once we're living together, I have your body available to me whenever I want it."

His boyish smile had me smiling back. If I hadn't seen him fighting during the attack on The Hollow, I would never have believed there was a ruthless, merciless streak to his nature. I'd always thought I'd seen him at his harshest. The first day we'd met, when we duelled during the try-outs, he'd aimed some big bad electric bolts at me. It hadn't been until the attack, when I saw *exactly* what he could do with his gift of electrokinesis, I realised just how much he had held back from me.

That night, I'd learned just why so many vampires feared him. He'd killed without blinking, had been almost like a machine. Not once had he hesitated, faltered, or let any of his morals interfere. Not many people could block out their conscience like that. As someone who was still trying to perfect that technique, I was very much aware of how difficult it was.

Touched that he wasn't pushing me to give up my apartment, even though he probably didn't get why it was a big deal, I gave him a kiss filled with gratitude.

"If you *really* want to thank me, you can talk to Antonio about these weird dreams. Please, baby. For me." He gripped my hips and pulled me tighter to him, making sure I could feel the proof of his arousal. Like I already hadn't! He seemed to be almost permanently hard, but then, Jared was a randy bastard. Or maybe he just had a gratification disorder. In any case, I saw no need to complain.

"What's in it for me?"

His devilish smirk surfaced. "The same thing that's always in you. Exactly where it belongs."

I sighed at my personal assistant, who had fast become my best friend. His petulant, sulky expression shouldn't have made him seem more adorable than he already was. Even the indignant look he shot over his glasses made me smile. Watching him type crazily on his work computer, I realised I'd been dismissed.

Perching myself on the edge of his desk, I said, "Fletcher, don't be an arse. It's just that I don't want to look like a slut at my own Binding ceremony. Is that really that much to ask? If I had my way, it would be a small, simple, private event."

Fletcher – a fellow Brit – was fabulous to go shopping with, but he was never happy unless my cleavage was on show and every curve of my body was accentuated. Not because he was a perv. Being gay, the last thing he was interested in was my body. He was simply determined to get rid of my tomboy look but had taken it to the extreme. Having just heard that he had been secretly working with the designer of my ceremony dress, I had every intention of going to choose something 'off the rack' – to his utter horror.

"Sam, luv, you're going to Bind with the Heir of the Grand High Master Vampire. It isn't possible to keep something like that private and simple."

He was right, the smart little shit.

"It's a good thing that Antonio and his personal assistants are taking care of the plans and not you or there'd be about five people gathered in a garden tent."

He was probably right about that as well. Actually, I was glad that I didn't have to worry about things like colour schemes, table centrepieces, and chair covers. I'd be hopeless at it anyway.

"Come on, just trust me on this," he implored, giving me a pitiful look that was designed to eat at my defences. "I promise the dress is fabulous. And not to be a drama queen or anything, but I think I'll choke on tears if you reject it again when you haven't even seen it. I have a very fragile ego."

"Emotional blackmail? Oh now that's low."

"I prefer to think of it as a request said with love." Pouting, he gave me another pitiful look.

Rolling my eyes, I sighed. "Fine." It was hard to refuse that cute little face – especially when he had the Keja hypnotic allure. The breath whooshed out of me as, in vampire speed, he was out of his chair and wrapped around me, sniffling.

"I'm getting all emotional here." Pulling away, he fanned his face as if it would hold back the tears. "You won't regret it, luv, I swear it."

"I'm warning you now that if it turns out the dress is slutty, I'll slash up all your designer clothes."

He gasped. "You wouldn't."

"Oh I would."

"Now that's just bitchy."

I gave him a bright, totally unapologetic smile.

Returning to his seat, he asked, "So…have you decided what to give Jared as a Binding gift yet?"

I groaned. "Don't remind me." The tricky thing was that it was tradition for the couple to *make* each other's gift. I could just about make a sandwich. Sure, I'd thought about cheating, but then I'd feel like shit when Jared gave me his hand-made gift.

"You'll think of something."

I wouldn't bet on that.

"I'm so excited about all the entertainment for this week. I've seen the schedule, and it's fab. Are you looking forward to the ceremony?"

"Yes. And no. I mean, I'm happy that I'm Binding with Jared, but I'm not looking forward to being the centre of attention. I'm not impressed that I have to spend a week away from training the squad just to have time with snooty Master Vampires."

"They're going to test you, luv," he warned in a grave yet sympathetic voice. "You know that, right?"

"I know. Jared told me." It hadn't exactly come as a surprise. They would want to know that when the day came that I ruled alongside Jared, I was capable of protecting them, and that I was someone they could trust, respect, and follow. "I'll try not to kill any of them."

Fletcher cocked his head. "It's not just that that's bothering you though, is it?"

Again, he was right. It wasn't that I had my doubts about Binding with Jared. It was that I couldn't help worrying that he might back out. I had a number of reasons to worry about that. None of which I could talk about right then, because I felt that familiar *pull*. I felt *him*.

Turning, I spotted Jared talking to one of the other commanders further along the corridor, just as I'd known I would. As if he felt that same pull, his gaze found mine and he flashed me one of his devilish smirks.

"Why does he only smile at *you* like that?" griped Fletcher. "Then again, if he did smile at me like that, I'd probably blush like a virgin. Don't you just love his Californian accent – especially when it's spoken in that deep voice of his?"

I did actually, and as he liked my British accent, it worked out nicely.

Having exchanged a few more words with the commander, Jared was then striding purposely toward me. He walked like a man who knew what he wanted and would make no bones about trying to get it. He owned every step, filled the space around him with just his air of self-assurance.

"That bloke is a walking, talking advertisement for sex," commented Fletcher, sighing in appreciation. I had to agree. Jared's tall, perfectly defined body promised gratification. And delivered it.

Finally up close, he snaked his arms around my waist and dabbed a lingering kiss on my mouth. "Hey baby, I spoke to Antonio on my cell. Apparently, he was going to call me and arrange for me to meet with him, so I told him I'd be bringing you along." Most likely in response to my sigh, he gave me a pointed look. "You promised me you'd talk to him."

"And I will."

"Then let's go." I gasped when he lightly bit my earlobe before whispering, "If we didn't have this meeting, I'd drag you into our office and fuck you on my desk."

"You've done that twice already this week."

"Never gets old."

Fletcher was tidying the papers on his desk, *totally* listening to every word.

"Want to go swimming later? I have this fantasy of fucking you in the pool."

It was kind of intriguing, but I never ever gave Jared a 'yes'. Teasing him was too much fun. "Maybe."

Shaking his head at my teasing, he gave me another lingering kiss before simply nodding at our personal assistant and teleporting us to Antonio's mansion – the main building of The Hollow. Situated on an off-the-map Caribbean island, The Hollow was much like a gated community, and was surrounded by tropical rainforests. Inside were stores, bars, a club, and plenty of housing for all those vampires and humans who lived there. In the centre was a man-made beach for the residents to use, but there was a private beach for Antonio, his staff, and the legion to use. I most liked the mansion's private pool which was shaped like a bat with outstretched wings.

As usual, the meeting was taking place in one of Antonio's conference rooms. The only people seated at the long table were Antonio, his Advisor Luther, and his tracker Sebastian.

"Ah...Sam, Jared," said Antonio with a smile. His personal guards stood behind him as usual, while his two pit-bulls flanked him. "Come sit down." Before meeting him, I had expected him to have a very imposing, suffocating presence. But there was something very reassuring about this particular Keja vampire.

Having sat down and exchanged smiles and nods with everyone – and having given the dogs a brief stroke – I raised a brow at Antonio. "Are we early or is this supposed to be a private meeting?"

"Private. It is not work-related. I have some news for you, Jared." Antonio looked both sympathetic and hesitant. "Your mother...she passed away just last night. I believe the funeral will be taking place in a few days if you wish to make a discreet appearance and—"

"No."

The one word response took me totally by surprise. Not simply because he didn't wish to attend his mother's funeral, but because it had been so hard and resolute.

Antonio released a long breath. "I thought not. However, I felt it better to give you the option."

"How do you know she died?" I asked, suspecting Antonio had kept tabs on the woman but not understanding why he'd bother.

"As you know, a person must disappear when they have been Turned. Their family often reports them missing, and there are investigations and searches. In such cases, it is imperative to monitor the families and ensure that the investigations fail. The secret of our existence has to be preserved."

"Jared's parents didn't stop searching for him and Evan" – Jared's twin brother who was also a vampire – "all these years?" I frowned at the look he gave Jared. Again, it was sympathetic. Why be sympathetic about the idea that his parents hadn't given up on finding him and his brother?

Sebastian's tone was cautious. "You realise that Evan's response may be different from yours?"

Jared shrugged at the tall Keja who, as always, was dressed in an Armani suit. "His decision is his own. I won't interfere with his, just as he won't interfere with mine."

I'd never heard him sound so cold and hard before. "Jared, she was your mum, she—"

"She was Evan's mom," he corrected, "but never mine." And then the shutters went down. Apparently that was the only answer I was getting.

When it came to questions, Jared was seriously the artful dodger. I'd quickly come to realise that he was very guarded. Whenever I asked about his past, he would instantly shut down. It wasn't just his human years that he was vague about; it was his years as a vampire before joining Antonio's legion. Whenever I pressed him, he turned into an arsehole, literally emitting 'fuck off' signals, but I knew it was just to distract me from my questions.

It didn't seem that he was hiding deep, dark secrets. No. It was more like he didn't want to think on life before The Hollow. When we had Merged with each other during the attack, I had automatically had access to his thoughts, feelings, and memories. I'd known he was worried for me, had known that he loved me, but as for his memories…There had been nothing from before The Hollow. Nothing that he cared to remember, anyway.

His seeming inability to open up to me was one of the reasons why I worried that he'd find himself backing out of the Binding. Not that I thought he didn't care for me as much as he claimed to. There was no way I could doubt the extent of what he felt; it was all in his body language, in his vocal tone, the constant touches, the heated glances. And he had this way of looking at me like nothing else mattered. It was all extremely intimate. Powerful. Even disorientating at times.

The problem was that Binding didn't allow for mental barriers. It wasn't like marriage – the connection wasn't something that a person could later free themselves from. Even if the couple came to hate each other, the psychic link could only be broken by death. As such, there wasn't space for doubts. But if Jared feared being open with me, if he felt this need to hold back, there was every chance that he would back out of the Binding.

Maybe it would make sense for me to cut and run, but this was someone I cared about. If he was deeply scarred by something, I wanted to know what it was. He'd helped me with my scars. He had made me realise that my past as an unwilling consort for my Sire didn't make me dirty or unworthy; it didn't mean that I couldn't have a normal, sexual, and even loving relationship with someone else. With him. I wanted to do the same for him. "Jared—"

Ignoring me, he spoke to Antonio. "There's something that Sam needs to talk with you about." He turned to me then. "Tell him."

I narrowed my eyes at his swift change of topic. *We'll continue this conversation later*, I told him telepathically. I wasn't telepathic myself, but as Jared was, he could hear any thought that was directed at him by anyone. His nod was reluctant.

"I've been having these dreams," I told Antonio. "I don't think they're anything to fret about, but they're bugging me."

The powerful vampire cocked his head, making his thick, black hair drape over his shoulder like a curtain. "What kind of dreams?"

"It's always the same. I wake up, and there's this female vampire there who wants me to follow her into the living area. In there is a huge mirror, which turns out to be a doorway. Through it, I can see a bungalow situated in the middle of nowhere. She steps through the doorway and wants me to go with her, but I never go."

"*And* you sleepwalk to the living area every time you have the dream," said Jared.

"So you may not be dreaming at all," mused Sebastian, pursing his full lips.

Jared nodded. "Exactly."

Antonio exchanged a look with Luther before asking me, "Does she speak to you?"

"No."

Luther, who looked like he'd just stepped out of a J. R. R. Tolkien book with his long white hair and beard, leaned toward me. "What breed of vampire is she?"

"She doesn't have a red or amber tinge to her irises, so I'm guessing she's a Sventé. Wait, why are we talking about her like she's real?"

"Because it's possible that she is." Luther rested his joined hands on the table. "There is a Sventé gift that allows a vampire to invade dreams, but they can only enter the dreams of other Sventés. Dreamwalkers, they're called."

"And you think she might be a dreamwalker?" At his nod, I asked, "Why would she come to me?"

"If she needs help — which is my guess — she will try to contact someone who can aid her. As I said, dreamwalkers can only invade the dreams of other Sventés. You're the most powerful Sventé there is, and you are closely linked with Antonio. It makes perfect sense for her to reach out to you."

"Or," drawled Jared, "this could be a trap." Luther tilted his head, allowing that.

"But it could be someone who truly needs help. I can't ignore that," I told Jared. I sensed his anger before he even spoke.

"Don't think you're going there, Sam. Not a chance will I let you take that kind of risk."

"*Let?* Jared, don't be a wanker."

"I'm serious. If we find this place, we could be walking right into a fucking trap."

"And that's why we won't go alone. We'll take the squad."

Antonio quickly interjected, "Jared, I realise that Sam's safety is important to you, but you need to channel that protectiveness into watching out for her while on assignments."

I was expecting an outburst, but what Jared did was shrug. A shaft of smugness shot through him. It wasn't until he spoke that I understood why.

"The probability of us finding this place is second to none anyway. It could be anywhere."

"Actually, I may be able to assist with that." Luther's words naturally didn't go down well with Jared. "Sam, if you were to hold my hand while replaying the dream through your mind, there's a possibility that I can help."

I shrugged. "Sure."

"Sam," Jared bit out.

The overprotectiveness was unbelievably annoying, but sensing his anxiety and concern made some of my anger fizzle away. Holding his gaze, I again spoke to him telepathically. *You know you wouldn't stay behind if I asked you to, just as I can't, no matter how much this pisses you off. That's not who we are.*

You don't get what it would do to me if something happened to you.

I do, because I get just as worried that something will happen to you. So stop with the bloody sulking.

Leaning across the table, I took the hand that Luther offered. "All I need to do is close my eyes and recall the dream?"

"Yes, let it play out in your mind." So I did. A short moment after he had released my hand, his eyes flew open. "I need a pen and some paper."

In vampire speed, Sebastian disappeared out of the room, only to return with both.

After scribbling down some numbers, Luther slid the sheet of paper to Jared. "Coordinates. If you teleport there, you will find the building from Sam's dream."

Jared folded the sheet of paper and tucked it into his pocket. He then went to stand, but Antonio's words stayed him.

"There's something else, Jared." His tone made it clear that this 'something else' wasn't good.

Jared stiffened. "What?"

Again, Antonio's expression was sympathetic. "I had no choice but to grant her request. Understand that." There was disdain in the way he spoke of this woman, and that was seemingly all it took for Jared to know who Antonio was referring to. I felt his surprise quickly give way to anger.

Jared's words were spoken through clenched teeth. "I don't want her here."

Although I had no idea who this woman was, I strangely felt a prick of jealousy. "Who are you talking about?"

"Jared, you must have anticipated that she would want to meet Sam." Antonio didn't look pleased about that. "Given who you are, there was no way that she would not hear about the upcoming ceremony."

"She's not going anywhere near Sam," Jared stated firmly. "You contact her, and you tell her that she isn't to come here."

Starting to feel a little unsettled, I pressed, "*Who* is not going anywhere near me?"

"I don't think she will harm Sam," said Sebastian reassuringly.

"I don't care." Jared set his jaw. "She's not getting near her."

That was it. I'd had enough. Sucking the energy around me into my palms, I released an air blast harsh enough to have everyone's hair rising. "Who the fuck is 'she'?"

Jared rubbed my nape soothingly, but I wasn't soothed. "Magda is" – a heavy sigh – "the woman who Turned Evan and me."

"A *woman* Turned you?" This time, jealousy bolted through me.

Sensing it, he gently squeezed my nape. *Hey, you don't have to feel even the slightest bit jealous. I fucking hate her.*

Maybe that should have made me feel better, but it didn't. To me, 'hate' wasn't a measure of dislike, it was an emotion. A very strong emotion. To feel such a strong emotion for someone, they had to have affected you in a very deep sense. I had to wonder if she was more than just the woman who Turned him, if she was an ex-partner – maybe even the reason why he was so guarded.

Evan had once told me that Jared had never really liked a woman in more than a physical sense before me, but that didn't mean he hadn't. No matter how close you were to a person, there would always be something about them that you didn't know. There was really no 'knowing' anyone. Well, in my experience anyway.

Sebastian sighed, flicking his peppery black hair from his face. "She heard the announcement that the Heir has claimed someone. I think we can safely guess that she has not taken it well, though she says she simply wants to meet the woman you have claimed and to…"

"And to what?" I prodded, though I was pretty sure what the answer would be.

"To be present at your Binding ceremony, as is her right as the vampire who Turned Jared."

"And it's such a bad thing that she's present because…?" No one answered me.

"She *won't* be present." Jared's nostrils flared. "Fuck her rights."

"Why do you hate her so much?" He didn't answer me. So I kicked him under the table. "At least tell me why you're so determined to keep us apart?"

His eyes were sad. "Because she likes to hurt people who mean something to me." Again, the shutters went down.

Oh he was a pain in my arse.

Jared stood, sighing. "I guess it's time we go get the squad. First, I need to call Evan."

I could guess why: he wanted to warn his brother about Magda. As he went to the corner of the room to take the call, I arched a brow at Antonio. "If he's not going to tell me anything about this woman, can you at least shine a light on things?"

Antonio shifted uncomfortably in his seat. "I would prefer not to involve myself in what may become a domestic argument."

When I switched my attention to Sebastian and Luther, they both stood so sharply that the table shook and the pen came rolling down to me; I knew they were intending to scarper before I had the chance to question them. Cowards. Huffing at Luther, I handed him the pen. It was as he touched it that he gasped and his entire body tensed. The surprise in his eyes was quickly replaced with worry and unease.

"What?" I demanded, though my voice was shaky. He simply shook his head. "I know you had a vision, and it obviously spooked the hell out of you. What did you see?"

His smile was forced. "Yes, it was a vision, but it did not concern you."

"Bollocks." I leaned across the table. "You listen to me, Gandalf. I'm about to walk into what could potentially be a trap. If there's something to worry about, I want to know what the bloody hell it is."

"I'm sorry, Sam, but I fear that this is a path you must take."

"What's wrong?" asked Jared as he returned to my side.

I pointed at Luther. "It's him over there doing his 'riddle me this, riddle me that'." And right then, I didn't have the patience for it. "Let's go before I set his beard on fire."

Narrowing his eyes at the three Kejas opposite us, Jared linked his fingers with mine. There was a queasy sensation in my stomach, and then we were in the living area of his rather impressive apartment. He pulled me flush against him, locking his arms around me. "I'll go pack my stuff so we can drop it at your place before we leave. Are you sure I can't talk you out of going to check out the bungalow?"

"Nope."

Resting his forehead against mine, he exhaled heavily. "Just promise me one thing. Promise me you won't Merge with anyone."

Although vampires each only had one gift, Bestowers like Antonio could impart power to another vampire and, thus, allow them to develop another gift. He had done this for me once as a reward, and had done it twice for Jared. "It's one of my gifts—"

"And it's a dangerous one. The last time you used it, you nearly got too overwhelmed by power, and I almost lost you."

I grabbed the lapels of his matrix-style leather jacket. "Look, it's sweet that you're so determined to protect me, but I'm a big girl."

"Yes, and you're *my* girl. I want you safe and here with me. Promise me."

"I only use it as a last resort."

"*Sam.*"

A sly thought came to me. Ordinarily, I wasn't a sly person, but when needs must…"I'll make you a deal. You tell me about Magda, and I'll promise not to use that gift at any time tonight."

He narrowed his eyes. "That's a shitty deal."

"It's the only one you're getting. You close yourself off from me all the time, Jared. It's not fair. I trusted you with all my shit. Now I'm asking you to do the same."

After a long moment, he nodded and took a seat on his corner leather sofa. It was a minute or so before he finally spoke. "Evan and I already knew about vampires before we Turned. One night on our way home, we were walking down an alley, and we saw this guy chomping on some girl's neck. He heard us coming and looked up; his irises were glowing amber, and his fangs were showing.

"He told us to turn around, to forget what we had seen and take another route to where we were going. I could feel the power, the *push* in his voice, but…I don't know, it just didn't work. The same went for Evan. I know *now* that he'd obviously had the gift to hypnotise, but for whatever reason it hadn't worked on us. The vampire realised and started laughing. He seemed fascinated with us, and we actually became friends."

Sensing his reluctance to go on, I perched myself on the sofa beside him and nudged his knee with mine. He gave me a put-out look but continued.

"Evan and I went to a club with him one night. It was a place where a lot of vampires went. Magda was there. I'll be honest, I was a little mesmerised by her. It was mostly because of the natural glamour that comes with vampirism, I guess" – Hmm, not feeling good about Magda right now – "but it was never more than sex to me. She told me she loved me, but I hadn't felt the same. I'd *thought* I cared about her at the time, though. In truth, I'd really just been kind of…I don't know…a little infatuated with her."

Did that make me feel a little better? No. Although I'd never been a possessive person, I could be quite possessive with Jared and I even had my jealous moments. This was to be one of those moments.

"She said that she wanted to Turn me. I probably should have considered it. My job bored the hell out of me and it didn't exactly pay well. My apartment was a shithole. I owed a serious amount of money to some seriously bad people. But there was Evan. I wouldn't have left him like that. And, although I'd thought I cared about her, I still hadn't wanted to give up my life for her. So I said no. She looked pissed, and I thought she was going to Turn me anyway. Instead, she told me to spend the next day thinking it over. But I hadn't changed my mind, so I didn't go back to the club that night.

"It was later that same night that I got a call from Evan's cell. Only it wasn't Evan. It was Magda. She'd Turned him, Sam. She'd Turned Evan against his will. She said she'd done it for me, so that I'd have Evan when she Turned me. But she hadn't done it for me, she hadn't loved me. She'd done it out of spite because I hadn't gone back to her – I knew it, she knew it. But how could I have said no? It was my fault that she'd done it to him, how could I have left him alone to live that life? So I let her Turn me. She could have just Turned me and left Evan out of it, but she hadn't because she'd wanted to hurt me. She used Evan to do it."

Feeling his pain and guilt, I straddled him and cradled his face with my hands. "Evan would never blame you." The brothers were too close for that.

His arms immediately went around me. "I know. But the dumb fucker should. Instead, he jokes how weird it is that in both our human life and vampire life we were born on the same day, yet both times he was born an hour before me."

That was typical of Evan; he could find humour in just about any situation. "What happened after that?"

"Once he and I had a good hold on our bloodlust, we left her."

"Has she ever been in touch?" I couldn't envision her letting him leave without a struggle.

"In the beginning, she tried to track me down. But when none of the vampires she sent ever returned to her – courtesy of my gift of electrokinesis – she stopped sending any. So I haven't seen her since we left, and that was the way I'd wanted it to stay."

"I guess Sebastian's right. She won't be happy about us."

"No, she won't. And I don't want her near you."

"You don't need to protect me from her."

He started playing with my hair, stroking it and combing his fingers through it. "I know that. You're stronger and more powerful than she is. But I also know she'll try to play mind games with you. It's what she does. And she's good at it, because her gift is to sense a person's fears and insecurities. Underneath your bitchy streak, you have the biggest heart, and I don't want her playing with it. She's toxic, Sam."

Well *now* I understood why he was so concerned. Admittedly, he had good reason to be. I'd met someone with that gift once. In a bitch's hands, it could be very destructive.

"She'll feed your insecurities, and she'll do her best to come between us. I don't want that."

"I get why you want to keep her away from me and I grant you that, yes, her gift is notable. But so are both of mine. If she tries to play with me, I'll make sure she's sorry she did it."

He grinned. "So bloodthirsty…I love it. And yes, you can take care of yourself." His smile turned apologetic – *falsely* apologetic. "Having said that…Although you don't *need* me to protect you from her or anyone else, I'll always do it. I'll kill anyone who tries to hurt you. Make your peace with it."

Stubborn sod. But I was more stubborn, which was why I wasn't willing to drop my earlier question. Softly, I coaxed, "Tell me why you don't want to go to your mother's funeral."

Instantly, his entire body stiffened. "I just don't."

"You must have a reason."

He shrugged. "It's not important. She's not important. You are." He brushed his lips against mine. "I love your mouth."

"Jared."

He exhaled a long, heavy, tired sigh. "Why do you want to hear about it?"

"Why don't you want to tell me about it?"

Another sigh. He lifted me from his lap and placed me on my feet. When he was upright, he stepped away, releasing me completely. Just like that, I felt cold. Not simply because his body heat was gone, but because I literally felt frozen out. "We'll talk about it another time. Right now, we have other things to concentrate on."

Although I wasn't satisfied with that response, I said nothing as he headed for his bedroom to begin packing his things. One thing I could be sure of was that his relationship with his mother had been somewhat strained, but that didn't mean that her death was necessarily good news. And if he *did* find it good news, he'd undoubtedly feel guilty about it – that was the way Jared's mind worked. The last thing I wanted was him hurting, especially during the week of our Binding.

But I'd noticed the determined set to his jaw; it wouldn't matter how much I pressed him right now, I wouldn't get any answers. Fine. If he needed to think that I was going to drop it, then I'd let him think that. I'd lull him into a false sense of security where he thought question time was over, and then I'd probe again when his guard was back down.

Maybe that was a little ruthless, but Jared could be his own worst enemy sometimes. He needed to talk, and maybe even vent. So that was exactly what I'd make him do.

And he thought trying to freeze me out would actually work? I almost felt sorry for the daft sod.

CHAPTER TWO

(Jared)

Studying the abandoned bungalow – which happened to be in Ohio – I had the strongest urge to hoist Sam over my shoulder and teleport her back to The Hollow...but then she'd probably whip the fuck out of me. And not in a hot, dominatrix kind of way. That was something I knew from prior experience. She especially liked to whip my earlobes when I upset her. That hurt like a motherfucker.

With Sam being so feisty, I'd been expecting her to be pretty pissed at me for repeatedly dodging her questions. But she wasn't. Or, at least, it seemed like she wasn't. There had been no insults, no abruptness, no silent treatment – nothing. I'd even half expected her to say I couldn't move into her apartment, purely to make a point of just how pissed she was. But she hadn't.

What she *did* do – and was still doing even now – was watch me in a way that fucking freaked me out. Her expression was patient, expectant, and intense; like a predator waiting for just the right moment to pounce on its prey. She was sneaky like that.

I kind of liked the sneakiness, though. On anyone else, I wouldn't. But Sam never behaved sneakily in a malignant or spiteful way. Oh she could be merciless at times, but never malicious in any sense of the word. One of the things I couldn't help but love about her was that you always knew where you stood with her. There were no games, no lies, and no passive aggressive behaviours. She was straight, and blunt, and real.

It hadn't been until Sam that I realised I'd been kind of lonely, hiding behind an inflated ego that hadn't really been all that inflated. Well of course I'd been lonely – what else was going to happen if you avoided forming any type of connection with another person?

It was bad enough that I had a blood-link to Magda. That damn link meant that I could never really escape her unless I bonded with another vampire, replacing the link with another. But claiming a woman would have meant forming another connection, and until Sam, I hadn't even considered it. But, then, there had never been anyone like her in my life before. And she was staying in it.

In the beginning, I had feared what I felt for her, feared the strength and intensity of it. But not anymore, because I knew without a doubt that if I ran from this connection, I'd never find anything like it again, I'd never find anyone like *her* again. That wouldn't have meant I had to spend my life alone – I could still have had a relationship with a person who didn't have what amounted to power over me. But honestly, what was the point of giving your life to someone if they didn't feel essential to you, if they didn't feel part of you?

That was what she was to me – essential, necessary, vital…which was why I didn't want her in potential danger. In truth, my instincts told me that this wasn't a trap, but when it came to Sam's safety, I didn't want to risk it. Unfortunately I didn't have a choice in the matter, because the stubborn bitch had refused to remain behind. What I'd never tell her was that, although it pissed me off when she disregarded me like that, I perversely liked that she didn't always give me my own way. I'd always liked that about her.

The fact was that since becoming Heir, everything had come easy to me. But Sam had never done what the other women did; she hadn't been wowed by my position, she hadn't thrown herself at me so she could say she'd slept with 'the Heir', and she hadn't blindly obeyed me. Instead, she'd been patronising and disrespectful, and God help me, I'd found it sexy as hell.

Of course, I'd have wanted her regardless. She intrigued me on every level; had wriggled through my mental walls without either of us even knowing. She also didn't take any of my shit, which was why she was here with me and the squad, scoping out this damn place, instead of safe at home.

"I know this probably won't make you feel any less irritated," began Chico, who was squatted beside me in the thin forest that bordered the building, "but I don't get the feeling that this is a trap. Still, it's bothering me that there are only two guards. Making a place look easy to infiltrate is one of the oldest tricks in the book." As he always did when in deep thought, he started stroking his Johnny

Depp style moustache and goatee. I noticed that he was repeatedly clenching his free hand, and guessed that he was most likely eager to use his gift and emit some poisonous thorns from his palm.

If it *was* a trap, we'd soon find out. Denny, as one of his animal-mimic abilities, was able to make his body go soft as liquid much like a sea cucumber. Stuart, as a Shredder, was able to explode into molecules and travel in that form. This made both squad members excellent spies, and gave us a huge advantage at times like this. "We'll know more when Stuart, Denny, and Damien get back." Well, technically Damien *was* with us – in body, anyway. His astral self, however, had gone for a wander.

"I know it's not exactly strange for vampires to want privacy, but this is isolated even for them," observed Salem.

Chico nodded. "Unless they're happy to survive on the blood of each other and the local wildlife, they must have to travel miles before reaching any humans."

"In my experience, the usual reason for someone to isolate themselves so thoroughly is that they have something to hide." Sam growled as she elbowed Salem. "For God's sake, will you keep bloody still."

Salem just grinned. Much like David, he had an inability to keep still at times like this – like a boxer loosening up before a fight, he'd roll his shoulders and cock his head this way and that way. While with David it was nervousness, it was anticipation and excitement with Salem. As such, the gift of having a psychic punch that could knock a person into unconsciousness suited Salem just fine.

One might think that David was nervous of the situation. In actuality, the youngest of the squad was actually nervous of his gift. The ability to produce a psionic boom that caused extreme pressure on the skull, completely overwhelming the brain and leading to a temporary coma, was undoubtedly a weighty one to have. If the blast was strong enough, it could even cause death. Sam's coaching had helped him dramatically, but he still feared accidentally harming or killing one of his fellow squad members.

"Hey, here comes Stu and Den," announced Max quietly, as he hopped down from a tree. I frowned at the flirty fucker who, as usual, sat too close to Sam for my liking. While once-upon-a-time he did it because he thought he had a chance with her, now he just did it to piss me off. It worked. If he wasn't such an asset to the squad in that he had the gift of sensory paralysis, I might have transferred him to another squad. Actually no, I couldn't have. Sam was protective of them all and would never have allowed it. She was good at getting her own way.

A trail of molecules and a small puddle of mush suddenly approached where we were hiding. Seconds later, the molecules reformed into Stuart, and the mush was once again Denny.

"I've done a lap of the perimeter of the forest," Denny informed us. "There's no one around other than us."

I nodded. "Okay, what about inside?"

"The inside isn't exactly well kept, but it's liveable." Stuart flicked his shoulder-length blond curls from his face. "There are four vampires; one female, and three males. They're not alert. Two are lounging around playing poker and watching T.V, and the other two are fucking. There's also a basement."

I didn't like the tone he used when speaking the latter words. "And?"

"This is where it gets bad. Down there are two rooms and eight cells."

"Cells?" echoed Sam. "Could you see what they contained?"

Stuart took a long breath. "Vampires. Three are females. Five are males. And they are all deformed and crazed."

"Deformed and crazed?" I repeated. Unease spread around the entire squad. "You can't deform a vampire. We're immortal, we don't change on a cellular level…so how the fuck could they be deformed?"

Stuart shook his head and shrugged. "Your guess is as good as mine. There was only one who was relatively lucid. A female Sventé."

"Long dark hair and green dress?" asked Sam.

"That's the one."

Now I really, really wanted to take my stubborn female back to The Hollow. "What about the rooms in the basement?"

"The first room had four male vampires inside – I got the feeling they were scientists by the terminology they were using. I didn't really understand much of what they were saying, other than they were disappointed that their latest 'experiment' hadn't been successful, and they would have to find a new 'subject' soon."

"That doesn't sound good," the telekinetic Harvey muttered, anxious.

Max looked at him incredulously. "Dude, none of this sounds good."

Suddenly Damien's head snapped up and he exhaled heavily.

"Hey, welcome back," said Reuben, slapping Damien's back.

"Well?" I prodded.

"The only outdoor guards are the two vampires you can see standing on the roof," said Damien. Although the bungalow was a fair distance away, our enhanced vision allowed us to see them. "They're not very vigilant, so I think it's safe to say that they don't think anyone of any threat is going to come along."

And wasn't that dumb of them. "Good, they're no more prepared than the ones inside." I looked again at Stuart. "What about the other room in the basement?"

"I couldn't get inside it. The door and wall were both made of steel, like a panic room. I couldn't hear any movement at all. It was soundproof."

Well now I really, really, really wanted to take my stubborn female back to The Hollow. Clearly she sensed it, because her voice was then in my head.

If you want to keep both of your bollocks, behave.

If you get hurt, I'll spank your pretty little ass and strap you to the bed when we get home. All I got in response was an amused snort – probably because she happened to like it when I did that.

"Do you think these scientists have been trying to come up with some kind of drug that can severely harm us, like chemical warfare or something?" asked Butch, his tone casual. But that was the thing about Butch; he could stand there plotting someone's death while looking as cool and calm as if he were watching a movie. He liked violence even more than Salem did, he just hid it better. I imagined that it therefore galled him to have a defensive gift as opposed to an offensive one – even though the ability to negate and deflect anything that came at him was a substantial gift to have.

Although Butch's theory wasn't a bad one, considering how many vampires liked to battle over territory – particularly the High Masters – I found myself shaking my head. My instincts simply weren't in agreement, but nor were they offering any theories of their own. "Reuben, I need you to do your thing on David, Salem, and Chico."

With a respectful nod, the highlander lookalike – who I had to agree with Sam wasn't the brightest bulb – used his gift of power augmentation to amplify those of three of his squad members. Using only the briefest touch, Reuben had made Salem's psychic punch, David's psionic boom, and Chico's poisonous thorns all fatal.

"Good. Stuart, give me a layout of the bungalow."

Having drawn a rectangle in the dirt with his finger, Stuart explained while sketching it. "The place has a side entrance. When you open the front door, you're in a hallway. The first room on your left is the living area, the second on your left is the dining room, and the one directly ahead of you on the opposite side of the bungalow is the kitchen. There's only one right turning, which is parallel to the dining room, and it's actually a continuance of the hallway. Once you make that right turn, you have a room on either side of you – one being a bathroom, and another being a tiny bedroom. You also have two doors in front of you. One of them is the master bedroom, and the other is just a standard sized bedroom."

"And the basement?"

"The hatch is in the kitchen. There's actually a back entrance to the bungalow and it leads straight into the kitchen, so we could just sneak—"

Easily reading where his thoughts had taken him, I raised a hand. "No, we need to eliminate all the guards before entering the basement. Where exactly are the poker-playing vampires lounging?"

"The living area."

"And the other two?"

"If they're still fucking, they're in the master bedroom."

Sam asked, "From what you've seen, do you think it's possible to save the vampires that are contained in the cells?"

Stuart blew out a breath, shaking his head. "No, Coach. The Sventé from your dream is lucid, but she doesn't seem stable, she looks like she's deteriorating fast."

I felt the disappointment that travelled through Sam, but I resisted trying to give her any comfort. With the guys, she was 'Coach', and she wouldn't like showing any weakness in front of them.

"Reuben, Damien, Harvey – I want you guys to cover the back entrance, just in case anyone from the basement tries to surface and make a run for it." I doubted that anybody would. If these vampires were here to guard and hide something, the last thing they would do was run before at least trying to fight us off. "Chico, Salem, Denny, Stuart – once we're inside, I want you four to deal with the vampires in the bedroom. Before we do anything, though, Salem and Chico – I want you both to deal with the guards on the roof. Do it quickly and quietly. We want the whole thing to be over as quickly and quietly as possible. We have no idea what kind of gifts the vampires in that place have. We can't afford to give them any warning that we're here."

They both nodded, slinking away. In a tense silence, we all watched as Chico and Salem moved with a predator's grace toward the large bungalow. Unseen, they reached the building and leaped up onto the roof from opposite sides. Before either of the guards could react, Salem threw an uppercut toward the first guard – I could almost see the ripple in the air as the psychic energy flew at its target. At the same time, Chico lifted his hand and released several thorns from his palm – all of which hit the second guard in the chest. The guards were then nothing but ashes.

"Okay, people, time to move," I announced. "We get in, kill the vampires inside, and extract the female Sventé if she's rational enough."

"Then we burn shit down," declared Sam. "If they've been creating any funky stuff, I want it to be completely and utterly destroyed. If it's harmful to vampires, it needs to go. Butch, I need you to stay with David the whole time." The natural born killer nodded.

It wasn't that David was the weakest link – far from it. He was, gift-wise, the most powerful. But that made him an immediate target of any enemies in combat situations. As Butch was able to use his gift to project a deflecting shield, he often remained with David – extending his shield around them both. That way, David could simply concentrate on attacking rather than defending.

At vampire speed, but still stealthy in our movements, we got into position. I watched, fascinated, as Sam's delicate fingers prickled at the air around her, absorbing energy; ready to manipulate it in whatever way she chose. It was impossible not to be in awe of just how in control she was of all that power.

Stuart, I want you to slip inside. If no one's in the hallway, open up and let us in.

He exploded into black particles that swished under the front door. When it quietly opened, I entered first, followed quickly by Sam. The noise of the T.V. didn't drown out the dirty talk coming from the other side of the bungalow. Clearly those two were still at it.

One at a time, I told Stuart, Salem, Chico, and Denny as I gestured for them to enter. Once all four were inside they slipped past us, heading for the master bedroom. Max, Butch, and David then entered, closing the door behind them. Knowing that if we lingered our scents would reach the vampires in the living area before we did, I didn't waste any time in moving.

I nodded at Max to go slightly ahead as we all inched our way along the wall. Not because I wanted to use him as a living shield – although it was an appealing thought – but because his gift would give us the best chance at ensuring the other vampires in the building weren't alerted to our presence.

Once we reached the doorway, Max turned sharply and, with the simple act of closing his fist, stole the senses of both vampires before they had the opportunity to react. While the shock of it seemed to freeze and distract one of the vampires, the other reflexively used his gift – conjuring a knife and hurling it in our general direction. It hit Butch's shield, but Sam caught it before it could clang to the hardwood floor. As David swiftly raised his arms and splayed his hands, a psionic blast streamed from his fingertips and crashed into the heads of the vampires. Just like that, they were both ashes.

With a tip of her head, Sam gestured for us to follow her further inside. I was not even slightly impressed by her taking the lead. Yeah, okay, she was my co-commander and it was her job, but I didn't have to like it. The other four met us at the junction of the hallway, clearly having dealt with the sex fiends. Scanning my eyes over them, I saw that they were fine, other than that Salem's shirt had been singed and Denny's collar had been...bit?

Finally in the kitchen, Sam quietly opened the back door to allow Damien, Harvey, and Reuben to enter. We all stood back, giving her space as she carefully opened the hatch just a crack. Seeing that there was no one in sight, and not picking up any nearby voices, I gestured for her to fully open the hatch. Most likely pre-empting that I would try to take the lead, she threw me a cautioning look and positioned herself in front of the squad. Forced to be satisfied with shadowing the wilful female, I followed her as she slowly and soundlessly descended the wooden staircase. The squad remained close, all extremely alert.

As Stuart had described, there were four cells on either side of the basement – all of which had a single barred glass window that allowed a peek of what, or who, was inside. Beyond the cells were two doors; one made of thick wood, and the other of metal. I could hear muffled voices, but I couldn't distinguish any words, even with my enhanced hearing.

Positioning myself at the right hand side, I signalled for Chico, Salem, Reuben, Damien, and Stuart to stand behind me. The other five stood behind Sam on the left hand side. Having exchanged a nod with Sam, both she and I began to edge our way toward the far doors while the squad followed closely.

As I past the first cell, I peered through the window and inwardly winced at what I saw. A female Keja with grotesquely overgrown nails appeared to have torn out most of her hair. More disturbingly, she was eating it. I had no idea what she was ranting, as the cell appeared to be sound-proof. I had to wonder if the window was one-way glass, because she didn't notice any of us passing.

The vision within the next cell was no better. Another Keja was lying on the floor, clawing at an elongated face and then licking dribbles of blood from his fingers as the facial scratches healed. What was perhaps more troubling was that he had an extra arm. I didn't look through the next window, not wanting to see more.

Jared, I've found her.

Signalling for the squad to all remain in position, I hurried over to Sam and glanced through the window. The Sventé was exactly as Sam had described, although her limbs were abnormally long. Her back kept bowing from the floor, putting her body at an unnatural angle that made Sam and I wince. She wasn't fighting whatever was happening to her, as if she saw no hope. At least she wasn't crazed. Yet.

We can try to get her out, but not until we've dealt with the bastards in those rooms. She'd be a distraction we don't need. Plus, we have no idea if she would turn violent and attack anyone.

True, Sam allowed with a sigh. *Most of the captives appear to be attacking themselves.*

Startling us all, the wooden door opened and four vampires stepped out, laughing amongst themselves and totally oblivious to our presence. That obliviousness only lasted a second, though. The squad did what they had been trained to do; they attacked first.

Unfortunately, the vampire in front swiftly produced a protective wall of frosted glass – one so resilient that even my lightning bolt had no effect on it. That vampire *definitely* had to go – and fast. Sam must have been thinking the same thing, because suddenly fire was streaming out of her palms, weakening the glass. At the same time, Reuben placed his hands on it, drawing power from it. Their combined efforts weakened it just enough that my next release of electricity shattered it completely.

Before the vampire had the chance to produce another shield, one of Sam's thermal energy beams was buried in his chest. Milliseconds later, he was ashes…but not before the tallest of the three remaining vampires duplicated himself until there were ten of him. All of the clones stepped in front, acting as shields. Shit. Of course each and every one of us attacked with our gifts, but each time some of the clones turned to ashes, more would take their place.

Harvey, we need to separate them.

Without hesitation, Harvey made a motion similar to that of someone abruptly yanking open a set of curtains. Thanks to his telekinesis, the clones parted like the red sea – some flew into the walls, and others fell to the floor, exposing the three vampires. Not giving the vampire a chance to duplicate himself again, I sent a charge of electricity out of my palm, reducing him to ashes. His clones died with him.

One of the last two vampires opened his mouth and exhaled a swarm of bees – not nice. Sam absorbed the energy around her, and suddenly a gust of wind sent the bees forcefully crashing into the wall, killing them instantly. That same gust of wind should have sent the two vampires crashing into that same wall, just as Harvey's telekinesis should have knocked them over, but they hadn't even stumbled against either force.

It was then that I realised something, and I sensed that Sam was realising it at the same time. The second vampire was gripping the waist of the one in front of him, holding him in position. I'd heard of a vampiric gift that allowed immovability, and it seemed that the second vampire had that very gift and was keeping them both stable.

Knowing what Sam had in mind, I teleported to her and lifted her so that she was above the first vampire's level of height. She cracked her whip over his shoulder to wrap it around the throat of the second vampire, and tightened it enough to make him reflexively put his hands to his neck. Quick as lightning, yellowy-green ooze shot out of

Denny's thumbs and smallest fingers and engulfed the other vampire. Denny then bounced him to Salem, who delivered a fatal uppercut.

"And then there was one," drawled Sam as she stared at the remaining vampire. He didn't struggle against the grip of her whip as I would have expected. In fact, he didn't do anything at all…other than stare at Sam in utter fascination, which supremely pissed me off even though I could understand it.

Don't kill him yet. It might be worth questioning him a little first. I crossed my arms over my chest. "Just what did you do to the vampires in the cells?"

When he didn't answer, Sam began to circle him, whip still in hand. "Have you ever pissed blood? You will if you don't start answering our questions."

His voice was shaky. "I don't know anything."

Sam sighed sadly. "No, they never do. But I can guarantee that within the next fifteen minutes after we've had some fun with you, your thought processes will be much improved." When the whip caught his jaw, he jerked and whimpered.

I stepped closer to him. "Now, why did you hurt the vampires like that?"

"We didn't hurt them," he quickly objected. "We were trying to achieve something."

"And what is that exactly?"

"Something that no one has even thought possible," said an amused voice as the metal door slowly swung open. Four new vampires stood in the doorway in some sort of protective bubble. The two in front closely resembled each other with their inky black hair and squinty eyes.

I held up a hand, warning the squad not to attack in case whatever was thrown simply rebounded off the bubble and hit one of us. "Care to elaborate?" I snapped. "Care to explain how, and why, there are deformed vampires in those cells?"

The taller and sharper-looking of the two vampires only spared me a glance before his gaze locked on Sam. He seemed surprised and intrigued. "A Sventé with a Pagori power."

She groaned and rolled her aquamarine eyes. "I wish people would just get over it."

His mouth twitched into a smile. "A Feeder in full control of their gift. I cannot say that is something I have witnessed before. Your control…it is astounding. Inspiring, even. I find myself envying you, and that is not an emotion I am prone to experiencing."

"Well that's great, but we'd like to know why the bloody hell you hurt those vampires."

"Neither my brother nor I planned for them to come to any harm," the podgy vampire replied, looking offended. "Our experiments have simply not yet been fruitful and have caused negative side effects."

"Negative side effects?" echoed Sam, disbelievingly. "It's not like they've got the shits or something, is it? They're *deformed* and half out of their minds."

The podgy one spoke again. "Sometimes, when one is trying to achieve something grand, sacrifices must be made. And we *will* achieve our goal. Our work will be recognised by all of vampirekind."

Sam scowled. "I don't suppose you're going to tell me just what that goal is."

"Be assured that we only did to those vampires what they asked us to do. They knew the risks."

That made little sense to me. "And what, exactly, would make anyone prepared to risk becoming deformed?"

"The feeling of desperation does many things to many people."

And wasn't that the vaguest thing I'd ever heard.

Sam must have been just as frustrated, because she growled at them. "Are neither of you capable of answering a question without talking in code?"

The taller brother pursed his lips. "If you want answers, we shall do better than tell you, we shall show you."

The brothers exchanged a look that I didn't like, and I was ready to question them when I felt an echo of fatigue and disorientation through my connection to Sam. As she suddenly staggered beside me and lost her hold on her whip, I wrapped an arm around her to steady her. Utter panic overtook me. "What the—" Then something else hit me via our connection; an all-consuming, agonising pain.

Sam cried out and doubled over with the force of it. Feelings of being stabbed, gutted, sliced at, and having her insides torn apart were torturing and weakening her. Fury and fear raced through me as I reflexively struck the bubble with a discharge so high in voltage that the entire building shook. It didn't burst; only wobbled like jelly, oddly absorbing the electricity. Then, as quickly as it had come, Sam's pain disappeared.

She double-blinked and took a steadying breath. "Oh, you little fuckers." Most likely sensing that I was ready to charge at them, protective bubble or no protective bubble, she grabbed my arm. Looking at the brothers through narrowed, accusing eyes, she asked, "What did you do to me?"

The podgy brother cocked his head. "Something that has made every other vampire collapse in agony and froth at the mouth."

Again I went to charge at them, but again Sam stopped me, worried they would hurt me too. I growled, intent on finding some way to burst that bubble and kill them all.

The tall vampire gave me a cool smile. "Rest assured that we have not harmed her, we would never wish to make her ill. On the contrary, if this works – and I strongly suspect it will as she is so much stronger than any subject we have used before – it will make her beautiful and unique in a way that you could never imagine."

For a third time I moved toward them, but once again Sam held me back. I growled again. "Know this: I *will* fucking hunt you both down, and I *will* fucking destroy you both."

"It is understandable that you feel that way now. But I truly believe that this is something you will come to appreciate." He smiled at Sam. "I shall be seeing you again very soon."

The vampires had teleported away before anyone could say another word. Well great. Just. Fucking. Great.

Anger surged through me, wanting an outlet, *needing* an outlet. Realising that they had left behind the vampire who had been minutes ago bound by Sam's whip, I took him out with a lightning bolt. But it didn't make me feel better. The same feelings of dread and helplessness that I'd felt when she'd once Merged with me were now taunting me again. "See, this was why I didn't want you to come!" Oh yeah, logic told me that it wasn't her fault, but whenever she got injured, I reflexively took my anger and worry out on her.

Sam's mouth fell open. Then she punched my shoulder. "I didn't want them to hurt me, you sodding fruitcake."

"We have no idea what they did to you!" But if it was the same thing they had done to the vampires in those cells…Shit, shit, shit!

Denny swallowed hard, studying her from head to toe. "How do you feel, Coach?"

"Well and truly ticked off."

THE BITE THAT BINDS

(Sam)

The rage and fear riding Jared was beating at me, almost stealing my breath. He was practically vibrating with it. So when he tugged me to him and enclosed me in a hug, I went easily. Ordinarily, I didn't like having displays of affection in front of the squad. But Jared was close to snapping and, truth be told, I kind of needed him right then. I wasn't a person who allowed myself to lean on others, but that vampire's words had spooked the living shit out of me.

"We need to get you to Antonio. Maybe he can do something." Turning to the squad, he began, "You guys finish up. I want the whole place burned d—"

I tugged on his jacket. "Wait, Jared, the Sventé—"

"Sam, we need to get you back to Antonio."

"Jared, we came here for her."

"Exactly. If it wasn't for her contacting you, those fucking bastards would never have—"

"*Jared.*" I framed his face with my hands, seizing his gaze. "I know you're worried, and I know you're pissed, but whatever they did has already been done. That vampire said it wasn't going to make me ill. We have to cling onto that, because right now there's a female who is ill, and we need to talk with her."

"She might be able to give us some idea of what those motherfuckers were trying to do," Max pointed out. "Then maybe we can work out what they did to Coach."

Jared squeezed his eyes closed as if in pain, and I could feel that he was wrestling with his instinct to whisk me off somewhere safe. I kissed him lightly. "We spend five minutes talking to her, and then we go."

When he opened his eyes again, they were a little calmer. "*Two minutes.* You've got two minutes, and then I'm getting you out of here."

Any other time, I'd have whipped his ears off for speaking to me like that. "Yes, then we can go." Sucking energy into my palms, I released it as an air blast that was strong enough to blow her cell door open. As we all stepped inside, she didn't react other than to slowly turn her head to look at us.

When her eyes met mine, her frown melted away. "You…You c-came."

I wanted to go to her side and give her some form of comfort, but the eleven males with me were feeling mighty overprotective right then and had planted themselves in front of me. Managing to shove Salem aside just enough to have a clear view of the female, I asked, "What did they do? What's happening to you?"

She swallowed hard and her eyes drifted shut. "D-d-didn't work."

"What didn't work?"

Her words weren't audible even to vampire hearing.

"Do you have any idea who they were or where they would have gone?" Jared's voice was gruff with anger.

Without opening her eyes, she stammered, "O-Orr-in."

Jared frowned. "Orrin? Is that a name, a place, what?"

She gasped as a spasm hit, making her back bow from the floor. Even through her groans of pain, she heard my wince. Her expression was almost sympathetic when she looked at me. "Y-you c-c-can't help m-me."

"What were they trying to do?"

"Make...m-make me—" She was cut off as yet another bad spasm racked her body. It was agonising just to watch. Her eyes shut and she seemed close to drifting off, but then they fluttered opened again. "Kill me," she croaked out.

I stiffened. "No."

"Pain. Hurts." She cried out as a particularly violent spasm shook her body and her back arched so unnaturally that I heard a bone break. There were tears in her eyes when she looked at me again. "Pl-please?"

"I'll do it, Coach." Chico squeezed my shoulder.

Salem nodded. "Yeah, you go see Antonio. We'll take care of everything. We'll make sure there's nothing left of the place."

I might have told them to stop coddling me if I hadn't sensed that Jared was going to lose his composure any second now. No sooner had I slipped my hand in his than we were back in Antonio's mansion. We found him in one of his many posh parlours with Luther.

Jared didn't even give them a chance to speak. "Sam got hurt. I don't know what the fuck they did, but you need to do something."

Antonio double-blinked. "Hurt? Hurt how? And who are 'they'?"

"We have no idea." He told Antonio about what had happened, giving full details on the condition of the captives, and carefully quoting every word the brothers had said. "All we could really get out of the female Sventé was the word 'Orrin'. Do you have any idea what she could have meant?"

"I'll have my researchers look into it." Antonio studied me intently. "How are you feeling?"

I took stock. "Fine. The pain's gone. I don't feel ill. I don't feel any different at all."

Releasing a heavy sigh, Antonio shrugged. "I suppose all we can do is watch and wait."

"Watch and wait?" repeated Jared. "You've got to be kidding me. They could have done anything to her!"

"Exactly, it could have been anything. Sam says she feels fine. You say you do not know what their gifts were. I have nothing to go on. Until I know what type of help she needs, I cannot know who I need to summon to help her. I doubt that my own gift will do her much good, no matter the problem."

Jared scrubbed a hand over his face. "Maybe we should postpone the celebrations." Well that got my back up, and he obviously felt it because he raised a placatory hand. "I want that Binding ceremony, Sam — you know that. But I don't trust outsiders around you; not when those vampires said they'd be seeing you again soon."

I snorted. "They wouldn't be stupid enough to try to infiltrate The Hollow."

"Bennington tried it, and he was just as fucking weird as the brothers."

"They wouldn't even know where to find me. They don't know who I am."

"No," agreed Antonio. "But they will have known who Jared is. He's recognised worldwide; he needs to be. However, I do not believe it necessary for the Binding ceremony to be postponed. I appreciate that you are feeling particularly protective at this moment, Jared. I fully understand that, as does Sam. But she is very well protected here, and nothing can get in or out of here without my knowledge or permission. It is also worth noting that having the High Masters here for your ceremony will mean that she is even better protected than usual. And I know that the last thing you really want is to postpone the ceremony."

It was a few moments before Jared exhaled a heavy sigh and nodded.

Distracting myself from the shard of pain I'd felt at hearing him propose to postpone the ceremony, I asked Antonio, "How could they have mutated those vampires like that?"

"There are vampires who have the gift of genekinesis and similar abilities which allow them to manipulate a person or animal's DNA. In fact, my Sire's life-partner – who you will meet at the informal gathering tomorrow evening – has such a gift. But these gifts would not work on vampires. It is a shame that the female Sventé in the cell was not able to tell us more."

I thought about mentioning Luther's earlier vision, but there was a good chance that Jared would kill him for not having warned him. Instead, I waited until Jared was in deep conversation with Antonio before approaching Gandalf's doppelganger. He had remained uncharacteristically mute and made himself busy in the far corner of the room. "What's going to happen to me, Luther? The vampires tried to change me in some way. What did they do?"

His expression was sad, apologetic, and anxious. "Do you know what one of the hardest things is about having my gift, Sam? That sometimes I can see a very trying time ahead, but I also know that to do something would be to affect the future."

"There you go again with those sodding riddles. Is it something bad? At least tell me that much."

"That depends on what way you look at it."

"Oh for the love of God, Luther, throw me a bone here."

He placed a hand on my shoulder. "All I can tell you without possibly meddling with the future is that you have a difficult time ahead of you, Sam. I know you do not like to rely on others, but you must accept what support Jared tries to give you. You're going to need it." And then the confusing bugger walked off.

CHAPTER THREE

(Sam)

Panting and shaking with the aftershocks of my orgasm, I griped, "*Now* will you untie me?"

"No," mumbled Jared, who was using my breast as a pillow.

"You can't leave me to sleep like this all day."

"You're so wrong about that."

"We've had sex five times. You were supposed to have stopped brooding by now." Although Jared had long ago stopped snapping at me and pacing like a caged tiger, he hadn't quite calmed down. I could sense that he was trying to block what had happened from his mind in the hope of calming, but even five bouts of sex hadn't been able to mellow him. "Untie me."

"Could you shush? I'm trying to sleep here."

"*Jared.*"

"Hey, I told you that if you got hurt I'd strap you to the bed. You knew I wasn't kidding."

Trying a different approach, I softened my voice and injected a little sensuality into it. "But if you leave me all tied up like this, I can't wake you up in style at dusk."

A snort. "I'm offended that you think I'd fall for that."

"Well if you really insist on being a plonker…" Sucking the surrounding energy into my palm, I formed my whip and cracked it at him.

He flinched and rubbed the healing gash on his lower back. "Now that was just plain mean."

"It'll be your ears next."

Grunting, he untied one wrist, leaving me to free my other wrist and then my ankles. The second I relaxed back into the bed, he rested his head on my chest again. Then he flung an arm over me, cupping my hip possessively.

Although I very much wanted to disappear to dreamland where I wouldn't have to worry about anything, there was something nibbling at me. "I need to ask you something."

"Hmmm?"

"Are you having doubts about the Binding?"

He lifted his head, frowning. "Baby, why in God's name would you think—" As realisation dawned on him, he sighed. "I would never, *ever* have suggested postponing it if it hadn't been for what happened tonight. I'm on edge right now, and I don't like the idea of outsiders being around you."

"Binding is a big thing," I reminded him. "It's a lifelong commitment, and considering we're never going to die, you don't get one more serious than that. I never would have envisioned you being prepared to make that kind of commitment to anyone."

"In all honesty, neither had I, baby. But you're *it* for me. I don't think you get what it would do to me if you walked away. I'll always remember something you once told me. You said that sometimes people only love each other for a little while and then it's over. That plays on my mind all the time; I worry you might suddenly stop and decide to leave. Not that I'd *let* you leave me, but you get my point."

I had to smile a little at that. "I'm not going to leave."

"That's good. I'd rather not have to keep you here against your will."

"All that aside, I'd understand if you didn't feel like celebrating when your mum's just died." And down went the shutters. "You have to stop doing that."

He lowered his head to my breast again, nipping it lightly. "Sleep, baby."

"Talk, Jared."

A sigh. "Maybe tomorrow night. Now sleep. We only have one last evening to ourselves before all the guests arrive. After that, we've got a big week ahead with the Binding."

If Luther's vision was right, we had much more than a big week ahead of us. A part of me wanted to warn Jared, to talk to him about it. But doing that would risk Luther's life, and talking in riddles wasn't a reason to die. So I'd have to do as Antonio said…watch and wait.

THE BITE THAT BINDS

(Jared)

"So you have an assignment for us." Ordinarily, I'd be pleased. But this time, I didn't have even an ounce of enthusiasm. After what had happened in the bungalow, the only thing I wanted was to lock Sam in a room where no one could reach her. Seeing her in pain had knocked me into a hyper vigilant state that I couldn't snap out of, no matter how hard I tried. But the oh-so-stubborn female was insisting on going.

"Yes," replied Antonio. "Luther had a vision. Unfortunately, it wasn't entirely clear."

Like that was anything new.

Luther spoke to Sam. "As I once told you, my visions do not always make much sense. Sometimes, it is the feel of the vision that I am left to rely on. What I do know is that this is something that hasn't happened yet, but will happen very soon – in just a few hours' time, in fact.

"In my vision, there was a park. It was the evening. There were two women; one was a vampire, one was a human. A pregnant human. I could feel that the vampire had every intention of murdering the human, who she had bound to a tree. The vampire's rage and pain hit me hard."

That wasn't good. "Not to be disrespectful," I said to Antonio, "but surely you could select another squad to deal with this."

Antonio's expression was apologetic. "Believe me when I say that I would have assigned this to another squad had it not been for one thing – you and Sam were in the vision. To remove you both from the equation might have a very negative impact on what happens."

Fuck. Well now there was definitely no getting out of it. "Do you have any idea who the women are?"

Luther shook his head. "No. But when I have a vision about unfamiliar people, it means that one, or all, of the people in the vision will become important to The Hollow somehow."

"And you think the human will be important?"

Luther sighed. "I do not know."

I scrubbed my nape, agitated. "What is it you want us to do exactly? Obviously we can't allow the vampire to kill the woman, but then what? Do you want us to bring one, or both, here?"

"I trust that you will know what train of action is appropriate once you decipher the situation," said Antonio.

"If it's only two women we've got to worry about, I suppose it's not necessary to take the squad," Sam concluded, but I shook my head.

"I've had plenty of experience with Luther's unclear visions. They always seem like simple situations and turn out to be anything but." That was another reason why going on this assignment pissed me off.

Antonio nodded in agreement with me. "I'd recommend that you take at least three of the squad with you."

"Where will we find the two women?" I asked Luther. He handed me a sheet of paper with coordinates written on it.

"I believe it would be best if you left as soon as possible."

So that was exactly what we did. It turned out that the place from Luther's vision was actually a redwood forest north of San Francisco.

After hours of searching, I halted, sighing. "I can't hear or smell anyone nearby."

Sam stopped beside me. "Neither can I."

"This is the only area of the woods that we haven't covered," said Butch, his eerily dark eyes taking in everything around us.

"Maybe we missed them." David shrugged as he nervously ran a hand through his coppery hair. "Maybe we were too late."

"Or too early," suggested Chico. He said something else, but it didn't register as my hearing had locked onto a distant moaning sound. *Did you all hear that?* I asked Sam and the guys. They each nodded. *Be as quiet as you can – we don't want the vampire hearing us approach.* The guys stealthily followed Sam and I as we wound through the trees.

Finally, my vampire enhanced vision picked up the source of the sound in the far distance. Just as Luther had described, there was a pregnant human sitting against a thin, tall tree with her hands bound behind it. The plan had been to make the job quick – disable the vampire, save the human, and decide if either of them should be taken to The Hollow. Instead, I held up my hand, signalling for Sam and the guys to remain in position. I wasn't sure why, but every single cell in my body told me to wait, told me to listen. Sam arched her brow questioningly. I mouthed, 'Trust me', glad when she shrugged and focused her attention on the spectacle ahead.

The moaning had now stopped and the human was waking. Her forehead was creased in a way that hinted at pain – probably a headache. It was a few seconds before she realised that she was in fact tied to the tree. She struggled, but it seemed that the knot was very secure. That was when sheer and utter panic took over her face.

"You can shout for help if you want," began a voice, "but even if someone came, I wouldn't let them help you." A tall brunette stepped out of the shadows and stood directly before the human. Malice literally gleamed from her eyes. I could see even from here that her irises weren't glowing. If she was that pissed off but her irises weren't glinting red or amber, she had to be a Sventé like Sam.

"Who are you?" the human asked, her lips quivering. When the vampire didn't answer, she rambled, "Look, whatever Leon owes you, I can get it. But if you're mistakenly thinking – like others have before you – that if you call him he'll rush here like lightning to save me, you're going to be very disappointed. He's out of town, and he hasn't got the money to give you anyway. He spends what he steals before he even steals it, trust me."

"So you're the breadwinner?"

"I have to be, or we'd have nothing."

"For someone who's financially struggling, you're dressed very smartly, aren't you?" The vampire was right; the woman was clothed in a black maternity suit – jacket, pencil skirt, and a white blouse. "What's your name?"

The human seemed taken aback by the question. "What's yours?" she returned cockily.

The vampire's mouth curved into a smile. "Jude. My name's Jude."

"If I were you, Jude, I'd let me go. I've told you, I can get you your money."

"I don't want money."

"Well whatever you want, I can get it. But hurting me would be a really stupid thing to do on your part. You'd be upsetting my employers, for a start. You don't know who I—"

"Yes I do." Jude squatted down in front of her. "Maybe I don't know your name, but I know something about you...something I doubt that many other people know...You're a Scout." The human's eyes widened and her mouth fell open. "You really don't remember me, do you?"

When the human didn't respond, Jude explained, "We met in a supermarket. We both reached for a velour baby sleep-suit at the same time. You told me that you were so sorry, massaging your pregnant belly. You said you had eight weeks left before your due date, that you were having a boy. I told you that I had four weeks left to go, that I was having a girl. Any of this jogging your memory?"

The human still didn't speak, so Jude continued. "Just as I was walking away, I felt a sharp prick in my arm that made me flinch, but I never thought anything of it. Why would I? A few minutes later, I was suddenly dizzy. Uncoordinated. My eyelids felt like they had lead weights hanging from them. With blurred vision and shaky legs, I stumbled outside. I just kept thinking that I needed to get to my car and go to a hospital. To any non-dizzy person, driving would have seemed nothing short of suicidal. But for me, the equation had been a little different: something was wrong and my baby might be at risk, therefore I had to hurry to get to a hospital.

"Then a car pulled up and the window lowered. A woman asked me if I was okay, if I needed a ride to the hospital. I said no, but she kept insisting that I couldn't drive in my state. I would have said no again, but then I saw a toddler in a babyseat in the back of the vehicle, clapping his hands and grinning. It made me relax, made me think I could trust this perfect stranger. So I hopped inside the car. Seconds later, I passed out.

"When I woke up, two men and a woman, all wearing scrubs, were looking down at me. I thought I must be at a hospital...And then there was the most amazing sound. Crying, my baby was crying. I tried to lift my head and see, but my body wasn't cooperating. The only thing I saw was a mop of black curls. Then, just before I blacked out again, I heard a harsh voice order, 'Get rid of her quickly'."

I truly would never have anticipated that the conversation would swing in this direction. I mean, seriously...what the fuck?

"When I came round, I was in a wooded area, just like this one. It felt like warm water had been thrown over my stomach. I reached down and realised my baby bump was gone. My *baby* was gone. When I brought my hand up, I saw that it wasn't water, it was blood. I don't know how long I lay there crying before I got up. I staggered about aimlessly, fuelled mostly by shock. But I was bleeding so badly. I was dying, and I knew it. I don't think I got far before I fell again. But, unbelievably, someone found me. I begged them to help me, and they did; they made sure I lived. They said that if anyone had the right to live and get revenge, it was me."

I was betting this 'someone' had been the vampire responsible for Turning her.

"It wasn't until about six months later that I was…healed enough to go searching for you."

In other words, it had been six months before her bloodlust had been under a satisfactory level of control – although Sventés had a manageable bloodlust, all newborn vampires of every breed suffered from uncontrollable bloodlust. Had she been a Keja or a Pagori vampire, it would have taken her longer to control it.

"I searched and searched for you, but I don't think I ever expected to find you, no matter how hard I tried to track you. I almost pissed my pants when I spotted you earlier. I think the woman behind me thought I was having a seizure or something."

The human now had the look of someone who understood exactly what danger they had found themselves in. "Jude, what happened to you was…horrific. Awful. But I swear to you, I had nothing to do with it. I don't even remember us meeting—"

"Surely you're not suggesting I'd forget the face of—"

"No, no," the human quickly added, clearly conscious of the danger of offending Jude. "I'm not saying we didn't meet, just that I'm not so good with remembering faces, but I swear to you, I was nothing whatsoever to do with what happened to you."

Jude's crooked grin widened, but it wasn't a pleasant one. "That would be much easier to believe if" – she dragged up the brunette's blouse to reveal an artificial baby bump – "you were truly pregnant. What do they call these? Some antenatal classes use them, don't they?"

"Empathy Belly Pregnancy Stimulators," replied the human quietly.

I hadn't been expecting that. I sensed that Sam was equally surprised. She was also extremely pissed to the point that a silvery-blue energy ball had appeared in her hand. I imagined she was probably cooking up interesting ways for the human to die.

"You weren't pregnant when we first met either, were you?" Jude said to the human. "You'd been wearing this. It gives you an excuse to talk to pregnant women without looking suspicious. It's just two pregnant women comparing notes. Admit it, you're a Scout."

"If you're hoping I can tell you where your baby is, you're very mistaken. My role ends at drugging the women."

Slowly, Jude tucked her hand inside her knee-high boot and retrieved a jagged-edged knife about eight inches long. The moonlight glimmered off the steel implement. "So what you're telling me is…you're no good to me?"

"What I'm saying is I might have drugged you, but I didn't perform the Caesarean, I didn't take the baby."

Rage flashed across Jude's face, but somehow she remained calm. "Don't call it a Caesarean, *don't*. A Caesarean section is a medical procedure that's used with the mother and baby's well-being in mind. Having my abdomen ripped open and my unborn baby snatched from my womb – risking its life – wasn't a Caesarean." Jude seemed to be searching the human's face for something, probably remorse. "How do you sleep at night? How many women have you done this to? Don't you even care that innocent little babies are being taken from their mothers? For all you know, they're being sold to paedophile rings. What is it – can't you have kids of your own so you hate women who can? Or is it all about the money for you?"

A scorned look suddenly took shape on the human's pale face. "Who are you to judge me? If you want to wiggle that knife in front of me and threaten me, go ahead, do it. I just hope you don't think I can tell you where your baby is, or that you'd ever find it now anyway."

"I don't. I gave up hope after a little while. I didn't want to lose faith, it just went. To tell you the truth, she's probably better off without me. Better off not knowing that her mom's messed up and her dad's a rapist. But that's not the point, is it? She wasn't yours or anyone else's to take. If anyone was going to give her away, it should have been me." Pain was etched into Jude's face. "There would be no point in me having her back now anyway. I can't raise her. But neither can the people who she's been sold to, because they're just. Like. Me."

I shared a confused look with Sam. Surely Jude wasn't suggesting that her baby was sold to vampires.

Jude looked at her blade admiringly. "Being sexually attacked has a way of making you more cautious. After that day, I bought this knife and I carried it everywhere, except for that one day when you decided

I was going to be butchered and my baby was going to be taken and sold. I dropped my guard for that day – can you believe that?"

The human licked her lips nervously. Desperation was in every word. "Jude, think about this…you could hurt me or kill me, but what would it change? Nothing. It wouldn't get you your baby back. All that would really come from it, is you would end up with my employers and the police on your tail for my murder. Is that what you want? You sound like an intelligent person, someone who's been through enough. You need to let me go, and let all this go, and move on."

"I can't. Not until all the people who were involved and profited from the sale of my baby pays for what they've done."

Not wanting the human dead until I'd had a chance to question her, I turned to Chico, Butch, and David. *You three concentrate on the vampire. Sam and I will take care of the human.* In vampire speed, we were in front of the two women. Jude looked up; there was no surprise in her expression, and I had to wonder how long she'd known we were there.

"Oh thank God, please you have to help me!" begged the human. "She tied me up, she wants to kill me!"

I arched a brow. "Is that so?"

"She's insane!"

I folded my arms across my chest. "Well, the good news is, she's totally sane. The bad news is my fiancée here is a crazy, homicidal bitch and she wants to kill you."

As Sam's energy whip appeared in her hands, the human blanched, gulping and shaking. I wondered if she'd pass out.

Jude's face took on a knowing look as she studied Sam – who was totally focused on the human. "You're the Sventé Feeder." She seemed entranced by her. I could understand that. Sam commanded attention when she was fierce. The vampire's eyes eventually moved to me. "And you're the Heir." Her gaze raked over the three squad members who had surrounded her, lingering a little on Chico.

As I went to stand in front of the human, her eyes widened. I suspected that the red tinge to my irises was glowing.

"What are you?" she asked shakily.

I *tsk*ed. "I ask the questions. First, I want to know who it is you work for." If Jude was right and vampires had bought her baby, this was a situation that I needed to take care of – and fast.

"There's really no point in denying anything," said Sam. "Although…it wouldn't be so bad if you did, because then I could whip you silly."

I winced, offering the human a sympathetic look. "I don't envy you right now. I've been on the receiving end of that whip a few times – and not in a good way."

The human shook her head madly. "No, this isn't real."

Sam cocked her head. "Frankly, I find it harder to believe there are people out there evil enough to steal children than that vampires exist. But maybe that's just me."

"Vampires?" the human echoed, releasing a nervous laugh.

Jude huffed. "What, you didn't realise you've been working for supposedly mythological creatures?"

"What makes you think your baby was sold to vampires?" I asked Jude.

"Because vampires are running the operation," replied Jude. "Stealing human babies, and then selling them to vampire couples."

"Why would vampires do that?"

"How else are they going to have children unless it's to steal them?"

The human was shaking her head incredulously. "You're all crazy."

Sam sighed. "Admittedly, *I* am. So for every time you fail to answer our questions, I will crack this whip at you. This can be over quickly, or it can be prolonged. Totally your choice, though the latter sounds more appealing to me. It's part of the 'crazy, homicidal bitch' thing."

"But me…I'd rather skip the cliché 'I don't know anything' game." I seized her gaze with mine. "Who do you work for?"

When she said nothing, Sam cracked the whip, catching the human's earlobe. She cried out, flinching.

"Hurts like a son of a bitch, doesn't it?" It truly did; Sam was merciless with that thing. "We'll try this again. Who do you work for?"

The human spoke to Jude. "You aren't even a little concerned that there are people here claiming to be vampires?"

Jude tilted her head. "As I'm also one…No."

The woman cursed as Sam's whip slashed along her jaw.

"I believe you were asked a question." Sam's voice became even raspier whenever she was pissed. It sent a shudder through me every time.

Jude tutted. "I'd answer their questions if I were you. The worst I can do is kill you, but these guys…I have a feeling they have powers that will shock the shit out of you."

"Powers," the woman whispered.

I turned to Sam. "Show her."

Sam let her whip fade away, sucked more energy into her palms, and released it as a blast of air that had debris whooshing around and the tree branches swaying. Taking more energy, she directed a flame of fire at the human, which stopped just short of her body. The human, sniffling and sobbing, then watched open-mouthed as Sam shaped the energy into a silvery-blue energy ball, which she bounced from hand to hand.

"Amazing, isn't she," I said to the human. "I remember the first day I met her, she kicked my ass using that gift – taunted me the entire time, even called me a pretty girl. Now, if you haven't yet figured out that it's in your best interests to tell us what we want to know—"

"I didn't steal any babies!"

"Yes, we overheard you admitting that your role ends at drugging the mothers. So the question is…what happens next? It's more than obvious that the woman who offered to give Jude a ride to the hospital was involved. So where do we find her?" The human's attention had drifted to Sam – most likely because she had her energy whip back in hand. "I said, where do we find her?"

"I don't know—" She yelped at the feel of Sam's whip on her cheek.

"Wrong answer." If she had been anyone else, the scent of her blood in the air would have made my mouth water. But I couldn't think of anything more disgusting than feeding from someone as callous as this woman in front of me. "Come on, you must have a name at the very least."

"I've never met or spoken to her, I swear! I saw her from afar a few times when she drove away with a pregnant woman, sure, but that's all."

"What does she look like?" I knew that I could get this information from Jude, but I wanted to find out if the human was lying.

"Her hair was light blonde, but you could tell it wasn't her natural hair colour, because her roots were very dark. She had to be in her forties. She wore glasses."

I looked at Jude, who nodded.

"I swear that's all I know. Leon tells me when and where to go Scouting. When I find someone, I drug them and call him. As far as I know, he then contacts the Deliverer and she takes it from there. He's only ever referred to her as that, but he might know her name, I don't know."

"The Deliverer?"

"That's what they call her and the other women who do that job. They take a kid with them on purpose to try to seem non-threatening and trustworthy."

"This is a big operation if there's more than just one Deliverer." And didn't that just worry the crap out of me.

"Yes, but I don't know how big, and I don't know more than what I've told you. I'm too low down in the chain to be trusted with details."

"She'll be telling the truth about that," interrupted Chico. "In big crime organisations, they don't tell their employees any more than they have to know. They're going to be extremely careful if, on top of that, they have the huge secret of being vampires to keep."

I had to agree with that theory. "Then it's safe to say that the person we need to speak to next…is her partner." I turned to Butch, whose eyes were boring into the human. "Check her purse for some I.D."

After some rummaging around, Butch pulled out the human's driver's licence. "Janine Peterson. Her address is right here."

"Good. I guess…you're no longer of any use to us, Janine."

Her eyes almost popped out of their sockets. "No, please, I told you everything I know, I—"

Sam sneered at her. "You hadn't honestly thought you'd be allowed to go on your merry way, had you?"

"What are you going to do with me?" she asked in a low voice.

"Well, that's all up to Jude." I turned to the brunette behind me. "Sam will be more than happy to have her way with this bitch if you don't want the honour. It's up to you."

Jude straightened her shoulders. "No. I need to do this."

Sam let out a petulant whine. "But I had something so good in mind."

Smiling, I draped an arm around her shoulders and pulled her aside. "Next time." I looked back at Jude. "Once you're done, you're coming with us."

"To her place to see her boyfriend?"

"No. If this organisation is as big as it seems and vampires are involved, we need to speak with Antonio first." At her blank look, I elaborated, "The Grand High Master."

Nodding, she rose to her feet and went to squat before Janine, her knife back in hand.

Janine began to sob, but I wouldn't have been surprised if the tears were false. "I didn't steal her, Jude, it wasn't me—"

"No, but if you hadn't drugged me that day, I wouldn't have been taken to have my abdomen ripped open, I wouldn't have nearly died, I would never have been Turned into a vampire, and – most importantly – my baby would be with me, her mom, *where she should be*. What's more, others wouldn't have suffered the same fate. So the way I see it is…you've had this coming for a long time." With that, Jude sliced open Janine's throat. She didn't move an inch from where she sat until Janine's heartbeat had come to a complete stop.

Note to self: Never piss off Jude.

(Sam)

No less than twenty minutes later, we were back in the conference room. Antonio, Luther, and Sebastian had looked equal measures of concerned, enraged, and sympathetic as Jude told her story.

When she was done, Antonio sighed. "Unfortunately, vampires are just as involved in trafficking as humans are. In the case of vampires, they provide others with human adults and human children to be used as vessels or consorts. It's been going on for a long time, and I've been sending my squads to end these operations for years."

"Well, now there's a new type of trafficking, and it's a well-organised crime syndicate." Jude leaned forward in her seat. "Foetal abduction isn't so new for humans – this has been happening in countries like Columbia for years."

"For years?" repeated Sebastian, stunned and disgusted.

Jude nodded. "There's a high demand for children, particularly newborns. Countries where it used to be fairly easy to adopt from now have a lot of restrictions. Adoption's a lengthy process, and they'll seem like a life-time to those who are desperate for a child. Abducting newborns from hospitals is much more difficult now that the places are more secure and people are more alert and aware.

"In the case of vampires, adoption isn't an option. Kidnapping children isn't an option as something so bold can draw attention to the existence of vampires – no vampire would risk that. But *buying* a child provides little risk for them. Just as they longed to be parents as humans, they long for the same thing as vampires. The crime organisation that has specialised in trafficking has leaped on this. I suppose you could call it a niche in the market."

Sebastian shook his head sadly. "But…why would they do that knowing that they couldn't grow old with the child?"

"They most likely plan to Turn the child once they reach a mature age," said Antonio.

"Don't do what I first did." Jude glanced at each person at the table as she spoke. "Don't try to search for some logic. These people aren't okay upstairs or they would never have done this to begin with, no matter how much they craved to be parents."

"Why are you sure that vampires are behind this?" I asked her.

"At first, I hadn't been – it hadn't even occurred to me. I was determined to find the people responsible for what happened, and I thought it would simply be a case of finding out what the human authorities knew. They had naturally been looking into the deaths; just as with me, each woman had been left for dead in a wooded area. My gift is to erase memories, though I can't erase any more than twenty minutes. So I questioned a couple of FBI agents and erased their memories of me afterwards.

"That was how I learned all about foetal abduction, and also about the ranks within the organisation. The Scout's job is to parade around wearing pregnancy simulators and search for heavily pregnant women; they find out if the baby is mature enough to survive an op.

After being drugged, the women are taken by Deliverers. No one has uncovered where the ops are performed, but because of the careful incisions on each of the victims, it's believed that the Medics have extensive medical knowledge.

"But no one knows what happens after the Medics perform their operation. It was literally a dead end. There was *nothing*, no trace of anyone or anything. My Sire suggested that I let it go, but I couldn't. One day, I was at home watching T.V., and half a dozen Pagori vampires just burst into the apartment. I was warned to stop asking questions, to stop poking around; that if I didn't, they'd be back and I'd be dead. All I can think is that they thought I knew more than I did. Until that moment, it hadn't even occurred to me that my own kind was involved."

"Janine, the human, was shocked at the sight of us," said Jared, who had his arm hung around my chair and was playing with my hair. "She clearly believed humans were running the organisation. I have to wonder when the human roles end and the vampires take over."

I pursed my lips. "It might be reasonable to think that the Medics are definitely humans. The operations they perform cause a lot of bleeding. Surely that would be difficult for vampires, so maybe it's after then they take over."

Antonio nodded. "Yes, that's a good point. It would also explain why the trail of information is stale after that."

"It would also explain why the women are simply being dumped, left to die," said Sebastian. "Vampires would never be so sloppy."

"Who Turned you?" Antonio asked Jude.

"My Sire calls himself Kingsley, but that's his surname. I don't know his first name."

Antonio shook his head a little. "I cannot say I know him. Does he know what you've told us?"

"No. I knew he'd tell me to stop searching. I can't. As much as I respect you, I won't be able to stop if you ask me to."

Antonio held her gaze for a moment before speaking. "I won't ask you to give up. But you must understand that it is my responsibility to ensure that this organisation is shut down. That means sending Sam, Jared, and the members of their squad to further investigate and to deal with it appropriately. You may accompany them *only* if you are prepared to follow whatever orders they give you."

"I will," Jude vowed.

"If at any point you attempt to tamper with their memories, you will be sent back here, and you will be punished. Do you understand?"

She nodded. "I get it. I'm not interested in hurting anyone except for those responsible."

"No one will rob you of that opportunity," I assured her, "as long as you follow what orders we give you."

"I'll show Jude to one of the rooms in the Guest House," announced Sebastian.

"When Janine's partner returns from his trip, we'll pay him a little visit." Jared threaded his fingers through mine. "Until then—" He cut himself off midsentence and suddenly stiffened beside me.

Automatically tensing just the same, I asked, "What is it?"

His eyes shut as a shudder travelled through him. When he opened his eyes again, he locked them with Antonio's huge dark ones. "She's here."

"Magda," I uttered under my breath.

Jared squeezed my hand. "Don't worry. I'll make sure she leaves soon."

Oddly enough, a part of me wanted to meet the bitch, to see her just once to satisfy my curiosity. But another part of me wanted her to keep the hell away from Jared – particularly if she still wanted him. In any case, I'd most likely have to meet her before she'd be willing to leave without attending the ceremony. That was if she *would* be willing to leave. Somehow, I doubted it. My luck didn't stretch that far.

CHAPTER FOUR

(Sam)

Coaching. I was good at coaching, and leading, and fighting. I was not good at playing the hostess. Of course Jared, with his enviable charisma, was at total ease with greeting each of the guests as they arrived at the informal gathering that preluded the week's Binding festivities. Sod.

It was being held in one of the many grand parlours in Antonio's mansion. Soft music was playing on the piano and waiters were strolling around with trays of either tiny appetisers or flutes of champagne-flavoured NSTs. As these Nutritive Supplemental Tonics – a mix of blood and other vitamins – were only available at The Hollow, many of the guests had eyed them suspiciously, but eventually they all tried one. Personally, I quite liked them, but although they were quick to answer thirst, they didn't hit the spot like pure blood did.

In truth, this gathering wasn't particularly my scene. I wasn't comfortable with 'posh', because it wasn't what I was used to. I was an active girl. I liked combat, paintballing, fairgrounds, and anything that would provide a good ole adrenaline rush. All this just wasn't *me*. If all the entertainment scheduled for the upcoming week was like this, I doubted that I'd particularly enjoy any of it. I didn't feel that I 'fit' in this room, didn't feel that I was truly celebrating my own Binding. Instead, I was following the same customs as all those vampire couples who had come before me…and I was bored.

Also, it wasn't sitting well with me that here I was, hosting an informal gathering – even if it was for my own Binding – when it was extremely important to further investigate the foetal abduction operation. I was particularly worried that Janine's boyfriend might become concerned about her absence and decide to do a runner. But Antonio had pointed out that it was unlikely, considering that she hadn't been dead for long and her boyfriend was out of town anyway. The members of the legion who were watching over the apartment building had confirmed that he hadn't yet returned. Though it was difficult for Jared and me to pass on an assignment to another squad, we had both agreed that if Janine's boyfriend returned before the end of the gathering, another squad could deal with the matter. We didn't want to put our job before our relationship.

Pulling me from my thoughts, two familiar vampires waltzed into the room with their consorts. The two High Master vampires were the first of the five to arrive. Originally, there had been nine, but the other four High Masters had been executed for the parts they had played in the attack on The Hollow. Antonio hadn't yet appointed vampires to replace them.

The two High Masters that had just entered couldn't have been more different from one-another. Whereas Kaiser always wore a grim expression and had a militant way about him, Connelly had the friendliest face and a personality to match. Both of them had supported and fought alongside our legion during the attack on The Hollow.

"Jared," Connelly practically crooned after adding his gift to the mountain of others on the table beside the doors. "I must say, it's wonderful that you have chosen a life-partner. And such a beautiful one, too."

"Thanks," said Jared as he flashed me a proud smile. "I'd have to agree with you on that one."

Connelly turned that jovial grin on me as he took my hands in his and kissed both cheeks. "Samantha, it is a pleasure to see you again."

"You too," I said simply. See, I was no good at the hostess thing.

Kaiser, having also added a gift to the pile, gave both Jared and I a deferent bow of the head. "Congratulations to you both."

"Ah, I spot Antonio," said Connelly a little excitedly before waltzing off. Yeah, he was a bit of a 'kiss-ass', as Jared called him. His consort gave me a genuine smile before trailing after Connelly. Kaiser's consort was a little cool, but that was most likely just Kaiser's personality rubbing off on her.

Next to arrive was another High Master, Ricardo Maxwell – one who I knew Jared disliked. Still, Jared courteously accepted the vampire's gift and also his not-so-heartfelt congratulations. Ricardo's eyes slid to me, and although he bowed his head respectfully, that respect wasn't in his eyes. It hadn't been in the eyes of many others tonight, actually.

Not that I was surprised. The widespread view that Sventés were the lower breed was always going to be an issue. But it wasn't simply a prejudice thing in this case. Connelly and Kaiser had both witnessed me Merge with Jared during the attack. They both knew how powerful I was, and they would have no doubt relayed this to others. Still, as the large majority of the vampires here hadn't seen this for themselves, a lot of them would have come here with their minds already made up − believing a Sventé could never protect them.

Well they could go jump up their own arse holes for all I cared. The only reason their behaviour bothered me was that I knew it was agitating Jared. The tension and edginess caused by last night's events hadn't totally left him, and the last thing I wanted, or needed, was for something to set him off again.

Unfortunately, I received a similar greeting − or lack thereof − from Rowan Murdock, another High Master, and his life-partner Marcia. Sensing that Jared had just about had enough and was tempted to comment, I placed my hand over his clenched one and gently relaxed his fist. Ordinarily, I'd give him a discrete pinch in warning, but I felt a bit shitty doing that when it wasn't that he was being an arse; he was being more overprotective than usual because I'd been hurt by the brothers. It was pretty understandable, and I'd have behaved exactly the same way.

My mood improved somewhat when the squad, as a whole, arrived. Of course, each of them passed on genuine congratulations before heading for the champagne. I noticed that Jared had been a little stiff with Max, who found it as amusing as always. I doubted that I'd ever be able to convince him that Max no longer had any interest in me. But, then, I'd probably never be totally comfortable around someone who'd once pursued Jared, so who was I to judge?

Evan then entered with the last of the High Masters, Bran, and one of Bran's consorts. Immediately Evan enfolded me in a hug. I saw that Bran's consort, Alora, stiffened at that and I knew it was jealousy. Her body went even more rigid when Evan very subtly moved close to her. Although she wanted him, she had been resisting him. Maybe Evan would have let the matter go if this was just any woman. But the redhead wasn't just any woman. She was the vampire that he'd seen in the vision he'd had through Luther; she was the one he had been waiting for – and it had been a fairly long wait – she simply had no idea of that.

Despite all of the female attention Evan received on a daily basis, he had always been indifferent to it. Well, not always. Apparently he had seriously enjoyed himself in his first years as a vampire, but it had come to an abrupt halt when he saw her in the vision.

There was utter determination in his eyes whenever he looked at her. He fully intended to have Alora and he was ensuring that she knew it. If the way she was averting her gaze was anything to go by, she did know it, and she was a little uncomfortable with his attention. Of course she was uncomfortable. Evan was pretty easy-going, centred, and even-tempered, but he had a presence about him that made people take notice. He could be very focused and persistent, and if that focus and persistence was directed at a woman, it would undoubtedly have her squirming.

Bran had obviously noticed Evan's interest in her, but he didn't care. From what I'd heard via another of Bran's consorts, he actually batted for Fletcher's team. Whereas Fletcher was open about it, Bran – a very reserved, private, quiet man – clearly had no intention of being so open. Having female consorts was merely a smoke screen. I knew that was the only thing stopping Evan from taking Alora away from the High Master.

Considering that Bran wouldn't object to leaving her with Evan, I had to conclude that if there was some kind of resistance, it was coming from Alora. Apparently Evan was intent on crushing her defences. See, persistent.

"I haven't put my gift on the table." Evan's hazel eyes – so like Jared's, yet not – were twinkling in amusement as he spoke to me. "You'll get it soon."

Jared frowned. "The Binding gift is supposed to be for both of us."

Evan waved his hand dismissively, making Jared snort. But a smile quickly appeared on Jared's face when two more guests entered. A very tall, silver-haired Keja with a very regal air had strolled into the room with an elegant platinum-blonde on his arm. I didn't have to ask who they were. I'd heard that Antonio's Sire, Wes – who was also Bran's Sire – was attending with his life-partner, and I knew that Jared cared about Wes and was looking forward to seeing him. He basically thought of him as a grandfather. As such, he was the only person who I particularly wanted to accept me.

He was also the only person who had a snake draped over his shoulders. I mean, come on, what was that about?

Wearing the hugest smile that was filled with pride and affection, he patted Jared's upper arm. "It has been a while. Too long."

"That's your fault for not visiting more." Jared regarded the snake warily, making me smile. He then went to introduce me, but Wes dived into a conversation with him about something or other. Oh, nice. I chose to believe that it hadn't been a snub, but I still couldn't help feeling a little awkward just standing there.

As if sensing my awkwardness, the Pagori female on his arm untangled herself from him and came to my side. "I can only apologise for Wes' awful manners. He's simply very excited to see Jared again. He's just as excited to see you…although you wouldn't think so," she grumbled, shooting him an impatient but playful scowl that he didn't see. "I'm Lena."

I shook the hand she offered me, glad when she didn't bow her head. It freaked me out whenever people did that. The way I saw it, I was just little old me – powerful vampire or not, the Heir's chosen or not. "Sam."

Her eyes flickered between Jared and me. "The bond between you both…it is very strong."

"You have a gift that allows you to measure bonds?" I knew I sounded confused; I'd heard from Antonio that she was genekinetic.

Lena shook her head. "One doesn't need such a gift to see that your bond is solid. In fact, it's almost feral in its intensity. That is a very good thing. If you are going to spend centuries with someone, it is important that there are no doubts."

I totally agreed with her on that one, which was why I still had my concerns about Jared; the more he persisted in freezing me out, the more I feared he would back out.

He gripped my elbow gently. "So you've met Lena. Good." After exchanging smiles with the beautiful blonde, he gestured at the tall man beside him. "Sam, this is Wes. Wes—"

"I'm glad to see that this one has some cushion, as opposed to your past consorts," laughed Wes as he assessed me in my lavender sleeveless dress.

Cushion? I wasn't sure whether to take that as a compliment or an insult wrapped in charm. I didn't particularly like that he had spoken of me in the same context as a consort. As the female that Jared intended to Bind with, I was a hell of a lot more than that. Jared, however, didn't look like he thought it was anything I should be offended by. On the contrary, he was laughing along with Wes. Maybe, then, I was being a little sensitive.

"Nice to meet you," I said as we shook hands, making sure my handshake was firm.

"Likewise. Antonio has told me much about you. From the way he spoke of you and your presence, I imagined you to be much taller. Just how small – sorry, *tall* – are you?"

Ah, I was dealing with a master of backhanded compliments. I didn't think I was particularly small at all, but naturally I looked that way when stood next to this lanky bugger. "I see myself as the right height for kicking overgrown plonkers in some seriously interesting places." I said all this with the friendliest smile. Again, Jared hadn't seemed to notice the insults beneath Wes' words, or mine for that matter.

Wes' smile faltered only slightly. With a slight tip of his head toward the grey snake that was staring right at me, he said, "This is Toto."

Toto? He had to be kidding. He'd called a slithering killer *Toto?*

"Would you like to hold him?"

Of course I wouldn't like to hold him. What, did he think I was stupid? Hey, I had nothing against snakes. In fact, as someone who had been brought up by their snake-obsessed father to admire and respect them, I was able to appreciate each and every species. *However*, appreciating them when there was a glass wall between you and the snake was one thing. Holding an eight-foot long fucker was another thing altogether.

I was ready to tell Wes no; that he had succeeded in freaking me out like he'd obviously been aiming to do. But then I saw something in his expression that made me pause. Instinct told me that he wasn't trying to freak me out at all. This was some sort of test. Yes, yes, I knew he, like everyone else, would want to know that I was strong enough to one day rule and that I was good enough for Jared, blah, blah, blah. But how the act of holding a snake would answer either of those questions for him, I wasn't sure.

What I *was* certain of was that I had no intention of failing *any* test.

Pasting a fake smile on my face, I nodded. "Why not." I felt Jared stiffen slightly, and Wes clearly noticed because he gave him a reassuring smile. Remaining still, I allowed him to drape the grey snake over my shoulders. A pair of black eyes met mine, and then the snake stuck its forked tongue out at me, lightly flicking my cheek. 'Tasting' me, smelling me, I knew.

It was then that I noticed the inky-black colouration on the inside of his mouth. My eyes widened. "A black mamba. I'm holding a black mamba?" Oh shit.

"Did Antonio tell you about my gift?"

"No."

Very proudly, he explained, "My gift is to make pictures that I have drawn come to life. Amazingly, this can even apply to tattoos. Ever since I was a child, I have been fascinated with snakes. My four favourite breeds have always been spitting cobras, rattlesnakes, garter snakes, and black mambas. So…I decided to create a breed that blended the four together by tattooing an image of this snake on my chest."

Interesting and impressive, but also freaky.

"Toto has the narrow, elongated head typical of a black mamba, as well as the black colouration you see inside his mouth. He also has the tail of a rattlesnake, the ability to spit venom like a spitting cobra, and he can secrete a rather foul-smelling fluid from his post anal glands much like a garter snake."

Well that was just fantastic. He was going to fart on me, wasn't he? That was if he didn't spit at me…or maybe sink those lethal fangs into me. Yeah, it was probably a little hypocritical for a vampire to talk about fangs like that, but in my defence, Sventés didn't have fangs like Kejas did.

My nervousness increased when he suddenly began slinking down my body. And then something occurred to me. "He isn't poisonous, right?" I kind of got the feeling that Wes didn't like me, so it wouldn't have been surprising to find that he was hoping his pet would bite and kill me.

Wes' devious smile didn't put me at ease *what*soever.

"Is that thing going to hurt her?" Jared demanded.

With a 'pfft', Wes waved a hand. "It is merely a serpent, Jared."

That wasn't exactly an answer, was it? And I didn't trust this vampire as far as I could throw him. My nervousness rocketed to extreme levels when Toto's colour abruptly changed from grey to a brilliant blue that was typical of a blue racer snake. "What the—"

"He appears to like you." Wes sounded surprised, but pleasantly surprised.

"I'm flattered." If the hissing bastard went under my dress, I'd kill him.

"Something very fascinating about this breed I have created is that their colour changes with their moods – even while in tattoo form."

"Tattoo form?"

"Oh yes, I can turn him back to a tattoo whenever I wish to, just as I can summon him to appear in this form whenever I wish to. I find that when Toto is grey or black, he is alert and wary. I also find that when he is the blue shade that you see now, he is relaxed and content. I am indeed surprised as he is generally antisocial toward anyone other than myself."

"And yet you put him on me?" I said through my teeth. Wes merely smiled, but it was a genuine smile this time, and I realised that I had passed the test. That was great and all, but there was an antisocial, poisonous killer wrapped around my body. "Look, not to offend Toto or anything, but could you take him back? He's getting a little too close to my crotch than I'm comfortable with."

Wes' mouth twitched in a way that indicated he was holding back a laugh as he returned the snake to his shoulders. "I think I shall greet Antonio and Bran. It has been some time since we were all together." With that, he turned and walked away with Lena.

"I think that's everyone," I said to Jared, sighing in relief that I was alive and un-bit. "Can we go sit down now?"

"What about Fletcher and Norm?"

"Apparently they're intent on being fashionably late, so sod them."

Smiling, he dabbed my lips with his. "Sure, baby." But that smile disappeared as something over my shoulder caught his attention. Of course I'd known that there was an additional guest left to arrive. Well, 'guest' wasn't quite the right word. More like 'gate-crasher'. But I'd kind of hoped she'd fallen off a cliff or something. Clearly, there was no such luck.

Bracing myself, I slowly turned. So *this* was quite possibly one of the reasons Jared was so guarded. The cow had to be beautiful, didn't she? She couldn't just be a hideous heifer with oozing zits, overgrown hairy moles, and a big fat pimply arse. Instead, with her flawless pale skin, her long tumbling red hair, and curvaceous body, she was like a real-life Jessica Rabbit.

Her gaze – a heated, inviting gaze – didn't move from Jared even once as she approached, as if he was standing here all alone. It was a snub, and I knew it. Maybe, in addition to being a devious manipulator, she was a silly little mare who was curious to know what it would feel like to have my fist crashing into her face.

Even when she stopped in front of us, she didn't look at me. What cheesed me off most was that she actually reached out to cup Jared's cheek. He didn't back away. He did something even better. He growled so menacingly that everyone within hearing range froze. Just like that, most of the squad were gathered behind me.

She dropped her hand, but she didn't drop her sultry smile. "It's been so long, Jared. I've been so looking forward to seeing you again." Her consort didn't appear to like that, going by the scowl he was wearing and the jealousy shining from his eyes. It would seem that she had this one totally enamoured.

"I can't say I feel the same." Jared slipped his arm around me – a move that forced her to acknowledge my presence. She actually looked down her nose at me. That confirmed that she was, in fact, a silly little mare who was curious to know what it would feel like to have my fist crashing into her face.

I cocked my head. "Males who Turn people are referred to as 'Sires', so with you being a female, I guess that makes you…a 'Bitch'." Ignoring the muffled laughs coming from the squad, I gave her a winning smile.

Her answering one was thin and fake. "I have been looking forward to meeting you."

I almost snorted at that.

"Wait…is she a Sventé?" her consort asked disbelievingly, bursting into laughter.

Before I knew what was happening, my whip was in my hand and I'd cracked it around his throat, cutting off his laugh. Yes, I should be used to this by now and be easily able to shrug it off, but, well, I preferred not to.

Jared kissed my temple, grinning. "I think he's learned his lesson, baby."

I sighed. He was no fun. "Fine." I allowed the whip to fade away.

"A Sventé Feeder," said Magda to her red-faced, coughing consort. "I wouldn't have thought it possible, Brook. But, then, I wouldn't have thought it possible for Jared to claim someone, considering his issues with women in general."

There was an odd note to her voice that told me I was being baited. Obviously I wondered what she meant by that, especially since Jared was a mystery to me in some ways, and it got to me that I didn't know him as well as I wished to. But she would know that, wouldn't she? She was already using her gift against me.

Evan appeared then, wearing the mother of all scowls. He stopped at Jared's side, glaring at the woman in a way that said he'd happily kill her and think nothing of it.

"Evan," she crooned, "it is good to see you also."

"She's kidding, right?" he said to Jared, who tightened his arm around me.

"I heard about your mother. My condolences to both of you." To Jared, she then said, "I imagine, what with everything that happened, that you're not attending the funeral."

He'd be attending *hers* if she tried to touch him again. Slut. And here she was baiting me a second time. "Have you ever wondered what it would feel like to be on fire, Magda?" I asked casually. Her brow wrinkled. "Use your gift on me, and I'll use mine on you. That's how it's going to work. Don't test me on that. Unless, of course, you do have a curiosity about burning – I'd be more than happy to help you out with that."

"Someone seems a little jealous," said Brook.

I arched a brow at him. "Should I take that as an indication that you'd like to become better acquainted with my whip?" He swallowed hard, losing his smirk. Arsewipe.

"I think you may be right, Brook." Magda turned back to me, grinning. "I suppose it's only to be expected, considering I have a blood-link with the man you love."

I went nose to nose with her, smiling at the way it clearly unnerved her. So she wasn't as confident as she appeared to be. "Let's look at it this way: you need to use a gift to piss me off and make me jealous. All I have to do to have that effect on you is *breathe*."

Turning on my heel, I headed for the balcony, hoping to get a little fresh air. There was no point in acting as though her words hadn't had the desired effect. With her gift, she would know how they would make me feel. Annoying me even more, I knew she'd be enjoying it. However, what was pissing me off the most was that Jared had clearly opened up to her about his past when he had told me bugger all.

That was why I avoided his touch when he came up beside me. "I need a few minutes alone," I snapped.

"Don't give her what she wants, Sam."

It was too late. I already had. But if the wanker next to me had simply opened up to me like he'd opened up to her, I wouldn't be feeling like this at all. With that reasoning, all I wanted right then was for him to be far away from me. "I said, I need a few minutes alone."

He reached for me. "Baby—"

I pulled away. "*Don't* call me that." That was my kneejerk reaction whenever he upset me – to deny him the right to call me anything even remotely possessive. What complicated things a little was that his kneejerk reaction to that was to fuck me senseless to prove that I was his. At least he wouldn't be able to do that right now. Suddenly he caged my wrist with his hand and there was a queasy feeling in my stomach as he teleported us into one of the empty conference rooms in the mansion. Shit.

He shook his head at me as he removed his tie. "You said you wouldn't do this. You said you wouldn't let her come between us, but you are. You're doing it."

He was right. I was. And I hated myself for it, even as I couldn't help it.

"You know that I don't want her, Sam."

I snickered. "If I thought you wanted her, I'd be juggling your eyeballs right now. *This* is not about that."

He began to unbutton his shirt, but he didn't move his eyes from mine. "I'm not going to say it's unreasonable for you to be jealous and upset. If our positions were reversed, and I had to be around someone who had touched you and been inside you, it would be the hardest fucking thing I've ever dealt with. But I would *never* have let those feelings, or that person, fuck up what we have."

Ignoring the element of guilt I was feeling, I threw the question at him that simply wouldn't stop bugging me. "Why won't you go to your mum's funeral, Jared?"

He sighed and paused in his actions for a short moment. "Sam—"

Seeing what he was about to do, I pointed a finger at him. "No, don't you do that again. Don't you shut down again."

He shrugged his shoulders, suddenly defensive. "I just don't want to talk about her. Doesn't everyone have things they don't want to talk about?"

"Good point, yet irrelevant. I want to hear about her, I want to understand."

"Why? What the fuck does it matter? I don't want to go, and that's that."

"So Magda can know, but I can't?"

He double-blinked, removing his shirt. "What does *she* have to do with it?"

"You let *her* in."

"I didn't let her in, and I never would have. She doesn't know any details — only what emotions her gift allowed her to pick up." Obviously seeing the doubt in my eyes, he held up his hands. "Baby, I swear, she's the last person I'd let in."

Mollified, I went to say something, but it was difficult to keep on topic when looking at his well-defined, solidly built chest. The sod was well aware of that, of course. And then he lowered his zipper. The sound seemed to echo in the room. I didn't need to look to know that he was commando. "Don't think you can use sex to distract me."

"Would I do that?" he asked, all innocence.

"Yes, you would, and you are. Because you're an inconsiderate, selfish, cocky little bastard."

He pursed his lips as he considered that. "True…but I'm still going to fuck you, and you're still going to love it." And then he leaped at me.

CHAPTER FIVE

(Sam)

I moved quickly, but it wasn't quick enough to dodge his Pagori speed. Jared crushed me against a wall, mashing his mouth with mine. His kisses were possessive, raw, and punishing, and that familiar feeling of fire shot through me. Pulling back, he abruptly sank his teeth down hard into the crook of my neck, drinking deep. His moans vibrated against my skin, making me release moans of my own. I found myself clawing at the skin of his back, attempting to pull him tighter to me, even though we were as close as two people could be.

Need was in every movement as he yanked on my dress to free my breasts, cupping and squeezing them almost painfully. It wasn't just 'need' that was driving us. Anger and fear was feeding that need, making it become sheer desperation. I could sense that he was still being careful not to really hurt me; always bearing in mind how much stronger he was. It galled me that he could never completely let go with me, which added to the other feelings, making me almost frantic in my need to have him inside me.

Lifting my leg, he curled it over his hip and began rocking his hips against mine. I bucked as he used his thumb to send a sizzling jolt of electricity to each nipple, groaning at that perfect balance of pleasure and pain. Reaching under my dress, he slid my thong aside and did the same thing to my clit. He knew exactly how to make me mindless, and he always set about doing it.

Before Jared, I'd always thought foreplay was kind of overrated. In fact, it had often simply felt like going through the motions. But Jared never did the bare minimum to have me ready to take him, never made it seem like it was all simply a means to an end. I could always sense just how much pleasure he got from what he did to me, from the range of expressions that flashed across my face as my climax neared. Finally, I came, crying out and shaking.

His almost crazed eyes seized mine. "You are so fucking amazing to me." He speared two fingers inside me, swirling them around. "Nice and wet for me, just how I like it."

Then his fingers were gone, and he abruptly spun me to face the wall. Instinctively, I braced myself against it for balance. He shoved my dress up to my waist and, without any preamble, slammed into me. I cried out and arched my back as he buried every inch of himself inside me in one smooth stroke. He stretched and filled me in a way that no one ever had before.

When he didn't move, I squirmed. "*Jared.*"

His mouth was at my ear. "Feel how perfectly your body fits to mine. You were made to take me, Sam."

I squirmed again, trying to entice him to move. But still, he didn't. "Jared," I growled. "Don't tease!"

"Tell me you're mine, and I'll give you what you want." When I didn't, he teasingly flexed his cock inside me.

Well we could both play that game. I squeezed my muscles tight around him, smiling at his warning growl. "Make me come, and I'll tell you I'm yours." Instead, the cheeky sod spanked my arse. "Oh you—"

He *tsk*ed, spanking me again. "You know I won't let this go."

"I could just whip you senseless instead."

"Yes, baby, yes you could. But then you wouldn't get to come, would you?" His hands slowly, almost stealthily, skimmed over me. One then cupped my breast as the other wandered down to my clit, gently but expertly toying with it. "You know I love your spirit, and you know I love that you never back down, but you can't refuse me – the guy you'll soon be Bound to – the right to be possessive of you. You just can't. If I did that to you, what would you do?"

I answered without hesitation. "Carve out your liver, dice it up, and feed it to you." All right, so he had a fair point.

"Hear this, baby: I'll call you that whenever, and as often, as I want. Because you're mine and I'm yours. Isn't that right?" When I didn't answer, he gave me a particularly hard thrust. "You're mine and I'm yours. Isn't that right?"

After a short pause, I replied in a low voice, "Yes." Suddenly, I was flat on my back on the long table with my legs locked around his waist.

"I'm going to fuck you now. Fuck you hard and deep, so that all you feel is me."

It hadn't been a false promise. He began ruthlessly pounding into me, holding my gaze with eyes that blazed with possessiveness. At the same time, he was zapping my clit over and over with his thumb, and I was almost sobbing with the burning pleasure/pain of it. I could feel my orgasm creeping up on me fast, and so could he.

"I love feeling you come around me. Let me feel it, baby. Now."

A particularly hard zap to my clit knocked me over the edge and sent an explosion of sensation tearing through me, pulling a scream from me that Jared eagerly swallowed. Wanting him right there with me, I tore my mouth from his and bit into his shoulder, drinking him into me.

"Christ, baby." With a guttural groan, he slammed into me one last time and held himself still as he pulsed deep inside me.

He flopped forward, but landed on his elbows, careful not to crush me. Well I'd certainly never be able to look at this table again without smiling — which would make any future meetings in this room kind of interesting. With reverberations still racking our bodies, he rested his forehead against mine and gently kissed me, sipping from my mouth. "Don't pull away from me like that again."

I sighed. "I was just ticked off."

"I'll make sure she leaves."

"She's not going anywhere. She stays."

He jerked back to examine my face. "What do you mean, she stays?"

"If she wants to see our Binding ceremony, that's exactly what she's going to do." Because it would severely piss her off.

"You won't be able to hide your feelings from her, Sam," he told me gently. "You won't be able to pretend she's not feeding your insecurities."

Smoothing my hands over his shoulders, I joined them behind his neck. "I know that. She'll sense that she's getting to me. But she'll also see that I'm not going anywhere; that we're going through with that ceremony whether she approves or not. Besides, I wouldn't want to be robbed of the chance to use my gifts on her." Magda might have a bad attitude, but so did I, and mine was much worse.

It was a long moment before he spoke. "If she gets too much—"

"I'm not going to challenge her, Jared. I know what it's like to feel a blood-link die – I'd never been through more pain than what I had when I killed Victor. I don't want you going through that."

He looked a mixture of amazed and pissed. "You think I care about a bit of fucking pain?"

"You probably don't. But I care about putting you through it. See, this is how I feel when you try to protect me and I don't need it. It's going to work both ways."

He opened his mouth to say something, but then snapped it shut. "Come on, let's get back. People will be wondering where we are."

As we were both fixing our clothes, something occurred to me. "She probably felt it, didn't she?"

"What?"

"When we were shagging, she probably sensed it through your blood-link as you're still in close proximity."

He tilted his head and frowned thoughtfully. Then he shrugged. "Maybe."

What could only be described as an evil smile surfaced on my face. "Good."

He chuckled. "So merciless." Linking his hand with mine, he gave me a light yet still very possessive kiss before teleporting us back to the parlour. But he didn't teleport us to the balcony, or to the doorway, or to a quiet corner. No, he teleported us to the centre of the dance floor with a wicked laugh. The sod knew I didn't like slow dancing.

(Jared)

Before she could pull away from me, I aligned her body to mine, took her arms and curled them around my neck. I then slid both of my arms around her, settling one under the curtain of her dark hair that covered the bare skin of her upper back, and snaking the other down her body. It was with great reluctance that she joined in the dancing. As usual, I found myself enthralled at how snug she felt against me…even if she was stiff as a board. "Relax."

"I will when you move your hand from my arse."

"But it's comfortable there."

"You know I don't like slow dancing."

"Dancing is just like sex – get the rhythm right and you can't go wrong."

"We could just go back to the apartment and have some more sex?" she said hopefully.

"We can't leave our own gathering early." Could we?

"You know you want to," she breathed into my ear before nibbling on the lobe.

"None of your little tricks," I admonished with a smile, tapping her ass lightly but punishingly. Ignoring her scowl, I tightened my arms around her. When that scowl morphed into a grin, I narrowed my eyes. "What?"

Sam tipped her head toward her left. "I think I may have been right. I think Jessica Rabbit might have sensed us shagging."

Glancing briefly in the direction she had indicated, I almost laughed. If the look on Magda's face was anything to go by, Sam was right. Hell, steam might as well have been coming out of her ears. I personally didn't give a shit either way, but I could feel that Sam was smug. If that cheered her up, fine.

Nuzzling Sam's neck, I breathed her in, took inside me that vanilla scent that was tinted with honeycomb. It was the best smell in the whole damn world. My cock was in total agreement; it rose to attention when even a hint of it was in the air. I let my tongue flick out to taste her pulse. Her skin tasted slightly like her scent; like vanilla and honeycomb, and like energy and mine.

"Stop it, or I'll get horny again."

I smiled at the breathlessness in her voice. I loved how sensitive her neck was. "I'm already there." Subtly, I ground my once-again-hard cock against her.

She laughed and moaned at the same time. The sound of quick, purposeful footsteps had us both swerving to see our personal assistant coming toward us.

"I've been looking for you." Fletcher's perceptive eyes scanned both of us. "Been for a bonk, I see."

"What's your excuse – *you* being my best friend – for being so late?" she snapped.

"Oh chilax, will you."

"Chilax?" I chuckled, confused.

"It's a mix of 'chill' and 'relax'," Fletcher quickly explained. "Norm and I were busy preparing your gift from us."

"Gift?" Sam repeated. "Maybe you're forgiven. What do you mean by 'preparing'?"

A huge and very self-satisfied grin spread across his face. "Come see."

Exchanging a smile with Sam, I walked with her hand-in-hand behind Fletcher. The other guests followed as Fletcher led us out of the parlour, down the everlasting pristine hallway, and out of the mansion. I frowned as I immediately scented fire and the unmistakable smell of meat cooking.

As we neared the white sandy beach, Sam gasped loudly. There was Norm flipping burgers, hotdogs, and steaks on a barbeque grill. Not far from the grill was a large bonfire around which some members of the legion stood drinking beer-flavoured NSTs. There was also a reggae band sitting there expectantly, waiting to be given the signal to play. And, in a typical beach set up, Norm and Fletcher had decorated the space with bamboo tiki torches, colourful lights, and lantern garlands.

Fletcher elbowed Sam. "Well, what do you think? I knew you'd be bored and miserable as hell in that parlour – ooh, no offense, your Grandness." His expression was one of total innocence when he smiled at the Keja vampire not far behind him.

Antonio's mouth twitched. "It's quite all right."

Fletcher mouthed 'phew' at Sam before speaking again. "Anyway, I knew you'd be more comfortable having a gathering like this."

She hugged him tightly. "Thank you."

Sensing Sam's spirits instantly lifting, I nodded my thanks at him. In all honesty, I'd have preferred a barbeque on the beach to champagne in a grand mansion any day. It seemed that everybody else did, too, because the atmosphere became much more relaxed and there was a lot of laughing as opposed to formal chatter.

Fletcher had even set up a beach bar and elected Damien to be the cocktail barman, ordering him to wear a brightly coloured shirt that matched the ones being worn by the reggae band. He didn't look too happy about that. Not only was Norm serving hotdogs, burgers, and steaks, but also baked potatoes, salads, and kebabs. None of it went to waste.

Hell, they'd even arranged for party entertainers to do fire eating and fire juggling. To add to that, they had provided beach balls and water guns for the more immature members of the legion – the ones who weren't so unbelievably childish that they were burying each other in the sand, anyway. Yes, Fletcher and Norm had pretty much outdone themselves. I knew they'd mostly done it for Sam because they adored her, but I was still grateful.

Relaxing with Sam between my legs on one of the many beach loungers that were gathered around the bonfire, I laughed as Wes told funny stories about Antonio's first years as a vampire. Apparently, he hadn't been much different from me back then. I wondered if maybe one of the reasons he had selected me to be part of the legion was that he had seen something of himself in me.

"Evan," drawled a sultry voice that had the effect of nails on a chalkboard to me. "Aren't you going to tell us some stories about what Jared was like in the early years…maybe even his childhood?"

Of course Magda had known exactly what she was doing, just as she had known that Sam would instantly tense up. What Magda hadn't known – I doubted that any of us had been expecting it – was that her hair was suddenly going to catch fire.

Eating her kebab, Sam watched in an almost detached interest as a screaming Magda shot up from the lounger beside ours, patting her hair. Then, still looking bored, Sam raised her hand and sent a gush of water at Magda, calming the flames.

With her soaking wet hair plastered to her head, a quivering extremely-cheesed-off Magda honed in on the amazing female between my legs.

Sam merely shrugged one shoulder delicately. "I did warn you." How she managed to keep a straight face when the majority of people around her – including me – were shaking with silent laughter, I had no idea.

Somehow, Magda remained dignified as she left with her consort in tow. That was when everyone erupted into laughter again, not bothering to keep their laughs quiet this time.

Sensing Sam's smugness, I couldn't help smiling. Cupping her chin, I turned her head and brought her face to meet mine, speaking against her mouth. "You enjoyed that, didn't you?"

She gasped in mock horror. "You can't seriously be insinuating that I enjoy inflicting pain on another person?" She jiggled her head. "All right, I did. But she's not a person, she's a bitch who hurt you, so I don't give a fuck."

Who wouldn't love a girl who'd set someone on fire for you?

The person who was laughing the loudest was actually Wes. He even nodded approvingly at Sam. I felt that she was surprised by it. I wasn't. Earlier, I'd noticed that Wes was testing Sam. It might have ticked me off if I hadn't been one hundred percent positive that nothing he did could faze her.

Sure, a huge part of me had wanted to tell him to back off and leave her alone, but then she'd have whipped my ass for fighting her battles for her. However, if she hadn't passed his test I would have definitely stepped in, because the guy would have then done everything he could to separate us. I'd never let anyone, or anything, do that. Not even her.

(Sam)

Pain. So much pain. Every single part of me hurt, just as it had when the brothers had done something to me. I wanted to cry, I wanted to scream, I wanted to curse and writhe in sheer agony. But I couldn't.

I couldn't move at all, not even to open my eyelids.

I had expected Jared to sense my pain, to wake and help me. But I could hear him breathing evenly beside me, totally relaxed. Whatever was happening wasn't simply paralysing me, it was interfering with my connection to Jared. And didn't that just spook the crap out of me, increasing my panic.

The whole thing made me think of 'intraoperative awareness' – incidences when people who were anaesthetised could see, hear, and feel but were unable to move or communicate this in any way. Despite feeling like someone's hands were tearing into me and rummaging around in my abdomen, despite feeling as though those same hands were crushing my insides, I couldn't give in to that primal urge to scream.

Instead, I screamed in my head at the feeling of invisible, harsh, merciless fingers torturing my body and poking inside my head. Then, suddenly, the pain stopped, and I jack-knifed to a sitting position, panting as utter terror continued to flow through me.

Jared's hands framed my face, searching my expression. "What is it, baby? Bad dream?"

"No, I woke up to this horrible pain. I was hurting all over, but I couldn't tell you, I couldn't move."

He crushed me to him, kissing my temple. "You sure you weren't dreaming?"

"It wasn't a dream."

His voice was like a blade. "Was it the same pain you felt when the brothers hurt you?"

I nodded. "Do you think Antonio's researchers will find out anything?"

"If there's something worth finding out, those guys will find it." The confidence in his voice made me breathe better. If they were so good that Jared relaxed at the mere thought of them, they had to be extremely capable.

"What do you think the brothers did to me?" My voice was quiet, almost vulnerable.

Jared squeezed me tightly. "I swear I'll find out what they did, and I'll get them to fix it."

"I know."

It was only an hour or so after breakfast that I, Jared, Denny, Max, Harvey, and Jude were stood outside the block of apartments where Janine Peterson lived – or had lived – with her boyfriend. Ten minutes before, Antonio had informed us that the boyfriend had returned from whatever trip he had been on. Jared had teleported us all there, and now it was time to get some answers.

Jude was obviously raring to get those answers, but Jared and I had instructed her not to interrupt our interrogation. Providing she didn't interfere, the boyfriend would be all hers once we were done questioning him.

As we ascended the graffiti-covered stairs, we past many drugged humans – some of whom were injecting themselves right there, right then. Although I wasn't a Keja, I – like all vampires – had an otherworldly lure that made humans take notice. And they *did* take notice of each and every one of us. I was pretty sure that if Jude and I had been on our own, we would have been attacked – not that our attackers would have gotten very far, of course. The 'fuck off' looks that Jared and the squad were wearing hadn't been ignored. Wise of the humans.

Finally outside the apartment number on Janine's driver's license, we didn't bother knocking. Nor did we force our way inside. The last thing we needed was to have a door we couldn't lock behind us, as that would allow others to glimpse inside. There would be much worth seeing tonight, and although it was unlikely that any human – particularly a drugged one – would have been believed if they had reported what they witnessed, it was always important to be careful.

One thing that science fiction had got right was that there were indeed human government divisions that fully believed vampires existed, and these divisions were absolutely intent on getting hold of one. Maybe they even had caught a vampire at some point, but if they had, they weren't content with just the one. They investigated each and every report that even had a hint of vampirism to it, no matter how small or how ridiculous, in the hope that it might lead them somewhere. It was best to not help them out with that.

Seeing that the hallway was totally clear, Denny reduced himself to mush and slipped under the door. When the door opened enough to allow us all to enter, we then locked it behind us. Instantly we found ourselves in a small, cluttered living area that stunk heavily of smoke, sweat, stale food, and the distinctive scent of cannabis. Refraining from balking had been a challenge for every one of us.

At the sound of a toilet flushing, our heads whipped around to our left. One of the three doors further down the hallway opened, and out stepped a tall, gangly guy with dark unkempt hair and skin almost as pale as mine. Upon seeing us, he – Leon, I remembered Janine calling him – froze.

The movement might not have registered to a human before it was too late, but it was like slow motion to a vampire when Leon reached behind him and retrieved a gun from the waistband of his jeans. He had barely had a chance to aim it at us when Harvey used his telekinesis to snatch the weapon and pull it to him.

Leon's eyes widened to saucers. To his credit, he didn't freeze with fear like others might have done. But before he could take more than one step backwards – I assumed he wanted to head for his bedroom where there was most likely another gun – Denny had sprayed yellowy-green ooze out of his thumbs and smallest fingers, trapping him. Denny then used the sticky ooze to bounce Leon from the hallway to the ragged sofa. At Jared's command, Denny didn't release the human from the grip of the ooze.

Jared and I stood in front of the sofa, looking down at him. My voice was deceptively pleasant. "You must be Leon. Glad you're finally back." The poor bugger looked like he might piss himself. I hoped not. The place smelled foul enough as it was. "I'll bet you're wishing you'd stayed away a little longer though, eh?"

He swallowed hard. "Whatever it is you're looking for, I didn't take it."

That statement was sort of the equivalent of a child suddenly saying 'Mummy, I didn't do anything with your scissors', and then you turn to find your curtains have been chopped up. "So Janine was telling the truth. You like to take what isn't yours to take."

"J-Janine?"

"Yes, we had an interesting conversation with her. She's a lovely girl. I noticed that she was pregnant. How long does she have left before the birth?"

"A month or so," he lied easily.

In my experience, most thieves were, in fact, good liars. I supposed they had to be. "How sweet."

"Look, I haven't done any jobs for months now. I've been trying to get myself clean."

"Tell me, are you a kleptomaniac, or are you just one of those people who are lazy and greedy and have a sense of entitlement?"

His brow crinkled. "Kleptomaniac?"

"A kleptomaniac is someone who is addicted to thieving. They get the same kind of high from it that a drug addict would get from cocaine."

His face scrunched up into a defensive expression. "It's not like the people I steal – *stole* – from can't easily replace what I took."

"And that's how you justify it to yourself, is it? Tell me, how do you justify helping unborn babies being stolen from their mothers?"

His mouth bobbed open and closed like a landed fish. Eventually, he shrugged, "I have no idea what you're talking about."

Jared snickered, crossing his arms over his chest. "I'm not sure there's much point in you playing dumb. We know about the criminal organisation. We know about the Scouts, the Deliverers, and the Medics. But there's more, isn't there, Leon? So much more. What we really want are names. Janine was quite informative, but she was unable to give us any names. She seemed to think that you, however, might just be able to."

Leon's eyes danced between Jared and me. "Janine wouldn't have said anything. She's not stupid."

"Are you sure about that?" I asked. "Are you sure she'd be so tight-lipped if, say, someone had done this right before her very eyes?" Using the energy I'd absorbed from around me, I manipulated it into my energy whip. Leon blanched.

"Janine had pretty much the same reaction," Jared told him. "But come on, are you really that shocked when you're wrapped in ooze and you watched someone take your gun without even touching it?"

Leon swallowed hard again. He was trembling now. "I snorted a lot of shit earlier."

"Ah, and you're hoping to convince yourself it's just the drugs?" I had to smile at that. "I can promise you right now, Leon, you are certainly not hallucinating or dreaming. I could pinch you just so you can be sure? Or maybe I'll just do this." I cracked my whip at him, catching his earlobe. Leon jerked, hissing.

"I recommend you get talking," said Jared, his voice grave. "I'm not a patient person at the best of times, but the last couple of days have tried me in ways you can't imagine. I'm not in a good frame of mind." He leaned forward, putting himself at eye level with Leon. "I want the name of the person who's running this operation." I knew that Jared doubted he knew a detail such as that, but it was always worth asking.

"What are you people?"

Jared's smile wasn't nice. "You don't want to know. Trust me on that. Now, I believe you were going to tell me his name."

"I don't know his name, I don't know any names."

Jared rolled his eyes. "It's like groundhog day. They always say the same shit." He gave Max a short nod. Understanding, Max opened his fist and closed it – robbing Leon of the ability to speak. When the human realised that not one of his words were at all audible, his eyes almost bugged out of his drawn face.

Jared's unpleasant smile returned. "We wouldn't want anyone hearing you scream, would we?" With that, he raised one hand and placed his fingertips against Leon's forehead. Leon's mouth opened in a silent scream as currents of electricity zinged through him, making his entire body shake. Ten seconds later, Jared stopped. He signalled for Max to give Leon back his ability to speak. "His name."

Leon, panting and shaking his head, said, "I swear I don't know. I can't tell you what I don't know."

Jared sighed. "Max." Once Leon had again lost his ability to vocalise, Jared again repeated his torturous process. It was fifteen seconds this time before he stopped and allowed Max to undo what he'd done. "I want his name."

"Please, please, please listen to me. I don't know his name." Seeing that Jared was again about to give Max a signal, Leon quickly cried, "*But I'll tell you what I do know, I swear.*"

I cocked my head at him. "And what is it, exactly, that you *do* know? It better be good, Leon."

"My part in the whole thing is simple. I receive a text message with the name of a shopping mall or something like that. I send Janine there, and I wait for her to contact me with a description of the woman she's drugged. I relay this info to the Deliverer in a text message. That's all."

That's consistent with what Janine said, I reminded Jared. "You must know the Deliverer's name, at the very least."

"I don't, I've never once heard her voice. I only know she's a woman because Janine saw her from afar a few times. We only communicate using text messages, and I delete them afterwards like I was instructed when I first got the job."

I arched a brow. "Oh yeah? And what were these instructions?"

"Wait for text messages, don't act until I receive any, never talk of the operation to anyone, and only ever drug the women with the drug that they leave with the money."

"So how do you get the drug and your wages if you don't come face-to-face with anyone?"

"Every month, I'm sent a text message with the address of wherever they've hidden the money and the drug. Sometimes it's in a public bathroom, sometimes it's in a phone booth, or hidden in a bush near the local park. I never know where the stuff's going to be, and I never see anyone. These people are very secretive. Paranoid, even."

Jared sniggered. "You expect us to believe that you've never seen even *one* face, you've never heard even *one* name?"

"I haven't, I swear—"

Sighing in annoyance, Jared nodded at Max. A stream of words came out of a petrified Leon, but none were audible. "Oh, you've remembered something." Instead of electrocuting him, Jared again nodded at Max, who returned Leon's ability to speak. "What's that now?"

Leon was almost sobbing. "When I first met the person who

recruited me, she introduced herself as Wendy. Janine's description of the Deliverer matched the Wendy I spoke to: a middle-aged blonde who wore glasses."

I knew he was telling the truth about that part at least. It was the same description that Jude and Janine had given us.

"Where's your cell phone?" Jared asked him.

"The kitchen counter."

I retrieved the phone. "Is the number saved in your contact list?"

Leon nodded. "Under the name 'Del'. Short for Deliverer."

I exhaled heavily and gave him a bright smile. "Well, that's all. You've been quite helpful. More than I thought, considering you lack a conscience."

He sneered. "You can be moral and law abiding when life's going good. I'll bet none of you know what it's like to have nothing, to be so damn hungry you were rummaging through a garbage can, to just need one hit."

I knew more about poverty than he thought, but I had no wish to explain myself to him. I shrugged. "Then I guess we're doing you a favour by letting our friend here end your pitiful existence." His face became a question mark. "Leon…Meet Jude."

CHAPTER SIX

(Sam)

Looking at myself in my oval mirror a few hours later, I groaned in exasperation. When Fletcher had knocked on the door and thrust a shopping bag at me, I'd known what would be inside, and I'd known it would be revealing. Of course if Fletcher was here, he would have disagreed; he would have said that the blood-red satin dress was 'flattering' and 'skin tight'. In reality, it was revealing.

Wearing a crooked smile, Jared came up behind me and curled his arms around my waist. "As much as I love this dress on you, it's making me want to take it off and have my way with you."

"I fully plan to take it off, it's too revealing."

He frowned. "No, leave it on. It's not revealing, it's flattering."

I groaned again. Now Fletcher's little phrases were rubbing off on Jared. Wasn't that special.

He just chuckled. "Cheer up, baby. We're about to go on a dinner cruise as part of the celebrations for our Binding."

"I know. But I can't help feeling guilty for enjoying myself when that organisation is still up and running." Jude hadn't taken it well when I told her that we wouldn't be calling the Deliverer. We didn't want to do anything that would be considered out of the ordinary for Leon, and he'd said that *she* contacted *him*. So we needed to wait for the Deliverer to get in touch before we could make our next move, but naturally Jude's patience for vengeance was running low. I couldn't blame her for that.

Jared nuzzled my neck. "I know what you mean. I feel bad shoving this matter aside, but how else are we going to enjoy this week unless we keep the assignment and the celebrations totally separate in our minds?"

I sighed. "All right, smart arse."

Having let Jared talk me into not changing my dress, we then headed for the beach. I should have guessed that Antonio – the flashy sod – wouldn't have just any yacht, but a luxury almost futuristic-looking one. The interior was more like a five-star hotel; it had a spacious lounge, a classy dining area, and several private cabins. Additionally, there was an outer dining area on the deck where two long tables were set up and a band was waiting. Wow, Antonio had gone all out tonight.

While the squad, the Master Vampires, Fletcher and Norm sat at one table, the High Master Vampires sat at the other with me, Jared, Evan, Antonio, Luther, Sebastian, Wes, and Lena. Just as they had at the informal gathering, Marcia, Rowan, and Ricardo were quite standoffish with me. They even went as far as to ignore my presence at the table, running their gaze along everyone but me as they spoke.

The fact that no one had stepped in to defend me would speak volumes to these prats – Jared, Antonio, and the others all believed me capable of protecting myself. Still, I could feel Jared's frustration, knew that he wanted to say something anyway, but a few cautioning pinches from me stopped him.

To my surprise, it was Marcia who was the worst. She had some nerve, considering that she wasn't even a powerful vampire; she was simply Bound to one – quite different. I wanted to seriously dislike her, but it was hard to dislike someone who was a silent partner in many human charities. I was in the same situation with Rowan and Ricardo. Neither of them were what anyone could call 'bad people'.

Rowan, though largely unpleasant, had his good points. I had learned that the reason he had such an extensive bloodline wasn't because he was quite the biter. It was that whenever he had encountered a human who knew a little too much about vampires, he hadn't immediately killed them as necessary. He had given them the choice: death or vampirism. Not many would want to be responsible for so many vampires. But despite that his numbers were large, he continued to make this offer.

In his human years, Ricardo had been a priest. He had done a lot of good back then. Even now, although he wasn't the nicest soul, he still had a kindness about him. He was the most supportive Sire out there. He was sure to remain in contact with each of his vampires, always helping those who might need it. They all respected him and followed him, which wasn't always the case with Sires – I was a prime example of that.

Marcia's words pulled me from my thoughts. "I imagine this kind of extravagance is something you had not encountered until coming here." It was a jab, and had Jared still been sitting next to me as opposed to talking to one of the Master Vampires on the neighbouring table, he'd have said something. No doubt she had purposely waited until he was absent. "I heard that you lived in a poverty stricken area of London. Is that also where your Sire is from?"

I casually took a sip of my red wine-flavoured NST, hiding my irritation. "I'm actually not sure where Victor *was* from."

"Your Sire is deceased?"

"Yeah. A crazy bitch killed him." I saw that Antonio, Sebastian, Luther, and Evan were fighting the urge to smile.

"I have been told that the physical pain of losing a Sire is almost unbearable." Connelly's comment came out sounding like a question.

I shrugged. "It was far from a tickle."

Marcia sighed. "Well, I suppose if you're going to base yourself in an area that has a high crime rate, you're going to meet your end sooner rather than later. I imagine that is why you came here. You sought sanctuary after his death."

"Sam's here because I recruited her," interjected Sebastian, agitated. "She was made Jared's co-commander because she earned the position. It is a job that she is very good at."

Rowan clenched his fists. "But she is a Svente."

I gently swirled my NST as my eyes flickered from him to Marcia. "I was wondering…You know when you act like this, do you feel much like those kids in the Harry Potter books that are prejudiced against muggles?"

Holding out his hands, Rowan said, "See this from our perspective."

"But then I'd have to ask Jared to jam my head all the way up my arse."

Apparently Rowan decided to ignore my comment. "You are of the weakest breed, both in terms of your physical capabilities and your gift. Yes, granted you have a powerful gift, and you are in control of it. But will you always be able to control it? That is the question. If you were a Pagori, I might be inclined to think so."

I snorted. "If I was a Pagori, we wouldn't be having this conversation."

Ricardo leaned forward. "I will be honest with you, Miss Parker. I believe you have some good qualities. You appear to be bright, strong-willed, and bold. They are qualities that I admire. I can see why Jared is taken with you, particularly as you also have…physical attributes." Everyone ignored Marcia's snort. "But that is not enough for me."

I smiled. "Oh I don't know. Haven't you heard what they say about us? Once you've had a Sventé, you'll never go back."

Evan's laugh didn't wash down well with the three idiots. "Let me save you all some time. You won't win an argument with Sam, and you won't make her feel like she isn't worthy of Jared or the position that she'll soon have."

"We do not wish to argue with anyone," Ricardo assured him. "We simply wish to express our viewpoint."

"*And* point out that Jared could do much better for himself than a common girl who can barely speak proper English," said Marcia, huffing at me. "I suppose you are a product of drug addicts then, are you? I'll bet you later became one, too. I'll bet you went down the road of prostitution to pay for your addiction. I wouldn't be surprised if that is how you came to be a vampire. You took the wrong type of client."

I gasped as if in awe of her. "Wow, how did you guess that so accurately? Do something else. What shape am I picturing in my head?"

A loud laugh burst out of Evan while Antonio, Luther, and Sebastian chuckled silently. Even Bran and Kaiser appeared amused.

"Insolent!"

"You couldn't come up with anything better? Seriously?" When she opened her mouth – most likely to insult me further – I raised a hand to stop her. "It's all right, Marcia, no need to apologise. I've been called worse by better, if I'm honest with you."

Rowan straightened in his seat. "I would appreciate it if you would not insult my partner."

"Tit for tat, and all that," I said, shrugging.

"How about you learn some manners," suggested Marcia, sneering.

"How about you just act like adults?" I proposed. "What do you think?" I took another gulp of my NST. "There is, of course, the other option – you can piss off." Rowan spluttered, apparently unused to anyone speaking to him that way. I looked at him sympathetically as he tried stuttering a comeback that made no sense. "Ah, is your battery running out?"

"Everything okay?" asked Jared as he returned to his seat.

Unsurprisingly, the three cheeky sods forced smiles and nodded at him.

But Jared wasn't dumb. *What did they say to you?*

Most likely exactly what you're thinking they said. There's no point reproaching them. I'm not going to win them over unless I'm prepared to do some kind of power-demonstration. No way am I proving myself to three toffee-nosed twats.

Toffee-nosed? he repeated, amused.

In other words, they're snobs.

After a three course meal and a lot of NSTs, most of the guests were up and dancing – even the three whiners, unbelievably. What inspired Damien to take the microphone and do a rendition of Michael Jackson's 'Billie Jean', I wasn't sure. But it had been a hell of a laugh watching him do the artist's signature moves. My laugh kind of died when Magda got up and sang Peggy Lee's 'Fever', staring at Jared the entire time. Did she have no shame?

Jared, however, didn't look at her even once. Oh he was well aware that the song was for his benefit, but he was playing dumb and focusing totally on me. Maybe a big reason for that was he could sense the homicidal urges I was having.

Obviously having guessed her game, the squad had gathered around my table supportively; joking around to distract me. So when Magda approached, she had a hard time trying to make any sly comments over the noise they were making. But the bitch was persistent, and that persistence finally paid off.

I had to grit my teeth when I heard, "Jared, do you remember the time when you and I made love to that song?"

The feel of both mine and Jared's anger shooting through my system almost had me throwing a fireball at her. But then Denny, who was standing in front of her, did the sweetest thing. He farted at her.

Now, having anyone fart at you would be bad. But as Denny was able – as one of his animal-mimic abilities – to release anal musk like a skunk…well, that was a bad moment for Magda. She nearly fell to her knees as the stench hit her. Her coughs and balks were drowned out by the laughs coming from me, Jared, and the guys. It was hard for me to stomach the smell, but the satisfaction I got from watching that bitch nearly pass out from a musky fart just purely diluted it. Even her consort looked like he wanted to laugh as he teleported her away — most likely because he disliked the attention she gave Jared and kind of thought of it as karma.

"Denny, I will love you forever for doing that," I told him.

A beaming smile took over his baby-face. "I wasn't about to let her get away with that remark."

"It's my turn next time," declared Chico. At my quizzical frown, he huffed. "She can't do shit like that to our Coach and think she'll get away with it. That's not how things work around here. Next time she tries something, she'll find a dart in her ass. I might even ask Reuben to strengthen my gift before I do it. That way, she won't just pass out, she'll croak." He said it all so casually, as if we were simply discussing the weather.

Aw. "You lot are the best." At Jared's growl, I quickly added, "Of course you're the best of them all." He snorted.

"How about a dance, Coach?" asked Max, his lips twitching. He'd said it purely to rile Jared. It worked.

"Not a fucking chance, Slaphead." Jared possessively placed his hand on my thigh. Of course his reaction absolutely delighted Max, who instantly went into a fit of laughter. Feeling protective of Jared, I decided that a little crack of the whip to Max's earlobe would be fun. I sucked the energy around me into my palms, and...and nothing. So I tried again. Nothing. Nothing fucking happened.

Sensing my confusion and anxiety, Jared turned to me. "What's wrong?"

"I don't know." Again I tried to manipulate the energy, but again it didn't work. So I tried shaping the energy into a ball instead...but still nothing. I was feeding on the energy in the same way that I always did, but I couldn't do anything with it. "Shit."

"What, what is it?"

"Something's really wrong. My gift isn't—" And then a burst of energy shot out of my palms, sending me and my chair flying backwards with the impact. Crashing into the wall behind me, I bounced out of my seat and fell on my hands and knees on the deck.

Jared was there in an instant. "What the fuck was that?"

"*That* was a tank of energy needing an outlet." An outlet that I hadn't been able to give it. Oh those fucking brothers had a lot to answer for.

Well this was fun. Although the conversation centred round me, not one person was addressing me. Jared, Antonio, Luther, Sebastian, Wes, Lena, and Evan were all pacing around my living area while I sat quietly on the sofa. Even the normally composed Antonio seemed unable to sit down. I could see panic on each and every face. It was the same panic that I was feeling.

Lena sighed. "For someone to have changed her to the extent that it is interfering with her gift, they must have changed her at a fundamental level."

"What level?" Jared was pale even for him. The incident had sent his protectiveness into overdrive, and he looked on the verge of snapping.

"It would be the same as for me to alter a human's internal system so that they can no longer digest their food. Sam can feed on the energy around her, but she cannot shape or control it. Much like a human would vomit in the case of being unable to digest their food, Sam had an abrupt release of the energy that she had absorbed."

"Isn't that what happens when a Feeder first develops their power?" Evan asked me.

"Yes," I replied. "Because we don't even realise we're absorbing energy, and when we do, we can't control it."

"So, what, she's digressing?" Jared asked Lena.

She exhaled heavily. "I truly have no idea, though it would appear so."

I finally asked her the question that was taunting me. "Will I lose my gift?"

Her expression was sympathetic. "Possibly."

Silence hit the room, and I felt as though I'd been dealt a blow to the chest as the breath practically whooshed out of me. My gift wasn't simply an ability to me. It was part of who I was. The truth was that I'd be kind of lost without it; it would feel like losing a part of myself.

Knowing that, Jared came and squeezed my shoulder. "How about your ability to Merge? Has that been affected?"

I exhaled heavily. "Let's find out." Standing, I placed my hand on Jared's chest and attempted to meld into him. Nothing. Well fuck a duck. Half-sighing, half-growling, I slumped back down onto the sofa.

"Has there been anything else happening to you that is out of the norm?" asked Antonio, his tone sensitive.

"Pain," I told him, swallowing hard. "There was this awful, unbearable pain…but I couldn't move, couldn't scream, couldn't do anything. Jared didn't even sense it through our connection."

The look on Antonio's face told me that that wasn't good at all. "I would say, then, that Lena is right. What's happening to you is happening on such a fundamental level that it can interfere with almost anything; your gifts, your body, and even your connection to Jared."

"Will it stop the Binding from working?" Jared's voice was low.

"No," Antonio assured him. "Nothing could do that."

Lena nodded in agreement. "It is likely that whatever is happening will be over before the ceremony anyway."

Jared, who was far from placated by the answers he'd been given, scrubbed a hand over his face. "There has to be someone who can help. Someone who can undo what's happening, or who can at least tell us what's happening."

"The only people who can help with that are the vampires responsible," Lena told him. "Had Sam been human or an animal, I could have aided her in some way. But my gift, though strong, is not that powerful. Technically, this particular gift should not be as strong as to have any effect on a vampire."

A thought came to me. "What if we had Reuben enhance your gift, make it stronger, would that do any good?"

She cocked her head as she considered it. "I cannot say for sure. It's worth a try, I suppose."

Jared's enthusiasm and hope was almost visible. "I'll go get him." Then he was gone.

Evan turned to me, sighing. "Hard seeing him like that, isn't it? Jared's usually so self-assured and at ease." I nodded. "He's scared of losing you."

"I don't think I'm dying, Evan, I really don't."

"I don't either. But if this situation was the other way around, if Jared was in pain and losing control of his gifts, would you take any chances? Would you allow yourself the luxury of trusting that he'll live?"

No, I wouldn't. "In other words, you want me to not give him a hard time about the overprotectiveness." Evan's smile was sheepish. I sighed. "Fine."

We all smiled as Jared returned with good ole Reub.

"Ah, Reuben," drawled Antonio. "Good of you to come."

My squad member nodded at him before running his gaze over me. "Coach, you okay? That was some release of energy back there. Don't worry, we didn't tell anyone that your gift went weird, we just said that you and Jared were having a fight."

"Focus, Reuben," said Jared. "We need you to use your gift on Lena."

"No problem." One brief touch to the shoulder had Lena's gift more powerful. "Is there any other way I can help?"

I shook my head. "Hopefully, we won't need any more help."

When Jared reached for him, Reuben raised a hand and headed for the front door. "I can get back to my apartment myself. You guys look like you need to be together right now."

Wasn't he lovely? "Thanks for coming. See you tomorrow." He nodded and left.

Lena shook her head a little. "Strange how different, stronger, I now feel."

"Do you think you're strong enough to help Sam?" asked Jared.

She inhaled deeply. "I can try. I would appreciate it if no one speaks while I study her." She came to sit beside me on the sofa, but she didn't touch me. Her attention was all on me, though her eyes seemed slightly out of focus. Minutes later, she took a deep breath and graciously accepted the NST that Sebastian was holding.

"Do you see DNA strands?" I asked.

"It's like looking at numbers and equations. I see what adds up, and what doesn't, in which case I can spot abnormalities. I see weak points, and I see strong points; therefore I know a person's strengths and weaknesses. I am able to shuffle the numbers around, make different equations, thus making a person stronger or weaker or different. Providing those equations make sense, there will be no problems."

"So...the brothers' equations weren't adding up," I surmised. "That was why the vampires they held were deformed."

"Yes. If a being has too many weak points, it is impossible to significantly strengthen them. So it might be reasonable to assume that the other vampires hadn't been strong enough to undergo the changes. The brothers were clearly hoping to strengthen you in some way, but I do not understand what they were trying to achieve. What I can tell is that they have tried to change you at a dramatic, massive level. The problem is…some of the equations aren't adding up. Where your gifts were once strong, they are now weak."

"What else?"

"As you know, when a person is Turned, their body changes in many ways. As they go through the transition, sensory organs are improved so that vision, hearing, and sense of smell are all enhanced. The circulatory, skeletal, and muscular systems also change, making the body much more resilient. But if a body is frozen in its development on a cellular level, does that really make it stronger? Personally, I do not believe so. It appears that the brothers have managed to…*un*freeze parts of you in order to make changes. But I cannot explain what they are, I'm sorry."

Lena's gaze danced between Jared and me. "My main concern is not the changes that are taking place. I'm not proud of this, but when I first began experimenting with my gift, I was very advantageous. I tried to change too much too quickly. The result…it was not pretty."

Jared narrowed his eyes. "What do you mean by that?"

"I mean that in those cases, the animals' system sort of went into…well, I suppose you could say 'override'. It began to shut down in some areas, protecting itself, and trying to rectify these problems. The problems were not always completely rectified even with my help to undo what I had done."

Jared went even paler. "So the animals died?"

"No. But they became brain damaged. One slipped into a coma from which it never awakened."

"And that could happen to Sam?" Jared ran a hand through his hair. "Can you help in some way? Can you undo anything of what they have done?"

"I'm sorry, but I doubt I will be able to make much difference, as I do not understand what it is the brothers have done to Sam's DNA. The only thing that will allow me to have any effect on Sam, a vampire, is that her development is no longer frozen. At best, I can slow the process, ease the side effects, but the changes will ultimately be made unless you can find the brothers and make them reverse the process."

"I will find them, I will. If there's some way you can help Sam in the meantime, please, just do what you can."

"It will be painful, Sam," warned Lena.

"I don't care, do what you can." The pain was quick in coming. It was exactly like the pain I had felt earlier, but this time I could move and I could scream. And I *did* scream. The entire time, Jared spoke to me telepathically. The pain was so bad that his words were pretty much background noise, but still it helped to hear his voice.

What felt like hours later, the pain vanished abruptly. Somebody thrust a NST into my hand, and I drank it all in one go.

Lena patted my arm. "I'm sorry about the pain."

"Don't be. I'm just grateful for any help anyone can give." And I truly was, because after everything that she had told me, I was at risk of shitting my pants.

Antonio stepped forward. "I think it may be best to keep Sam's problem very quiet. Currently, a lot of the vampires are nervous of a Sventé being their source of protection once I have given up my position. The only thing making them keep an open mind is that her gifts are so powerful. For them to find out that her gifts are no longer under control, that she may actually lose them…"

Jared cursed, now pacing in front of me again. "If only you'd had some kind of vision, Luther…It's kind of odd that something this serious wasn't—" He stopped at the shifty expression on the tribute to Gandalf's face. "What do you know?"

"Jared," Luther implored; his expression pleaded with him to understand.

"You had a vision," Jared immediately realised. When Luther exchanged a look with me, Jared glanced at me and narrowed his eyes. "And you knew he'd had a vision."

I didn't deny it. He was always going to find out at some point. I'd just kind of hoped for more time.

Jared came to stand in front of me. His voice was strained with anger. "Let me get this straight. You knew something might happen, but you went to the bungalow with me anyway."

"I cannot interfere with people's paths, Jared," Luther insisted.

Jared twirled around to face him. "Really? Okay, let's look at this path she's taking. She has unbearable pain, she's losing control of her gifts, and two guys did something to her that made other vampires deformed and crazed! Explain to me how that path is a good thing."

He advanced on the Keja vampire until he was almost nose-to-nose with him. "You need to tell me what you know, and you need to do it now. I don't want to hear any of your cryptic bullshit. Tell me! Tell me so that I can fucking fix it!"

Luther's small smile was gentle and apologetic. "I'm sorry, Jared. You know that I would do so if I could."

I honestly feared that Jared might hit him, but instead he snapped, "Fuck it. Fuck all of you." Without even a glance at me, he teleported away.

(Jared)

Of course I'd known that lazing on a sun lounger on the empty beach wasn't going to calm me, but I'd sort of expected to feel better after an hour alone. Apparently I was expecting a little too much from life lately. See, I'd *expect* that the woman I loved would have some sense of self-preservation, but no. I'd *expect* that if there was something I needed to know – particularly if it was somehow related to her safety – then I'd be told about it. And I'd *expect* Sam not to keep something so important from me, but, again, no.

Sure, I knew why she hadn't told me – she'd known that my protectiveness would have hit critical levels and that I'd have done everything I could to stop her from going with me to investigate her weird dreams. Was that really so damn wrong of me, though?

I even understood why Luther hadn't mentioned the vision. So many times over the years I'd seen him quiet and subdued, and I'd known he'd had a vision that he couldn't share. Each time, I'd deeply sympathised with him. After all, his gift had to be more of a curse sometimes. But if that vision somehow concerned Sam, I was never going to be so understanding, and he'd known that.

So, yeah, I could understand why neither of them had told me beforehand. The question bugging me now was…why hadn't Sam mentioned this *afterwards?* She wasn't exactly someone who would care about risking my wrath. She'd snort and flip me off if I yelled at her. So why keep this from me? Why keep me out like that?

Unfortunately, none of that could distract me from the bone-deep fear circulating through me. Yes, the brothers had assured me that Sam wouldn't become ill, but if their 'equations' weren't adding up, then there was every chance that something bad would happen to her, even if they hadn't meant for it to.

This whole thing sucked.

The scent that suddenly drifted downwind to me instantly made my blood boil. This was not what I needed. "I don't know why you're out here and I don't care, just go."

A very scantily dressed Magda sat gingerly on the lounger beside mine. "I sensed your anger and fear, Jared. Naturally I was going to come to you."

The false concern in her voice nibbled at what patience I had left. "Not now. I really don't want to have to deal with your shit right now."

"Did it ever occur to you that I might wish to make amends?"

I snorted. "No, because you don't. What you want is to play games. It's what you're good at."

"You used to think I was good at a lot of things."

"I also used to think that vampires didn't exist." I enjoyed watching that practiced sultry smile fall from her face.

"If I thought you were happy with Sam, I would wish you well" – Yeah, right – "but you're not happy. You may seem it at times, but you're not truly happy. A Binding is life-long. I would hate to see you trapped in a stale relationship."

"Really? Strange, because that's pretty much what you'd wanted when you Turned me all those years ago."

Her eyes flared and her irises were suddenly glowing amber. "What we had was not stale. When I revealed what I was to you, I had two choices. Turn you at some point, or kill you – that is how it works, and you know that. I chose the first option and I do not regret that."

"And that's all it was? You Turned me purely to save me from death?" My words were dripping with scepticism. Magda wasn't a stickler for rules. She would have gotten a kick out of risking punishment.

"Of course. You know this, just as you know that what we had was not stale. You may wish to believe that it had been, you may prefer to think differently, but you know in your own mind that it was not."

"I *know* that you used me, just like you use everyone else around you. I *know* that, to you, I was just a toy. I *know* that you didn't Turn me to save me, or because you cared; you did it out of spite, just as you Turned my brother out of spite. *That's* what I know."

"It wasn't out of spite, but I can see why you might think that. I was hurt when you didn't return to me. I panicked. I didn't want to believe that you had stopped caring for me and I convinced myself that the only thing in our way was Evan being human. I used him to tempt you, yes, but not to hurt you. I would never have wished to do that."

And wasn't that the biggest load of shit I'd ever heard. If I hadn't known her as well as I did, though, I might have fallen for that act. "Why are you here, Magda? Here at The Hollow? I know you don't like that I'm Binding with Sam, and I know you get off on trying to separate us, but you have to know that your schemes won't work. So why stay?"

"As I said, if I can be convinced that you're truly happy with Sam, I shall no longer interfere. But if she continues to upset you as she clearly has now, well…"

I growled at the threat in her voice. "You stay away from Sam."

Magda rolled her eyes. "These growls and warnings are wasted on me, Jared. You have a blood-link to me, you would never hurt me."

She really believed that? Wow. "There are only three people in this world that will never come to any harm from me. Sam, Evan, and Antonio."

"You do not wish to harm me, Jared," she insisted, inserting authority into her tone. She might have Turned me, but she had no authority over me as far as I was concerned. "You were happy with me. Granted, I made a mess of things—"

"That's putting it lightly, don't you think?"

"—but before that, you were happy with me."

Again, there was authority in her tone that was much like a subtle *push*. I looked at her curiously. "What do you think you are, a fucking Jedi?"

"You made love to me as no other man before, or after you, has done."

I slowly sat upright on the lounger and swung my legs over the side, facing her. "Let's get one thing straight, Magda. I fucked you, but that's all. Only with Sam has sex ever been anything more than that for me."

Anger flashed on her face. "Perhaps it's that way for you. But is it that way for her? Does she truly feel as strongly for you? If so, I have to wonder why you aren't happy and why you are currently so angry."

I knew she was playing mind games with me and it made me want to slap her – female or not. I almost did when she grabbed my arm. Instead, I shook off her grip. "Yeah, I'm pissed with Sam," I admitted. "I'm pissed with her big time. In fact, I get pissed with her a lot, just as she does with me. But I still love her, and that's not going to change." I stood sharply, almost unbalancing the lounger.

"You say these things…but you have not totally opened yourself up to her, have you? You persist in holding back from her, even though it hurts her. Odd, then, that you claim to love her."

But Magda was wrong. I wasn't holding back from Sam, although that was how both women saw it. Telling Sam about my past would mean going back to that place in time in my head, and it would mean taking Sam there with me. I didn't want her being touched by that shit.

Similarly, I didn't want her to see the anxieties that lurked very deep inside me in spite of my efforts to get rid of them. I was broken in many ways, but I'd done a good job of hiding it, of denying it even to myself. It didn't matter that I knew those anxieties were needless – when you were told things every single day of your childhood, those things had a way of embedding themselves inside you; lurking there, and appearing to torment you at your low moments. *Knowing* that none of it was true didn't make it completely go away. And if your own mother couldn't love you, it was so easy to believe that nobody else was ever going to.

I didn't want Sam to have to hear about that woman. I didn't want Sam spending even a second of her life thinking about her. It would feel like I was letting my mother taint her just as she had tainted my human life. Of course I wasn't dumb; I knew that I would have to tell Sam everything at some point – mostly because she would never let it alone. Was delaying that such a bad thing?

Teleporting back to the apartment, I found Sam already in bed. I thought by her even breathing that she was sleeping deeply, but when I finally slipped into bed, one eye peeked open.

"You still angry?" Her voice was a little croaky.

"More angry than I've ever been about anything in my fucking life." I was pulling her to me even as I said it.

"If I'd told you about Luther's vision, you would have tried to stop me from—"

"Yeah, and as much as it pisses me off, I do understand why you didn't tell me. But you could have told me afterwards, Sam. You could've, but you didn't; that's what hurts. On some level you were punishing me, weren't you? You didn't tell me because you wanted me to know how it felt to be shut out."

I could tell by her expression that she hadn't really considered that. After a few seconds, she sighed. "Maybe. But if I was, I hadn't actually realised it. It does hurt me that you don't share stuff, especially this thing with your mother, because it's obviously something big to you."

My arm contracted around her. "I don't mean to hurt you. I would never want to do that. Not ever."

"But you don't trust me with the details," she assumed.

I cupped her chin and tried to lift her face to mine, but she resisted. "Hey, hey, hey, look at me. *Look* at me." Sighing, she did. "It is not that I don't trust you. You, Evan, and Antonio are the only people that I do trust. I'm asking *you* to trust *me* here. I will tell you what you want to know. I will. Just don't ask me to bring up this shit now. There is so much going on around us, interfering with our ability to enjoy our own Binding. Can we just shove this aside until afterward? Can we at least shelf this one thing?"

Could I at least have the luxury of not thinking and talking about the woman who had given birth to me, but done little else for me? That was the real question, but it would be revealing too much. Sam had a very curious nature and was drawn to mysteries. She wouldn't be grateful to know only a few things. No, her curiosity would drive her to ask for more details.

"All right," she eventually replied. "But you have to promise that you *will* tell me eventually."

I nodded, wishing she hadn't said that, and wishing she wasn't looking at me with an expression that said 'I'll need more than a nod'. "I promise."

"Good." Abruptly, she sank her teeth into my chest. Her hand closed around my cock and she pumped as she drank from me, not stopping until I exploded over her hand. I was more than happy to return the favour.

CHAPTER SEVEN

(Sam)

I was surprised to find Wes and his snake on my doorstep at dusk. "Everything all right?"

Wes gestured to a small gift-wrapped box he was holding. "I have something for you."

Not comforted by his impish expression, I nevertheless stepped aside to allow him to enter.

Jared, who was seated on the sofa drinking a NST and eating toast, looked up from his breakfast. "Hey," he greeted simply, and then his eyes went to the box. His expression – complete with the questioning brow – mirrored my own.

"I have a gift for Sam. As I believe you will benefit from it to an extent, I suppose it can double as a Binding gift from Lena and I."

Curious, Jared rose from the sofa and went to take the box, but Wes shook his head and turned to me. "Firstly, may I ask how you slept?"

Translation: Had there been any more pain? "Actually, I slept really well."

His smile was wide. "That's good to hear." He held out the gift to me.

Not liking the roguish look on his face, I eyed the prettily wrapped box suspiciously. "What is it?" I asked dubiously.

"That's for you to find out, my dear girl. Here, open it."

Sighing, I took the box and carefully placed it on the coffee table. Just as carefully, I removed the wrapping paper, only to find a wooden box. Taking off the lid, I felt my eyebrows crash into my hairline. "Wow, a pen – just what I've always wanted." Of course he was giving me a pen. Why wouldn't he give me a pen? Clearly his antenna didn't pick up all the channels.

"This fountain pen is what I use to draw pictures or tattoos.

Using it as an outline, I then project the image in my mind onto paper, skin, or whatever my 'canvas' is. A needle is not necessary and would not work with vampires anyway as the skin would heal too quickly."

I had to refrain from backing away when Toto leaned toward me, but he didn't touch me. Instead, he flicked his forked tongue out at the box. Then it snapped into place. "Oh you're bloody joking."

Jared frowned as the same realisation hit him. "You're giving her a snake?"

"Like Antonio, I reward those in my service who have truly earned it." Wes turned back to me. "I have only ever done this for my most prized warriors."

I might have felt a little flattered by the sentiment if it wasn't for the twinkle of mischief in his eyes. "I don't know if 'warrior' is a word that could be used to describe me."

"Of course it is. Trust me, you will be more than happy with my gift. These snakes are such intelligent creatures. And so uniquely beautiful – not only in appearance, but in temperament. They are loyal to their…I suppose you could say 'owner'. I am certain that Jared will be happy for you to receive anything that adds to your protection. Strikers are particularly protective."

I raised a brow. "Strikers?"

"That is what I have named the breed. He will guard and protect you, just as Toto does me."

I probably would be better not asking, but, I had to. "And you picked the name 'Striker' because…?"

"You see, in most instances it is easy to tell when a snake is feeling uneasy or threatened. This breed always appears calm and docile, but it is forever alert" – a little like Butch, then – "and it will strike so quickly, not even a vampire would have seen it coming."

Well wasn't this special. Common sense advised me to tell him to shove that pen up his arse and sod off, but something in his eyes made me pause. He really, really wanted me to accept this gift, really wanted me to have this added protection. It wasn't like I didn't need protection right now, was it? Finally, I nodded. He smiled in satisfaction, while Jared gave me a look that said 'Fair play to you'.

I led Wes over to the dining table and gestured for him to take a seat. He did, but stopped me when I went to sit beside him. "It would be better if you could stand due to our differences in size."

Oh again with the 'size' remarks. "Whatever," I grumbled.

"Are you happy for me to draw him on your arm? I'm quite certain that Jared will object to me sketching anything on your chest."

Jared threw him a playfully dark scowl. "You got that right."

I held out my arm, watching in fascination as he took the pen from the box on the table and began to draw. "You said 'him'. Does that mean you're drawing a male?"

"Yes," confirmed Wes. "He will be physically identical to Toto, though much shorter. He will grow with time. Growth, for Strikers, is an extremely slow process."

"So he'll be a baby?"

"No, he'll be what you might call an adolescent. But this will not make him any less lethal. Size makes no difference with this breed. In tattoo form, however, he will always remain the same length."

Jared came to stand beside me, watching closely. "Does it hurt?" He ignored Wes' impatient look.

I shook my head. Strangely, the pen left a tingling sensation as it moved on my skin. It wasn't pleasant or unpleasant, simply a sensation. Although the ink was black, other colours appeared in the intricate drawing, and I realised that Wes was projecting them onto the image.

It was an hour later when Wes was finally finished. A very detailed four-inch long, piebald snake was then twined around my upper arm. The brown patches on his pure-white scales were small and spaced far apart.

"Before I bring him to life, you need to give him a name. He will not simply be your guard, but a pet; an individual in his own right with a personality all of his own."

After a moment, I said, "I quite like Dexter."

"Why 'Dexter'?" asked Jared with a smile.

I shrugged. "I just like it. Or I could name him Slick, or Conan, or Boomer."

Jared chuckled. "No, Dexter's good."

"Yes, I rather like it myself," said Wes. "Now, Sam, stay as still as you can for me."

Fighting the urge to tense, I held still and waited. Wes did nothing other than stare at the image. Then, suddenly, heat travelled up my arm. Seconds later, there was a live snake where the image had been. Only it was five times the length that it had been as a tattoo, making it one and a half foot long.

He had a good look around before his black eyes locked onto me. I would have expected that I'd be shuddering and backing away. Instead, I was smiling at him fondly – like a crazy person.

Wanting to be sure I didn't startle him, I slowly raised my hand and lightly ran a finger over his coffin-shaped head. Amazingly, he leaned in to the touch, still staring at me. His gaze was intelligent, observant, and curious. I almost shit my pants in surprise when his colour abruptly changed to the same brilliant blue that Toto had earlier been. "So that means he likes me, right?" I asked Wes without moving my gaze from Dexter.

"Yes, it does."

"He's actually kind of cool." Jared took a step toward me, and Dexter's head shot around to face him. Just like that, his colouring went to jet black and his tail rattled slightly. I remembered Wes saying something about Toto being grey or black whenever he was wary. And obviously the rattling tail wasn't a good thing.

"Whoa," said Jared, freezing on the spot.

Wes held up a hand. "He's just being cautious as he doesn't yet know you, and he's intent on protecting Sam. It's instinctive for him."

Jared looked slightly placated. "Why does it feel like he's assessing me?"

Wes smiled. "He most likely is. Come closer, so he can get a better feel for you."

I almost laughed at Jared's 'Do you think I'm stupid?' look. "Oh behave. You face big, bad vampires all the time. He's just a snake."

"With venomous fangs. Did you forget that part? And he spits, too. I like being able to see, thanks."

I rolled my eyes. "Come here, you big Nancy."

Jared tried his best to seem cool and calm, even moving with a very casual, cocky strut. "What do you want me to do?"

"I need him to get used to you. I don't want him thinking I need protecting from you, so just sit down on this chair near me. But *slowly*." Once Jared had done as I asked, I took his hand in mine and waited. At a steady pace, Dexter slinked his way down my arm and up Jared's. "Don't tense." To Jared's credit, he didn't.

Much like Toto had done to me, Dexter flicked out his tongue, 'tasting' Jared. It had to have been at least a full minute before he returned to my own arm, switching back to a brilliant blue shade. "You've passed muster, by the looks of it."

"He didn't change colour again until he was with you."

"Yes, but he didn't bite you."

Jared jiggled his head. "Fair point."

I looked at Wes. "What do I feed him?"

"He's totally independent; perfectly capable of catching a rodent. Taking him into the rainforest regularly would be good for him so that he can feed himself. Do not feel guilty returning him to his tattoo form. He will be just as content in that form as he is in this."

"How do I turn him back?" I didn't particularly want to, but I'd have to soon enough.

"All you need to do in order to get him to change from one form to another is repeat the word 'novo'. It's Latin for 'change'."

"That's it?"

"Yes. Try it now, as practice."

Feeling a teensy bit guilty, I nonetheless repeated, "Novo." Instantly, Dexter seemed to melt into my arm and was back in his four-inch long tattoo form.

"Whoa!" exclaimed Jared – and not just because of how strange it had been to watch Dexter change. No, what was stranger was that the tattoo was moving.

That mischievous twinkle was back in Wes' eyes. "You'll find that he'll often move around your body like that, just as he'll also change colour while in tattoo form."

"Does it feel weird when he moves?" Jared asked me.

I shrugged, chuckling. "I can't feel anything at all. But I can sense his mood. He's…content." So Wes was right. Dexter was just as happy as a tattoo.

Wes slapped his knees and rose. "Well, I shall let myself out."

Just as he reached the front door, a thought occurred to me. "Wait, just what exactly does his venom do?"

Mischief returned to his eyes. "If he spits the venom, it will cause irritation to the skin and eyes, but will eventually wear off – unless the victim is human, in which case it can cause blindness. A single bite would not be fatal to a vampire, but it wouldn't be pleasant. There are, in fact, three stages."

That didn't sound good. "Stages?"

"Each stage is only temporary and should wear off after a few hours. Stage one is blindness. Stage two is mental disorientation. And the final stage is paralysis."

I shouldn't ask, I know, but… "And if a second bite is delivered, what would that do?"

Wes shrugged. "Merely cause excruciating, cry-wrenching pain, which is then soon followed by death."

Of course it did.

To look at Fletcher's skinny frame, you wouldn't think that he had the strength to cut off a person's air supply merely by hugging them. I struggled inside his hold, managing to wheeze out, "Fletch, I'm fine."

"You're not fine and you bloody well know it." The Empath pulled back, wearing a stern expression. "I can sense that you're a mess right now. I want to know everything, lady. Don't leave a single thing out." So we went inside my office, and I revealed everything – the brothers, the pain, and my problems with my gifts.

Fletcher shook his head and put his hand to his chest. "This isn't good for the heart. I think I feel a palpation coming on."

"I'm trying not to worry. I really, really am, because I know that Jared will sense it if I do. He's in a bad enough state as it is." It was nice not having to pretend for just a little while.

"Well of course he is. He loves you and he's used to saving the day and having all the answers. He's so worried about you, it actually hurts me to feel it. And—" Hearing the tap-tap-tap of high heels coming down the corridor, he groaned. "Oh here comes Widow Twankey. She's intent on trying to put a spanner in the works, isn't she?"

I laughed. "I call her Jessica Rabbit, but Widow Twankey's better, without a doubt."

Seconds later, wearing a superior grin and a dress that left nothing whatsoever to the imagination, Magda strode inside. Seriously, someone needed to tell her that she wasn't the only one with a pair of tits. "I was hoping we could talk."

On receiving a nod from me that said I'd be okay, Fletcher strutted past Magda, snarling, and left the office. Of course he'd be eavesdropping, as usual.

I arched a questioning brow at her, being sure to look disinterested.

"Hi again, Sam." When I didn't respond, she sighed. "I feel like you and I got off on the wrong foot. Truly, I am not the enemy. In fact, I can help you understand Jared much better. I thought you and I could spend some time together and get to know each other."

"Oh you did? Well see, here's the thing. I don't want to get to know you. I have no reason to. If Jared had wanted me to, I'd have made the effort. But as he doesn't…well, I'll just tell you to fuck off."

"Aren't you curious to know what he's keeping from you?"

"I'm curious to know why you don't own any decent clothes." I heard a snort of laughter from behind the office door.

"Jared always liked them."

I could tell by her smug expression that she thought that was all it would take to set me off. Sure, I was pissed, but I was *not* about to give her what she wanted. "Do you want to know what he likes better? When I bite the head of his dick. Yeah, my Sventé saliva does the trick every time."

A sound came from her that sounded suspiciously like a hiss. "I didn't need to resort to tricks."

"No, you needed to Turn his brother before he would stay with you."

"He could still have said no, but he didn't. He chose to Turn, chose to be with me."

"He chose to be with Evan – dress the situation up with a pretty bow if you like, but that fact remains. Now," I drawled, leaning forward. "I'm going to make myself very, very clear, and if you have any sense in your messed-up head, you'll listen. Jared is not yours. He does not want to be. He has absolutely no interest in you, and I can't say I blame him. If I'd been in his position, I'd rather have sucked cow snot through a straw than go back to a manipulative, calculating, devious bitch."

She snickered. "You're jealous of the blood-link, aren't you? That's why you're being so hostile toward me."

Jealous? Yes. Hostile? Pfft. "When I'm being hostile toward you, you'll know it in those precious seconds before I punch a hole into your chest searching for a heart that's probably not there."

"I really am sure that I told you to stay away from Sam." Jared's tone was flat, cold.

Magda twirled to face him, spluttering. "It's natural for me to have an interest in a person who wishes to Bind with one of my vampires."

"I'm not one of your vampires," he objected through clenched teeth. "You may have Turned me, but I cut my ties with you a long time ago."

She shook her head, looking almost desperate. "You'll always be linked to me, Jared. Running away wasn't going to get rid of it. Dim it, yes. But you'll never get away from it."

His words were quiet, but not soft. "Oh, but I will when I Bind with Sam. My blood-link with her will replace the one I have with you; you already know this." In a blink, he was stood behind my chair with his hands on my shoulders.

"Yeah," I agreed. "So get out." To my surprise, she did.

Jared dragged me from the chair and pulled me against him. "You okay?"

"Agitated beyond belief," I answered honestly, relaxing in his hold. "But this will all be worth it when she feels the link die. My conscience goes asleep when she's around." He didn't smile as I'd thought he might. Instead he sighed, resting his forehead against mine.

"She's only just getting started, Sam. This is just a taste of what you'll have to deal with. I don't want our time together being spoiled by her. I don't want her causing problems for us."

As I met his gaze, I realised something. "You're waiting for me to leave you, aren't you?" I knew why: it was hard to trust that someone you wanted so much could really want you back.

"I'm waiting for you to try. I won't let you go."

"There are only two people who have the power to mess this up. You and me. I have no intention of doing that and neither do you."

"We're tight, I know that. But she only needs one crack, Sam. One crack and she's in."

I smoothed my hands up and down his t-shirt. "And if she gets in, I'll kill her. But the only way she can get in is if we aren't as solid as we think we are. We could look at this as a test. If she manages to mess this up, it was never going to go the distance and the Binding would have been a mistake."

He shook his head. "That's a nice way of looking at it. But you're wrong, baby. She's poison, and it doesn't matter how strong a person's body is, poison can still have the intended effect. It can still hurt and it can still kill. Like I said, all she needs is one crack. One crack and that poison will get into our relationship and spread."

"No."

"She's getting to you. If she gets to you badly enough, she'll get in here" – he gently poked my temple – "and she'll poison your mind. She can make you destroy what we have."

"I'm too strong a person for her to do that." Even I heard the doubt in my voice. With everything that was going on, I wasn't at my strongest. Still, I insisted, "She can't do that. It's not possible."

He gave me a gentle, sad smile. "Neither is a vampire becoming deformed or crazed."

A knock on our office door was quickly followed by the entrance of Antonio, Luther, and Sebastian. I was glad. A distraction was just what both Jared and I needed right then.

Antonio gave me a soft smile. "How have you been?"

"No more pain, if that's what you mean."

"Good. You will both be glad to hear that my researchers were able to clear up the meaning of 'Orrin'. As it turns out, Orrin is a Pagori vampire living in L.A. He is not a Master Vampire, but he has Sired a large number of vampires." Antonio placed the folder of information on my desk. Inside it was a photograph of a blond, blue-eyed Pagori.

"That's not either of the brothers," I said.

"It's possible that he does not know the brothers at all, that 'Orrin' isn't a person and, instead, stands for something."

"Still, it's worth following this up."

The grinding of Jared's teeth was audible. "Sam, please don't tell me that you think you're going."

I gave him a pointed look. "Jared, please don't tell me that you're going to be a prat."

He cursed. "I don't want you leaving The Hollow while you're ill. Fuck Sam, vampires aren't supposed to *be* ill."

"I'm not ill, it's just that my gifts are playing up."

"And there's the unbearable pain, remember. I don't want you out there while you're vulnerable."

"Vulnerable to what? We're just visiting a Pagori vampire in L.A, who may or may not be linked to the Brothers Grimm. Besides, I have Dexter."

Antonio neatly stepped in. "Sam is right, Jared. This isn't an assignment. You will simply be paying another vampire a friendly visit."

Naturally Jared hadn't been happy with that response, which was why he sulked the entire time we gathered the squad, and right up until we reached the gates of Orrin's Spanish style duplex in L.A. Although we had taken the entire squad, we decided it would be best to leave most of them outside so that we didn't appear threatening. As Antonio had said, this was supposed to be a social visit, nothing more.

Jared's knock was answered by a large, sleazy-looking Pagori who I would bet had an affinity for banjos. He ran his gaze over Jared, myself, Max, Salem, and Denny, scowling. When his eyes focused again on Jared, he demanded, "Who the fuck are you?"

Ignoring his tone, Jared simply said, "I'm here to see Orrin."

"And who—" Realisation must have dawned on him, because his eyes widened and he spluttered. "Jared...For a second there, I didn't recognise you. Come in."

Entering, we found ourselves in a small, bright hallway. Branching off it was a living area on our left side, and a dining area on our right side. In both rooms, a number of vampires were lazing. They tensed at the look of Jared, but bowed their heads respectfully.

Have you met any of them before? I asked Jared.

No. But they'll recognise me as being the Heir. Antonio made sure that would be the case worldwide.

"I'm Rudy, by the way," the large vampire informed us after chasing the vampires out of the dining room. "Take a seat. Can I get you anything before I go tell Orrin that you're here?"

Jared shook his head. "No thanks."

Rudy nodded and left the room.

No sooner had we all seated ourselves at the large, glass dining table than Rudy returned with the lanky, blond Pagori from the photograph. He wore a timid, shy smile as he walked toward us. He had an awkward way about him, much like one of those school geeks who totally lacked social skills. Not that my social skills were much better.

"Jared," he greeted simply, shaking his hand. "A pleasure to meet you."

Jared nodded. "Likewise. This is my fiancée, Sam, and three of my squad."

Orrin must have looked at me a little longer than Jared was

comfortable with, because he stiffened beside me. Personally, though, I didn't feel that Orrin was ogling me. His gaze was studious, searching.

"It's an honour to meet you all." Having taken a seat directly opposite Jared, Orrin again smiled shyly. "I'm not in trouble, am I?"

Jared returned the grin. "No, nothing like that. I'm hoping that you can help us with something."

Orrin suddenly looked eager, perhaps flattered that the Heir would come to him for any assistance.

"The Grand High Master is looking for a vampire with a certain set of skills. Namely, someone with the ability to alter DNA. But he needs one strong enough to alter the DNA of vampires. We know that one of your vampires has that gift. We'd like to borrow him for a short time."

I thought that was quite clever of Jared. Vampires could be quite protective of those they had Turned. Therefore, if Jared had said that he wanted to punish any of them, Orrin would most likely have concealed their location.

Orrin scratched his nape. "I don't have a vampire with a gift that strong. However…put him and his brother together and you have a force powerful enough to achieve that."

"It requires two of them?"

"Yes. Quinn can manipulate DNA, and Wyatt has the capability to freeze and unfreeze things. Vampires are physically frozen in their development, but if Wyatt can very slightly affect that, it enables his brother to play with DNA."

I hadn't thought of that. "Where can we find them?"

Orrin's expression was sheepish. "I'm afraid that's something I can't help you with. Once the Trent brothers realised how strong they were, they felt that they didn't need their Sire or anyone else. They felt that they were quite capable of starting their own line. I heard that they were seen in Vegas a few days ago. I doubt it was really them, though. They prefer solitude."

I strongly suspected that it *had* been them and that they were trying the trick of hiding in plain sight.

"Do you want me to have a few of my guys search for them?" Orrin seemed keen to help, clearly wanting to impress the Heir.

Jared waved a hand. "That's not necessary. There are other vampires on the list that we can approach." Very smart of Jared to not seem desperate. Besides, now that we knew their names and a little more about them – including where they were last seen – it was very possible that Sebastian could track them much faster than Orrin ever could. "Thanks for your time."

Back at The Hollow, Jared and I relayed all of the information to Antonio. Going by the strain in his expression, I suspected that he was sincerely looking forward to getting a grip of the Trent brothers and making them pay for what they had done. Well he'd better get in line.

"Sebastian, I do not need to stress to you the importance of the brothers being found," said Antonio. "Track them as best and as fast as you can, but do not act when you finally find them. Simply report back to me with their location."

With a nod, the tracker left.

Antonio looked between Jared and I. "You should both go and get ready for tonight's entertainment. We shall see you soon."

Ah, yes, the Opera. So not my thing, but I was willing to keep an open mind.

I had expected to find Fletcher waiting outside my apartment with a shopping bag containing a revealing dress, as he normally was. Instead, I found Evan, smiling like the cat that got the cream. Nope, that wasn't good.

CHAPTER EIGHT

(Sam)

I'd never liked those 'I know something you don't' smiles, and I especially never liked them when they belonged to Evan. He was a great bloke and all that, but he was also a sneaky bugger. I immediately narrowed my eyes.

Jared, who knew his brother well enough to know what that look meant, groaned. "Okay, what did you do?"

Evan shrugged innocently. "Who says I've done anything?"

"Spill it."

"Bro," whined Evan, putting a hand to his chest. "I'm hurt that you're so suspicious. Secrets aren't always bad secrets." He looked to me for some kind of character back-up.

"Yeah, I'm with Jared on this one, Ev. It's never good when you're smiling like that."

He seemed delighted rather than offended. "Ready for your Binding gift?" he asked me.

"Should I be worried about what it is?"

"You're going to love it."

Jared shook his head at his twin. "Do I at least get to come and see this gift that's *supposed* to be for both of us?"

A little patronisingly, Evan patted him on the back. "Sure. You'll love it too, because it's work-related. But it's mainly for Sam." He peered down at my feet. "Oh good, you're wearing cross trainers."

I frowned. "What does that have to do with anything?"

That smile was back. "You'll see."

Excited in spite of myself, I followed him down the hallway where we came across Fletcher. He was holding a shopping bag, surprise, surprise.

Evan spoke to Fletcher. "If anyone asks, they'll be gone most of the evening. And they'll be having way more fun than they would have at the opera-thing that Antonio's got planned."

Jared exchanged a baffled look with me before asking his brother, "Gone *where* all evening? And *why* will we be gone all evening?" His twin merely winked in response.

Fletcher put his hands on his hips, studying Evan over the rim of his glasses. "Hang on a minute, why are you smirking like that? What have you done?"

"I'm only taking Sam to see her Binding gift from me."

My best friend's expression morphed into one of intense curiosity. "Don't think you're leaving me behind."

To my surprise, Evan's smile faltered a little. "Are you sure you're not too busy, Fletch?"

"When there's a gift involved? Not at all."

A very impish grin spread across Evan's face. "Okay then, if you want to come, by all means come."

Now I was even more suspicious...but I was also more intrigued. Curiosity won over, and I followed Evan out of the building. When he led us into the rainforest, I went from curious to 'what the fuck?' Still, I remained silent as he took us deep into the rainforest, in the direction of what the legion immaturely called 'the four tits' – basically, they were four mountains clustered together, surrounding a huge stretch of land.

Evan came to an abrupt halt when we neared the narrow opening that lay between two of the mountains, leading to the land nestled between all four. The excitement on his face made me smile, despite my impatience. "You ready?"

I shoved him. "Move out of my way so I can get through and see what it is."

"No. You have to close your eyes."

"Ev, don't take the piss. I don't have much patience left."

"Just do it."

Releasing a put-out sigh, I nonetheless did as he asked.

"Bro, Fletch – both of you stay quiet until I've told her to open her eyes." He took my hand and guided me through the narrow opening. I heard Fletcher gasp and sensed Jared's surprise and...awe? That made me even more desperate to look. Finally, Evan brought us to a halt. "Now, Sam, do you remember a month ago you told me how you thought the legion would benefit from having a tactical field to train in? Look."

When I opened my eyes, I gasped just as Fletcher had done. Tactical field my arse. It was more like a small, abandoned village. The only thing stopping it from looking real was that the buildings were made of plywood. And of course no one has gas drums and piles of tyres just lying around here and there, do they. There was even a bus and several other vehicles lining the 'streets'. "How did you do all this in a month?"

"I designed it, but every squad member and every one of the commanders – other than Jared, because I didn't tell him about it – all came together to help me build it. Like it?" My smile must have been answer enough for him, because he chuckled and curled an arm around me. "Then you're going to *love* what I've got planned for the next six hours." He slipped his free hand into his pocket and fished out a single, spherical, gelatin capsule.

Anticipation shot through me. "Paintballing?"

He chuckled again, nodding. "Paintballing. I got one of Antonio's guards to teleport all the necessary equipment here. The squad will arrive any minute. They're eager to play; they've been looking forward to this for weeks."

I hugged Evan tightly, laughing at Jared's playful growl. "I haven't been paintballing for years."

Stroking a finger through his collar, Fletcher cleared his throat. "This isn't really my scene, luv. I'm more of a pacifist."

I gripped Fletcher's hand. "Oh please stay. It'll be a laugh. Honestly, it's addictive, you'll love it."

Just then, Chico entered through the narrow opening, followed closely by the rest of the squad…and someone I really hadn't wanted to see.

Fletcher curled his upper lip in distaste. "What's Widow Twankey doing here?" She didn't appear to appreciate that nickname, though she probably had no idea he had named her after a pantomime dame that was always played by a man.

Salem, who I then noticed was holding her lower arm, frowned down at her. "We found her wandering aimlessly. Apparently, she's looking for you, Coach."

Fletcher snorted. "Yeah? Well she can sod off."

Magda lifted her chin, scowling at Fletcher. "As I told Sam, I think it would be good for her and I to spend time together if she intends on Binding to one of my vampires. Besides, if she's going to one day be responsible for my protection and the protection of all vampirekind, it is only fair that I get to know her."

Jared, Fletcher, and Evan all went to object, but I held up a hand. "No, she's right." I smiled brightly at Magda. "If you'd really like us to become better acquainted, there couldn't be a more perfect time. You can join us for a few games of paintballing."

Magda gaped. "Paintballing?" Going by the distaste coating that one word, she thought this kind of thing was beneath her. I sensed Jared's amusement.

"Don't worry. I'm not one of those really competitive people who take it too seriously." The guys all snorted, knowing me too well.

Magda straightened to her full height and forced a smile. "I accept your invitation."

"Invitation?" repeated Fletcher. "What planet are you on? This is gate-crashing."

"Nah," disagreed Evan, "it's important that she and Sam bond." He winked at me, humour lighting his eyes. "Come on, let's go get kitted up." He led us all to a small hut where, as I'd expected, he'd kept the supplies. "First, I want to talk you all through everything. I know some of you haven't been paintballing before – particularly Fletcher, Reuben, Damien, and David—"

"And me," Magda informed him.

Evan nodded. "And Magda. But don't worry, you'll all enjoy it. You'll be split into two teams, and the aim of the game is to complete each mission without getting shot by a paintball. It's as simple as that." He shrugged to emphasise the simplicity of it, but then he held up one finger as he continued.

"There are rules for the game. I know that some of you will have big advantages because of your gifts…and that's why rule number one is that none of you are to use your gifts at any time. Rule number two: if you are hit, you do not need to leave the game unless you've been hit in the torso or the head – they're the only areas that would have any real effect on a vampire. At that point, you simply raise your gun, declare that you're hit, and head to 'the dead zone' – no one is to shoot at or go near this zone. I'll show you where it is in a minute.

"If you're hit in the head, it's considered a fatal shot and you will be eliminated from that particular game. If you're hit in the torso, you need to only spend ten minutes in 'the dead zone' before you can return to the game. But unless the paintball breaks and leaves a mark the size of a quarter, it doesn't count. And nor does paint splatter, which means that although the paint grenades will do well at distracting the other team, they won't count as 'deadly'. Rule number three: do not take off your safety mask unless you're in 'the dead zone' or unless the game has ended. Rule number four: you must allow surrenders. And the final rule: no bodily contact. This is not about combat. That all understood?" Everybody nodded.

Ten minutes later, all of us were dressed in camouflaged overalls and padded gloves. It was when Evan pulled out a bag and handed it to me that I understood exactly why he'd been wearing that smile earlier. Inside was a pink tutu, a headband with pink horns attached, and a white 'L' sign. Bastard. In seconds, I was dressed like an army slut. Of course everyone thought it was hilarious, even Jared.

I snarled at my fiancé. "Thanks a lot, Judas."

Evan huffed at him. "I don't know what you're laughing at." He then pulled out another bag. Jared's face fell when his twin fished out a Borat-style, lime-green, lycra mankini. Then it was my turn to laugh.

"You're fucking kidding me." Jared shook his head. "No way."

I put my hands on my hips. "Oi, if I'm going to look stupid, you can as well."

He stood, seething, as his brother and Fletcher helped him put the mankini on over his camo gear. The icing on the cake had been when Harvey took a photograph with his smartphone. Jared made a dive for it. Obviously having anticipated that, however, the others held him back as Harvey dashed off to hide the photographic evidence of us looking like plonkers.

Once the laughing had died down, Evan clapped his hands twice to get everyone's attention. "Okay, let's split you into teams. Sam and Jared will each be a leader, which places them on opposing teams. I'll be refereeing, since it wouldn't be fair to have two commanders on one team."

My team ended up consisting of Fletcher, Chico, Butch, Harvey, David, and Salem. As such, Jared had Reuben, Max, Denny, Damien, Stuart, and Magda. The bitch was staying as close as physically possible to Jared, of course. I shot her a 'you better watch yourself' look. She returned it, although she did seem nervous. She should be.

"We're going to be playing lots of different games," began Evan, "but before we start, we'll do what's called 'walk the field'. This way, you can all familiarise yourselves with the place, see where everything is. You'll find that on opposite sides of the field are the base camps, which are also the starting points for each team."

It was as we were walking around that Evan explained, "The first game is called 'Ammo Retrieval'. In the centre is the tallest of the buildings, which has the sign, 'Bed and Breakfast'. Inside there is a crate of ammunition. Your objective is to retrieve the crate and take it back to your base camp. The team that manages to do that wins. Simple. If you claim the crate and think you have the time to stop, feel free to reload your paintball guns, as there are pods of pellets inside the crate."

Having completed the walk through and studied the field – which was absolutely bloody brilliant and topped every Binding gift we'd been given so far – we returned to the supply hut. Evan gave us all the necessary equipment: a protective mask, semi-automatic marker, hopper, smoke grenades, paint grenades, a pod pack – which looped around the waist – and two spare pods of pellets. Magda also had to swap her high heels for a pair of spare boots that were too big for her dainty feet. We then each tied coloured ribbons on our sleeves; blue for Jared's team, and yellow for mine.

As each team was ready to split and enter their assigned base camps, Jared smacked a kiss on my lips. I could feel the excitement thrumming through him. "Good luck, baby. You're going to need it, since we both know I'll win."

"Sure, sure."

"I mean it, baby, don't expect any mercy. I'm going to beat your sexy little ass at this."

I patted his arm. "It's sort of cute that you really believe that."

He laughed and jogged away with his team. Magda gave me a sly smile before trailing after them. She honestly thought it would bother me that she was on Jared's team? Okay, it did bother me. But I would rather that she wasn't on my team, since I planned to shoot the crap out of her.

Our base camp was a detached bare house on the border of the field further down from the supply hut. Jared's base camp – also a detached house – was on the opposite side of the field. Due to the streets of buildings, their camp was out of our line of vision, just as ours was out of theirs. As the 'B and B' was in the centre of the field, both teams were equally far from it.

In base camp I turned to my team. "Right, although this is

supposed to be all about fun, please understand that I have every intention of winning this. You all with me on that?" Everyone other than Fletcher nodded enthusiastically. "Good. When we need to get into position, I've found it often works best to form a 'U' shape. Any volunteers for the front? I'll need two. I'd happily offer, but I'm not too proud to admit that – as a Sventé – I'm the slowest here."

"I'll do it, I used to play this a lot as part of my police training," said Chico.

Salem raised a hand. "I'm fast, and I have a real good aim."

"Me too," claimed Butch.

I shook my head. "No Butch, I want to keep you as protected as possible. You're the fastest here so you're the obvious person to be responsible for getting the crate back to camp. Chico and Salem can lead. You and I will take up positions behind them. Then Chico can pave the way for you to get inside that 'B and B'."

I looked at the other three. "I'm going to put you all at the rear so—"

"Luv, I'll be no good at this," declared Fletcher. "I'm too scared to get hit. I've heard it really hurts."

"It's not that bad. It's like a hard pinch."

"I don't like hard pinches. Seriously, luv, I'll be hopeless at it."

"Paintballing isn't really that difficult. It's about ducking, diving, creeping, running, and crawling."

"I'm no good at stealth. I'd give away my location in seconds."

He was probably right about that. I sighed. "I'll tell you what: you stay back here and defend our camp. I doubt anyone will get past us but if they do, shoot them."

He nodded, appearing both relieved and nervous. "I can do that." It wasn't so much a statement as it was him trying to convince himself of that.

"Great. Now, I have a few rules of my own. These will help us as a team. One, don't ever go off alone. I'm not saying stick to someone's side. I mean, don't wander away from the rest of the team. You won't last long if you do. Two, don't hang around in one spot, keep on the move. If you don't, you're liable to be seen. Then all someone has to do is get a good enough angle on you to shoot you. Three, never stand out in the open; you want to be under cover as much as possible. When you move, you move to more cover. Four, always have your gun up, ready to fire. Lastly, enjoy yourselves."

Harvey cocked his head. "Do you think Jared will cheat and use his telepathy? You know how competitive he is. He won't want to lose."

I had to agree with that, but I strongly doubted that he would cheat. "The glory would mean nothing to him if he did that, so no. Right, to sum up…Until we reach the street where the 'B and B' is located, we have the luxury of running without being seen. Let's make that count. Once we reach that street, we form the U shape and we shoot any fucker in the way, covering Butch so that he can go get our crate." The boys all nodded, somehow managing to look serious and giddy at the same time.

At that moment, Evan's voice rang out. "Both teams ready?" Hearing Jared and I respond with 'yes', he then shouted, "Three, two, one…Game on!"

As one, we sprinted at vampire speed past the first street and the second, but stopped at the corner of the next one. Knowing that the other team would have reached the opposite end of the street at the same time, I didn't hesitate in getting everyone into position. Following my hand gestures – after months of training, they knew my signals well enough – Chico and Butch crossed over to the other side of the street. Chico slipped inside the second building along while Butch took position behind the car at the corner of the street, placing him a little distance behind Chico yet close enough for them to watch out for one-another.

At my signal, David and Harvey positioned themselves behind a row of gas drums in the middle of the road, keeping at the rear. Satisfied with their locations, I gestured for Salem to run on ahead of me as we kept close to the buildings on our side. On reaching the second house along, he hid behind a large pile of tyres there, while I dashed inside. As we had all moved at vampire speed, it had taken mere seconds.

Inside the house, I headed quietly up the stairs. Once on the second floor, I went to the balcony and crouched behind a gas drum there. My enhanced vision allowed me to spot some of the other team, but unfortunately I didn't have a clear shot. There was no order to where they were positioned…but that was Jared's plan, I realised – unpredictability. He figured that if I couldn't guess where any of them were, I couldn't move into position to pick them off. It wasn't actually a bad strategy. He wasn't going to win, though. Not a bloody chance.

Wanting the other team's attention on my side of the street to give Butch the best chance at slipping into the 'B and B' without being noticed, I jumped up and leaped over to the next balcony. Although I'd moved at vampire speed, the others saw me clearly, and paint pellets headed for me. But the moment I landed on the balcony, I'd rolled to the gas drum for cover.

My move seemed to have sparked the rest to act, because suddenly people were darting from spot to spot, and pellets were flying through the air. Knowing better than to stay in one place, I quickly darted down the stairs. Flat against the wall near the entrance, I took a quick peek outside. Salem had moved from his position near the tyres and was now squatted behind a gas drum further along the street. He was also exchanging shots with Stuart, who was crouched behind a car. Although there was a little paint on Salem, it was only on his leg.

Some sixth sense beat at me, telling me to look up. I did just in time to see that Damien was lying on the roof of one of the buildings across the road, aiming his marker at an unsuspecting Chico. I didn't have a good enough angle to take the shot, but Salem did. "Salem, ten forty-five."

Without hesitation, he swerved and shot. The pellet hit Damien's shoulder, surprising him; he lost his balance and tumbled down the roof, onto the balcony…and right into Chico's line of fire. A second later, there was a splat of yellow paint on his mask. Damien held up his gun, growling, "I'm hit." With that, he marched off to 'the dead zone', grumbling to himself.

One down, six to go.

Distracted, I almost didn't notice that not only was Max training his marker on Harvey – typical, since they didn't get along very well – but he had a nice, clean shot. Quick as lightning, I turned sharply and rained pellets at him, forcing him to take cover. Although a few hit him, they didn't catch him in a fatal spot. Cursing silently, I darted to the car outside and hunkered behind the wide-open-door.

"Harvey, learn to hide better!" I called. His cockiness was his downfall sometimes. This proved to be true when, only seconds later, he stood with his gun high above his head, declaring that he'd been hit…by Max.

Of course, Max was absolutely delighted. That was until Salem managed to hit him in the torso, temporarily cutting him out of the game. Much like Damien, he grumbled his way to 'the dead zone'.

Two down, four left to go. But I didn't have time to laugh about it, because suddenly pellets were hitting the car I was hiding behind, catching my sleeve. I tucked myself in tighter, avoiding the spray. I quickly realised that the pellets were coming from two directions. A peek to my left told me that Reuben was one of the arseholes responsible. No way would I give the two teammates a chance to flank me – which was exactly what they were trying to do. While one shot at me, the other advanced forward, and vice versa.

I took a smoke grenade out of my pocket, and flung it over the car. Five seconds later, it exploded. I wasted no time in rushing around the car, delivering a fatal shot to Reuben's mask, before leaping onto the balcony above. However, rather than staying up there, I quickly scampered down the stairs. I was right to do so, as no sooner had I moved than paint pellets were being fired.

Startled by movement in my peripheral vision, I almost shot David. Likewise, he almost shot me. We both sighed. I'd have been as embarrassed as all shit to have to walk out of there, declaring I'd been hit by a member of my own team, *and* that I'd hit him too.

Gesturing for him to follow me, I went to leave the house. I had barely taken a step when an array of pellets came flying my way. I managed to dodge most of them. The ones that made contact had only hit my leg and foot.

I turned to David. "While I shoot, you run to the pile of tyres outside. Once you're there, you take over firing. I'll head to the gas drums a few feet away from you. Got it?"

He nodded. The second I popped out my head and gun and began shooting, David rushed out as instructed. As I pulled back, David started firing. Bent over, I ran to the gas drums, giving David a grateful and approving nod. As David continued exchanging shots with Stuart, I glanced around the gas drums, only to quickly pull back as Magda fired shots at me from behind one of the cars.

Thankfully the bitch had a crap aim. She was even dumb enough to look *over* the car rather than *around* it. Truly, it was a wonder that she was still in the game. It wouldn't have surprised me if she'd been hiding there the whole time, simply waiting for me to come near.

I was about to finish her when a better idea came to mind. Yeah, okay, it would be best to take her out of the game, but this would be more fun. I grabbed one of the paint grenades and threw it at the car, satisfied at her outraged cry when it exploded all over her. I probably should have been ashamed that my laugh had sounded more like a cackle, but whatever.

The problem was that this would have given away my location to anyone around. Wanting to quickly reposition myself so that no one could get a good angle on me, I headed over to a pile of tyres. An array of pellets zoomed at me, but I managed to take cover before they could land on me. Something told me that the person responsible had been my fiancé. A quick peek to the right confirmed my suspicion.

That wasn't great news, because Jared had a real good aim. We fired some shots back and forth as I took in the angles around me, looking for fresh cover. I didn't pop out of the same place each time, hoping the unpredictability would keep me in the game – and that it would make the bugger frustrated. Sometimes I'd peek out of the top left, sometimes the low right, and so on and so on. At one point, I stuck my head out on my right, and then dived to my left and fired. But the trick didn't work because he was too bloody fast. Fucking Pagori speed.

My focus flew to David as he stood upright with his gun held high and a blob of paint on his mask. Crap. I nearly had a sodding heart attack when Salem appeared beside me. I jabbed him with my gun. "You little shit."

"Look." He pointed at the 'B and B'. I looked in time to watch Butch hurrying inside it, while Chico covered him by pinning Denny in place with pellets. Meanwhile, Salem was shooting crazily at Stuart, who was squatted behind a car beside the 'B and B'. Had Salem not pinned him in place like that, Stuart would have been inside that building at the same time as Butch.

"We need to cover Butch as he runs with the crate," I told Salem as I reloaded. I had every confidence that Butch would get the crate in a matter of seconds. I was right. As soon as he appeared in the doorway, Salem launched a smoke grenade. Butch waited only until it exploded before he sprinted out of the building. He hadn't taken his gun with him, trusting that those of us left – me, Salem, and Chico – would cover him as he ran. We did.

It took the other team a few seconds before they realised what was happening and started firing at him. Salem, Chico, and I ran backwards, exchanging shots with Jared, Denny, and Magda. Although the other team had now redoubled their efforts, so had we.

Unfortunately, though, it wasn't long before Jared picked off Chico – the fucker. Pissing me off even more, Magda almost took me out. Time to get rid of the bitch. A well-aimed shot to the head eliminated her from the game. But – fuck it all! – a well-aimed shot from Jared took Salem out of the game no more than a second later. It seemed only natural to then turn on my fiancé, who at the same time turned on me, and we eliminated each other simultaneously. He dived on me then, knocking me to the ground and lounging on top of me, laughing.

Chuckling myself, I turned my head to watch Butch, ready to yell in victory as he reached base camp – something he was literally seconds away from doing. Although Denny was chasing after him, his shots were going wide and it looked like we had definitely won. But then Max – who I'd forgotten was only out of the game temporarily – appeared from around the corner of the last street and shot Butch right in the head.

Growling, Butch halted and dropped the crate at his feet.

Jared and his team started cheering and clapping, but Evan *tsk*ed. "Until you get the crate to your own base camp, you haven't won, guys."

Shrugging and laughing, Max and Denny both walked toward the crate. Startling all of us, there was a loud battle cry and Fletcher came charging out of our base camp, firing a series of pellets that seemed to go in every direction. Miraculously, some of his totally inaccurate shots caught Max and Denny's masks.

Cheers rang out from my team.

"Fletcher, put the crate in our base!" I shouted.

Nodding, he dragged it into the small building and then came back out, mask off, grinning like a Cheshire cat. As the cheers rose in volume, he adjusted his glasses and curtseyed.

Maybe it was childish, but I whipped off my mask and laughed in Jared's face. "How do you like that?"

He removed his own mask, appearing stunned. "How did I forget about Fletcher?"

I'd forgotten about him, too. But I wasn't about to tell Jared that. I smiled, joining my hands around his neck when he kissed me. "All part of the strategy."

He kissed me again. "Well played. But I *will* win you at the next game."

I gave him a sympathetic look. "I'll allow you to have your fantasies. I sure hadn't thought that wearing a mankini would be one of them, though."

His smile was quickly replaced by a scowl.

I began teasing him about the mankini again when we woke the next evening – even going as far as to call him Borat. That got me a punishment in the form of him pinning me down and shagging me until I came so hard I saw stars – ha, like that was a deterrent. We were lying in the bed, still reverberating with the aftershocks, when I noticed that he was staring. He did that a lot, never feeling uncomfortable as if it was totally normal to just stare at someone. I playfully snapped, "What?"

He flashed me an innocent smile that quickly turned roguish. "I like looking at you. I like looking at you, knowing I know this body better than even you do. Like knowing you belong to me." His kiss captured and muffled my 'I belong to myself, thank you very much'. When he pulled back, he had the oddest expression on his face. "That's not you touching my leg, is it?"

I looked down the bed to see that Dexter had made his way from the living area to the bedroom and was now slithering his way up the bed. I giggled. "Maybe he's starting to warm up to you."

"More like he's jealous that I'm touching you," grumbled Jared.

Yeah, Dexter often hissed at Jared, not yet comfortable with him.

"I'd appreciate it if you moved him away from me. He's heading in a direction that I'm not happy about."

Smiling, I gently coaxed Dexter over to me. He came easily. "Only *I* get to bite that part of you."

A devilish grin took over his face. I'd just joined my lips to his when we heard two distinct beeps. And we knew just which mobile phone was beeping. Swallowing hard, Jared retrieved Leon's mobile phone from the kitchen drawer and brought it to the bed. "It's from 'Del'."

This was what we'd been waiting for. This was what we'd been stressing over since meeting Jude. This was also something that was going to cause a humungous argument between Jared and me. "I'm not staying behind."

"There is *no* way you're going on this assignment, Sam."

"Oh I think you'll find I am."

"Oh I think you'll find you're not."

And on and on it went.

(Jared)

A full hour. I'd spent a full hour trying to make the homicidal bitch listen to me, trying to make her see reason. What had she done the entire time? Smiled indulgently at me, much like a parent would at a teenager having a tantrum. "Sam, you can't expect me to be okay with you going out there helpless."

"I'm not helpless."

"Really? Conjure your whip. Go on."

I watched as she absorbed energy into her palms, just as she had done thousands of times before. As I'd anticipated, nothing happened. Well, *one* thing happened: a stream of energy shot out of her palms in the form of water, drenching Luther.

Wincing at him in sympathy, she said, "Sorry, Gandalf."

Dignified, he wiped at his face. "It's quite all right."

I gestured at the soaking wet Advisor. "And *that* is why I want you to stay behind."

She snorted. "Tough titties. I'm going. Everything shouldn't always come down to my gifts...unless you're saying they're all I have to offer?"

The woman always knew what cards to play. "Of course I'm not." I truly wasn't. To me, she was intelligent, skilful, determined, tenacious, strong, resilient...*and still not going*.

"I won't send off my co-commander and my squad on a risky assignment while I stay home all safe and sound. Jude doesn't have an offensive power, yet you haven't objected to her going."

"Jude isn't the woman I intend to Bind with."

"No, she's not, but you wouldn't allow any person to go on an assignment unless you thought they were capable enough to handle it. So am I to take this as you think *she's* capable, but I'm not?"

Damn, how did she do that? How did she take something I'd done or said, twist it around, and use it against me?

"You have so little faith in me, do you?" That smile was back. She knew I was struggling with this one, and she was enjoying it. Of course I could declare that neither female was going, but in that case there would be uproar – particularly since Jude was out for blood. "You believe I'm weak like those Master Vampires who've come to supposedly offer their congratulations to us?"

"Stop twisting things." I was ashamed to say that had come out sounding a little petulant. She appeared to have enjoyed that, too. "I just want you to be safe. If you can't properly defend yourself, you won't be safe. Right now, as much as it pains us both, you can't—"

She held up a finger, wearing a look that reminded me of one of my old school teachers. "Quiet now. It's your own time you're wasting."

Chuckles burst of both Antonio and Luther. How supportive of them.

"So I'm the only one who cares whether or not she's safe?"

Antonio quickly sobered. Well, sort of – he was no longer chuckling out loud, but his body was still shaking with it. "You know Sam's well-being is of great importance to me. If I believed, for even one moment, that she could not handle this assignment, I would insist that she remained behind. But Sam is right; there is more to her than her gifts. You are simply unable to look at this objectively and I understand why. Bear in mind that you will not be facing vampires, but humans. Sam may not be a Pagori or a Keja, but she is still significantly stronger and faster than any human."

Before I could respond, Sam said brightly, "Now that that's all sorted, why don't I tell you my plan?"

Plan? Why did I get the feeling that I wasn't going to like this?

"You remember I took Janine's artificial baby bump after Jude had killed her, right? You never wondered why I wanted it?"

Oh shit.

CHAPTER NINE

(Sam)

I would have thought that seeing a pregnant woman stumbling out of a supermarket would get a reaction out of people. Most hadn't even noticed, wrapped up in conversations or using their mobile phones. Out of those that did notice, only one person had asked if I was okay. Some had looked at others, trying to judge if they would act or thought it necessary to. It seemed it was that whole bystander apathy thing.

It was as I reached the parking lot that a vehicle pulled up beside me. One of the tinted windows of the grey Volvo wound down just enough to show me a concerned face. This sure looked like our Wendy – if that was even her real name, of course. Approximately ten minutes ago, Jared had sent a response from Leon's phone; giving a description of me as the pregnant woman who had been drugged.

"Is everything all right, hon?"

I continued to stagger at a slow pace as I slurred, "F-fine." It was at times like this that I wished I'd been paying a little attention in drama class.

"You look like you need to see a doctor."

"Really, I'm fine," I slurred again.

"You're not fine, hon. Come on, jump in, I'll take you to the hospital."

"But my car—"

"You can't drive like that. You're close to passing out. It's important you get to a hospital fast...as long as you don't mind listening to a two year old recite his ABCs all the way there," she added with a laugh. Yes, Wendy had brought along a toddler to look unsuspicious. I wondered if he was her child or she'd borrowed him like the weirdo that she was.

Once the familiar mush by my feet had wriggled through the

cracks of the rear door and was inside the vehicle, I said, "Okay, thanks." For show, I fumbled and stumbled as I got into the Volvo.

"Don't worry about anything, hon. You just rest. I'll get you help."

If I'd been adhering to Jared's proposal, I would simply have waited patiently until he and the rest of the squad stopped the vehicle. But as my own plan had been more popular – more popular to everyone but Jared – I would be continuing the 'I'm in agony and disorientated' act, allowing her to lead me and the others right to the Medics.

Jared had insisted that the Deliverer would have easily told us their whereabouts. After a bit of torture, she most likely would have done. But that would have taken time. We couldn't risk the Medics deciding to leave as this was our best chance at getting to them. I knew that Jared was still pissed, but he had been slightly placated by my keeping Denny with me.

During the entire journey, I was sure to moan in pain, and to appear as if I was drifting in and out of consciousness. Instead of taking us to an isolated spot, as I would have expected, Wendy took us deeper into the city. Once we reached a row of industrial warehouses, she stopped the car. She paid me no attention whatsoever as she took her mobile phone from her purse and dialled a number. "Outside" was all she said.

Moments later, there was a loud crashing sound as one of the yellow roller doors opened. Three people, all in scrubs, came dashing out with a flatbed trolley. Wendy lit a cigarette and watched with a bored expression as they – all humans, I detected – placed me on the bed and wheeled me toward the building. Shame I wouldn't get to see her face when Denny materialised in front of her.

Thankfully, the little boy in the backseat was asleep. As instructed, Denny and Chico would immediately hand the little boy over to the police.

I was surprised by the interior of the warehouse. The large, bare space was much cleaner than I'd been expecting. In the far corner was a large white lorry that, at first glance, seemed like an average heavy goods vehicle. It was actually a mobile hospital.

The three humans – two men, one woman – lifted the bed into the vehicle with a practiced ease that made my blood boil. Just how many women had they done this to? Just how many bodies hadn't yet been discovered?

They took me past a supply station, a small lab, and a curtained area that contained a baby incubator and cot. Finally, they halted and I saw that we were in an operating suite. They transferred me from the trolley to a standard hospital bed, arranging my body in the position that they wanted.

The dark-skinned male took a place at the bottom of the bed. "Right, let's get this over with." He didn't sound happy to be doing it. At least he had a conscience, even if it was tiny.

The woman, having taken a place on my left while the other male was at my right, rolled up my sweater, and gasped at the sight of the Empathy Belly Pregnancy Stimulator.

Before any of them could react, I bolted upright and backhanded the Medics on either side of me, sending them crashing to the floor. In a blink, I was then behind the dark-skinned male, holding one of the scalpels to his throat. "Surprise," I drawled. "Bet you never seen that coming, eh? Shit yourself?"

"I d-don't understand what th-this is a-about," he stammered. "I sw-swear I haven't t-told anyone anything." So he thought I was one of his employers, most likely based on me being 'different'...which meant he had detected that something was 'different' about them.

"I'm not one of your employers, but I am like them. In fact, this lot are just like them as well," I added as Jared, the squad, and Jude entered the suite.

The female Medic took one of the scalpels and hurled it at them. It hit Salem in the chest, who merely peered down at it in bemusement. Rolling his eyes, he tugged it out and slung it on the floor. I had to give her credit for trying to fight back.

"Sandra, no!" chastised the human I was restraining. "Just cooperate. You too, Mitch," he told the other male Medic who was now being held by Reuben.

Salem tangled his hand in Sandra's hair and dragged her to him, pinning her wrists behind her back with one hand. Neither she nor Mitch struggled.

Jared came to stand in front of the dark male, shooting me a brief glance. *Nice work, baby.*

See, I'm not helpless just because my gifts are on the blink.

I can see that. Although there was amusement and affection in his tone, his expression was hard as stone. "What's your name?"

"Erik."

"Well, Erik, I'll get straight to the point. I have a few questions for you." Jared held up his hand, showing the human the trickles of electricity that were playing around his fingertips. "Answer them correctly and I won't have any reason to demonstrate just exactly how much this will hurt. Play dumb and, well…we'll find out if you can hit the high notes. Are we clear?"

Erik, stinking of fear, whined, "If I tell you anything, they'll kill me."

"Ah, but if you don't tell *me* anything, *I'll* kill you. That's if the beautiful female behind you restrains herself long enough to let me. I should probably point out that she has homicidal tendencies. Oh, and you may have noticed the totally pissed off woman at the other end of the suite, glaring at you. She had her baby taken from her."

"Is this the one that cut you open?" I asked Jude. She nodded, looking fiercer than I'd ever seen her.

Jared scratched his head, giving Erik a falsely sympathetic smile. "Yeah, I think it's safe to say that you're not leaving this warehouse alive. I won't lie to you about that. Denying Jude her vengeance isn't something I'm prepared to do. *But* I'm prepared to skip the 'torture' part of the interrogation if you answer me honestly and quickly. Think you can do that?"

Startling all of us, Erik abruptly leaned into the scalpel and sharply twisted his head, slitting his own throat. Releasing the gargling human, I jerked back.

Butch sighed. "I guess he didn't think he could."

Max cocked his head. "If he'd rather die than talk, they had to have scared him even worse than we have."

Jared shrugged one shoulder. "No matter. We have two others here who can help us with our enquiries." At a leisurely pace, he strolled over to Mitch. "I'm hoping that you'll be more cooperative."

"He looks like a helpful person," I said, as I joined Jared.

"He does, doesn't he?"

The words burst out of Mitch. "I don't remember anything." When Jared went to move, he shouted, "It's true, it's true! They did something to me."

Jared crossed his arms over his chest. "Explain."

"I can't, not all of it, because I don't remember. I just know that they put some kind of block on my memories."

"A block?"

"A block, or they erased them or something. They did the same to Sandra. The only one of us who really knew anything was Erik, but that was because he'd saw stuff that he wasn't supposed to see. He would never tell me any of it. He said it was safer for me that way." His expression was poignant as he looked down at the body of his ex-colleague.

I turned to Jared. "Is that possible?"

"Yes. It's a little like Jude's gift, only much stronger. Whereas Jude can only delete the last twenty minutes of memory, these people can choose which memories they want to delete and there is no time limit."

"So we have nothing," said Jude through her teeth.

"Not necessarily," interjected Stuart. "See, the brain is made up of so many compartments that it would be impossible to completely erase a memory. It's a little like a computer. When you delete things, it simply goes into the recycle bin, so it's more like the vampire *suppressed* his memories. One memory can trigger another to resurface."

I nodded. "Okay. So how do we get to those memories?"

"We use Antonio's top interrogator, Ryder," announced Jared. "He can do a mind swipe. Basically, he has a psychic hand. He uses it to sift and browse through what's there. If there is anything at all left of those memories, he'll find it."

Cool gift, but… "If he's that good, why doesn't Antonio send him on assignments? It would be a hell of a lot easier to get answers if we had someone like him with us."

"Ryder never leaves The Hollow. He's only five months old, so he's not in control of his bloodlust yet. Antonio keeps him isolated, just as he would with any newborn."

"We'll have the Deliverer, too," David reminded us. "She might know stuff."

"Then let's get these humans to The Hollow." When Jude stepped forward, her eyes flashing with anger, I gave her a pointed look. "Jude, you *will* get your vengeance, I promise you. But we need Ryder to sweep through their memories first. We need what info they have so we can find out what they know. Once we have it, they're all yours. Okay?"

Her nod was reluctant, and I couldn't blame her for being so impatient.

"There's something I want to know first." Jared turned back to the male Medic. "What were you going to do with the baby once you had it? Is there someone waiting for it right now? Bear in mind that I'll know if you're lying to me."

"No one's waiting. We can't do it at a moment's notice, so we were always given a week to get a baby. Once we had one and we were confident it would survive the Caesarean, Erik would send a message on his cell phone and then they'd message him with a location for him to drive to with the baby. He never took me or Sandra with him."

"Good," I said. "No one will suspect anything if this lot doesn't show up with a baby today. When is the latest they'll expect to be contacted?"

"In four days."

"Think Ryder will be done within four days?" I asked Jared.

"Let's hope so." Jared sighed. "This place needs cleaning up. We don't want human forensics finding Salem's blood or any traces of us. It would probably be easier to just teleport it to the ocean or something. First, I want Harvey, Max, and Damien to search the vehicle. Look for any files or paperwork or anything that might even *seem* important. If I'm tied up, one of Antonio's guards will teleport in and pick you guys up in a couple of hours."

I looked at Salem, who was still holding Sandra, and at Reuben, who was still restraining Mitch. "When we get back, take them straight to the containment cells. Make sure they're put in separate ones. Ask Denny to do the same with Weird Wendy."

Once Jared had teleported everyone, with the exception of Harvey, Damien, and Max, back to The Hollow, he and I made a quick stop at our apartment.

"I need to get this Belly and these clothes off," I grumbled, not too happy with having splatters of Erik's blood on my sweater. Catching sight of myself in the large oval mirror, I stopped. A pang of sorrow ran through me as I realised that this was the closest I would ever get to being pregnant. Never would I look like this, never would I know what it was like to carry and raise a child – *my* child, mine and Jared's child.

I hadn't considered whether I'd ever want kids before now. Although I wasn't the most maternal person, I would rather not have had the choice taken away from me. Now that it was, I realised exactly how much I had wanted a child someday.

Obviously having sensed my change of mood, Jared appeared and slipped his arms around me. "What is it?"

I twirled in his hold. "Just thinking."

"About what?"

"Don't you regret that you'll never get to have kids?" I didn't like the way his face seemed to shut down.

He backed away, shrugging. "I don't think I'd have been good at parenting anyway."

"Why do you say that?"

He sighed, shrugging again. "I just don't. Some people shouldn't have kids." And with that odd little comment he disappeared back into the living area.

Suspecting it was something to do with his mother and making a mental note to ask him to elaborate later, I changed into my white tank top and combat pants. It was then that we sought out Antonio. To my surprise, he wasn't in one of his parlours. He was sitting on a bench in his indoor botanical gardens with Luther, Wes, and Lena. As usual, his guards and dogs also lingered close.

After hearing Jared's account of what had happened, Antonio shook his head sadly. "I was hoping to find that Jude was wrong about vampires being involved in such an awful thing. I think it is now safe to say that she was correct. I'll get Ryder to…"

Antonio's voice seemed to fade away as my attention was snagged by the pulse beating in Jared's throat. I couldn't seem to look away from it, I felt literally mesmerised by it. Watching it throbbing had me licking my lips, had my stomach clenching. Then everything went black.

(Jared)

Shock seized and froze my entire body as Sam suddenly dived on me and latched on to my throat. It was nothing like her usual bites. There was nothing teasing or sensual about the way she sunk her teeth down hard, gulping my blood like she'd die on the spot if she didn't. Antonio tried to pry her away, but she locked her limbs around me and growled.

She fucking growled!

Worse, in spite of the pain, her Sventé saliva was making me horny as shit and I was going to come in my jeans if someone didn't detach her from me quickly.

It took the combined efforts of Antonio, Wes, Luther, and the guards to wrench her away. She fought their hold – kicking, scratching, and punching them. All the while, she hissed, growled, and snapped her teeth. Her pupils were completely dilated and she was shaking. She looked…crazed. The bottom fell out of my stomach as a heavy weight hit my chest. Shit, no.

I cupped her chin hard, but she managed to escape my grip. Then she curled her upper lip at me; it was a warning and a challenge. I framed her face with my hands, holding it still. "Sam, stop!" She didn't. "Sam, I said stop!" My words didn't even seem to register. Her focus was now solely on my throat. If the others weren't still restraining her, she'd have been latched on to my throat again.

"Maybe you should try slapping her," suggested Wes.

I shot him a scowl. I had no intention of hurting her. But that did give me an idea. Not knowing what else to do, I released a small harmless electrical discharge – something I hoped might snap her out of it. Her body jerked, but not in pain, in shock. I did it again, and again, and again, breathing a sigh of relief when her struggles stopped.

Reason and rationality soon returned to her eyes, and she glanced at us all oddly. "What the fuck?"

"Let her go." Dubious, the others slowly released her. I curled my arms around her and kissed her hair. "I don't know what the hell just happened. It was like you flipped or something."

"Flipped?"

"You acted much like a newborn vampire," said Wes. "You were wild."

She swallowed hard as anxiety and worry flashed on her face, but she quickly blanked her expression. "I'm deteriorating, aren't I?" It wasn't really a question.

Antonio patted her back. "Let's find out, shall we?"

Five minutes later, after Reuben had once again amplified Lena's gift, she and Sam sat on the bench as Lena studied her. I held Sam's hand, needing to touch her. Nothing had ever shocked me more than when she leaped at me like that. Nothing. Watching her in pain was awful, but looking at the only woman I'd ever loved and seeing nothing of that woman there...That was ten times worse.

Finally, Lena took a long breath and sat back. After taking a few mouthfuls of the NST that the guards had given her, she began to speak. "Your DNA has changed since I last looked. As last time there were certain equations that didn't add up, I had expected – after what just happened – to find that those equations made absolutely no sense. But it is not that at all. In fact, those equations almost add up perfectly. What has changed is that these equations have become more complicated."

I didn't like the sound of that. "What does that mean?"

"It means that rather than her body going into 'override' and fighting the dramatic changes, it is...entering the next stage of the alterations."

"I don't get it. How can she enter the next stage without fully completing the first stage?"

"It is similar to the predicament of a caterpillar. If you were to open the cocoon, it would die. It has to be able to have the strength to free itself or it will not have the strength to fly away." Lena placed her hand over Sam's. "However, do not take that to mean that you will die – or fly, for that matter. My point is, you don't yet have the strength to move on to the next stage, but your body has done it anyway. That is what most likely caused you to experience such an attack of bloodlust. Your body feels the need to compensate, it needs to replenish. Perhaps it would be a good idea for you to drink a few more NSTs a day than you would normally do."

Antonio stopped in his pacing. "Does this mean that she is not deteriorating?"

"My opinion is that, on the contrary, she is strengthening. She is simply not seeing or feeling anything of these changes because the alterations are not yet complete."

"When will they be complete?" I asked Lena.

"That, I do not know. But it was not all that long ago that I first looked at her DNA, and already there have been big changes. Give it a few days." She smiled at Sam. "So how do you like your new pet?"

Sam's smile took over her face. "He's gorgeous. I've named him Dexter."

Lena chuckled. "I look forward to meeting him. When you take him into the rainforest, take some tropical vine branches back to your apartment and create a jungle set-up. That's what Wes and I did for Toto."

I couldn't believe they were talking about vines and pets in the middle of a conversation like this. Unreal. But sensing that Sam was spooked by having blacked out, I didn't try bringing the matter up again. She wasn't the type who liked to talk about stuff until she had sorted things through in her own head, and I knew she needed a little time to do that.

So I pretended that I bought the relaxed act, pretended I didn't know how scared she was. Even when she wanted to take the damn snake for a walk…well, a slither…in the rainforest, I continued pretending, and I didn't try coaxing her to open up. But after watching her stare at her office desk for two hours, I couldn't keep quiet any longer.

She was so lost in her thoughts that she didn't notice I'd crouched beside her chair until I rested my hand on her thigh. "Baby?"

Turning to look at me, she double-blinked. "Sorry, what?"

I gently moved her hair away from her face. "I know you're scared, just like I know you'd prefer to pretend you're not scared, but you have to have faith in Sebastian. That guy could find God if you asked him to. He'll come through for you, I promise you. And then I'll get those brothers to put everything right."

"I have faith in all of you. It's just…it freaks me out that I lost control like that. Worse, I don't even remember it. I hurt you."

"You didn't hurt me."

"Jared, I bit you without permission." For vampires, that was a sort of rape. Cursing, she got to her feet and started pacing.

Feeling a shadow of her guilt, I pointed hard at her as I stood. "You do not have to feel bad about that. You don't need my permission. I'm yours."

"That's not the point."

No, it wasn't the point. "Still, I don't care. Do you hear me? I don't care."

"And what if it hadn't been you? Not only could I have hurt someone else, but I'd have drank from someone else, and don't tell me you wouldn't hate that."

Of course I'd hate that; I wanted her to feed from me, no one else. "But that wasn't really you, Sam. That wasn't my Sam. That was bloodlust taking over."

"That freaks me out as well. But the worst is the 'not knowing'. If I knew what they had done to me, I could deal with it. I'd probably be pissed and scared, but I could deal. Not knowing is harder." Looking defeated, she backed into the wall and sighed.

I went to her and slid my hands into her hair. "I hate seeing you like this."

"I'm entitled to sulk now and then. You do it all the time."

I smiled at that, kissing her softly, teasingly, making her mouth chase mine. "You do know that even if you grow five heads, I'm keeping you, right?" Her laugh made me relax a little. I licked along the seam of her mouth, wanting entry again. "Let me make you forget for a while. Let me make you feel good." The second she opened for me, I slipped my tongue inside, seeking hers. Quickly the kiss went from soft to demanding; it sent fire sizzling through us both as it usually did.

She sucked on my tongue, knowing I liked it, knowing it made me think about how much I loved her sucking something else. Tricky bitch. My hands drifted down to mould and squeeze what were, without a doubt, the most perfect set of breasts. I nibbled and drew on a nipple through the cotton of her tank top, teasing the other nipple by sending sparks of electricity to it through my thumb. Her husky moans made my cock so hard it hurt. But this wasn't about me, it wasn't for me.

I dropped to my knees and, in Pagori speed, got her naked from the waist down. Hooking one shapely leg over my shoulder, I shot her a promising smile and started suckling on her clit. I slid my tongue between her folds, groaning at how wet she was, and licked my way back to her clit to suck on it again. Then I was flicking it with the tip of my tongue, loving that I could *feel* a hint of the pleasure that was coursing through her. She repeatedly moaned, clenching her fingers in my hair to the point of pain, but I didn't care.

I let my hands snake up the back of her thighs to cup that luscious ass that seemed to fit perfectly in my hands. All I wanted right then was to pull her to her knees and impale her hard on my cock. But I didn't. Even though her scent was driving me insane and I was hard as a fucking rock, I didn't. Even though her addictive taste was feeding that need to be inside her, I didn't. This was all about her.

I flicked and fluttered my tongue along the tips of her opening, knowing she loved it. She shifted her hips, trying to take my tongue inside her. Any other time, I'd have teased her for a while, but not today. I gave her what she wanted, spearing my tongue inside her, alternating between swirling it around, and thrusting it in and out of her.

I could sense the friction building in her, knew she was about to come. I started at the feel of something else – a wicked sense of self-satisfaction. Confused, I asked, *What's with the smugness?*

Even her mental voice sounded breathy. *Magda just walked in, stared open-mouthed, scowled at me, and then stormed back out.*

That made me smile. *No doubt Fletcher knew what he was doing when he sent her in.* As an Empath, he probably had a real good idea of what was going on.

Of course he did. Now get back to work.

Chuckling, I moved my mouth back to her clit and sank two fingers deep inside her. She jerked and groaned as her muscles gripped them tight.

"Jared, no teasing this time," she insisted, her voice huskier than usual.

I plunged my fingers in and out of her as I circled her clit with the tip of my tongue. "Tell me what you want, Sam. Tell me how much you want it."

"You. In me. Now. I need it."

I withdrew my fingers and lazily sucked the moisture from them, smiling at the way her glazed eyes flared. Standing, I lifted her and perched her on the edge of her desk. She practically attacked my jeans, tearing at the buttons. My chuckle turned into a groan at the feel of her soft fingers curling around my cock.

But when she started running her hand up and down my length, I stilled her hand with mine. "You do that and I'll come before I'm inside you." I would have undressed, but I was aware of how much she liked it when I fucked her with my clothes on. Gripping her thighs, I angled her hips just right and slammed home, forcing myself deep. Her muscles clamped tight around me. "Oh fuck." Nothing in the world beat being inside her. Nothing.

She locked her legs around my waist and bucked hard, telling me what she wanted. I gave it to her, clenching my jaw as I took her hard and fast; never easing, never slowing, yet always remembering how much stronger I was than her, always careful not to hurt her. Not once did I move my gaze from hers. I loved to watch the way her aquamarine eyes went out of focus, like she was drunk. Drunk on pleasure.

"God, baby, you feel so fucking good around me." I fused my lips with hers, tangling my tongue with hers. When her eyes drifted shut, I tore my mouth away. "Uh-uh, Sam. I want those eyes open. Look at me."

Her lids flickered open. "I need to come."

"I know you do. And I'm going to make you come." The awkward bitch closed her eyes again. "I said I want those eyes open."

She actually slapped my arm. "I can't help it."

Punishingly, I bit her lip, lapping up the drop of blood that surfaced. I watched her gaze dance to my throat, *felt* what she wanted. "Do it, baby." She shook her head, and I knew why. She was still pissed at herself for what she'd done earlier, so she was denying herself that pleasure now. "Do it. Bite me."

"No," she snarled. "Just make me come."

"Not until you drink from me."

"Oh, you bloody bastard!"

"If you want to come, do what I said."

She didn't. Of course she didn't, she was too damn stubborn. So I stopped.

Her mouth dropped open. "What are you doing?"

"I won't let you punish yourself, Sam. You want to drink from me, and I want you to drink from me, so do it."

"Piss off, you twat!"

"You know I don't care how much you insult me." If anything, it was amusing. "You know I won't let this drop. Come on, baby." I punched my cock into her once. "Give us what we both want."

"I hurt you!"

"You took what was yours. Do it again now. I'm sure as hell going to." I bit into her neck at about the same time that I began pumping my cock in and out of her. But I didn't take more than four gulps. "Your turn." Seeing that she was close to caving, I – sneaky though it was – parted her wet folds and tipped her so that my pelvis was hitting her clit with each thrust. "Bite me. Take what's yours."

With a moan of begrudging surrender, she sank her teeth into my throat, and it felt too damn good.

"Shit, Sam." Rewardingly, I hardened my thrusts and upped my pace. The effects of her saliva started to speed along my orgasm, and

I knew I wouldn't last much longer. I knotted a hand in her hair and tugged her mouth away from my throat. Seizing her gaze, I demanded, "Come for me now, baby, come around me."

Her eyes fell closed as her climax slammed into her, triggering my own. I closed my mouth over hers, swallowing her scream and groaning/growling into her mouth as I exploded inside her. The woman was fucking amazing. And she was all mine.

Waiting for the aftershocks to subside, I rested my forehead against hers. "You okay?"

She smiled dreamily. "If I didn't already love you, I would after that. God, you're good."

I laughed. "My ego adores you."

"I probably shouldn't feed it, since it's big enough."

"Oh no, you should definitely feed it."

She softly shaped my back with her hands. "I'm sorry I hurt you earlier. Even if you don't care that I did it, I'm still sorry."

"I know you are. I'd hate myself if I ever hurt you. I'd rather die than do it. But like I said, that wasn't really you."

"What if it happens again?"

"I don't think it will. Not if you do as Lena said and drink more than you usually do. Our refrigerator is already stocked full of NSTs. And I'm *totally* fine with you drinking more from me than usual…especially if it means a lot more sex."

"If we shag any more than we already do, there's a chance your dick will fall off."

I shrugged. "It'd be worth it. You're good in the sack." She just shook her head, like she pitied me. I kissed her lightly. "Come on, let's go for a swim in the pool before we go for the meal. We'll see if you're good in the water, too." Before she could say no, I teleported us to the bottom of the pool. I got a huge slap for that.

CHAPTER TEN

(Jared)

I was jealous of a snake. That was something I never thought I'd say.

Yeah, it was true. The second Sam had returned Dexter to his tattoo form, my mood had dramatically improved. In my defence...Okay, maybe there wasn't really much of a defence if you were jealous of a pet. It was probably fair to say that it was immature and a little unreasonable. But when that pet hissed at you every time you moved to touch your fiancée, it got annoying *fast*. There were only two reasons why I wasn't tempted to slice up the slithering little shit – Sam adored him, and he was, as Wes had predicted, extremely protective of her.

With everything that was going on right now, she needed protection. Not simply because her gifts were acting up. No, it wouldn't be long before Ryder reported to Antonio with the info he had been able to retrieve from the Medics and from the Deliverer. As soon as he did, Sam would insist on being part of whatever happened next. I was kidding myself if I thought I could stop her. As she had told me over and over, sitting in the background wasn't who she was. Dexter would help me ensure that she was well protected...which meant I couldn't kill him.

Earlier, we had read the file that Antonio's researchers had compiled about the brothers. Born into a very prestigious family, they had been given the best of everything all their lives. Both of them had shown great aptitudes for science at an early age and had won many awards in that subject in school and university. One of them had been married and had a son, while the other had been in a relationship with their gardener – male gardener.

It wasn't clear how they had found out about the existence of vampires, but it was apparent that they had gone to Orrin and had requested to be Turned – not the other way around. Considering that Orrin had Sired many vampires, it was reasonable to assume that he'd had no qualms about Siring two more. Consistent with Orrin's story, they had only remained with him for the first year. Then they seemed to have gone off alone to begin their own bloodline.

We weren't any the wiser about the foetal abduction operation either. Unfortunately, neither Max, Harvey, nor Damien had found any documents in the mobile hospital that might help with the investigation. I had heard from Antonio that although Ryder was doing well with the captives, he hadn't yet acquired all of the info we needed. Being relatively newborn meant that Ryder wasn't fully in control of his gift yet, so it would take him a little time.

Although I was eager to shut down the operation, I was also grateful for the small reprieve; grateful that Sam and I were able to spend one whole evening with each other. Yeah that was selfish and shitty of me, but I wanted Sam to be relaxed and happy during the week of our Binding. At the moment, she was far from it. Still, she was smiling as we entered the large dining room where the oriental meal was being held.

Our designated waitress led us over to a circular table where several people already sat. Antonio, Luther, Evan, Wes, and Lena greeted us both with, literally, open arms. Bran and Kaiser were cordial, albeit a little stiff. Ricardo, Rowan, and Marcia, on the other hand, were welcoming toward me but very curt with Sam.

I was well aware of why, just as I was well aware that the pinch she gave me was a 'don't say anything' warning. Yeah, yeah, I knew she liked to fight her own battles and I knew it was important that she did so in this instance. While I respected that, it made me want to strangle her sometimes. Who would want to sit back and do nothing while people were being rude to their fiancée?

"The room looks amazing, doesn't it?" Sam said to me. At that moment, she looked truly happy, and that was all I wanted.

She was right; it really did look amazing. Hanging from the ceiling were several zodiac spirals, an oriental dragon garland, and large red and gold lanterns. The walls were decorated with large oriental fans, amazingly detailed wall scrolls, and bamboo borders.

"That centrepiece is gorgeous," she said, pointing at the red paper and bamboo oriental lamp that matched the napkins and table cloth.

"It is set up beautifully," agreed Marcia. Her expression turned devious as she went to continue.

Sam stopped her with a raised hand. "Marcia, I'm happy. Don't spoil it by speaking."

"All I was going to say was that the quality of food at The Hollow must be very different to what you were used to before coming here."

Sam nodded in agreement, but both her self-suffering sigh and her sad tone were forced. And they all knew it. "Yes, it's quite appalling that I was raised on fish, chips, and mushy peas. Still, I wasn't completely deprived. There was a Chinese takeout near my flat, and it had a lantern a bit like these. The lantern had splatters of barbeque and curry sauce on it, but the beauty was still there."

Rowan shuddered. "I do not know how people could eat from places like that. They're unclean."

"Nonsense," objected Sam with a wide smile. "Germs build up your immune system. I never caught any of the diseases that my neighbours had…Other than the time I had oral herpes after one of them forced a kiss on me. That hadn't been pleasant."

My mouth twitched into a smile. That was my Sam. She played the game with them, and she played it better.

Rowan grimaced. "I have a feeling that you are not being truthful, Miss Parker," – oh he was on the ball, wasn't he – "but, in any case, it is disgusting to talk of diseases at a dinner table."

"No more disgusting than your attitude."

Marcia placed a hand on her partner's arm. "Should we expect anything more from a girl whose origins are like Miss Parker's?"

Sam regarded her curiously. "Have you ever visited that website greatlyinneedofalife.com?"

Marcia bristled. "I have a life, thank you."

"Really? You seem a little too fascinated with mine. I mean, really, are you capable of talking about something that isn't related to my childhood or where I grew up?"

"*Did* you grow up?" quipped Rowan.

Sam simply looked at him with pity. "Aw, Rowan, didn't anyone ever tell you that in order to be a smartarse, you need to be smart? If you're not, it just makes you an arse."

Even Ricardo laughed at that.

"I could tell you that I was raised by parents who were addicted to crack. I could tell you that I sampled the stuff myself at a very early age. I could also tell you that I'd had a boyfriend who was not only a drug dealer, but a pimp – *my* pimp. But that would merely be telling you what you want to hear. You want reasons to disapprove of me. The truth of my childhood is, in fact, quite different. Not great, but nothing like that. But, see, I don't have to explain myself to any of you, and I won't. I don't crave the respect of people that I have no respect for."

Marcia crossed her arms over her chest. "You cannot expect us to respect someone who dislikes us so very much."

"In all honesty," began Sam, cocking her head. "I don't dislike any of you, you just piss me off. Still, you're entitled to your opinions, and you're clearly full of them. But like it or not, I'm going to Bind with Jared, and I'm going to one day be responsible for your protection." She leaned forward, whispering, "So you might want to be nice to me, because I have a vengeful streak."

Smiling, I kissed her temple. "I can vouch for that. I've been on the receiving end of it more than once."

"You're right about one thing, though," Sam told Rowan. "I have ended up a little like my parents. A workaholic. Yes, my parents actually have jobs. In fact, they run their own business. It's a small business and it doesn't do very well, but they work hard for a living. What do all of you do again? Oh yeah. Absolutely nothing."

It was at that moment that the waiter brought over the first course, effectively ending that conversation. I had noticed that Ricardo, Rowan, and Marcia appeared to be looking at Sam a little differently, as if considering her through fresh eyes. The problem was that even if they grew to like her, they wouldn't fully accept her until they were confident that she could protect them. Thankfully they didn't know that, at the present moment, she couldn't properly protect herself, let alone others.

In spite of the awkwardness at the table, conversation came easy and no more insults were exchanged. In fact, the mood even improved when Harvey brought over his smartphone to show his snaps of the paintballing games – I tried to snatch it before anyone saw the ones of me wearing that damn mankini, but Harvey had too good a grip on it.

Of course Magda had to try to ruin the good mood, didn't she?

Standing behind Marcia's chair, Magda greeted everyone individually, leaving Sam until last. "Good evening. Enjoying your meal?" Her expression said that she sincerely hoped that the answer was no.

Sam fiddled with the chopstick in her hand. "Still a bit sour that everyone turned on you at the end of paintballing? Karma doesn't taste all that nice, does it?"

I could understand why Magda snarled at the comment. Just the memory of her standing there, squealing, while a seemingly endless amount of paint pellets showered her…Ah, good times.

"That behaviour was uncall—"

"Oh Magda, Magda, Magda," began Sam. "We all know that you're only over here to insult me because you want Jared and you're jealous – it's old news. So why not just run along and nobody gets hurt. Okay?"

"You may think that you are clever, Sam. But all I see is an insecure, green-eyed, bitter, hot-headed individual." Madga's self-satisfied grin faded when Sam simply shrugged. I had to admit, I was surprised by her composure too.

"At least I don't have a chopstick sticking out of my eye." And then she lunged across the table, chopstick in hand. Yep, that was more like my Sam. If Magda hadn't scampered so fast, she would have ended up in sheer agony. God, I loved this woman.

(Sam)

Taking some time to calm down after Magda's little jibe, I'd gone out onto the empty veranda. I was actually enjoying the solitude, which was new for me. That peace and quiet didn't last long, though. Hearing footsteps approach, I swivelled my head to see none other than Ricardo. "Hello there, Rick. Lovely night, isn't it?"

A muscle in his jaw ticked. "My name is Ricardo."

"Right, that's what I said."

"You are very rude." He didn't actually sound that annoyed about it.

"And you're looking for reasons not to like or approve of me."

"You're a Sventé. That is reason enough."

"It's reason enough for you to worry that I might not be able to guarantee you're protected," I granted, "but it doesn't give you reason to insult me. And you know it."

His gaze skidded away, almost as if he was slightly ashamed of that. Nah. "Perhaps if you and Jared had been truly devoted to one another, I could accept you. But I know the truth of things. I know that you both sleep with others."

"Let me guess who told you that…The tribute to Jessica Rabbit. Am I right?"

He peered down at me, frowning. "Yes."

"It didn't occur to you that she just might be talking tripe to cause problems?"

"I will admit that jealousy does funny things to people, but surely she would be too protective of one of her vampires to cause him any pain."

I snickered. "You'd think so, wouldn't you? But no. The fact is that Jared would never be unfaithful to me. That bloke is loyal to a fault. But, of course, you already know that. You simply want to justify your behaviour. And you need to justify it to those Master Vampires over there who you Sired, don't you? You need to keep supplying them with reasons not to accept me."

He stiffened. "My vampires will always follow me."

"In the past they have, yeah. But you know as well as I do that they will only continue to do that if you continue being someone they respect. Refusing to give your approval to Antonio's Heir…That's not exactly admirable behaviour, Rick."

He inhaled deeply, as if seeking for calm. "It is Ricardo. And as you said, I am entitled to my opinion."

"Yes, you are. But it would be wise of you to keep that opinion to yourself and to allow them to decide for themselves what they want to do. They've been obedient so far, but they're not a flock of sheep, they're people with their own minds. This is a very delicate and important matter. Many of them respect Antonio and Jared. I doubt that they'll want to offend them by leaving before the ceremony. That is what you have every intention of doing, isn't it?"

He studied me through narrowed eyes. "You are very perceptive."

"I'm not going to tell anyone about your plan to leave, if that's what you're wondering. To be frank, I couldn't care less if you scuttle off in the day when everyone's asleep, or whether you dance a bloody jig after the ceremony is done. But you should have a long think before you ask your entire bloodline to leave with you. Yep, they have you to protect them. But what if something happened to you in the future, what then?" I rose from my chair. "I know what it's like to have no one to turn to. Don't put them through that." Then I left him standing there alone, hoping he made the right choice.

Instinctively, I made my way to Jared, who was in a corner with his twin. On hearing Evan's words, I halted a footstep away.

"I went. To the funeral, I mean."

As the twins had their backs to me, I stayed where I was, hoping to hear more before Jared sensed me.

"I knew what you meant." Jared's tone was flat, lifeless.

"But then I asked myself what the hell I was doing there, and I came straight back."

Jared frowned at him. "You had every reason and right to go."

"No. No, I didn't. How could I pay my respects to someone that I didn't respect? I don't like the way people think that we're supposed to love our parents simply because they're our parents. If they didn't live up to their end of the deal, why should we live up to ours?"

"She was good to you." I'd never heard Jared's voice sound so small before. He almost seemed…lost – a total first for him. It made my chest ache.

"Not for the right reasons, but it took me a while to see that." Evan shook his head. "I honestly don't know how you can't hate me just a little."

Jared chuckled, though there didn't seem much humour in it. "That was one thing she never succeeding in doing, wasn't it? Causing a divide between me and you proved too much, even for her."

"I know how you think, so I'm pretty sure you've felt bad that you didn't go to the funeral. Yes, she was our mother, but she didn't act like one. What I'm trying to say is that you aren't harsh for not going. I just want you to know that."

"I don't feel bad for not going. I feel bad that I *don't* feel bad…if that even makes sense."

"Don't feel bad. You shouldn't. She doesn't deserve the satisfaction. She'll be looking up at this, laughing in delight, so stop."

When Jared raised a brow questioningly, his twin shrugged.

"Yeah, she was good to me," he allowed, "but she's burning in hell for sure." Both then chuckled, and turned. When Jared's eyes landed on me, they instantly narrowed. I could tell by his expression that he knew I'd been eavesdropping, and he wasn't happy about it.

Evan smiled widely. "Hey there, calmed down yet?"

"No. That's why I still have this." I held up the chopstick.

"The look on Magda's face when you dived at her...Priceless." A nudge from one of the Master Vampires made Evan turn.

As I looked up at my fiancé, I sighed. "You're never going to tell me about your mother, are you?" I'd heard the strain in his voice, sensed the pain and anger he felt at merely thinking about her.

Jared's face hardened. "I've said I will, and I will. Just not until after the Binding."

"But *when* after the Binding? A month later, a year later, ten?"

"Sam, I told you—" He stopped on hearing Antonio call his name. "I'll be back in a minute." But we both knew he wouldn't.

Laughing, Evan turned away from the vampire and double-blinked at the empty space beside him. "Where'd he go?"

"Do you mean physically or mentally?"

Evan's expression morphed into one of concern. "What's wrong?"

"He's shutting me out again, the bastard." There was no venom in my voice because a part of me felt sorry for him. But apparently there was enough frustration that Evan decided to subtly lead me out of the room and into the ballroom adjacent to it.

The second the door was closed, he pressed, "What do you mean, shutting you out? Don't tell me you guys are letting Magda get to you. I really thought you were both coping pretty well with that."

"We are. Sort of. But that's not what this is about anyway."

"Then, what?"

"Answer me something. Is it a lot to ask him to talk to me about your mother, about why he wouldn't go to the funeral? If it truly is, I'll let this go. For now. But if it's not, tell me so that I can kick him up the arse and *make* him tell me. This isn't about my curiosity anymore. I heard his voice when he spoke of her, I heard him say he's feeling bad. I want to help him. He won't let me."

Evan ran a hand through his hair, looking like he would rather be anywhere but there with me at that very moment. "You can't understand what our mom was like, Sam."

"Then help me understand. He won't tell me anything, Evan. I just want to be there for him."

There was a long pause before he finally spoke. "If this was any other subject, I'd tell you to go to Jared, I wouldn't get involved. But this is a sore subject for him. I'm pretty sure he'd have told you eventually, but not now. And *now* is when he needs to talk about it, whether he likes it or not."

He led me over to one of the large circular tables, taking the seat opposite me. He then took a long, preparatory breath before starting. "Our mother...She wasn't a mom to Jared, Sam. To understand why, you have to understand what she was like. Ever met a narcissist before? I mean a true narcissist."

"No."

He smiled sadly. "That's the thing, you probably have; you just hadn't known it. Narcissists have two faces. They're one person in public, but a completely different person behind closed doors. Of course, no one other than the people living behind those doors with them will have any inkling there is more than one side to them.

"Lorna Michaels was totally obsessed with herself, had a sense of entitlement, couldn't empathise with another person, used and manipulated everyone around her. Her needs always came first. In some ways, she was like a spoilt child. And the vanity...she was so superficial; all about looks and appearances."

When he hesitated to continue, I knew he was debating whether to send me to Jared. "Please, Evan. I need to know."

Sighing, he nodded. "Because she was so nice to everyone else, they all thought she was amazing; a regular martyr who would do anything for anybody. Some kids even used to say that they wished they had my mom. They didn't know about the outbursts, the emotional abuse, or the physical abuse. But we did. Or, more specifically, Jared did, because it was only really him who suffered from it. Occasionally I was the focus of an outburst, but that was only if I'd tried to defend Jared or disobey her. Lorna Michaels had to be obeyed, and that was that."

Already I wished I'd been at the funeral just to do a celebratory dance around the headstone, singing 'Ding Dong the Wicked Witch is Dead'. "And your dad?"

"I don't remember him being home all that much – he was either at work, or out drinking with his friends. He was a 'woe is me' person, too wrapped up in his own misery to give a shit about anybody else. I think that was why their marriage was so bad – they were both attention seekers, and neither liked it when the other was getting all the attention. It was almost like sibling rivalry. But my mother would *never* have given him a divorce. No, other people weren't allowed to know that we were anything but the perfect little family. She let him have his work affairs as long as he was discreet about it. After all, she had secrets of her own, didn't she?"

"Why did she hone in on Jared?"

"When she gave birth to us, I popped out easily enough. But he hadn't turned, so she'd needed a C-section. And she was sure to tell him on a regular basis that she wished she'd never had him because she hated the scar. I think she would always have chosen just one of us to dote on. Apparently, it's typical of narcissists to, on a subconscious level, pick a golden child and a scapegoat. The golden child can do no wrong; the scapegoat can do no right."

Weird. "And she chose Jared to be the scapegoat because of the scar?"

"I don't think so. I think it was because she couldn't mould him into the person she wanted him to be. She tried to make us both extensions of her. Tried to control us – our every move, our every feeling, our every thought. With me, it worked in some ways. I wanted her attention, and the best way to get it was to agree with her, mirror her, do whatever she wanted. But Jared wouldn't let her control him."

And didn't that make me proud as hell.

"No matter how much she punished him, she couldn't break him. She couldn't get into his head and take control. Personally, I think it was because of the hurtful comments she made. Instead of trying to seek her approval, he'd rejected her in his mind as some kind of defence mechanism. Because of that, she simply couldn't get in. She actually made the job harder for herself, it was like a vicious cycle – the more she demeaned him to try to weaken him and take over, the more he rejected her and the tougher his defences against her became."

"You said there'd been physical abuse." A part of me didn't want to hear it, but this was Jared, and I couldn't help if I didn't understand.

Evan swallowed hard. "It was more about control, wanting us to fear her enough that we'd be easier to control. Oh she was nice to me, but she still terrified me. I'm ashamed to say that I didn't help Jared in the beginning. It wasn't that I hadn't wanted to. Sometimes, I'd get an urge to pull her away from him, but then I'd feel guilty because she was my mom and she was always good to me."

With a disbelieving look on his face, he continued, "See, I thought she was great, because she thought *I* was great, and she'd tell me how I was her best boy, and that we were so alike and special. But with Jared, she was cold, aloof, distant, and abusive…except when people came around. Then she'd talk about her '*two* best boys' and put him on display. And he'd have to perform. The punishment was so severe when he didn't that he learned it was easier to act the perfect family when people were around."

"What kind of punishments?"

He inhaled deeply. "One of her favourites was to lock him in our tiny shed – this was after she'd beaten the shit out of him. Even when it was winter and ice cold, she'd lock him in there, not even bothering to give him a coat. Yeah, she did lots of cruel crap like that. Other times, it would be mind games. She'd ask him to imagine what it would be like if she let 'The Bad Man' take him away and keep him, to imagine what that man would do to him. Or she'd pretend that she couldn't hear or see him, would act as if he wasn't there, like he didn't exist."

It was hard speaking while there was a big, fat lump in my throat. Just imagining him as a little boy being huddled in the corner of a cold shed, or repeatedly talking to his mother only to be completely ignored and made to feel like a ghost…Twisted bitch. "Didn't he ever tell anyone?" I couldn't imagine Jared ever suffering *anything* in silence.

"He told our aunt, but she didn't believe him. Why would she? Lorna was so nice to everyone, and she made him out to be 'troubled' and an 'attention seeker' with a 'vivid imagination'. She was cunning like that."

As he went on, Evan grinned; it was all pride. "He managed to get his revenge in subtle ways. He'd realised that she liked it when he flinched or cried, so he never did it for her. No matter what she did to him, he wouldn't cry, wouldn't ask her to stop, wouldn't even wince. Nothing. *That* got to her, because it was a reminder that she might be able to physically overpower him, but she still hadn't got in here." He tapped his temple, still grinning. "And denying that to someone who fed off misery and pain…it was probably the best form of revenge."

His grin faded as he went on. "I should have spoken up with him, should have told my aunt that Lorna was lying. I should have got him help. I wanted to, I did. But, like I said, *then* I'd feel guilty, because I'd sort of felt indebted to her. That was how she made me feel."

Hearing the shame and guilt in his voice, I patted his arm. "You were just a kid, Evan."

His chuckle was humourless. "He always says the same thing. But I still should have helped him. He's my *twin*."

"You didn't know any other way. To you, that was probably normal."

"I was eleven when it finally clicked in my head that it wasn't right. When I started spending time at my friends' houses, I saw how other parents were, how the kids were treated equally. But the real turning point for me was the time when I went inside one of my friends' homes with him and we found his dad beating up his brother. The first thing my friend did was jump on his dad's back and try to help his brother.

"That was when I really started to defend Jared rather than just divert her attention from him. We started to spend lots of time together and we became really close, and maybe that was a lot to do with being the only two people who knew the *real* her – we were each the other's validation that we weren't crazy for thinking that this supposed martyr was truly, well, evil."

"I'll bet she didn't like you two becoming close."

"No, she didn't. She turned on me big time, and she did some mean shit to me, too. But I was still the golden child, no matter what. Jared, on the other hand…She made it clear to him in as many ways as possible that he didn't matter to her, that he wasn't even a person. I'll tell you one thing that I remember. It happened when we were in our teens. We got quite a bit of female attention at school. I'm not being boastful here, I'm just—"

I held up a hand, smiling. "No, it's okay, I can fully imagine. I'll bet Jared loved that."

"Actually, he didn't. He hated attention back then. *Hated* it. He didn't trust anyone, he thought everyone was fake, he expected everyone to try to use him, or to fuck him over. He even hated his looks, because he looked so much like Lorna. He couldn't bring himself to respect many of the girls who rallied around him because most were as superficial as the bitch that gave birth to us. *But* he wasn't bitter or a total asshole, he was just very guarded and even quiet. He never really showed emotion…probably because at home, emotions had always got him in deep shit."

It was at that moment that I realised that I *had* been asking a lot of Jared when I wanted him to talk to me. But how was I supposed to know that this was such a hot button for him? Still, I felt like crap for pushing him.

"Mom's friends used to tell her she must be so proud to have such handsome sons. She'd say of course she was. One of those friends used to flirt a lot with Jared, who was freaked out by it and avoided her as far as possible. When she got a little too heavy, he went to Lorna and told her to keep the woman away from him. Wanna know what she said? She told him to give her friend the little fling that she wanted. She actually told him to fuck her friend, which he didn't, and that got him punished."

"Please tell me that you're joking." When he shook his head, I asked, "How old was he?"

"Fourteen."

My jaw practically hit the floor.

"She didn't see people as 'people', Sam; especially not him. Jared was just a thing for her to use and manipulate. When Magda turned out to be exactly the same, it did something to him. It changed him. Something in him just…went. Although he hadn't cared about Magda, he'd *thought* he did at the time. What's more, she'd told him that she loved him. That was something he'd never had before. But she just became another woman that hurt, used, and betrayed him."

Had I ever wanted to hurt Magda more than I did right at that second?

"When he was made Heir and the spotlight was on him…That was what he'd always wanted. Not necessarily the spotlight itself, but recognition, acceptance, and respect. And, yeah, he got a lot of female attention too. But, again, they didn't want *him*. They wanted the Heir, they wanted to use him. It didn't even bother him; he'd come to expect that from people, had convinced himself that women were users and manipulators. There'd never been anyone to make him think differently."

The click in my head was so definitive that I was surprised it hadn't been audible. "So, basically, all that prejudice…it wasn't because he thought women were the inferior sex. It was because he was angry at women in general."

Evan nodded. "But you…you didn't care that he was the Heir. You didn't jump into his bed. You were going to require some effort on his part, some respect, and he liked you enough to give you both. I don't think either of us can appreciate how hard it must have been for him to take the chance of letting you in, knowing you could hurt him. I imagine it was a while before he even realised he'd let you in enough to care about you. He'd probably convinced himself it was all physical, that sex would make it go away."

Thinking back to the way Jared had behaved in the beginning, how Fletcher and I had mused that he seemed to be sulking over my refusal to shag him, I thought that Evan might just be right about that.

"Now do you see why he's being so protective, Sam? You've been the exception to every rule. You're the total opposite of all those women who used him. You're something he hadn't imagined existed, something he needs and *will* be determined to keep. If you are at all worried about Magda, don't be. He would never want her or anybody else. Nothing in this world could stop him from Binding with you. Nothing."

And if Evan was right about that, I'd been worrying for absolutely no reason. Jared hadn't shut down because he had doubts, he had shut down for reasons deeper than I would ever have imagined.

"I know the protectiveness is driving you crazy, Sam, but you won't get him to tone it down. Not with how scarred he is, not with how determined he is to never lose you. If you really do love him, don't ask him to change. Just…indulge him in this. Not all the time, but at least sometimes. Especially while your gifts don't seem to be working."

I nodded. "Okay, that's fair."

Evan looked at me beseechingly. "Now can you understand why he hasn't wanted to talk about our mother?"

"Definitely."

"Don't think his confidence must therefore be all an act. It's not. Jared fought hard to keep what she tried her level-best to take from him. And it must've been hard. To be told everyday – and by your own mother, the person who's supposed to love you – that you're nothing, you'll never be anything, you're bad through and through…it's like brainwashing. But like I said, he'd formed defences against her, and those defences kept him going. He became emotionally independent at a very young age, and the only person other than me who he ever allowed himself to care about was Antonio."

The man who'd saved him. "Ah, hero worship."

Evan chuckled. "Antonio was kind of like the dad we'd never had. He was the positive influence that Jared had really needed at the time. Up until that point, I was the only person that Jared had ever let fully 'in' to his life. Actually, that's not true. Antonio had *barged* his way in. When he sees potential in someone, he won't let it be left untapped."

Very true. I knew that from personal experience.

"Jared had resisted at first because, as I said, he'd become emotionally independent at a young age. Maybe that's admirable, but it wasn't good for him. I wanted so much for him to let another person into his life. The great thing about Jared is that once he does, once they're 'in', he doesn't hold back from them. He'll give them whatever they want or need, he'll kill or die for them. But no one ever really sees that part of him, because he doesn't let them. But he let you. And that should speak volumes to you."

It did, and now I was crying. I did *not* cry, but here I was crying.

"Please don't cry. Teary women scare me. It's—" Evan cut himself off when the door suddenly swung open, and in strode Jared.

Oh bugger.

CHAPTER ELEVEN

(Sam)

Jared halted at our expressions, but it was when he saw me scrubbing tears from my cheeks that understanding flashed on his face.

Evan got to his feet, hands raised in a placatory gesture. "I had to tell her, Jared. It was important that she understood."

Jared did something I would never have seen coming. He simply nodded, giving Evan a half-smile. I almost felt Evan's relief, who returned the smile and gave me a wave before heading for the door. Further surprising me, Jared patted his brother on the back as Evan past him and left the room. Leaving us alone.

Sighing, Jared shrugged. "Now you know."

"Yeah, now I know." In vampire speed, I was pressed up against him, wrapping my arms around him. Of course he did that man-thing and struggled. "This isn't sympathy, you macho sod, this is me wanting to hug you because I love you." He settled then, curling his arms around me. "I understand now why you didn't want to talk about her, but it felt like you were pushing me away."

He shook his head, sliding his hands into my hair. "No, baby, not that. Never that. Do you want to know what my two biggest fears are?"

"What?"

"That something bad will happen to you, or you'll leave me. I'm not going to do anything that might make either of those things happen. Oh I'm not saying I'll be a ray of fucking sunshine, or that I won't screw up sometimes. But I would never do anything that would hurt or push you away. Understand?" He relaxed a little when I nodded. "I'm just not good at talking about stuff, at talking about feelings and whatever."

That made me remember what Evan had said – emotions had always got Jared into shit. Of course he wouldn't be comfortable having to tell me anything. "If she wasn't already dead, I'd kill her for you," I told him with all seriousness.

That got a hint of a smile from him. His hazel eyes smouldered with possessiveness and adoration when he looked down at me. And then my eyes filled up again. He gently swiped the tears away with the pads of his thumbs. "Hey, don't be sad for me."

"I might have homicidal tendencies, but I'm not made of stone."

"No, you're definitely not made of stone."

"I don't like crying. It makes me feel weak." And then more tears came. Again, he wiped them away.

"One word I would never use to describe you is 'weak'."

"I thought you did in the beginning, when I first came here; that you arrogantly thought I was weak just because I was female. But it was your mother and Magda who'd created the prejudices, wasn't it?"

He tilted his head. "With you, it was never really prejudice. It was panic. I knew that if I let you in my life in any capacity, even as a squad member, everything would turn upside fucking down. I'd had an immediate reaction to you, felt instantly possessive, and I hadn't liked it. I hadn't known what to do with it."

He dropped a gentle but lingering kiss on my mouth. "I'd just never met anyone like you before. You're not superficial or fake. You're upfront about whatever flaws you have, you don't pretend to be anything but who you are. That's drugging to me." He dabbed another kiss on my mouth, smiling this time. "But you didn't want me."

"Correction: I didn't want to be another of your consorts."

"You know, in all honesty, I truly hadn't understood your problem over the consorts in the beginning. Women had always used me, and they still did then, so I hadn't seen why I couldn't do the same." His arms contracted tight around me. "But that could just be because I'm an asshole."

"I heard you telling Evan you felt bad. Why?"

"I don't care that she's dead, Sam. I hated her. Some people might say that's not surprising—"

"That's because it isn't."

"—but there are lots of people out there who were hurt by their parents and yet they still loved them. I wasn't capable of giving her that unconditional love. I resented the way everybody bought her act, resented having to be part of that act, resented that everyone believed her lies that *I* was the one who needed help – the regular problem child – and *she* was the poor mother having to deal with me. She was my mother, and I hated her."

I gave him a hard look. "She didn't deserve your unconditional love, Jared. No one has the right to treat anyone the way she treated you – mother or not. In fact, your mother should be the one person who would *never* do it. How could you ever expect yourself to love someone like that?"

"But I should still care that she's dead, shouldn't I? I should care that it was only Evan she was looking for all these years, never me. But I don't. The only thing I've been mourning is the mother that I never had, that I wished I'd had." He sighed as his eyes took on a faraway quality. "You know, sometimes, I even think I'm like her."

I tugged on his shirt, bringing his focus back to me. "No, no you're not."

"Vain. Can't admit when I'm wrong. Can't seem to form the word 'sorry'. Can't give a compliment."

"Hey, lots of people are vain to some degree. And you're not actually as vain as I first thought you were."

He shook his head adamantly. "No. After coming here and becoming Heir, I forgot who I was and where I came from."

"Because you wanted to," I finished quietly.

He sucked in a breath, and I realised he hadn't looked at it that way before. Finally, he nodded. "Yeah."

"As for the other stuff…No one likes to admit when they're wrong. But you know in your own head when you're in the wrong and you care that you're in the wrong – that's what differentiates you from that bitch. 'Sorry' would be a nice thing to hear from you occasionally, but I prefer your current mode of apology, which is to fuck me senseless."

That got me a smile. "And if you can't give compliments it's because you don't know *how* to, because no one ever gave them to you. What would I do with a load of compliments anyway? Flattery means nothing to me. Actions mean something to me. And you act like you care. I *feel* that you care."

"Of course I care." He sucked my bottom lip into his mouth and gently bit down on it. "You...you're like a patch. You make the anger go away. Until you piss me off, which you do a lot."

I thumped him in the stomach, shaking my head. "Plonker."

"You love me really," he wheezed out, leading me toward the door.

"Yeah, well, you love me."

"Yes, I do, which is why I get so pissed when you fight me on trying to protect you."

I shot him a playful, petulant scowl. "How about this: I'll accommodate this protective streak you have, and you stop freezing me out."

His brows arched, and I felt his suspiciousness. "That deal sounds fifty/fifty. For you, that's a first."

I shrugged. "It's not like I don't need a little help right now, is it?"

"Hey, soon enough your gifts will be working again and you'll be kicking ass like you usually are. Mine, included."

I chuckled as I exited the room, almost not seeing Magda until it was too late. The gloating smile on her face told me something that made my stomach sink: she'd heard Jared's comment about my gifts. Oh shit.

Rather than saying anything, she simply turned and headed back to the dining room.

Obviously having reached the same conclusion as me, Jared growled warningly, "Magda."

Without breaking stride, she peered at him over her shoulder and winked. This wasn't good. Hand-in-hand, presenting a united front, Jared and I re-entered the dining room. Seeing that she had made a beeline for Marcia and Rowan, I cursed. Smoothly but quickly, Jared and I walked to our table where only Antonio, Luther, Wes, and Lena sat.

"She knows," Jared told Antonio as we returned to our seats. At Antonio's confused frown, he elaborated, "Magda. She overheard me talking about Sam's problem with her gifts."

Antonio cursed, which raised everybody's brows since he wasn't one for swearing. "Once she informs the others, we will have a huge problem on our hands."

"What exactly is it that you think they'll do?" I asked.

"Cause a riot," he replied. "What you have to understand is that this is much like humans having the right to vote for who is president, or prime minister, or whatever they term the ruler of their country. Up to now, no one has objected to you, despite their reservations. Yes, Marcia, Rowan, and Ricardo have issues with you, but they have not publically rejected you. If enough people were to do so, a voting would be held. If the outcome was that most of vampirekind had decided to vote against you, one of two things would have to happen. Jared must choose another life-partner—"

"That will never fucking happen," Jared vehemently stated.

"—or I would have to choose another Heir. It is vampire-law."

"Shite," I uttered. I'd always known that Jared might be under some form of pressure to 'do better' than me, but I hadn't imagined that he might lose his position. *That* wasn't an acceptable path to me.

Wes growled. "Is there no way we could just kill her before she has the chance to talk?"

"I'm pretty sure that ship has sailed," said Jared. "She went over to those three moaners. Now she and Marcia keep looking over, smirking."

Crap, crap, crap. "No prizes for guessing how this is going to play out." And what else could we do but sit there and wait for the shit to start?

So we sat and we waited. And waited. And waited. And waited. Nothing. Not a bloody thing. "Do you think that maybe she hasn't told anyone?"

Jared, who was holding my hand and massaging my pulse-point with his thumb, shrugged. "It could be that she's trying to make us sweat, keep us wondering and worrying."

"She does like mind games," mused Luther.

"Let's find out." Keeping hold of my hand, Jared walked toward her with a determined stride that I saw made Magda hitch in a breath. Whether it was from arousal or anxiety, I wasn't sure. "What the fuck is your game?" he demanded quietly.

The weird witch smiled at him and patted his chest. At his growl and my hiss, she dropped her hand. "There is no need to panic, Jared. I told you, I only wish you happiness. If I can be convinced over the next few evenings that you are happy with Sam, I will not reveal what I know."

"I could just slit your throat now before you do," he gritted out.

"You could…but I'm not the only one with the knowledge, so that will do you no good. Like I said, I simply want to be assured that you are content."

He shook his head, glaring at her through narrowed eyes. "You're playing some sort of game…I'm just not sure what it is yet."

"Always so suspicious and eager to distrust those around you," said Magda, shaking her head sadly before shooting me a smug smirk. Working those hips, she waltzed away. Oh I could kill that bitch happily if I didn't know it would put Jared through absolute agony.

He turned to me. "What do we do now?"

"I agree with you, she's up to something, but I don't know what. So we wait."

"I'm *sick* of waiting."

I knew what he meant but was afraid to say aloud – he was sick of waiting for whatever changes were happening to me to finally take shape. "So am I, but what else can we do?" Nothing, there was nothing.

(Jared)

Sam was draped over me when I woke up after a restless sleep. Unable to resist touching her, I ran my hand along the length of her spine. My hand then crept lower and cupped her ass. I knew that fondling a sleeping person was a little low, but in my defence, it was the most luscious ass. I smiled as I recalled biting it. My smile widened as I remembered promising her I was going to fuck that ass one night, and she'd responded with, 'You'd never catch my arse to fuck it'. She was probably right.

Then it all hit me. Reality hit me. Our problems hit me.

Those precious seconds I had each evening when I first woke up, thinking about nothing but the woman in my arms, were the best. For those few seconds, nothing was on my mind but her. Everything felt as normal as it usually was. For those few seconds, I forgot that we had more issues than we knew what to do with.

Feeling her stir, I tightened my arms around her. "Hey, sleep well?"

"I feel like I only shut my eyes ten minutes ago," she mumbled against my chest.

I sighed. "I know what you mean."

"Do you think we'll hear from Ryder tonight?"

"I'm more worried about if Magda's blabbed yet."

"Maybe she's telling the truth and she won't say anything."

I snorted. "Do you really believe that?"

"No, but a girl can dream."

After we had both drank some NSTs, I followed her into the shower, where I took her hard like the good fiancé that I was. Hey, I'd take her slow if she didn't always bitch at me to go faster.

After a few hours in our office, taking care of a couple of minor issues, we headed for the huge training arena for the evening's entertainment: a gladiator-style dinner show. It was tradition that three of the High Masters would each pit five of their best legion members against the others in a series of events. It was usually pretty entertaining, so I was looking forward to it. I knew Sam was equally eager – anything with a little violence tended to keep her interested.

Inside, most of the guests were already seated, nibbling on the appetisers that had been laid out on the long counter-style tables. For the purpose of the show's theme, the seating had been divided into four sections. One section was for Rowan's bloodline as five members of his legion were partaking in the challenge. The second section was for Ricardo's bloodline since his legion was also involved. The third section was for Bran's bloodline, who usually won. And the fourth section was for all neutral parties.

Our particular seats were on the middle tier of the neutral section, giving us an excellent view. Seated closest to us were Evan, Antonio, Luther, Wes, Lena, Fletcher, and Norm.

Fletcher leaned in. "Widow Twankey's sitting on Rowan's side, next to Marcia. Have you noticed?"

"He's talking about Magda," explained Sam, having sensed my confusion.

"Maybe we've finally succeeded in alienating her." Fletcher looked utterly delighted. "The paint pellets most likely helped with that."

"And the chopstick incident," said Norm, laughing.

Yeah, and that was what worried me. The last thing we needed was that woman to be extremely pissed off. But apparently news of Sam's attempt at taking out Magda's eye had gone around like wildfire…and everyone thought it was hilarious. And that Sam was a lunatic.

Magda wouldn't exactly be happy to be the subject of a joke. Although…she looked quite happy right now. Excited, even.

Not willing to give that woman the satisfaction of ruining the evening for me with her 'let's keep them on eggshells game' – honestly, what other game could it possibly be? – I switched my focus back to Sam. I kept that focus mostly on her as we watched the show. The first event, like the remaining seven, tested the strength and physical endurance of the contenders.

As I'd anticipated, Bran's legion seemed to be the obvious winners right from the beginning, though Ricardo's contenders weren't too far behind in terms of points. Considering Bran was, for all intents and purposes, my uncle, I was obviously supporting him.

Not that I'd give my support to the other two bastards. I had to admit that I was really enjoying watching their faces turn various shades of purple each time their legion members lost at an event. Of course, I cheered along for Bran's vampires with everyone else, gloating a little. I didn't even care if that was petty. These guys had snubbed my fiancée, so fuck 'em.

After the eighth event, Rowan's legion was eliminated from the challenge due to having the lowest amount of points. Out of Bran's five contenders, the one in the fittest shape was selected to go against one of Ricardo's vampires in the final, eliminating, challenge: a duel. Whichever side won the duel would win the overall contest.

Both vampires had impressive gifts, and the duel was filled with explosions, fire, bright lights, smoke, and rain. When Bran's vampire won, cheers from both his section and our section filled the arena.

Only then was dessert finally served – the most amazing chocolate and caramel sundae, which I spoon-fed to a laughing Sam. Maybe that was why I hadn't noticed Magda making her way down to the centre of the arena until she clapped to gain everybody's attention.

Fletcher groaned. "Oh what's that mental heifer doing now?"

"In honour of this tradition, I propose there be a friendly challenge between a guest and someone from the host's side. Yes, ordinarily the hosts are left to be the hosts. But why not have a tiny duel to top the evening off? I would like to challenge…Miss Samantha Parker, the Heir's fiancée."

(Sam)

Oh joy. I heard all the mutterings and gasps around me, but I didn't move my eyes from Magda. "So *this* is why she hasn't told anyone. She planned to challenge me, knowing I couldn't properly defend myself." If she had told people that I was weak, they wouldn't have counted her win as a genuine one. "Bollocks."

Norm guffawed. "What the hell is she thinking? With your gifts, she doesn't have a chance. It's like the wheel's still turning but the hamster died a *long* time ago." Well of course he would think that. He didn't know about my current problem.

But Fletcher did, and he shrunk into his seat. "I don't think I can watch. My heart can't take it."

"There'll be nothing to watch," stated Jared. "This is not going to happen."

I grabbed Jared's arm. "I have to do it. If I don't accept the challenge, I'll look weak."

He cupped my chin. "And if you do accept it, you'll look weak. You can't win this, not without your gifts. You're strong, baby – so damn strong – but she's a Pagori. Biology makes her stronger than you."

"But not more agile. Maybe I can play on that." I had at the try-outs, and it had worked then.

"Actually, I have an idea," said Antonio. To Magda, he called out, "Your proposal to honour the tradition is a good one. But I feel that a challenge with Sam would be unfair to you, for she has very offensive gifts."

"As do I," said Magda, just as her arm melted into a blade.

I winced. "Not. Good."

"My Sire was a Bestower, like yourself, your Grandness," explained Magda. "He once bestowed another gift upon me."

And wasn't that just wonderful. The fact was that she had boxed me into a corner. If I didn't come out clawing, it would be totally against my nature. But I wasn't too keen on having that blade piercing through my body. She wouldn't kill me, couldn't, but she *would* make a spectacle out of me.

Jared was right; she was a lot stronger, and there was every chance that I wouldn't beat her. But there was also a chance that I would, because there was more to duelling than the physical side of things. A good strategy was just as important. And Magda wasn't exactly a full shilling, was she? Strategizing wouldn't be her strong point.

In any case, I didn't have a choice. Sighing, I went to stand but Jared put a restraining hand on my thigh. "Baby, don't."

"She can't kill me," I reminded him.

"But she could hurt you, and I'd rather step down from my position than give her the chance to do that."

"I know you would, and I love you for it, but this is something I have to do. Not everything comes down to my gifts." Before he could teleport me away, I called out, "I accept the challenge." I stood, adding only loud enough for Jared to hear, "And so does Dexter."

He double-blinked, then smiled a little, but worry still filled his eyes. "That snake better live up to its expectations. If you get seriously hurt, he becomes a purse."

I gave him a light tap over the head as I past him.

Wes shot me a concerned look, squeezing my hand supportively. "Let Dexter help you. Wind him around your waist, or put him on the ground. Either way, he will do his best to protect you."

I hoped he was right. Making my way down the stairs, I felt all eyes on me, felt the anticipation of some and the expectations of others. This was so crap. I'd been really enjoying myself up until this point. That fact alone made me want to skin the bitch alive. *And there was every chance that my new emerald-green dress would be ruined. If she had a bunny, I'd boil it.*

When I came to stand opposite her, keeping a standard thirty feet between us, she gave me a wide, smug smile. She was clearly confident she was going to win this. Unfortunately, she had every reason to be. The only plan I could come up with was to repeatedly dodge her, which would serve two purposes; remaining unharmed, and frustrating her so immensely that she made a mistake.

"I'm looking forward to this, Sam."

"I'm not the easy target that you think I am, Magda." Ignoring her snicker, I quietly said, "Novo." Then Dexter was draped over my shoulders – yeah, he'd gone for a wander from my arm to my shoulders in his tattoo form. There were gasps and sounds of appreciation, but I was more interested in the nervous gasp that flew out of Magda. Ha. Carefully, I placed Dexter on the ground. He didn't move away from me, just as I knew he wouldn't.

Most likely in response to my anger and the clear danger of the situation, he turned a dark-red and hissed loudly. His tail was going crazy, too. Much like the black mamba, he was able to raise a third of his body from the floor. Handy.

I returned my attention to Magda then. We stared at each other, feet slightly apart and clenching our fists, much like a pair of cowgirls ready for a shootout. As I always did in a duel, I let everything else around me fade away. I honed every single one of my senses on her, intending to predict her movements as best I could.

"You don't have a hope in hell of winning this," taunted Magda. She almost sang the next words. "I *will* defeat you."

I gave her a pitying smile. "Oh, you and your wishful thinking."

That was all it took to make her move. She hadn't needed to come very close to take a swipe at me with that jagged-blade-for-an-arm. I ducked with vampire speed, making my action blurred, and then stood tall again. Without giving me a reprieve, she attempted to slash at my chest. Bitch.

I dodged the move, smiling in satisfaction as Dexter spat venom at the blade, making it sizzle. Magda cried out in pain and pulled her arm back, quickly changing it back to skin and bone. Oh, so it turned out that even when her arms were steel, she still felt the pain. Interesting. And gratifying.

I watched, morbidly curious, as the blisters slowly healed. Only then did she morph her arm back into a blade and take another swipe at me – this time aiming for my feet. I jumped high, missing the jagged blade by mere inches. Crap, she was a lot faster than me. The reason that I wasn't separated from my feet was that I had my Sventé agility. A lot of people underestimated it, but having the dexterity of a leopard came in handy at times like this.

Another thing in my favour was that you could always count on a Pagori to stupidly rely on their immense strength. It meant their movements were often a little clumsy. And as Magda's movements were fuelled by anger, her forceful swings were very clumsy.

"Give it up, Sam. Save yourself the embarrassment of being beaten to a pulp."

"You're just upset that I have bigger tits than you." Apparently those words hit a little too close to home, because her red irises practically smouldered. "Aw, don't be upset because you like my boobs. Be upset because Jared likes them."

Suddenly, both of her arms were steel; one was a blade, the other was a spike. Wasn't that nice. I repeatedly dodged them: ducking, diving, leaping, and jerking backwards – always remaining out of reach. As I'd hoped, she became more and more frustrated. As such, she became clumsier and clumsier.

I knew that people would be wondering why I wasn't using my gifts, might think I was simply toying with her with the intention of using them later in the duel. If I could just get her close enough for Dexter to take a chunk out of her, I could act as though I was ending the duel early for that reason. She wouldn't be in a fit state to fight me once his venom was in her system.

Magda must have guessed that, because she did her best to stay far away from Dexter and me. None of the venom he spat managed to reach her. I thought about signalling for him to leap at her, but I didn't want to risk that blade slicing him in half. Well then I'd just have to piss her off so that she charged at me. "Shame I didn't bring my chopsticks."

"Bitch."

"Thanks."

"I've just thought of a great idea—"

"Wow, beginner's luck."

"—why don't *you* come at *me* this time? Or do you only know defensive moves?"

Wearing a daring smile, I winked. "Oh I've got plenty of moves. Just ask Jared."

Picking up on the insinuation, she hissed louder than Dexter. Then she was rocketing at me so fast that the effect was more of her disappearing and then materialising right in front of me. Although I'd been expecting it and had flipped backwards out of her reach, she still managed to slice at my chest with the tip of the blade. I cursed with the pain. She might have charged at me again had Dexter not spat venom in her face.

Crying out, she staggered back, scrubbing at her eyes. Not willing to play nice, I chose that moment to lunge forward and deliver a fast, hard uppercut. The force of it sent her somersaulting backwards. Her vampire grace meant that she landed steadily on her feet, but she looked dazed enough to slightly placate me.

In some sort of Matrix style manoeuvre, she abruptly jumped into the air and darted at me with her leg ready to strike. Again, she was fast. But with anger driving her, her movements had been too brisk to be anything but inept. I – though just barely – captured her foot, and spun her entire body clockwise so that she did a lovely spinning flip. Her back met the ground with a loud thud and there was a harsh crack that made me wince.

"He doesn't love you, you know," she said as she sprung upright, snapping her dislocated arm back into place. Ew. "Not really. Jared's too scarred and guarded to let anyone past his walls. You might be snuggled up against those walls, but you haven't got through them."

I knew what she was trying to do: make me lose it so I rushed at her the way she had at me. Poor cow really thought I was daft, didn't she? "Don't take this the wrong way, but you make me think of a pigeon that keeps flying at a glass window. No matter how hard the knocks are, you just keep on hitting it – totally missing reality. The reality in this instance is that you can't mess this up for us. Keep trying, though. It's funny as shit to watch."

Magda laughed. "You're the one who isn't facing reality, sweetie. In a way, I actually feel sorry for you."

"Aw, bless your little black heart."

"Whether you like it or not, that link I have with him makes me closer to him than he is to you. And you hate that, don't you? He still wants me. That's why he's so desperate for me to leave. He doesn't trust himself around me…and neither do you."

"You know, I really wish I'd brought my Gullibility Test Kit with me. I've got a feeling you'd have passed with flying colours."

I could always count on this mental case to react in anger. Growling, she charged at me. I could have ducked and swept her feet from under her with one whip of my leg. That had been the plan, anyway. But what I hadn't known was that at that very second, an all familiar agony would assail my entire body. Helplessly, I fell to my knees, narrowly missing the blade aimed at my chest. But I didn't miss the spike that pierced through my shoulder.

If I hadn't already been in unbearable pain, I might not have screamed, but with so much agony tearing through me, I couldn't hold it in. I knew that no one would know about the other more excruciating pain, I knew that they would all simply think Magda was defeating me. Hell, she *was* defeating me. But there was nothing I could do.

My peripheral vision picked up Dexter lunging at her. More pain – this time, emotional – seared me as I saw her backhand him with the blade, sending him crashing into the wall. Instead of darting at her again, he remained limp. Oh I'd fucking kill her if he was dead – even if it meant somehow coming back from the afterlife, I'd fucking end the bitch.

I screamed again as she repeatedly twisted the spike, tearing into the wound and preventing it from closing. I could feel the blood spilling down my dress, just as I could feel tears filling my eyes. To add to that, I had the sensation of invisible hands clawing their way into my abdomen, ripping me open, snapping my intestines, and trying to pull my stomach out of my body. Only twice before had I felt anything like it; in the bungalow, and that evening when I'd woken, paralysed, by torturous sensations.

Abruptly, Magda yanked the spike out of my shoulder. "Fight me," she hissed.

Even through the pain, I understood why she'd pulled back. The duel would be ended if it looked as though she was attempting to kill me. No one would intervene as long as it looked like nothing more than a battle of strength.

"Get up," she spat.

I told myself the same thing, but my legs couldn't support me just then. Not while those invisible hands were still ravaging my insides and poking around in my head. Unexpectedly, a harsh kick to the face sent me tumbling onto my back. Blood gushed from my now-broken nose. *Twat!* What bothered me more than the blood was the nauseating crunch I'd heard as the cartilage snapped.

Looking up, I saw a spike once again aiming for me. Somehow, I rolled onto my side out of the way, still clutching my abdomen. The spike missed me, making Magda curse with frustration. Apparently, it also inspired her to deliver a hard kick to my back. Oh the witch!

"I told you I'd beat you. Look at the great Sventé Feeder curled up like a foetus on the ground. You're *nothing*. And now they'll all see that. Now Jared will see that. He deserves better than you, and he'll see that too."

Striving to ignore the relentless aching, I struggled to get back onto my knees. But I must have looked feeble, because she merely laughed, sure of her dominance in the duel.

"You tell yourself that you don't believe that he wants me, Sam. But truthfully, it plays on your mind, doesn't it? It plays on your mind that maybe, behind all his anger, there lies some lingering desire for me, even some lingering feelings. Oh you believe he means it when he says that he doesn't want me. But you worry that he's only kidding himself, don't you? You worry that he's trying to convince himself as much as he's trying to convince you."

Each word was like being stabbed at with a hot poker. The cracked cow was right. I hadn't acknowledged any of this until now, but it was true. I'd always worry that I'd lose Jared, because that was what happened when you loved someone, when you knew you'd be a shell without them. It wasn't distrust. It was fear, pure and simple.

Hating her so much in that moment, I used every ounce of energy that I had into making my body move. Trying to set aside the pain somehow, I sprang to my feet. But a shoe slamming into my kneecap had me back on my knees only a second later. Then there was even more pain as the spike drilled into my uninjured shoulder. As she had with the other, she twisted it this way and that way.

"Beg me to stop, Sam. Beg me, admit defeat, and I'll stop."

Not bloody likely. She had to be off her rocker. Pain or no pain, she would never get that from me.

"Do it."

Instead, I peered up and scowled at her. "Fuck you, you demented, unhinged crank."

The spike went deeper into my shoulder, scraping bone and tearing through more muscle. I squeezed my eyes closed against the pain, thinking that I might actually pass out with it. But then something happened. The torturous abdominal agony...it went. The sensation of invisible hands went. The feeling of being torn inside out went.

Where all that had been, there was something else in its place: power.

CHAPTER TWELVE

(Sam)

Strength blasted through my veins like a hot wave, invigorating me, energizing me, galvanising me. My eyes snapped open with the shock of it. Whatever Magda saw on my face made her gasp and back away, taking that sodding spike with her. My nose quickly snapped back into place, and each of my wounds swiftly closed over. It was then my turn to gasp – that kind of instant healing shouldn't have been possible for injuries as severe as those. I'd had giant holes in my bloody shoulders, for God's sake.

I inhaled a long breath, filling my lungs, as I took stock. Physically, I was fine. More than fine. In fact, I felt better than I'd ever felt. But inside…inside I felt…different. *More*.

Effortlessly, I jumped to my feet. Lifting my hands, I saw that they were literally sparkling with energy. That wasn't all. Those same silvery-blue glimmers of energy played around the surface of my entire body. As I wiggled my fingers, tiny sprinkles of it peppered the air. It was like I was dripping silvery-blue fairy dust.

I didn't know what any of this meant, but I knew two things. One, something very fundamental had occurred. Two, I was *so* much stronger than I'd been before. But it wasn't *bad* strong. Not like when I Merged with someone and felt engulfed by the power or threatened by the measure of it. No, I was simply…*more*. That was the only way I could explain it.

Testing myself, I played with the energy that was spilling from me, shaping it into my much beloved whip. It buzzed against my skin, leaving tingles as I threaded it through my fingers – God, I'd missed that. Hence my huge smile.

Two things, however, were quite different about the whip. Not only was it longer, but it had occasional flashes of ultraviolet – whatever the hell that meant. Curious as to just how long the whip was, I spun it around my body again and again, as if preparing to crack it at Magda. It was able to loop around me three times. This was just bloody brilliant.

Still experimenting, I lashed the whip at the ground. Tremors practically rumbled along the earth – nothing that would cause a crack, but enough to unsteady a person. Seeing the utter shock and horror on Magda's face made my smile widen. She knew she was due some payback. "Didn't see this coming, did you?" I cracked the whip at her, leaving a diagonal laceration from her collarbone to her hip.

She jumped and gave a loud cry at the burn of the lash. With stunned eyes, she peered down at the tear in her dress, as if expecting it to be an illusion or something. She cried out again as the whip slashed her thigh.

"Fight me," I insisted, just as she had me.

To her credit, she straightened her shoulders and met my gaze. But that boldness disappeared when the whip caught her cheek. Without giving her a second to recover, I slashed at her mouth, watching in satisfaction as blood dripped down her chin. I noticed then that her wounds weren't healing as quickly as they should – or as quickly as wounds from my whip had in the past anyway.

"Come on, Magda. Where did all that bravado go? Of course, if you've had enough, you can always just admit defeat and beg me to stop. But I won't stop, so it's hardly worth it."

I cracked the whip again. This time, I wrapped it around her waist, using it to slam her against the ground a few times. When I released her, she dragged herself to her feet, coughing and cradling the back of her head. Then the psycho actually launched herself at me, aiming that spike at my stomach. Bad move. In under a millisecond, I allowed my whip to fade away and remoulded the energy into a shield. She ricocheted off it, ending up on her backside.

"Ooh," I said with false sympathy. "That hadn't been wise, had it? But, then, none of this had been wise. You should have known that."

She quickly got to her feet, but before she could make another move, I was directly in front of her and shoving her hard in the chest with the palm of my hand. She zoomed across the arena and crashed into the far wall. I heard stunned gasps all around me. Of course they were surprised. So was I. A Sventé vampire should not have that kind of strength.

Apparently deciding to copy my move, she bounded at me in

vampire speed so that she was up close and personal. Having dodged the fist that was fast heading for me, I spun and kicked her hard in the face. Maybe it was a little cruel to be so satisfied at the sight of her broken nose, but 'tit for tat' and all that.

Movement in my peripheral vision snatched my attention. A fierce looking Dexter had joined my side and had elevated his head and a third of his body from the ground. Focused on Magda, he flattened his neck and opened his mouth – exposing the inky black colouration – before emitting a hollow hiss. Yeah, he was well and truly pissed. I cocked my head at the neurotic woman who appeared to be contemplating lunging at me again. "You know what, I think I'll let Dexter have you."

I took a small step backwards, handing power over to him. Before Magda had a chance to properly process my words, the snake abruptly struck and bit into her chest. Wow, Wes hadn't been kidding when he said that this breed was fast – the movement had been a complete blur.

She cried out in what seemed to be a mixture of shock, anger, and pain. Still, the dumb crank came at me with her blade flying high. Using more of the natural energy that was coating my body, I directed a flame of fire at the blade – a flame that was wilder and hotter than any I had released before. She squealed and quickly cradled her arm against her chest, which was now back to skin and bone…and blistering again.

Noticing how her now bloodshot eyes were going in and out of focus, I gave her a falsely sympathetic smile. "That's stage one coming on: temporary blindness."

Panicked, she stumbled backwards with her arms spread wide. "What's happening?"

"It's Dexter's venom. It can do some extraordinary stuff…as you'll soon find out." I could tell that her eyesight was now totally gone. Dexter, who was weaving in and out of my legs, hissed repeatedly at her while his tail rattled like crazy. "I could be wrong, but I'd say that ticking off a venomous snake was a really bad move."

Suddenly she started to sway and stagger, holding her hands to her head.

"Oh that's just stage two kicking in: temporary mental disorientation."

Making strange keening noises, she continued to stumble around for a minute until eventually she fell flat on her back. "Make it stop."

"I couldn't even if I wanted to. You didn't stop when I was in excruciating pain, did you? Maybe a nice, compassionate girl would, nonetheless, try to help you. But I'm not a nice, compassionate girl – especially when it comes to people like you. And *especially* when you seriously hurt my fiancé. I have a huge fucking issue with that."

It would be true to say that if she hadn't Turned him, he wouldn't be mine now; that if she hadn't betrayed him, he might never have left her. But I was just selfless enough to prefer for him to have never gone through that pain than for him to be here with me.

Seconds later, she wasn't moving at all other than to breathe. The little devil on my shoulder thought that that was a real shame. "It appears that now you've reached the third and final stage: temporary paralysis. Horrible that. I had a taste of it a few evenings ago. At least you're not in severe agony at the same time. It's always best to be grateful for small mercies, I think."

I crouched down beside her. "Do us all a favour; bear something in mind for future reference. Being sly doesn't get anybody anywhere. In my opinion, you should know that by now. It lost you Jared, and it lost you this fight, and it'll also lose you the long-term fight. Maybe you were right in what you said before; maybe he does deserve better than me. But I ain't going anywhere. Get used to it." I stood then, addressing the entire arena. "All of you get used to it. Or piss off home, whichever."

(Jared)

Back at our apartment, all I could do was squat in front of the sofa and stare, open-mouthed, at my beautiful fiancée…and wonder what in God's name was going on.

The crowd had barely begun cheering when I'd teleported to her and then took us both home. Watching her duel with Magda, watching her in agony, had been an agony all on its own for me. It had taken Antonio, Luther, and Wes to keep me from intervening. Of course I'd understood their actions; if I *had* interfered in what Magda had implied was nothing more than a friendly challenge, it would have greatly undermined Sam. That would have seriously brought her suitability as a future ruler into question, making things ten times worse than what they already were.

Still, all I'd wanted was to step in and end the duel. And then I'd no longer had to. Well, it seemed that the intended changes were complete, but I was still none the wiser about just what had happened to her.

"What?" she demanded for, like, the twentieth time. "Why are you staring at me like that?"

Dexter, who was settled on one of the vines, lifted his head at her tone. That snake had definitely earned his stripes as far as I was concerned. He didn't hiss at me for being so close to her, so maybe he was coming to figure out that we had a common interest – keeping Sam safe.

Exhaling a heavy breath, I handed her a small, handheld mirror. Shooting me a put-out look, she snatched it. The feistiness…That was typical of my Sam. Having her irises glint a unique mercury shade…Not so typical of my Sam.

She gaped, looking from me to the mirror. "What's all that about?"

That had been my question since the second she'd looked up at Magda with those irises glowing while energy seemed to coat the surface of her body. Even now, wisps of it clung to her fingers. I cupped her nape. "How do you feel, baby?"

Shaking slightly, she placed the mirror on the coffee table. "I'm okay."

"Any idea why energy seems magnetised to you?"

She glanced down at her hands, swallowing hard. "I think it's just because I'm stronger."

"I think we can safely guess that when you're pissed, it's going to basically envelope every inch of you, just like it did at the arena." I massaged her nape, unable to stop staring at her. She had always been stunning to me, always so very tempting. It wasn't that she was suddenly even more beautiful. Other than the striking mercury ring to her irises, not one physical detail about her was different. Not one. Yet, she now had this entrancing effect.

God, this was all so damn weird.

The knock at the door hadn't come as a surprise. Nor had the entrance of Antonio, Luther, Evan, Wes, and Lena. All five stopped and gazed at Sam, looking a combination of spooked, awed, and anxious.

"What's happened to me, Lena?" Sam's own anxiety hadn't leaked into her voice, but I could feel it.

Just as she had last time, Lena sat beside her and took a minute or so to study her. Just like last time, I held Sam's hand the entire time. When Lena eventually lounged back into the sofa, Evan handed both her and Sam a NST. They drank them gratefully.

"Well?" I prodded, panicky.

Lena put her empty bottle on the table. "The changes to Sam's DNA are, as you have probably guessed, complete. Her body is, once again, now frozen in its development — which means there will be no more alterations. The equations, despite being quite complicated, all add up perfectly."

Then why did she appear so worried? "Lena, what exactly has changed?"

She turned to Sam. "Maybe I should have considered that this was what the brothers were trying to accomplish. Truthfully, I wouldn't have thought such a thing would ever be achievable so, therefore, I hadn't at all considered it."

I had to grit my teeth to prevent a growl from seeping out. "Hadn't thought *what* was possible?"

Lena sighed. "By making his tattoos of snakes come to life, Wes effectively makes a crossbreed. And so have the brothers."

My mouth once again dropped open as the implications settled into my brain. The others wore similar expressions.

Antonio shook his head. "That is not possible."

"I wouldn't have believed so," said Lena, "but the brothers are very powerful. Being as strong as she was before, Sam was the perfect subject for them to use. Her strength and power got her through the changes, and now she has evolved into a blend of all three vampire breeds."

"It explains the physical strength she displayed in the arena," mused Evan before turning to Sam. "When you sent Magda flying through the air to the other side of the arena with just a palm heel strike…Only a Pagori could have done that."

"It also explains the compelling allure she now has," said Antonio, cocking his head as he studied her intently. "It is much like that of a Keja."

I scrubbed my forehead with my hand. "The mercury ring to her irises?"

Lena shrugged. "My guess is that it is much like a marker. A red ring to the irises is the mark of a Pagori vampire, just as an amber ring is the mark of a Keja. Perhaps this would be the mark of a hybrid, if it was a breed in its own right."

"Thirst-wise, how do you feel?" I asked Sam, giving her hand a light squeeze.

She frowned thoughtfully. "A little thirsty, but all right."

"You don't feel a slight discomfort at the back of your throat?" I asked. That was typical for Kejas whenever they were thirsty. Sam shook her head. "You don't feel agitated and restless with the thirst?" That was normal for all Pagori vampires.

"I don't feel any different than I usually do when I'm thirsty. Just…thirsty."

Looking utterly amazed, Antonio shook his head. "Pagori strength, Keja allure, and Sventé manageable bloodlust…A perfect combination."

I slid my gaze to the suspiciously quiet Luther. "You knew this would happen, didn't you? You knew this was how she would change?"

"In all honesty," began Luther. "I wasn't sure of anything. I had no idea if investigating the bungalow would have had any bearing on what happened during my vision."

"So what exactly did you see?"

"In my vision, you and Sam and the squad were all engaged in a battle in an open field — how far ahead in the future this is supposed to occur, I have no idea. The vampires you were all up against were very strong. Sam was significantly stronger and much more powerful. Of course, I knew that this should not be possible, that the mercury glow to her irises were unnatural, but I had to question whether alerting you would be a positive thing or not. Your response would have been to lock her away to keep her safe. I knew, however, that if she was not so strong during the battle in my vision, she might be harmed. Perhaps even killed. I was not prepared to take that risk. I hope you can understand that."

Yeah, I could, which meant I didn't have an excuse to punch him for not giving me any kind of heads-up.

Sam sighed, forcing a smile. "Well, at least all this power helped me kick Magda's arse."

"And as for that bitch," I growled. "She is leaving *now*."

Sam laughed a totally humourless laugh. "No, Jared, she's not."

Literally mystified, I demanded, "Are you fucking kidding me?"

"She stays."

"Sam, she hurt you badly out there!"

"I'm fine."

"That's not the point! She challenged you, knowing you wouldn't be able to defend yourself. She's been messing with your head since she got here. I don't want her hurting you any more than she already has."

"She stays."

I shook my head. "If she doesn't leave, I'll end up killing her anyway."

She appealed to me with a look. "Jared, listen to me. I despise that woman, I despise her more than you can ever imagine. I want to do a lot of things to her, but the best form of revenge I know is to make her watch while we Bind, and make her feel as your connection to her dies and you form one with me. If she's far away, the pain will be massively dulled, but if she's near, it will be excruciating. And I know just how excruciating, because I've been through it myself. I want her to suffer like she's made us suffer, physically and emotionally. Yeah, that makes me a huge fucking bitch, but I never claimed to be anything else."

"Sam," I groaned.

"I *need* to make sure she suffers, Jared. This is the one way guaranteed to do it."

She was right about that. It didn't mean I had to like it. "Everyone out," I gently, but firmly, ordered. "Sam needs some space while she works everything out in her own head."

Nodding, they all gave her smiles, nods, and waves as they left.

She peered up at me, looking more vulnerable than I'd ever seen her. It literally tore at me. "You always know what I need. It freaks me out."

"*That's* what freaks you out? All this stuff has happened, and that's what freaks you out?" I'd never understand this female. Ever. I ran a hand through my hair, blowing out a breath. "I'll leave, too. Give you some time to yourself." The last word hadn't even escaped my mouth before I was dragged onto the sofa and Sam was suddenly straddling me. Not only that, but my shirt was gone. Christ, she was a *lot* stronger and faster now.

"No. I want you to stay." Fitting her body to mine, she lightly nipped the curves of my mouth.

"So you can delay having to process stuff?" Well, in her defence, it was heavy stuff.

"Yes," she admitted, and I felt how hard it was for her to show any weakness. "But also because I want you inside me," she whispered huskily as she rocked her hips. "Make me forget for a while."

Again, she nipped at my mouth, wanting me to open for her. Without hesitation, I did. Then she was thrusting her tongue into my mouth, tangling it with mine. Fire tore through both of us, just like it always did. I angled my head, needing to go deeper, needing more of her even though I knew I'd never get enough.

When she rocked her hips again, I growled into her mouth and scrunched her hair in my hands. Sharply I tugged her head back, wanting access to her neck. I swirled my tongue in the hollow of her throat and found myself groaning. Her skin fizzed slightly, like when I ate honeycomb or sherbet, but ten times better and damn addictive. I distantly wondered if it was something to do with the high concentration of power that now lived within her, but at that moment it wasn't important.

I licked, nipped, and kissed my way around her neck, loving how she melted against me. That was pretty much the only time that Sam was ever pliant – in or out of bed. God bless her sensitive neck.

Needing her skin against mine, I peeled off her dress and unclipped her bra. My mouth literally went dry at the sight of her in just her panties. She really did have the most amazing body – a body I'd craved and ached for since laying eyes on her, a body I'd never tire of touching or looking at. I knew it better than she did; knew every curve, every hollow, and every sensitive zone.

She gave me the most sinful yet somehow still angelic smile. Only Sam could have pulled off something like that. And I knew in that moment that if she *had* fallen ill, if she had died, I would have stayed alive only long enough to kill the bastards that took her from me. After that, I'd have followed right behind her.

Some might call that cowardly. To be honest, I couldn't have given a shit what others thought. If I'd been forced to be without her, I wouldn't have truly been alive anyway. She was too essential to me, too much an integral part of me, for me to ever exist without her.

Grasping her hips, I raised her so that she was balanced on her knees, putting my mouth level with her breasts. As my hands roamed over every inch of her that I could reach, I licked a path from nipple to nipple, pausing to circle the taut buds but resisting the urge to suck on them. Of course I was aware that it would drive her crazy, and that was exactly why I did it.

Ripping her panties off, I drove two fingers inside her, curving them to target her g-spot. At that exact moment, I finally closed my mouth around one of her hard nipples. As I teased her g-spot, those soft moans grew louder and she firmly held my head to her breast. Taking the hint, I suckled harder, occasionally grazing the nipple with my teeth. She repeatedly bucked on my hand, hinting for me to deepen my thrusts. I didn't. I'd learned early that it wasn't a good idea to always give her what she wanted.

"Deeper," she insisted breathily. I shook my head. Narrowing her eyes, the sneaky bitch started riding my hand. Even sneakier, before I could chastise her for it, she mashed her mouth with mine, slipping her tongue inside. See, Sam knew me just as well as I knew her. And she knew that regardless of how much I loved touching her, and regardless of how much I loved licking every inch of her, it was her mouth that I loved the most. Kissing me and letting me possess her lips was always a guaranteed way of distracting me.

When she sucked hard on my tongue, I knotted a hand in her hair, and yanked her head away, growling. "Don't do that again unless you're going to suck me off."

"Next time," she said as she lowered my zipper impatiently. My cock – which had been rock hard since the second she straddled me – sprang out, and slapped her clit. With a firm grip, she worked her hand up and down my entire length over and over, keeping her eyes locked with mine. Again her irises were glowing. Only this time, it was with arousal, not anger.

"Does it freak you out?"

I knew she was talking about her eyes. "Nothing about you could freak me out."

"I mean, does it look bad?"

I shook my head, grunting as her grip tightened. "Totally the opposite, baby, I promise you." I could see that she wasn't convinced, but it was true. I went to position her above my cock, but she grabbed my hands and hung them over the top of the sofa.

She actually tutted. "Oh no, *I'm* in charge this time."

Because she needed some control over something, I realised. I had to wonder if there was also a part of her that wanted to test exactly how much stronger and faster she was now. That was okay. She wouldn't have to know that I'd be topping from the bottom.

"Don't even think about topping from the bottom."

Awkward, mind-reading minx. "As long as you quickly put me inside you, I don't have a problem with that."

She hovered above the head of my cock, but she didn't sink down. Instead, she began tantalisingly rocking back and forth, back and forth. At the same time, she nibbled on my throat, teasing me with the possibility of biting down and drinking from me. Then one of her hands was cupping my balls, squeezing with just the right amount of pressure. I loved all of it, sure, but there was only so much a guy could take. The next time she rocked back, I gripped her hips and surged up inside her. Both of us groaned as her muscles clamped tight around me. Christ.

"I said that I was in charge this time." She again draped my arms over the sofa, which was sheer torture for me since I ached to touch her.

"Then take control. Fuck yourself on me, Sam." The request came out with a ring of authority that turned it into an order. Yeah, well, handing over total control wasn't my thing. "I want to watch you fuck yourself on me."

"Good…because I want you to watch." Slowly, with her eyes locked with mine, she began rocking her hips, moaning softly. She dragged her nails down my chest, taunting me to move and try to touch her. I had to clench my fists against the urge to do it, the urge to cinch her hips and help her to up her pace. But I knew I wouldn't be able to keep my hands off her for long; I could no more ignore the urge to touch her than I could ignore the urge to breathe, or sleep, or drink blood. It was that basic.

She soon fell into a steady rhythm, impaling herself on me over and over. I loved seeing her like this, loved watching her breasts bounce jauntily, loved the husky moans erupting from her throat. I grunted between clenched teeth as she paused to rotate her hips…Fuck. Then she stilled, smirking, confident of her power.

Returning that smirk, I flexed my cock inside her, making her groan; reminding her that I could still tease her, even without touching her. In an agonisingly slow movement, she began to rise on my cock, stopping when just the head was inside her. Then, smiling wickedly, she slammed herself down on me.

"Son of a bitch." No longer able to hold back, I grasped her waist and began lifting my hips to meet her hard, fast, downward thrusts. Her head fell back as she groaned loudly. Over and over I slammed her down, not having to be gentle anymore, not having to worry about hurting her now that her strength matched mine. "Look at me while you ride me, Sam." I had to see those gorgeous eyes; see them glazed over, giving her that sex-crazed look that always made my balls ache. With the mercury glow to her irises, the effect was even more intense.

Both our movements suddenly became more erratic, frantic even. And with me not having to hold back, this particular fuck – love or not, this here and now was a pure, hard fuck – was like none we'd had before.

Dipping her backwards, I bit down on her nipple, drawing blood and drinking it. That was when I discovered something that made me unable to pull back straight away – her blood tasted different, had a delicious syrupy quality to it that hadn't been there before. Still, I didn't take much, because I wanted to lift my head and stare into her eyes again. "Make me come, Sam."

I wouldn't have thought her bouncing could have become any harder or faster, but shit, was I wrong. Then, just as I felt her muscles beginning to flutter around my cock with her approaching orgasm, she bit into the crook of my neck, taking long, greedy swallows. That was it – I was gone. My climax slammed into me so hard, I was surprised it hadn't hurt. Her head fell back and her body arched as she screamed my name, shuddering with the force of her own orgasm. Then she collapsed onto me, still shaking with the aftershocks.

It was a minute or so before my brain switched back on and I could form words. "That was fucking amazing."

"It really was," she practically slurred.

"Your blood tastes different. And your skin." I breezed my hand up and down her smooth, slender back. "In a good way," I added quickly. All I got in response was a lazy, aloof 'hmm' sound. Apparently, she was close to nodding off. I kissed her hair. "Sleep, baby." After the eventful evening she'd had, she definitely needed it.

Me, on the other hand…I doubted I'd get to sleep any time soon. Not with how confused and anxious I still was.

The brothers were right in what they had said; what they had done to Sam had made her stronger. But, was that really a good thing?

Sam was, to my knowledge, the only hybrid in the world. Sure, people might admire and respect her for it, but these people might also want her, want to use her to create more like her. With Sam's saliva, they could Turn humans into vampires who were as powerful as her. Yes, the brothers could do that without Sam, but only providing they could find someone as strong as her to use.

In any case, would it really be wise to create more hybrids? That would be to make them a breed in their own right. And they would become a ruling breed, without a doubt. It went without saying that the other breeds would feel threatened by this new, much more powerful breed. They might all decide that, therefore, the best thing to do would be to unite, and to kill Sam and the brothers before any more like her could be created.

Given that, maybe it would be better not to announce her new condition to others, and to instead allow people to think that her strengthening bond to me was what was making her stronger. Or something to that effect, anyway. It wasn't like they would ever suspect the truth, because it seemed too impossible to even be true. But then, so had a Sventé with a Pagori power.

CHAPTER THIRTEEN

(Sam)

Opening my eyes at dusk, I found Jared's gaze locked on me. I didn't get my usual boyish smile. There was a combination of adoration, mystification, and anxiety in his odd expression, making me frown. His words distracted me from quizzing him about it.

"You kicked me out of the bed in your sleep."

My eyebrows flew up. "Say again?"

"You were mumbling something too. What was your dream about?"

Thinking hard, I quickly remembered. "The brothers. I dreamed that they'd come for me now that the changes are complete. They will, won't they?"

"They're eccentric enough to try. I won't let them take you." He ran the pad of his thumb along my cheekbone, seemingly drinking in every detail of my face like nothing else existed.

"It's the Keja allure," I reminded him, feeling a little sour that the person I loved was only gazing at me like that because of some preternatural enchantment.

Frowning, he shook his head. "It's you. Just you." He nipped my bottom lip. "You've never had to do anything to make me want you. It's…almost visceral." As if to demonstrate that, he then hooked my leg over his hip and surged inside me. Every thrust was smooth, deliberate, and sensual. Not once did he even slightly up his pace. No matter how many tricks I tried, he didn't speed up, didn't move harder, didn't handle me with anything but reverence. I sensed why. He was determined to remain in total control of himself, intent on proving to me that he wasn't swept away by any Keja allure; that he was inside me for no other reason than that he wanted to be there.

When he finally came, it was with his eyes locked tight to mine. "It's just you," he repeated, his voice husky. "Don't ever doubt that."

As if to ensure that I didn't, he did the exact same thing again in the shower. Or maybe that was just because he had an overactive libido.

It was as we sat at the breakfast bar, drinking NSTs and eating cereal, that there was a knock at the apartment door. No sooner had Jared opened it than the entire squad barged inside and piled in the kitchen. They all seemed to sag in relief when they saw I was fine. Then they were all staring, open-mouthed. Not so much in admiration of the new allure, but in surprise – despite the occasional compliment, they really thought of me as one of the boys as opposed to a woman. It had only ever been Max who behaved differently on that score.

Currently, his face was scrunched up in confusion rather than admiration. "Is *this* and your super strength good changes or bad changes? I mean, yeah, power's good but for you to actually *change* in any way, like with the irises…" He let the sentence trail, knowing we'd get his point.

I shrugged. "I don't know." I addressed them all as I said, "I can't say much about it. Not because I don't trust you lot, but because – as Ryder will soon show – there are other ways of getting information from people. All I will say is that these changes will only be temporary."

Harvey frowned. "What's with the mercury rings to your irises anyway? Don't get me wrong, they're nice." He smiled at Jared's growl.

Sighing, I shrugged again. "No idea." I felt bad that I had to be so secretive. This was my squad, and there had to be total trust between us all. I didn't want that to change but if they felt slightly embittered by my failure to be totally open with them, it might just happen.

As if he had guessed my train of thought, Chico patted my back once. "Hey, we get it. You're trying to protect us and protect yourself." The others nodded.

"Yeah, we might not know what's going on," began Damien. "But it's obvious that it's some weird shit. Unless it's something we *need* to know that you're not telling us, then only then is it a problem for me. But I trust that you'd tell us if we did need to know." Again, the others nodded.

I smiled at them. "Thanks for getting it."

"So, I'm guessing Magda's nothing but ashes now. Which one of you killed the bitch?" asked Max. When neither Jared nor I responded, he narrowed his eyes. "She's still alive? Tell me that you guys have at least sent her packing."

When he again received no response, each of the squad either cursed, sighed, or groaned in annoyance. Well of course they did: they all had big hard-ons for Magda — and not good ones.

"In a couple of evenings, she'll be gone," I stated. "I'm pretty sure she won't bother me in the meantime. Not after what happened last night."

Unfortunately, my words didn't seem to have placated them. In fact, Max looked about to have an outburst. The sudden ringing of my mobile phone distracted everyone. Not in the mood to hear any of the squad rant and support Jared's argument that she should leave, I took advantage of the distraction and quickly scarpered to the bedroom to answer my phone.

(Jared)

I sighed at Sam's retreating back. She'd known that we would all gang up on her, attempt to pressure her into changing her mind. Luckily for her, she'd been saved by the bell — or cell, as the situation might be.

"Why are you keeping Magda around?" demanded Max in an abrasive whisper. "Please don't tell me you still have feelings for her or something. Coach doesn't deserve—"

I held up a hand, barely refraining from balling said hand into a fist and smashing it into the guy's jaw. "Whoa there, Slaphead. The only thing I feel for Magda is pure and utter contempt, so get your facts straight before saying shit like that."

"You're saying it's *Coach* who wants her to stay?" asked David. "Why?"

Realisation appeared to dawn on Chico, and he sighed tiredly. "Coach is as ruthless as they come, isn't she?" The others all seemed to understand too…bar one.

"I don't get it," said Harvey. No surprise there. He was great at forming strategies, but common sense seemed to be something he lacked.

"I want her gone," I explained, "but Sam's determined that she stays. She wants Magda to be in close proximity when she feels the blood-link break so that she can't escape the physical pain of it. I've tried talking her out of it, but Sam thinks of this as the worst possible revenge."

"I hate to say it, but she's right," said Salem. I nodded, sighing.

"We'll get going," announced Chico. "See you later." Giving me respectful nods, the squad then left the kitchen, heading for the front door.

Max, however, lingered. "You swear that you don't still have feelings for Magda? That you're not going to betray Coach like that?"

I snorted. "I'm not even going to credit that fucked-up question with an answer. And what does any of this have to do with you anyway? Still have some delusion that you and Sam will get together?" If he did, I'd have to rid him of that very quickly.

"No." The tension left his body, and he exhaled heavily. His tone was no longer confrontational when he spoke. "Look, I cared about her. Still do a little; I admit that. But I don't care about her the way you do. To you, she's all there is. For me, it was never that intense. If you want the truth, when you two got together I was more upset with myself than the situation."

That surprised me. And confused me, actually. "With yourself?"

"Like you, I have a guard up. Don't deny that you have it. I can see it in another person. Coach is a great girl, but I hadn't been able to lower that guard for her. I'd wanted to, but I couldn't. Maybe, in time, that would have happened, but maybe it wouldn't have. And I can't help thinking that if I can't lower my guard for someone as great as her, then I'm never going to lower it for anyone, am I?"

Huh. I sure wouldn't have guessed that *that* had been his issue. Odd how we could be similar in having a guard up like that, and yet we were still so different – unlike him, I didn't resent the protective walls I had. Figuring honesty deserved honesty, I told him, "I'd never wanted to let my guard down, never wanted to let other people in. So maybe if letting someone in could still happen for me, it's even more likely that it can happen for you. I know I'd never have done it for anyone other than Sam, though."

He seemed to consider that for a moment. "So what you're saying is that it's a matter of finding the right person?"

I shrugged, thinking it was kind of strange to be giving advice to a guy that I'd happily strangle. "Maybe."

"Like fate?"

"I'm not sure if I really believe in that, but, yeah, I guess — taking into account the large population — there's a probability that each person's going to have someone who's well suited to them. Just because you're a prick doesn't mean there isn't someone out there who won't find that a problem," I added, smiling.

He laughed. "You're a prick, too, you know."

"I know. But I wouldn't hurt Sam. You don't need to protect her from me, and you should note that it pisses me off when you try."

"I'm not protective of her because I want her. She's someone I look up to, who I admire, who's given me a lot of the strengths that I have. I treated her badly at the beginning, and then again when she got together with you. I feel like I owe her for all of that, for who I am now, but it's hard to give something back to someone who's ten times more powerful than you."

Yeah, I got that. "The thing is…if you tried to repay her for anything, she'd tell you that she doesn't give to receive and then she'd bitch-slap you. Believe me, I know."

He chuckled. "You're probably right." He went to leave but then turned back. "Whether you believe me or not, I am happy for you guys."

"Good. It means I don't have to slit your throat."

Rolling his eyes, he waved and left.

It was a moment later that Sam returned to the kitchen. "That was Antonio," she said, hopping onto the bar stool to finish her cereal. "He was just letting me know what rumours he's let circulate that will explain to everyone why I'm suddenly so strong. They're all now under the impression that a few weeks ago, as a reward for defending The Hollow, he had used his gift of bestowing power on me so that I could develop another gift. The general belief is that this has finally manifested itself by simply making my present gifts and qualities stronger."

I had to give Antonio full points for his creativity and quick thinking. "People are buying it, without question?"

"He said it seems that people don't particularly care why I'm suddenly so strong; they're only interested insofar as it means I'm capable of protecting them. Some had wondered about the mercury ring to my irises, apparently, but Antonio had suggested to them that my having a large amount of power inside me was bound to be visible in some way."

"I suppose they're likely to believe it, since they have no reason to think Antonio would lie to them."

"He said the same thing. I think he feels bad about it and I can understand that, but they can't know the truth."

"They won't. Besides, the brothers will be found soon enough and then they'll return you to the way you were."

"You don't like my new qualities?" she teased.

"I like *all* your qualities, but I don't like anything that puts you in danger."

"Good, because this Keja allure has the potential to severely piss me off."

Same here, since the ogling would now be worse than it already was. Not that Sam realised just how much people drooled over her. But I'd sure as hell noticed, and I'd sure as hell…strongly suggested…that they didn't do it again. "People are going to wonder about the Keja allure, too."

"Antonio's already on top of that. He told everyone that the new mesmerising effect was a Binding gift from one of the many vampires in his bloodline. No one's going to question that either — the ability to impart bewitching glamour isn't an uncommon gift to have."

True enough. One of Magda's vampires had had that very gift and had used it on her, which had been the main reason why she had been able to have me so infatuated with her once-upon-a-time. It was probably why Brook was so infatuated with her, too. On that topic…"You're sure I can't convince you to banish Magda back to the hole she crawled out of?"

Sam shook her head. "Nope. I think I've proven that I don't need protecting from her. So drop it."

I shrugged unrepentantly. "I told you, baby, I'll always try to protect you, even though I know you're perfectly capable of protecting yourself." Watching her lick a stray cornflake from her spoon, I couldn't help feeling a little jealous of that particular piece of cutlery right then. As if she sensed that, an impish grin surfaced on her face. "You're a tease. Do you know that?"

She copied my unrepentant shrug. "It's not my fault you're a randy bastard with a one-track mind."

"Come on, let's get ready for tonight's entertainment. I have a feeling you're going to love it."

THE BITE THAT BINDS

(Sam)

At any other time, I would have been seriously irritated by the way my previous non-supporters were suddenly giving me respectful nods or admiring smiles – of course I was glad to be finally accepted as the last thing I wanted was for Jared to have to step down from his position as Heir, but it was annoying to know that I was around such two-faced, fickle people. One demonstration of power and they all wanted us to be chums. *I don't bloody think so.*

But at this moment, I didn't give a shit. As Jared had predicted, I was loving tonight's entertainment. I'd always wanted to go to a Caribbean street party, so this was an absolute treat for me. Jared also seemed to be truly enjoying himself as the colourful floats and parades wound through the streets of The Hollow, lending an extraordinary level of energy to the evening. It was even affecting Dexter: his tattoo form was slinking around and I could sense how stimulated and animated he was feeling.

Live music, torch lights, and flamboyant, vibrant, feathery costumes all added to the feel of the evening. The atmosphere was light and fun, made all the more better by the smells of various Caribbean delicacies that were being prepared at each of the food booths – all of which were delicious by anyone's standards. There were also craft tents and game stalls, as well as the occasional sideshow.

Every single resident of The Hollow was allowed to be part of the celebrations. And they really *were* celebrating the Binding now that I'd been totally accepted. Just like the masqueraders, they all practically danced their way along the streets, going from stall to stall, and tanking themselves up on food and rum flavoured NSTs.

With our bodies meshed together, swaying sensually to the rhythm of the music currently playing, Jared and I watched the parade in total awe. Taking the hand that I'd had curled around his neck, he held it in front of him, turning it this way and that way, admiring the speckles of energy that dripped from my fingers like fairy dust.

"I think it's because of how hectic the night is," I told him. "So much positive energy around us." I shaped it into a silvery-blue energy ball, surprised by how substantial it looked. Curious, I told Jared, "Hold out your hand."

His brows arched in surprise, but he did as I'd asked. Carefully, I rolled the ball onto the palm of his hand. Rather than immediately disintegrating as it should have done since Jared wasn't a Feeder, it remained in shape.

Jared jerked his head back. "Wow. Does the energy always buzz against your skin like that?"

I smiled. "Yep. Feels odd, but nice, doesn't it?"

He smiled in agreement, watching with me as the ball stayed as it was for a good ten seconds before visibly weakening, until it sort of winked out.

"My whip's stronger as well."

"Which means it will hurt more. That would be a good thing if you didn't use it on me."

"Let me have my way in all things and I'll never have to."

His snort told me that that would never happen. But then, things would be boring if it did.

I smelt the High Master Vampire before he tapped my shoulder. Swerving around, I felt my eyebrows fly up as Ricardo and his consort bowed their heads respectfully. I repeat, *respectfully*. "Are you taking the piss?"

Ignoring my question, Ricardo spoke in a courteous tone. "I thoroughly enjoyed the challenge last night. That was an impressive display of power. I have to say, it was quite ruthless of you to toy with Magda and allow her to believe she was winning the duel for a while. I admire that."

"So you're staying for the ceremony?"

He cocked his head. "In all honesty, I think that I would have stayed regardless. You may be, by far, the least polite person I have ever met, but I strangely find myself liking you."

Oddly enough, I was quite happy about that. Although Ricardo hadn't exactly been friendly at any point, I didn't dislike him. He had been looking out for his bloodline, and that wasn't something I could fault him for. In fact, it was a shame that all vampires weren't like that. I'd certainly have appreciated it if Victor had been like that. "You know something? I like you too, Rick."

His smile shrunk slightly. "It is Ricardo."

"Right, that's what I said."

It was at that moment that Bran, Connelly, Kaiser, Rowan, and Marcia approached. Oh joy.

Connelly smiled affectionately at us. "I do not wish to anger you," he said to Jared, "but it is impossible not to comment on how beautiful the mercury glow is."

Well of course my irises were glowing – Jared had been grinding against me for the past half hour as we swayed, whispering sensual promises into my ear, so it was hardly surprising that I was horny. I wasn't impressed by the fact that my arousal would be so easily evident to others. I could now relate to the plight of blokes and how they were unable to hide their arousal.

Jared laughed at Connelly's comment. "I can't blame you for that."

"Yes, it is very unique," said Bran. "I have to wonder if it was wise of Antonio to bestow power onto someone who was already extremely strong."

Kaiser grunted his agreement. "Does it feel uncomfortable to have such an immense quantity of power inside you? Does it make you feel bloated?"

I shook my head. "It feels kind of…uplifting."

Rowan spoke then. "I admit to feeling placated now that I have seen just what you can do."

I snorted. "Forgive me if I'm not bowled over by the comment, considering you've been a bit of an arse."

His mouth twitched into a smile. Not an ugly smile, but still self-satisfied and slightly mischievous. "But – as it turned out – it wasn't anything you couldn't handle, was it?"

Seeing that Marcia's smile matched his, I realised something. "You two had been baiting me, hadn't you? You'd wanted me to lose control, to show you my gifts?"

Marcia jiggled her head. "That was partly the motive. But it was also important for us to see if you would easily turn on your own kind. In the past, leaders have ruled by instilling fear – punishing anyone who disagreed with their decisions or dared to question them. We want to feel comfortable voicing our thoughts, want that assurance that we will be heard and not punished."

That I could understand. Antonio ruled in such a way, and it had always worked. Everyone respected him for it.

"You gave as good as you got," continued Marcia, "but you did not physically harm any of us. That spoke volumes about what kind of leader you would be."

Huh. "I still think you're a bit of a snob."

Marcia laughed, sounding delighted. "Not something I haven't heard before. Much like you, I do not believe in changing who I am to suit other people."

That was something I could respect. Having exchanged nods with both Jared and me, the five vampires walked away.

"Since I arrived at The Hollow, I've been constantly tested one way or another," I griped to Jared.

He smiled. "You think it was any different for me? Although I'd passed the try-outs and earned a spot in the legion, I hadn't been promoted to commander straight away. That came later, and it hadn't been easy. I wasn't appointed as Heir until after I'd intercepted a direct attack on Antonio – twice. I hadn't expected him to give me that position in a million years. There are lots of vampires in the legion who are older than me and have served him a hell of a lot longer than I have. Everyone was curious as to why he would select me. They knew I was powerful, but that hadn't been enough for them to be comfortable with me."

"So they tested you?"

"Yep, just like they tested you. They were rude, they were patronising, and they repeatedly goaded me. One of them even challenged me. Not like Magda challenged you. No, they challenged me for my *position*. That was something I wasn't prepared to lose."

"Who?" I'd kill the twat.

"You haven't met him, because he's dead."

Oh, good.

"He was a very old, very powerful, very well-known vampire, but I won. And I ensured that I made a spectacle of this bastard who had been a huge problem for Antonio over the years – no swift, clean death. I fought fairly, but I didn't make it quick and painless. And no one forgot that. They didn't want a leader who was dishonourable, but nor did they want one who gave mercy to those who didn't deserve it. You did that very same thing to Magda, and no one will ever forget that either."

Hearing my name being called, I turned my head. My eyes widened when I noticed two very familiar faces dancing on one of the floats passing us, waving like crazy. "Oh dear God."

Jared's gaze followed my line of vision and he laughed. Who wouldn't? The feathery, sequin-covered eye-masks that they had clearly made themselves should have made Fletcher and Norm look completely daft, but they somehow suited them. It was their idea of dancing that was so amusing. It looked more like they were hyperventilating.

Having jumped down from the float that they had clearly hitched a ride on, they both dashed over to us. As usual, Fletcher gave me a tight hug. "Isn't this party bloody brilliant?"

"I know, it's amazing. I love it."

Norm, too, gave me a hug. Pulling back, he studied my eyes and smiled knowingly. "The mercury's glowing."

I tensed. "Tell me the truth. Does it look bad?"

Jared groaned in frustration, tugging me to him and enfolding me in his arms again. "I've told you, it looks anything but bad."

I huffed. "You would say that – you like sex."

Laughing, Fletcher agreed with Jared, "It doesn't look bad at all. It looks quite sexy actually."

"Sexy," repeated Norm, though he was looking directly at an unsuspecting Jared – it wasn't an uncommon thing.

Unlike Jared, Fletcher hadn't missed that and he shot his boyfriend a scowl that swore repercussions.

Norm snickered. "Oh *you* can look, but *I* can't?"

"I'm pleased we've sorted that out," replied Fletcher with a cheeky smile that made Norm gape in outrage. Turning back to me, Fletcher said, "Widow Twankey's nowhere to be seen. Does that mean she's gone?" When I shook my head, he gave me a castigating look. "You must have a screw loose to keep her around. Well, at least she's not here at the party."

Right at that moment, I couldn't have cared less where she was. With Jared wrapped around me and the fabulous atmosphere, the woman didn't seem important. We continued to dance and eat and dance and eat…right up until sunrise when the street party finally ended, culminating in an amazing firework display.

Even if the street party hadn't been so incredible, we would still have enjoyed the night. We had a list of reasons to be happy. I had been totally accepted by all so there was no longer any worry that Jared may have to step down from his position. Magda and Brook were very wisely keeping a low profile. There had been no more bouts of excruciating pain or attacks of bloodlust. And my gifts were now under total control – not to mention stronger.

But our contentedness only lasted until dusk when we received a message from Antonio, summoning us to meet with him. Ryder had got the information we needed.

CHAPTER FOURTEEN

(Sam)

I was glad to be meeting with Antonio in this particular room of his mansion. In the centre of the huge space was a large glass aviary. Inside, with the many trees and plants, there were canaries, rabbits, guinea pigs, and lots of different types of birds. Making it even nicer, a tiny stream bordered the entire aviary.

This room was where Antonio came whenever he felt overwhelmed by things; he'd once said that the peaceful space relaxed him. So, as always, he and Luther were wearing beaming smiles as they watched the animals scurrying around. At my entrance, the dogs immediately came to sniff and nuzzle my hands. Jared received merely a fleeting, dismissive look from them, which made him snort.

"So what did Ryder find out?" Jared gruffly asked Antonio. He never bothered with pleasantries when he was in this kind of mood. And why was he in a bad mood? He'd been hoping that Ryder wouldn't retrieve the relevant information until after our ceremony. Yeah, I could understand that. But I'd rather have the whole thing over with before then, as it would mean I could totally relax and have nothing on my mind other than the ceremony. Hopefully this peaceful place would work its wonders on Jared.

Antonio's mouth twitched in amusement at Jared's abruptness. "I believe there is plenty that you should be able to use to shut down this operation once and for all."

"Good." Somehow, that managed to sound like a growl.

I elbowed Jared hard. "Snap out of it. You said sex would cheer you up. Clearly that was a load of bleeding shite."

He released a long-suffering sigh. "Fine. Tell us what Ryder found out," he said more calmly.

Antonio nodded. "The Deliverer, Wendy, did not know much at all. She was merely given the position by the Medics, and was told not to ask questions. She didn't. The Medics, on the other hand – Sandra and Mitch, I believe their names are – proved very useful."

The powerful Keja settled himself on one of the benches before continuing. "None of them had known each other prior to becoming Medics. Erik had been struck off the medical register for misconduct. Mitch had been in an accident that left him with a tremor in his hand, which meant he could no longer be a surgeon and so he lost his job. Sandra was in medical school but struggling to pay for it herself.

"One thing that applied to all of them was that they were financially struggling. Erik and Mitch had lost big jobs, but still had big mortgages and families to support. Sandra worked part-time as a waitress, but some of her wages were going to her mother, who was an alcoholic and mostly drinking it away."

A part of me could sympathise with that, but I didn't feel that it could possibly excuse anything that they had done.

"Each was recruited separately. They were teased by a stranger with the idea of a job that would be the answer to all of their problems. They were then given a card and asked to call if they wished to talk about it more. Each of them did. Separately, they were collected and taken to a detached house. There, they were informed exactly what they would be required to do and asked if they had problems with this. These people are known as the Handlers."

"I take it the Medics didn't have any issues."

"Sandra had had her doubts, but apparently because of her own childhood, her belief was that children would be better off with financially comfortable families. She was assuming that the babies were going to such people. Mitch had simply needed the money desperately as he was extremely close to losing everything. Erik had been scared and intimidated into saying yes after, without their knowledge, watching one of the vampires feeding on a human."

No wonder he had been so petrified of us.

"After accepting the position, all of them had their memories altered so that they remembered only what they needed to remember. Erik had, at one point, seen fangs after meeting with one of the Handlers, and it had sparked the other memories to resurface. He therefore knew exactly where the babies were going, and exactly who they would be going to."

"Yet he didn't stop?" Jared's expression morphed into one of disgust.

"It wasn't sitting well with him. Many times he had considered going to the police, but he was in too deep and he had a wife and twin daughters. Apparently, though, the vampires had noticed the guilt, so they had frightened him by telling him that if he talked, they would drink his wife dry and sell his children before then killing him."

My eyebrows rose. "I suppose that explains why he was prepared to slit his own throat rather than tell us anything."

"Was Ryder able to get us any names?" Jared asked Antonio.

"Yes. The name of the person who did most of the talking was 'Zeke'. The one with the gift of meddling with memories was 'Blake'." Antonio smiled slightly as he added, "Ryder did sketches of them, but he's no artist, so don't expect too much."

"This house that Erik, Sandra, and Mitch were taken to," I began. "Did Ryder manage to get an address?" I wasn't optimistic about that.

Antonio's smile was smug. "Fortunately, as Sandra was familiar with that particular area, she was able to recognise the avenue." Oh, fab.

Jared nodded approvingly. "Were there any other names? Anything that could be linked to the vampire who's running the operation?"

Sighing disappointedly, Antonio replied, "They merely referred to him as 'the boss'. They talked to each other about 'Lynne' and 'Moira', both of who I suspect take care of the babies."

"Then Lynne and Moira die too," I said simply, to which Jared nodded.

Antonio rose from the bench. "I suggest you leave promptly. Regrettably you'll be missing tonight's entertainment, but I will not have you miss or delay the ceremony – it *will* happen in two evenings' time. Tomorrow evening must be a time that you can relax and prepare for it. As such, if all is not resolved tonight, I will hand over the assignment to another squad." He held up a hand when both Jared and I went to speak. "I appreciate that this is a sore spot for every squad, but I will not let your work interfere with your Binding."

We gave Antonio 'fair enough' nods. He was right; we couldn't place an assignment before our Binding, no matter how delicate this particular assignment was. That simply made me more determined to end it tonight.

Okay, so the plan had been simple enough. Using the same technique we used at the secluded bungalow, we get inside, kill the occupants, and rescue anyone that needed rescuing, if applicable.

Of course, at first we needed to find out just how many people were inside, where exactly they were, and what it was they were doing. That was where Stuart would come in. From the roof of the late night café on the corner of the avenue, we had been able to tell that the gated house had plenty of security cameras. That wouldn't be an issue as nobody monitoring the footage would notice Stuart travelling around as molecules. His role was to get inside, investigate, and report back with whatever information he found.

There turned out to be a huge problem with that.

"What do you mean you can't get near the house?" I asked him. Jared and the squad all huddled closer on the roof.

Stuart looked at me helplessly. "The building's surrounded by some kind of psychic alarm. I might not have noticed it, but a guy in the legion has the same gift and he's placed one around his apartment so that if anyone even gets close to his door, the activity will trigger the alarm. You can't see the alarm, but it makes a really low buzzing sound. I probably would have ignored the noise if it hadn't been so familiar."

Harvey flapped his arms. "So now what?"

"There's something you guys should know," began Stuart. "I heard two voices talking. One of the windows had been slightly open. Anyone passing wouldn't have heard it...if they hadn't been a vampire. They were talking about picking up a 'package' shortly to take to 'Moira', and that 'the boss' was impatient. They were also frustrated that some of the other 'Docs' hadn't contacted them with a 'package' yet."

"He obviously means Erik, Sandra, and Mitch, then," said Jude, her eyes gleaming. The woman knew justice was close, and it was making her both anxious and restless.

"By package, they clearly mean they're going to pick up another baby soon." Jared sighed. "Well, if we can't get in there, maybe the best thing would be to wait for them to come out. Then we follow them. We let them lead us to Moira and Lynne."

"*And* we stop that baby from being sold," stated Jude.

Jared nodded. "This ends tonight."

Enter the new plan…

That plan entailed me sitting in the passenger seat of a car that Jared had parked outside the café. Courtesy of the vampires that Antonio sent, we were in possession of four cars that had been 'borrowed' for the night. It was a given that if we screwed this up and the vampires realised that someone was onto them, they would disappear and we might possibly lose any chance of getting to them or the person behind the op. Worse still, that would mean not only would babies continue to go missing and their mothers be killed, but we would be unable to track the children that had already been sold. None of that was acceptable to any of us.

With all that in mind, it was agreed that in order to follow the Handlers without attracting their attention, we would need to be extremely careful. While watching from a car seemed beyond cliché and could often attract suspicion, Chico had been right when he said that a car parked outside a café wasn't going to look suspicious. As an added precaution, he had instructed me to go shotgun, reading a newspaper; that way, it would simply look as though I was waiting for someone.

Inside the café, Jared was having a coffee at one of the tables near the window with David and Butch, who would soon be using the car that was parked beside mine. All three of them were very subtly monitoring the target. Of course, a human would have extreme difficulties with monitoring from such a long distance, but our enhanced vision gave us that advantage. What we had to bear in mind was that Zeke and Blake also had that advantage and would be able to see us as clearly as we could see them – hence all the cautiousness.

Helping the situation, Stuart and Denny were hovering near the house in their alternate forms, ready to report back with any movement from inside the building. As the house was on a one-way street, it had made it possible for Chico and Jude to wait in another vehicle around the corner – the Handlers' car would have to drive in their direction, and so Chico could pick up the tailing from there.

Salem and Reuben were waiting at the bus stop that was one hundred yards in front of Chico's car, who would pick them up as he passed by. Chico felt that for all four of them to be sitting in the car on watch would attract the attention of passers-by or neighbours, and attention wasn't what we needed. I wasn't all that convinced that so much cautiousness was necessary, but as he had been on stakeouts before, I trusted his intuition. Apparently, he had been on a couple of stake-outs that had been ruined by simply a nosy old woman seeing a strange car parked near her home. These days, people were wary of strangers hanging around. They had every reason to be.

Max, Harvey, and Damien were sitting in another car in the parking lot of a store located not far away, awaiting telepathic contact from Jared. Basically, everyone was in position, and all we needed now was for the Handlers to get moving.

Soon enough, a trail of molecules entered through the open window of the car. Taking a sneak peek around me and satisfied that no one would see anything, I quietly said, "You can change back."

A second later, Stuart was lounging on the backseat with his head rested on his hand. "We have movement. The two guys from Ryder's sketches were putting jackets on and switching off the T.V. I reckon they'll leave any minute now. From what I could gather, they're the only people in the house."

Time to move, I told Jared.

Quickly yet still managing to appear casual, he, Butch, and David abandoned their coffees and headed for the door. They would have managed not to attract any attention if they all weren't so bloody gorgeous. One of the women in the café actually said something to Jared as he passed, which I imagined was a line of some kind.

"Slut." I hadn't realised I'd spoken aloud until Stuart started laughing. I shot him a scowl, but he just laughed harder. "Your time will come, Stuart. Then I'll be the one laughing." He just gave me a dismissive, 'sure, sure' look.

A little of my irritation must have been showing on my face, because the first thing Jared did when he hopped inside the car was give me one of his 'whatever it is, I didn't do it' looks. I merely snorted.

"They're leaving," announced Stuart. We all looked in time to see two male vampires exit the house.

"Those are definitely the guys from the sketches," stated Jared. "I'll warn Chico and all the others to get ready to move."

THE BITE THAT BINDS

Obviously having heard Jared's telepathic announcement, Denny travelled in his alternate form to the car beside ours, wherein Butch and David were already waiting. Once inside it, he returned to his human shape on the backseat.

We all remained very still as the Handlers' black SUV drove by. I had no idea whether or not they took a look at us, because I focused on my newspaper to avoid any chance of eye contact. When I saw in my peripheral vision that they had turned the corner, I looked up again. It was only then that Jared – having known better than to immediately slip behind the SUV – started the car. At a steady pace, he exited the car parking lot and followed after the SUV. Butch kept close behind us.

As Jared drove along another street, keeping a fair distance between us and the Handlers, my enhanced vision was able to spot Chico's car up ahead, tailing the SUV from the front. I guessed that was one way to avoid suspicion, though following from the front seemed a little complicated to me.

A left turn took us all onto a very busy road.

Jared exhaled a loud sound of annoyance. "We could have done without the heavy traffic."

He was right. Keeping the vehicle in sight would be much easier for us, but that didn't mean we could afford to leave a lengthy distance between us and them. Doing that would be to risk losing them in the traffic. So, as advised by Chico, Jared kept two car spaces between us and the Handlers as he drove. He was careful not to remain directly behind them by changing lanes every now and then. At one point, Max and Butch positioned the cars either side of the Handlers, so that we had all effectively boxed the SUV in.

About ten minutes into the pursuit, we came to a roundabout. Startling the hell out of me – and I'm pretty sure it equally startled the others – the Handlers didn't take the first, second, third, or final turn; they instead continued to circle the roundabout…leaving us no choice but to drive on ahead of them, or expose that we were following them. Bollocks.

Chico, too, had been forced to take the final turn or expose himself. In the visor, I was able to see that the SUV actually circled the roundabout three times. At that point, they then took the same turn that we had taken, placing them six car spaces behind us.

Stuart took the words out of my mouth. "What the hell was all that about?"

"Chico thinks they're testing to see if anybody's following them," said Jared.

"They've sensed that they have a tail?"

"It's more likely that they're doing a standard test. Chico said a lot of guys do things like quickly change their course, or enter a public building."

I thought it wasn't a bad idea, actually. "Circling a roundabout…I wouldn't have thought of that."

"Chico's pulled over up ahead," Jared told us. "He's going to fall in from behind and take our place at the rear of the Handlers. We're going to now take his place at the front."

"Oh, right," I said. "I suppose the question is, though…how do you follow someone from the front?"

"Well, according to Chico, I shouldn't watch for signals. He says that most drivers take a couple of seconds before flashing the light to signal that they're turning. I should watch the driver and the tyres." So that was exactly what Jared did. And he did pretty well at it. That was most likely a lot to do with the fact that Jared's vision enabled him to observe very well.

But then the Handlers turned down a side-street.

"Shit," Jared uttered.

"It's okay. Chico or one of the others can stick with them." But Stuart was wrong. Chico didn't stick with the Handlers. He instead stopped just before reaching the corner, where Salem hopped out and proceeded to follow the Handlers on foot.

Having crossed the intersecting street, Jared made a somewhat illegal U-turn and drove down the opposite side. He parked outside a Chinese takeaway, placing him parallel with Chico. It was at that moment that Salem had returned to Chico's car.

"They've parked at the end of the one-way street," revealed Jared, obviously having telepathically heard the info from Salem. "Apparently there's a white van waiting there. A van that looks a lot like the mobile hospital that Erik had."

"Stuart, time to go spying." My announcement was met with an excited smile. Then Stuart reduced himself to molecules that went zooming out of the slightly open window and across the road. "Where are Max and Butch?" I asked Jared.

"One of them is parked at the end of this road, and the other is waiting at the end of the other side."

I understood why; this way, both possible routes that the Handlers could take were covered.

"Nervous?" Jared suddenly asked me, and I understood that he wasn't talking about the assignment.

I smiled. "Not in a way that means I'm unsure. But I'm nervous of being the centre of attention. And of seeing the dress that Fletcher played a part in designing."

Jared's brows arched. "He did? Good. I always like the stuff that Fletcher picks out for you."

"That's because you're a pervert."

He gave me an unapologetic, devilish grin. "So you're not going to try to run on me?"

I shook my head, still smiling. "You're stuck with me."

"I like being stuck to you."

Just then, the molecules returned to the backseat. "They've just collected their 'package'," revealed Stuart, angrily, once he shifted back. "How can people sell *babies*? How can they kill their mothers and sell their babies? It's fucking sick."

"You'd be surprised what people would do for money," said Jared, "especially those who want it there and now – which seems to be the case with the vampire running this op. He wants a lot of cash, and he wants it fast. I'm guessing he has to be young in vampire years. The longer a vampire has lived, the more time he's had to accumulate money. An older vampire wouldn't need to do this, or to take these kinds of risks."

Stuart leaned forward. "Do you think he wants it fast because he *needs* it fast?"

"No. Maybe he was used to a certain lifestyle as a human and he wants it back. I'm willing to bet that he was involved in criminal activity as a human and this is the only way of life he knows."

"Good theory. Hey, maybe when he was a human he was involved in an operation where he had a role similar to Wendy's, and maybe he saw too much and they Turned him rather than kill him."

"Maybe," allowed Jared. He stiffened as he added, "We have movement."

The Handlers turned out of the side street and crossed the intersection, placing them on our side of the road.

I took a long breath. "Right, let's go slaughter the fuckers."

Jared slipped behind the SUV. "Sounds like fun."

As before, he kept two car spaces between us and them as we followed the SUV down more roads. It wasn't long before Chico was once again in front of them, and Max and Butch had taken a place on either side of them. Jared did all the usual things; he sped up when he needed to, he slowed down when necessary, and he switched lanes often. Always he managed to keep the Handlers in sight, and all without drawing attention to himself.

Things got a little worrying, though, when we started to enter a rural area. Although, on the upside, it meant that the traffic wasn't hectic, it also meant that we would stand out more. Obviously sensing my concern, Jared spoke reassuringly.

"It's okay. Chico's giving me some advice." Listening to that advice, Jared kept a reasonable distance between us and the SUV as he drove; only closing some of that distance when turning corners so that he didn't lose sight of the SUV. Once back on a straight section, he pulled back, giving them a wide berth again.

Butch and Max followed that same example, keeping far behind us, as parallel surveillance would arouse suspicion at this point. The thing with rural areas was that everybody tended to know everybody, and strange vehicles would attract attention. Four strange vehicles…Not great.

"We need to all split up," I said. "The next time we come across somewhere that would be a good idea to park and conceal the cars, tell them to pull in. We'll catch up with them after we've seen where the Handlers stop."

Jared nodded. "Good idea." He was quiet for a short moment, and I knew he was communicating with the others. "I've also told them that if we see another good hiding area on our way, we'll tell them to head to there."

About fifteen minutes later, the SUV took a right turning. Jared sped up until he reached the corner.

"It's some sort of converted farmhouse," said Stuart.

Rather than stopping, Jared kept going straight.

"Want me to go take a closer look?" At Jared's nod, Stuart switched to his other form and flew out of the window.

Jared puffed out a long breath, clearly agitated. "There's nowhere to park around here. Not unless we want to stick out like a sore thumb, anyway."

"Maybe we should head back to the others. The campground they stopped at isn't that far away. It's not like we can't get back here quickly if we need to."

Nodding, Jared did a U-turn and passed the farmhouse. "Stuart said there's no psychic alarm around the house."

Good. "I suppose that means that it wasn't a precaution for all those involved in the op, it was simply added to the Handlers' home."

"It's most likely Zeke's gift as we know Blake's gift is to mess with memories."

I was about to say something else, but Jared held up his index finger, gesturing for me to wait. I guessed he was talking to someone telepathically so I remained quiet, waiting for him to finally pass on the info.

"Stuart said there are two female vampires in there, who I'm guessing are Lynne and Moira. He said there are also five male vampires – he's not sure whether they're serving as guards, but if they are, they're not acting very vigilant. That means that, with Zeke and Blake, we're facing nine vampires in total. I'd say we have a very good chance of ending this now."

"The rest of the squad will be happy to hear that." It turned out that I was right. They were extremely happy to hear that, as was Jude.

She made a good point, though, when we were discussing strategies. "I'm not comfortable with having a big battle around a baby."

I sighed as I leaned back against one of the cars. "Neither am I."

"Then our priority has to be to get the baby out of there, and to do it fast," said Jared.

Harvey, who was standing beside him, nodded. "Like in paintballing."

My brows flew up. "Say again?"

"During our first round of paintballing, our objective was to get inside a building, obtain something, and quickly get it out again, right? This is pretty much the same." That was my Harvey – full of ideas.

"Very true," said Jared, looking impressed. "So, we cover the fastest here – which is, hands down, Butch – while he slips in and out with the baby."

"The vampires in there will surround the house as best they can," Chico pointed out, "which means they might not be so preoccupied with the baby."

Another good point. "I say we split into teams of two like we did at paintballing, but this time we work together. We come at the rear of the house from either side. The attack will not only mean the death of those vampires, but it will provide the perfect distraction for Butch."

Jared nodded. "Most importantly, we move *now* in case the Handlers decide to leave soon."

After Jared had relayed the plan to Stuart via telepathy, we all abandoned the four cars at the campground – planning to return to them after the attack. Quickly and stealthily, we made our way to the trees that surrounded the farmhouse.

Time to split up, Jared told me. *Stay safe, baby.*

You, too. Oh, and keep an eye on Jude. We don't want her doing anything stupid.

Don't hesitate to call on Dexter if you need to. It was an order. It was an order because he knew me well enough to guess that I was too protective of Dexter to want to expose him to this kind of danger. Yeah, I know that might sound kind of backwards since Dexter was supposed to be there to protect me. But every time I recalled him limp on the floor after a harsh blow from Magda, I felt ill.

Fine, I lied, knowing Jared would push if I didn't give him an answer.

I know that you're lying. Christ, you're so damn stubborn.

Then why bother me? Ignoring his flow of curses, I led my team – Chico, Butch, Salem, David, and Harvey – to the trees that were on the left of the large stretch of land at the rear of the house. That placed us directly opposite the rest of the team, who were hiding in the trees parallel to ours. Despite my enhanced vision, I wasn't able to spot any of them – not even the glow that would undoubtedly be coming from their irises.

It was as I sat there studying my surroundings that I realised something; due to the many acres of land around us, this place looked a lot like an open field. The same open field that Luther had seen in his vision? I'd like to think not, but it wouldn't surprise me. In fact, I'd suspected that the attack in his vision would be something to do with the op. I'd just kind of hoped I was wrong. Great.

Although I heard two vehicles approaching in the distance, it didn't occur to me that the cars might be intending to stop at the farmhouse. Why would it? None of the others that had approached had stopped here. But not only did one of these particular cars do so, they both did.

I cursed silently. Nobody liked a spanner in the works, especially when the plan was ready to be put into action. Indicating for the team to remain in position, I silently hurried toward the trees that were closer to the front of the house. My new Pagori speed got me there in an instant. It still felt strange to be so much stronger, but at this particular moment, I wasn't going to gripe about it.

From my hiding spot, I could see that two cars had parked beside the Handlers' SUV. Four male Pagoris exited one vehicle, but didn't pass by the other; instead they waited just behind it. It seemed to be a gesture of respect, an acceptance of their position in the hierarchy of vampires there.

Two vampires exited the other car, and one of them then went to the rear door and opened it courteously. It was reasonable to assume, then, that this just might be 'the boss'. Well that would make sense. The only thing left to happen at this stage of the operation would be for the baby to be handed over to the Buyer, and it was probable that he would wish to be present at each transaction. This worked out quite nicely, as it meant we could kill him.

I cursed again when who was potentially 'the boss' exited the car.

Obviously sensing the cocktail of surprise, agitation, and anger circulating through me, Jared asked, *What's the matter?*

Their boss has arrived, and he's brought seven vampires with him. But that wasn't what had me feeling enraged. The rage was owed to the fact that we knew this person, we'd been in their presence, and had we known that they were behind the op, we could have ended this some time ago. At the idea of that, nausea swirled around my stomach.

What is it?

CHAPTER FIFTEEN

(Sam)

It's fucking Orrin. The vampire's walk was nothing like it had been at his home. Back there, he had seemed somewhat bashful and introverted – 'seemed' being the key word. The bloody bastard had played us, and he'd played us well. Now his walk was confident, purposeful, and imposing. In the place of the timid smile that he had worn for us was a harsh scowl.

Oh he was sooooooo going to die tonight. And very, very painfully.

The bastard, I'll kill him, growled Jared. I sensed that he was as frustrated with himself as I was with myself for not looking closer at this particular vampire, at not even considering him. All right, maybe it was fair to say that there hadn't been anything to make us link Orrin with this op, but had we paid more attention, we might have sensed his little act. Might have questioned just *why* he was putting on a little act.

Returning to my team, I took a calming breath. "The boss...it's Orrin."

Salem, who had gone inside Orrin's home with us a few evenings ago, blew out a breath. "I never would have guessed."

That made me feel slightly better. "He's brought seven vampires with him."

"That takes the people count up to thirteen versus sixteen," said Chico. "Still good odds, though."

Too pissed off to stall any longer, I contacted Jared again, staring at the spot that he and his team were waiting. *I'm ready to move.*

Good, let's do this.

Whereas usually I would have had to absorb the energy around me, things were very different after the brothers' meddling. Now the energy – both kinetic and solar – was already clinging to me, filling me. I let it buzz through me, invigorating me. *On three. One, two, three.* And then I manipulated some of the energy into a fireball and threw it. As I'd planned, it caught the clothesline that was hanging at the rear of the house, setting alight some of the garments pegged on it.

As we'd hoped, several of the vampires came dashing outside to investigate. Before they could even think to act, a bolt of lightning struck the small shack behind the clothesline. Suddenly all of them, other than one female, were there, ready to fight...and away from the baby. This not only gave Butch a chance to get inside, but it meant that the battle was happening away from the baby.

"Go," I told Butch, watching with satisfaction as he slinked through the trees, heading toward the front of the house. There wasn't room for optimism yet, however.

Jared was the first to attack. Remaining under the cover of the trees, he projected a massive lightning bolt at the vampires. The bolt hit one of them, reducing him to ashes. The hope was that the action would lure them away from the house and toward the trees. It sort of worked. Everybody other than Orrin and Blake began to move.

My mouth almost dropped open when Rudy – who I recognised from Orrin's home – swiftly changed into a white tiger. Well that could be a problem. One of the others – a muscular Keja – wiggled his fingers, and they suddenly turned into black, oily tentacles. Ew. Startling me more than any of that, however, was when another Keja faded, becoming invisible. No, not invisible, I realised as he turned toward where Jared and his team were hidden. When he moved, it was possible to see him ever so slightly. But when he literally dashed away, I couldn't see him at all. Apparently then, he was only slightly visible when he moved reasonably slowly – which wasn't something he was liable to do in an attack. Oh joy.

It was fair to say that this wasn't going to be at all easy. These vampires were clearly powerful...but so were we.

Not wanting all of the vampires to head for Jared and outnumber the rest of the team, I launched a powerful energy ball at one of them, hitting him in the back and making him burst into ashes. Simultaneously, Chico exhaled dozens of thorns in their direction; some connected with a dark-skinned Pagori. Instead of falling to the floor in agonising pain that would quickly lead to his death, however, he swerved...and exhaled thorns at us that were identical to Chico's. We barely managed to dodge them.

"Oh shit. He's a Syphon." That was definitely not good. Whatever gift we used against him, he would be able to absorb and use for himself. *Tell the others not to use their gifts on the dark-skinned Pagori, he's a Syphon*, I warned Jared. *The only way we can deal with him is with up close and personal combat, but you'll have to wait until his ability to exhale thorns has worn off.* The average time was somewhere between three and five minutes.

Great, he snapped. *I'll get Stuart to duel him.* That was clever, since Stuart had sparred with Chico often in order to improve the speed at which he could explode into molecules – when poisonous thorns were coming at you and you needed to dodge fast, your speed could improve very quickly. But I didn't have time to praise Jared for his decision as suddenly six vampires were charging at me and my team. Oh bugger.

The one that had decided to focus on me jumped in the air and hissed a large spray of water at me. Or, what *looked* like water. It was only when it hit the trees in front of me and the bark sizzled away that I realised what it was: acid. I slammed up my shield just in time, smiling at him. Again he hissed acid, seeming to think that it would dissolve the shield, but again it didn't work. Behind my shield, I tauntingly wagged a finger at him, just to piss him off.

I was about to reshape my shield into an energy beam and bury it in his chest when, distracting the hell out of me, Salem was suddenly flat on his back in front of me and clutching his abdomen. The vampire chose that moment to hiss acid at his face. Salem cried out as patches of his skin began to sizzle, smoke, and peel. Shit.

As a feral-looking Pagori leaped at Salem – I guessed it was the same vampire that had put Salem on his back in the first place – I pushed my shield outward, encompassing Salem. The Pagori rebounded off my shield and went zooming backwards.

Relentless – or stupid, whichever – the hisser once again tried to penetrate my shield with his acid. Before he could try it again, that very same vampire exploded into ashes, courtesy of a psionic boom from David. I gave him a brief nod of thanks then allowed my shield to fade away, and offered Salem my hand. "Can you get up?"

In answer, Salem ignored my hand and bounced to his feet. He didn't look good at all. Although his wounds were healing, they were healing extremely slowly and were obviously painful. But they didn't distract him from sending a vengeful, psychic punch hurling at the feral-looking Pagori. The force rippled in the air as it headed for the vampire, taking him out instantly. Salem's grunt of satisfaction would have made me smile if I hadn't, at that moment, sensed two vampires coming at me from behind.

I turned sharply, ready to fight them, when they were each abruptly lifted off their feet by an unseen force and sent colliding into a tree. Turning back again, I gave Harvey a nod of thanks. He barely had time to nod back before his attention was snatched by a vampire that was heading for him. I might have moved to help him, returning the favour, if green ooze wasn't suddenly being aimed at me.

It was very familiar green ooze, actually…as was the vampire spraying it out of his hands. "Denny, what the fuck?" I demanded, shocked. Everything in me rebelled against the idea of hurting a member of my own squad, but he had obviously been brainwashed into turning on us or something, because he was about to attack me!

Unsure of what else to do, I was ready to blow a gust of wind at him. But then the ooze stopped just short of reaching me and wrapped around an invisible, struggling captive. *That* was when it all made sense. The struggling stopped as a psionic boom sprayed out of David's fingertips and hit the invisible vampire hard. Like that, he was ashes inside the oozy web.

David's triumphant smile disappeared from his face, however, as a white tiger crashed into him, sending him sprawling onto the ground. It went to bite down on David's throat, but as David threw his arm up defensively, the powerful jaw instead locked onto his arm. He cried out through his teeth, shoving at the animal. I shot an energy ball at him, but the tiger flattened himself on top of David, effectively ducking from the impact. He couldn't escape David's other hand though as it pressed against his head. Blue sparks danced around the animal's large skull just a second before its entire body burst into ashes.

I ran to David, checking his arm. It was practically savaged; I could even see bone. "It'll heal, but with that kind of damage, it's going to be at least half an hour before it's properly healed."

"I'm not leaving the fight." His face was a mask of frustration and pain, but there was utter determination there.

I turned to Chico, who stood over us. "I need you to stay with him."

Ignoring David's petulant 'I don't need babysitting' comment,

Chico nodded.

"No, you don't need babysitting," I agreed. David's pride was a big thing. "But you're always an immediate target because of how powerful you are. This is no different than when Butch sticks with you. It's just having someone to watch your back, that's all."

Pure instinct made me look in a particular spot. There was Jared with black, oily tentacles trapping his wrists and ankles, pinning him to the ground. A large Keja stood, sneering down at him. *Fucking bastard.* In the space of a millisecond, I was on my feet and an energy ball was in my hand. I only barely managed to hold it back when the Syphon threw himself in my path, wanting to absorb the energy ball and have my power for a while. Sneaky little sod.

I had to assume two things from that. One, the ability to exhale thorns had worn off. Two, Stuart was hurt somewhere, or the Syphon wouldn't be running around freely.

Cursing, I sucked the energy back into my hand, disintegrating the ball. Eager to get to Jared, my instinct was to whip the shit out of the Syphon and get him out of my way. But I couldn't touch him with my whip, because then he'd have one of his own. And I couldn't attack him with my gifts in any way, because I couldn't afford for him to have them. But I needed him gone!

As an idea came to mind, I smiled. "Novo." The tattoo that had been twined around my waist was now a live, very ticked off snake. Like that time when I'd been up against Magda, Dexter's scales were dark-red and he was hissing angrily.

Unsurprisingly, the Syphon's cocky smirk faltered. Ha. He would know that though the snake was clearly preternatural, Dexter didn't have a gift that he could absorb. As such, if Dexter hurt him, he was fucked.

I had no idea what his plan had been when he took an angry step toward me, and I didn't get the chance to find out because that one step forward had been enough to set Dexter off. Abruptly, he struck at the Syphon, biting into his cheek.

The Syphon cried out in both surprise and pain, bringing his hand up to his cheek. "Bitch. You fucking bitch."

"Why thank you."

As he began double-blinking and shaking his head, I knew that stage one was starting to take effect. Any other time, I might have sat back and watched the show, but not now while Jared was in danger.

Instead, I cracked my whip at the vampire that was attacking Chico, winding it round his ankle. I then used the vampire as a bat, whacking the Syphon hard enough to send him hurtling in the air and crashing into the broken shack. He landed hard on one of the jagged pieces of wood and it pierced right through his chest. A loud groan escaped him just before he turned into ashes.

That groan had barely ended when my attention was back on Jared – he was still struggling against the tentacles that were pinning him to the ground. Worse, a scowling Pagori was bent over him with his arm pulled back, ready to punch. Not just punch Jared, but punch his fist into Jared's chest.

I lashed my whip at the Pagori, curling it tight around his throat. Then, practically feral in my anger, I dragged him to me with the whip. He clawed at it wildly, trying to free himself, but he froze when Dexter's head was suddenly only inches from his face. He actually whimpered, and who could blame him?

Dexter spat venom into his eyes, making him groan through gritted teeth and scrub his eyes madly. When he finally opened them and saw me standing with my elbow reared back, he knew what I was going to do but I was too fast for him to stop me, too strong for him to do anything about it. In under a second, his heart was in my hand, and then both he and his heart were ashes – something I wouldn't have been able to do if it hadn't been for the extra strength.

Snarling, I turned to Tentacle Boy, who had the sense to look worried.

There was no trace of that nervousness in his gruff voice, though. "You hurt me with that whip or you sic that snake on me, and I'll pull his limbs from his body."

"That would be a shame. He's good with those hands." Plan in mind, I went to absorb the energy of the Earth beneath my feet, but it had already come to me, waiting for direction.

Seeming to notice the mercury glow to my irises, Tentacle Boy stared at me studiously. "What are you?"

"Empress of the fucking universe." And then I caused a spike of earth to sprout from the ground between his legs and smack him hard in the balls. Blokes always did the same thing when that happened; they momentarily tensed and then all energy seemed to leave them as they dropped whatever they were holding and fell to their knees, cupping their balls, and that was exactly what he did.

Before Dexter or I could have any fun with the sod, a pissed-fricking-off Jared jumped to his feet, grabbed the vampire's head, and snapped it from his body. Swiftly, the Keja was ashes.

"Feel better?" I asked Jared, slightly amused by a move that was more about anger management than vengeance.

He frowned thoughtfully. "Yeah."

Looking around, I noticed that there appeared to only be a few of Orrin's vampires still fighting. The man himself was still standing at the rear entrance with Blake, watching the whole thing. The memory meddler was looking pretty nervous but Orrin looked cool as a cucumber, which made me wonder what his gift was.

The weird bugger clapped. "Impressive. Very impressive. Oh, and I do like that pet of yours, Samantha."

Do you think the squad will be okay taking out the ones who are left? I asked Jared. *Because I really want to hurt this silly little twat.*

Max is in a coma, Stuart's in a trance, and Damien – though fully conscious and still fighting – has a hole in his chest that's so huge, you could put your hand through it. How about the others?

I hadn't been expecting to hear any of that. *Salem's face has been burned with acid but he's otherwise okay. David's arm has been savaged by a tiger but Chico's watching his back so he can stay in the fight. Who's watching over Max and Stuart?*

Reuben, and Damien – the guy might be injured, but he sure can fight.

It was true: Damien had become great at combat. *Please tell me Butch got out with the baby.*

Yep, he's waiting at the campground. There isn't many of Orrin's vampires left now, and with Chico, Harvey, Reuben, and Denny still going strong, I think they'll be fine dealing with them.

Then let's have a chat with Orrin. Wait, where's Jude?

I'm not sure, but I have a strong feeling she's inside that house looking for the other female vampire.

That did sound like Jude. *All right, let's deal with him, but we can't kill him. He belongs to Jude.* With that in mind, I decided it would be better to return Dexter to his tattoo form – I couldn't guarantee that he wouldn't kill the bloke. "Novo." Instantly Dexter seemed to melt into my body, which appeared to shock the living shit out of Orrin. Good.

I cracked my whip at him, intending to trap him with it so that I could cart him inside the house. To my utter shock, the whip flew through him as if he wasn't even there, like he was merely a ghost.

"Much like you, Samantha, I have a substantial gift," Orrin explained, seemingly enjoying my confusion. "It has its advantages in many situations."

It was Jared who guessed. "Density control. You can manipulate the density of your own body. Rare."

Shit. *Now what do we do?*

Fuck if I know.

"That's right, Jared. You – fortunately for me, but unfortunately for you – cannot harm me. Even with all that power, Samantha, you cannot harm me. Nor can those talented men there."

A fleeting look allowed me to see that the squad were now the only ones remaining – though many of them were worse for wear – and they were beginning to gather behind us.

A click of Orrin's fingers was followed by the swift appearance of a stout, cheery looking female. "Moira, be a dear and take care of these people." He gestured to Jared and the squad.

Suddenly the squad began to drop to the ground, one by one. Instinctively, I brought my shield up and extended it around Jared before the woman could place her focus on him – which appeared to agitate the hell out of Orrin. "What did you do to them?" I demanded.

"Don't be alarmed, they're merely in a very deep sleep. After a few hours – it differs from person to person – they'll wake again. It's a useful gift to have when you're caring for babies." He signalled to Moira to return inside. A nervous Blake went with her.

Jared asked the very question that was bugging me. "Why didn't you get her to do that at the beginning?"

"I wanted to see what Samantha was capable of. And it's not often you get the chance to observe the Heir and his own personal squad in action." Orrin gave me what I guessed was supposed to be a reassuring smile. "I had considered plucking you out of harm's way so that we could leave a little sooner, but I was confident that you would escape it unscathed. And I was right, wasn't I?"

I had to have heard him wrong. "Excuse me, but it sounds like you have the impression that I'm going somewhere with you."

"Well of course you are. You think I don't know what the brothers did to you? You think I didn't play some part in what happened?"

"What do you mean?" growled Jared. Yeah, it had been dumb of Orrin to admit that in front of a very protective Jared.

Orrin sighed. "The brothers are what you might call...I guess sociopaths, is probably the best term." And wasn't that the pot calling the kettle black. "They know what's right and wrong, they just think the rules don't apply to them. It's what makes them such good scientists – no guilt or ethics to interfere.

"They're both obsessed with the idea of glory, of making a discovery or an achievement that no one else can match. Their goal is to create the ultimate vampire – a blend of all three. Unfortunately, the brothers can be a little eccentric and unpredictable, but the right amount of motivation and the right amount of adoration from me had them focusing on the task."

He looked as though he actually expected us to praise him for that. Snort.

"Unfortunately, none of their experiments turned out well. I admit, I didn't actually think they would be successful." He tilted his head as if in thought. "Maybe they can find a way to amplify my gift so that it's strong enough that I can manipulate the density of other peoples' bodies, too." He shrugged.

That gave me an idea. *Call Reuben*, I told Jared.

Baby, I don't know if you've noticed, but he's in dreamland right now.

So wake him up using your telepathy.

I don't think that'll work.

Try, I growled.

Hey, don't get pissy with me.

I can't just – You know what, we can argue later. Just try to wake Reuben, and tell him what to do. I addressed Orrin then, hoping to keep him talking. "I can understand why the brothers would want to create a hybrid – it's all about glory, all in the name of science. But what's in it for you?"

His smile was creepily wide. "Tell me, Samantha, what vampire out there wouldn't pay – and pay very well – to become as powerful as you?"

"So this is about money?"

"Isn't that what makes the world go around? Come on, you're a Sventé. Or, should I say, you *were* a Sventé. You know what it's like to be seen as the weaker breed, to *feel* the weaker breed, to be dismissed, and to be targeted. If someone had offered to make you stronger, given you the opportunity to help yourself, wouldn't you have jumped at their offer?"

I did kind of get his point. After all, that was exactly what I *had* done. Sebastian had appeared with his offer to get me out of my shitty situation and find something better, and I'd taken it. But this…this was a little different. "I'm surprised at you, Orrin – and not in a good way."

"Surprised, how?"

"See, it's not a shock that the brothers haven't looked beyond their goal – they have tunnel vision. But you…I would have thought you'd have been able to see the bigger picture. How can you not see the complications and possible consequences of what you've done?"

He narrowed his eyes. "I don't follow."

"That's my point. Let's say I was to Turn a human. They're not going to become a Sventé, they're going to become just like me. So will other humans I Turn, and any humans that *they* Turn. The same applies to any vampires that the brothers work their magic on. Before you know it, you have a new breed of vampire. That's not good."

Orrin inhaled deeply as he considered that. "I don't see why it would be a huge problem. Sventés, Kejas, and Pagoris have co-existed well enough. Why would the introduction of a new breed be such a bad thing?"

"Because this new breed will be stronger. A lot stronger. That's a threat to the status quo. Although it chafes most, they do accept that Pagoris are the most powerful of the three breeds, they accept that Kejas are a close second, and that Sventés are the weakest. They accept that that's the way of things. Introducing a stronger breed will unsettle everyone. Sventés will worry that they're now easy pickings. Kejas won't like that they've gone a step down in the hierarchy, now being in the place that Sventés once had. And Pagoris, so used to sitting on the throne, won't like that they've lost that throne. They'll all want to react, and it won't be pretty."

Uncertainty briefly flashed on his face. "The point may be moot since, for all I know, you're no longer able to Turn humans. I will take you to the brothers and let them look at you. They can tell us more."

The bloke lived in another reality if he thought that would happen. "Here's the thing…I don't have any intention of leaving Jared or the squad to go anywhere, let alone with you. Shame, isn't it."

He was quiet for a moment, studying Jared intently. "We could take him with us, I suppose. But not conscious. Jared is too powerful for us to take any risks with him."

"*Jared* is right here," snapped my fiancé. "And Jared isn't going to let you take him or Sam anywhere. It's really that simple."

"I didn't come this far to allow you or anyone else to be a hindrance. Samantha comes with me. I assure you, she'll come to no harm."

Jared snickered, crossing his arms over his chest. "The brothers said the same thing. Then she went through nights of agony and all kinds of weird stuff happened. Forgive me if I'm not reassured."

"Then look at it this way: harming her would totally go against what I'm trying to achieve. Therefore, it makes no sense that I would hurt her, does it?"

Scepticism dripped from Jared's smile and voice. "And I suppose you're going to let me and the guys go free."

Orrin jiggled his head. "If Samantha agrees to drop her shield and come with me, I shall agree to simply have Moira put you to sleep for a while – long enough for Samantha and I to be gone. I do not like to kill for killing's sake."

Unreal. "But you don't mind mothers being butchered and their babies being sold?"

"That's just business, nothing more." He returned his attention to Jared. "You know what it's like to yearn for things like power, respect, and status. Unfortunately, nobody came and took me to the Grand High Master. I had to get those things for myself. And I have." He seemed to take pride in that. "Once Samantha agrees to drop her shield, Moira will put you to sleep long enough for Samantha and I to leave."

I cocked my head. "And just what would make me agree to drop my shield? There's no point in threatening me. You can't get inside this shield to reach either of us."

"No," he allowed, "but I can always ask Moira to make the squad's sleep more permanent. She can do that, you know."

"I don't believe you. I think you're just calling my bluff."

"Do you really want to take that chance? Do you really—" He gasped as two strong hands manacled his ankles. Lying on the ground behind him was a drained-looking Reuben. Orrin managed to kick him aside, but it didn't matter because Reuben had touched him long enough to have the desired effect.

"My good squad member there has the ability to temporarily amplify a person's gift," Jared told Orrin. "He can also make it temporarily weaker. You feel it, don't you? See how quickly you're becoming substantial?"

Orrin peered down at himself and smiled. He was *beyond* weird. "It's an admirable gift." He focused on me, losing his smile. "I suppose you're going to kill me while my gift isn't working."

I pursed my lips. "No. But someone else is."

Jared locked his hand around Orrin's throat and dragged him inside the house.

"If you're looking for the child—"

"Don't worry, Orrin, the baby is safe and sound," assured Jared as we stopped inside the kitchen. "I'm not sure I can say the same for Moira, though."

He definitely couldn't say the same for Moira, considering that Jude was in the hallway holding her beloved knife and that it was dripping with blood. Looking a combination of irate and keyed up, she slowly began advancing toward us. Her gaze never moved from Orrin, who Jared was holding directly in front of him, presenting him to Jude.

"Good ole Moira won't be joining us," she told Orrin when she came to stand before him. "Which is a shame, really, because I'd happily kill her twice. If you're thinking that the memory guy might run to your rescue, I've got news that'll kill that dream. He jumped into one of your SUVs about five minutes ago. Couldn't get away fast enough. You just can't get the staff these days, can you?"

In a rather sluggish movement, Jude ran the tip of her blade down Orrin's chest, over his navel, and continued downwards. It finally came to a stop when the tip was pressed against the space between his bollocks and his arse hole.

Orrin gulped. Of course he did. Right at that moment, Jude looked far from sane...and fully capable of relieving him of his crown jewels.

Shakily, he asked, "Who might you be?"

"That's not important," Jude told him calmly. "What's important is that you're in agony when you die. It'll never match the kind of agony I went through when my child was taken from me. No, nothing can match that. But it can certainly be damn well close." And then, as if to demonstrate that, she thrust the knife upwards.

Jared winced, though not in sympathy with a screaming Orrin. He winced again when she twisted the knife before withdrawing it. *Damn, that would hurt.*

"I'll take it from here," Jude told us, though her gaze hadn't left her victim.

Had I not seen what an accurate shot she was with that knife, I might have worried about leaving her alone with him in case he tried to fight her off and make a run for it. It was like she and that knife were one entity.

Understanding that she needed to do this – and do it alone – in order to find some measure of peace, I gestured for Jared to release Orrin. The vampire dropped to his knees, still crying out in agony. "It should be about an hour before his gift begins to strengthen again," I told Jude.

Still, she didn't look away from him as she spoke. "Then I'll make those minutes count."

Taking the hand that Jared offered me, I allowed him to lead me out of the house towards where our squad was lying, still dozing – and snoring, in some cases. It seemed that Reuben had returned to dreamland.

As we were walking away, we heard Jude speaking again to Orrin. "Do you know what's great about how quickly you heal? It means I can do this to you over and over again before I finally kill you." By the sound of his squeal, she had just made that evident.

I was pretty sure the next hour was going to feel very long for Orrin.

It was impossible not to balk as I watched Harvey repeatedly poke his arm through the hole in Damien's stomach. Both seemed to think it was absolutely hilarious. The hole was slowly shrinking in size now that his body was healing, but it would be a few hours before it finally closed over.

They were the only squad members who weren't lying on one of the infirmary beds around them. The others hadn't yet woken from Moira's induced sleep, but their wounds had healed nicely.

Antonio came to my side, frowning at Reuben. "I do not think I have ever heard anyone snore so loud."

"Me neither," said Jared as he came up on my other side. Tension was still thrumming through him and I had a feeling he was thinking, just as I was, that if Moira's gift had been to induce a fatal sleep as opposed to a temporary one, the squad would be nothing but ashes now. It was scary to think that no matter how well we trained them, it might only take a vampire with a unique gift to kill them all – and us, for that matter.

Antonio exhaled heavily. "It is a relief to know that the operation has been put to a halt, but I still have to locate the couples who purchased the human babies who were taken from their mothers."

I doubted that that would be an easy feat. "I take it you're sending Sebastian?"

Antonio nodded. "Once he returns from finding the brothers, I will do so. I have sent out a message to all vampirekind that if these couples give themselves up to me, they will not be punished with death. If they do not do this, however, they will be executed once Sebastian has hunted them down – and he *will* hunt them down. That is something that I am certain about."

"What are you going to do with the babies once you have them?" asked Jared.

"The only thing I can do: I plan to hand them over to human authorities. Of course it is not possible to return them to their mothers, but they still have fathers and other relatives. It is up to the humans to return the children to the right families – that is something I have no control over."

"Poor Jude," I said quietly, looking at the woman in question, who was at the other side of the infirmary. She hadn't spoken a word since we got back. "Every single cell of her must want her daughter back even though she understands it can't happen."

"Yes, it has to be heart-breaking." Antonio sighed.

"Do you think she might stay, if we asked her?"

"If that is your way of requesting for a place to be made for her here, then yes."

Nodding my thanks at him, I walked over to where she sat beside Chico's bed. I'd noticed that they spent a little time together, but there was nothing going on between them as far as I knew. "Hi."

She smiled at me, but it wasn't a full smile. "Hi."

"How do you feel?"

She blew out a breath. "Tired. Tired in too many ways to count.

You know, I didn't expect that I'd feel better afterwards, so it's no surprise that I don't. But I guess I'm…relieved. I feel like I got vengeance for Holly, for the life she should have had."

"For the life you *both* should have had," I corrected.

"It's weird. Now that it's over, I don't know what to do. For so long, I've been running on a need for vengeance. Now that I have it, I feel…"

Seeing that she was struggling for words, I offered, "without purpose." She nodded. "You could stay. You could make a place for yourself here."

She glanced fleetingly at Chico. "Thanks. Maybe."

I doubted that she truly would stay. In fact, I wouldn't be surprised if Jude spent her life watching over her daughter, looking out for her from a distance. That was what I'd have done in her position.

Feeling that Jared was behind me, I turned to him.

"Ready to go?" At my nod, he took my hand in his and teleported us to the living area of our apartment. There, he pulled me to him, fitting me against him. Trapping my gaze with his, he slid both hands into my hair. "You're okay."

And that was no little thing, given just how powerful those vampires had been tonight. "Yes."

"If you had been one of the people lying on an infirmary bed, I really don't think I could have taken it." Of course he couldn't have taken it. He'd been pushed to his limits so many times already this week.

"But I'm not. I'm fine. And I'm here. With you."

Then he was on me. Mouths fused together, tongues tangling, teeth biting, we stumbled through the apartment – stripping as we went. We had only gotten as far as the kitchen when Jared ended the kiss. "I can't wait. I need this." With an impatient growl, he tore the only remaining clothes from my body – my jeans and panties – and slammed me against the kitchen cupboards. Just as impatient, I ripped open the fly of his jeans. His cock was hot and throbbing in my hand as I pumped fast.

He rested his forehead against mine. "Harder."

When I gave him what he wanted, he groaned loudly. But it wasn't long before he tried pulling my hand away. I resisted.

"I want inside you," he growled, again tugging at my hand. This time, I let him go. Then with our mouths again meshed together, he slid his hands to the back of my thighs, lifted me, and placed me on the countertop. When his probing fingers discovered that I was wet and ready, a growl of approval rumbled its way up his chest. "Just how I like it." Angling my hips just right, he slammed home, and my muscles rippled around him. "Christ, Sam."

He held himself still, giving me a minute to adjust to him, but I didn't want that minute. I scratched at his back. "Move, move, move."

He did. There was no teasing this time. His fingertips bit into my skin as he gripped my hips tightly, possessively, and punched his cock in and out of me. All the while, he groaned into the crook of my neck, whispering about how good I felt, about how amazing I was to him, about how much he needed to feel me come apart around him.

He wouldn't have to wait long for that, because the tension was quickly building inside me, burning me hotter and hotter, and sending me closer and closer to finding my release. But I didn't want to find it yet, didn't want it to end so soon.

Obviously sensing that I was fighting it, Jared sucked on my earlobe and began circling my clit with his thumb. "Let go."

I shook my head, trying to pull his hand away from my clit. The sod wouldn't let me. "I don't want to come yet. Please."

Ignoring me, he continued toying with my clit. "Give me what I need, baby. Come all over me."

I might have continued to fight it, but then his teeth sank deep into my neck, sending me hurtling over the edge and screaming. He didn't pull back after a few swallows the way he usually would. Instead, he kept on drinking, drawing out my orgasm. Only once I slumped against him, totally satiated, did he – with one final hard thrust – come deep inside me.

I wasn't sure how long we stayed locked like that, as I was pretty much drifting to sleep when he spoke.

"I love you, baby."

I smiled lazily against his shoulder. The fact that he didn't say it often only made it all that more fulfilling to hear. "And I love you," I more or less slurred.

"As much as I want to kill the brothers for what they've done to you, I was glad of it tonight. Glad you had that extra strength and power. They said that, didn't they? They said that what they've done would be something I'd one day appreciate. They were right."

Frowning at the bitterness in his voice, I lifted my head, seeking his gaze. "Hey, if you want the truth, I was glad as well." Not that I wanted to stay a hybrid, but it had certainly been an advantage.

Looking at me curiously, he shook his head in what seemed to be incredulity. "Since the first night I met you, you've had me messed up. You're my weakness — pure and simple. But you're also the only thing that I really couldn't live without."

"You won't have to," I assured him. But I knew as well as he did that with two sociopaths out there, wanting to get their hands on their 'project', I wasn't truly safe.

CHAPTER SIXTEEN

(Sam)

"Will you bloody relax, woman," Fletcher repeated for, like, the twelfth time as he flopped onto the sofa beside me.

Trying again, and failing again, to stop fidgeting, I huffed. "How exactly am I supposed to relax when it's my Binding ceremony tomorrow evening?"

"Well that's what this little Pamper Party was for." He gestured to the numerous females that were leaving my apartment after having given me several spa treatments. But even after a full body massage, some reflexology, a holistic facial, and an Indian head massage, I was still tense.

Not that the women weren't good at what they did. In all honesty, I wasn't a big fan of spas and massages, but I'd found these treatments surprisingly enjoyable. I simply wasn't relaxed. But, seriously, could anybody blame me for that?

I let my hand delve into the bowl of hazelnuts on the coffee table. One of the best parts of this little get together had been the nibbles, pastries, and cakes. Oh and the Butlers in the Buff who had served the snacks and NSTs…they'd certainly been a nice addition.

"You do realise that you're comfort-eating, don't you? Stressed or not, attacking pastries won't do you any good."

I threw Fletcher a dirty look. "Shut your noise, I'll eat what I want."

"I think you'll enjoy what's coming next."

The excitement in his tone had me instantly intrigued. "What is it?"

"We're going to have a pedicure."

And there went my intrigue. "That's it? We don't need manicures or pedicures – we're vampires, our nails are all perfect."

He gave me a cheeky smile. "Ah, but this is a different kind of pedicure."

"There's more than one kind of pedicure?"

As the door closed behind the last beauty therapist, he said, "So…are you going to tell me the *real* reason why you now seem to have the same enchanting glamour that Keja vampires have?"

The camp sod was too astute for his own good – it really was a good job that I adored him. There was no sense in lying to him, but I also couldn't tell him. Not that I thought Fletcher would blab. I just didn't want anyone plucking the info from his mind. "If I could tell you, I would. I'm sorry."

He grabbed my hand and gave it a reassuring squeeze. "I appreciate you not giving me an 'I don't know what you're talking about'; that would have hurt. But, if you're not going to tell me about that, you can at least answer my question of why you're so anxious about tomorrow evening."

"Doesn't every 'bride' have a last minute attack of the jitters, or whatever they call it?"

"There's being jittery, and there's being bloody petrified. Why are you so scared? What could you possibly have to be scared of?"

"The mysterious dress you've designed?" I offered. He'd brought it with him in a full-size protective bag which he'd placed in my bedroom.

He huffed at me. "Stop stalling, Lady Jane, and spill the beans."

Persistent little bugger.

"You're not having second thoughts, are you?"

"Definitely not."

"Are you worried that he's not going to show up? If so, that's daft. We can safely say that he'll be there."

"It's not that, it's just that…Binding…it's not like marriage. There's no divorce, no annulment, no get-out clause. Once you Bind yourself to someone, you have a life-long psychic connection to them that can only be broken if one of you dies. Even if the couple grew to despise each other or had come to care for somebody else, there's no getting out of the bond."

"And that scares you," he guessed.

"Actually, no. I thought it would. It probably should. But the idea that it can't be broken makes me feel more secure, strangely enough."

"I don't understand. What's the problem, then?"

"The problem is that Jared gets temptation thrown in his face constantly – you've seen what women are like around him. I'm not saying he's shallow, he's far from it, though I didn't realise that at first. But I can't help worrying that he might one day fall for one of them. Not because I don't trust him or because I don't believe he loves me. But because it scares me that I'd be able to *feel* what he felt for her. Knowing that he loved someone else would be bad enough. But to be able to *feel* it, and to have no way of saving myself from that…I couldn't deal with that Fletcher, I know I couldn't. I wouldn't need to kill myself to break the bond: it would destroy me."

Fletcher pulled me against him and locked his arm around me. Patting my arm, he gently said, "Yes, he has women throwing themselves at him all the time, which is daft of them since they know you could, and would happily, whip them to death. But who can blame them, really? I mean, he's gorgeous, he's powerful, he's got that dominant vibe going on, and he's the Heir – it's a combination that will have most females downright bloody horny."

"Fletch, you're not helping," I said dryly.

He held up his index finger. "Wait, I'm not done. What I was about to say before you rudely interrupted me, was that I've been around him when he's had women slobbering over him. Not once has it ever got him hot and bothered – I'd have sensed it. He actually gets annoyed about it. Sometimes there's even a bit of resentment there, but I'm not sure what that's about."

The latter made me think back to Evan's words of how Jared resented just how much attention his looks got him, of how he resented that he looked like his mother.

"Before you came here, Jared was hard. Cynical. You didn't need to be an Empath to know that. I wouldn't say he's changed. No, he's still like that in many ways. But my point is that he's not like that with you. When he's with you, he's relaxed. He trusts you. I'd say that's a big thing for Jared. I can sense that he's not a very trusting person, just as I can sense that he absolutely adores you. Oh, luv, if you'd have felt how beside himself he was when your gifts were on the blink, you wouldn't be worrying like this. If there was any doubt in my mind about his commitment to you, I'd be trying to talk you out of the Binding. I'm a meddling sod like that."

I smiled. "Yeah, you would do that, wouldn't you?"

"Yes, because I love you. And Jared does as well."

A knock at the apartment door had Fletcher bouncing to his feet. "This is going to be fabulous."

"Why do I get the feeling that this is more for you than it is for me?"

He gave me a wounded look. "I can't believe you'd even think that."

"So I'm right then?"

"Possibly." He opened the door, and a tall Keja with flowing sable hair and a large, silver cosmetics case strolled inside.

The Keja shook my hand. "Hi, my name's Rayna. I'm here to do your Swarovski Pedicure. Are you both having one?"

"What's a Swarovski Pedicure?" It turned out that it was when someone spent almost two hours applying individual Swarovski crystals to your toenails in a very intricate, beehive formation. And it was bloody great. I liked it so much that I even asked her to apply them to my fingernails as well.

Afterwards, Fletcher and I sat back and admired them with sighs of appreciation.

"These will look fabulous with your ceremony dress and shoes."

"Am I allowed to see this dress yet?"

Hearing the apprehension in my voice, he shook his head at me sadly. "I'm hurt that you have so little faith in me. But, yes, you can see it now." Obviously excited, he practically skipped to my bedroom.

I followed behind him, dreading what was about to happen. I would no doubt dislike it, and he would no doubt become upset, and then I would have offended my best mate. In the room, I found him standing before the bag that was hanging on my wardrobe door.

"Ready?" Without giving me a chance to answer, he tackled the zipper and pulled out the weirdest thing I'd ever seen. There wasn't a word to describe it. A mix of pink and purple, the organza gown actually had fairy wings and a magic wand.

"What's that?"

"A joke. Calm down."

I sagged in relief. "Sod."

"*This* is your dress." He carefully withdrew another dress and held it out at arms' length. Ducking under his arm in order to circle the garment, I literally couldn't say a word. Technically, I shouldn't like this dress. I mean, I'd envisioned myself in something reasonably simple but nice...maybe a white silk halter-neck that was just below knee-length, lacking even a hint of a train. This sleeveless, backless, floor-length dress was pretty much the opposite.

In the typical 'fit n flare' style, it was skin-tight all the way to mid-thigh before flaring out. It was definitely going to accentuate my already noticeable cleavage. And it was decorated with girly things like crystals and beads, and even had a clump of rosettes on one hip. But I absolutely loved it. That must have shown on my face, because Fletcher hung up the dress and started jumping up and down, clapping like a performing seal.

"I knew you'd adore it! See, you should have a little more faith in your mates."

"Is it satin?"

"Yep. Isn't the court train gorgeous? I had a feeling you still wouldn't want one, so I asked the designer to sew in a little loop." If he hadn't pointed it out to me, I never would have noticed it. "If you don't want the train, or you just want it out of your way while you're dancing, all you have to do is lift it by the loop and then hook it on one of the fake buttons near the small of your back."

I did the only thing I could do right then. I practically wrapped myself around Fletcher, hugging the breath out of him. Then we were both jumping up and down, squealing in delight – something I wouldn't normally do.

"Come on, you have to try it on. I'm convinced that it will fit, but it's best to make sure."

"Sam?"

Both mine and Fletcher's eyes widened at the sound of Jared calling my name. "He must've teleported inside. Don't come in! You're not allowed to see my dress!"

"Okay, I'll wait out here." I could hear the smile in his voice.

Fletcher and I worked as a team to quickly, but still carefully, return the dress to the bag. We both breathed a sigh of relief when the zipper was closed.

"Can I come in now?"

"Yes," I replied.

Opening the door, he went to walk inside, but then his eyes caught sight of something over my shoulder and he froze. "Whoa."

Realising what he'd seen, I chuckled. "Don't worry; that's not the dress. Fletcher thought it would be funny to make me think I'd be dressed like a slutty fairy at my Binding Ceremony."

Fletcher smirked. "You should've seen her expression, it was priceless." His smirk was replaced by a frown as he folded his arms across his chest. "Hang on a minute. You're not supposed to be here. You're not allowed to see her the night before. It's bad luck."

Jared rolled his eyes. "That's a human thing."

"She hasn't tried on her dress yet."

A shrug. "She can do it after I'm gone."

"She's *supposed* to be relaxing."

"You're suggesting that I'm not a relaxing person to be around?" This was asked with all the innocence of a five year old.

Fletcher sighed tiredly. "I won't get you to leave, will I?"

"No."

Adjusting his glasses on his nose, Fletcher sighed again. "I'll leave you two alone, then. Try not to bonk, all right? It'll all add to the anticipation for tomorrow evening."

As Fletcher dashed out of the room, Jared snatched my hand and tugged me to him before landing a very disorientating kiss on me. "Hey baby."

"I didn't expect you to come here. Aren't you supposed to be getting hammered with the boys?" That had sounded a lot more fun than a pamper party, but everyone was determined to keep us separated for this one night.

"You're more appealing."

"But that's not why you're here," I sensed, knowing him well.

"I guess I just wanted to check that you're okay…and that you're not having second thoughts."

"I told you last night that I wasn't."

"Yeah. But that was last night."

There was a glimmer of vulnerability in his eyes that I'd only seen once before – that night that I'd learned the truth about the bitch that gave birth to him. A vulnerability that *she'd* put there. Despite all his confidence, there was a lack of self-worth lurking deep, and it was clearly making him doubt that I truly loved him. I kind of wished she was alive just so that I could kill her. "I have *not* had an overnight change of heart."

"Even though you know everything about me, even though you know that I'm pretty damaged? It can't be an attractive idea to Bind yourself to someone with this many issues."

I slapped his arm. "Hey, I'm taking offense to that – I have issues of my own. But so what? I think it would be pretty boring to be one-dimensional anyway."

He smiled against my mouth. "Good, it means I don't have to tie you to the bed and hold you here against your will."

"You're not even joking, are you?"

"No. I can't let you go."

"Does this mean I can relax in the knowledge that you'll turn up to the ceremony?"

His all-too-perceptive eyes narrowed. "So I wasn't the only one worrying." When I shook my head in admission, he dabbed a drugging kiss on my mouth. "That's just dumb. I need you in more ways than you know. You were right in what you said; when I came here I forgot who I was and where I came from because I wanted to. You brought me back from that. If you go, I'll be tempted to forget again, because it's easier that way. I need you to keep me grounded. It sounds corny, I know, but you're like my personal little refuge. You can't leave."

"I won't. But note, for the record, that if you don't show up, I'll gut you like a fish."

His smile took over his face. "There's my girl." He nipped my bottom lip. "Open for me." When I did, his tongue immediately shot inside to find mine. In a dominant move that could have landed him in trouble if I wasn't in such a good mood, he tangled a hand in my hair and angled my head how he wanted – holding it there while he literally devastated my mouth.

When he pulled back to nuzzle my neck and lick at my pulse, I groaned. "You need to go, or we'll end up bonking."

"And that would be bad because...?"

"Fletcher's right; it'll add to the anticipation and stuff if we hold off tonight."

"You're mean to me."

"I won't be mean to you tomorrow night. Although...I will be biting you in some very interesting places."

His eyes were shining with humour and interest when he looked at me. "Oh I really hope you do." Having smacked one last kiss on my mouth, he released me. "Oh and Sam…I'll be doing the same." With a devilish smirk, he teleported away, leaving me tingling in all kinds of places. The sod.

A cold shower. That sounded like the best idea.

Unfortunately, it didn't work. I came out of the shower feeling more sexually frustrated than I had before I got in it.

I was just slipping my robe on over my underwear when there was a knock on my apartment door. Clearly Fletcher was back to help me try on the dress. I quickly scuttled through the apartment and opened the door – and growled at my two visitors. Before I could say a word, Brook grabbed my arm, and there was a very familiar sensation in my stomach as he – oh fuck a duck – teleported me, him, and Magda to a strange living room.

I had no idea where the hell I was, but I had a very strong feeling that I was no longer at The Hollow. Confirming that, the door opened and five male vampires entered. I recognised three of them. Two were the Trent brothers, and the other was Blake. Fucking great.

Abruptly, Brook shoved me into an armchair, holding me there by my shoulder. I had barely shrugged him away, fully intending to whip the crap out of these people, when I was suddenly paralysed. Literally. I couldn't move at all. Recalling what Orrin had said about one of the brothers having the gift of freezing things, I quickly realised what had happened.

"You'll have to do it quickly," Magda told the brothers, sounding desperate and anxious. "Jared will sense her fear, and he'll come to her."

"Do not worry," said the tallest brother. "It will not come to that. Blake."

The ex-Handler stepped forward, grinning mischievously. If I hadn't been frozen in place, I'd have snarled at him. "How much do you want gone?"

"Everything up until the day that she was recruited," the tallest brother told him. "I do not want her to remember anything after that day."

Oh shit.

Magda shot me an evil smile. "I should be getting back. I don't want anyone to notice that I was missing at the same time that she disappeared. Plus, Jared is going to need me to be there for him." She left with her consort, wearing a smug, devious smirk. Oh the bitch.

Blake put his index finger to my temple. Then, there was only blackness.

(Jared)

I felt like someone had punched me in the head – there was a heavy impact, there was a momentary disorientation, and then there was pain as my connection to Sam abruptly vanished. Not physical pain, but a crushing, overwhelming, agonising emotional pain as suddenly I could no longer feel her.

I should have been rushing out of the bar in a panic, but that same sense of panic seemed to be stopping me from moving. I was expecting to feel her again any second now, for the 'glitch' to fix itself.

"What's wrong?" Evan asked.

"Sam."

Concern was plastered across his face. "What's wrong with her?"

"I don't know."

"Go to her."

"I can't." Without our link, I couldn't take myself to her unless I could see her.

"What do you mean, you can't? Don't tell me *your* gifts are now acting up, too."

Shaking myself out of my shocked state, I teleported to our apartment, right in the spot that I'd left her only half an hour ago. The room was empty. "Sam! Sam!" In vampire speed, I raced through the apartment, coming to an abrupt halt when I saw that the door was open. I dashed into the hallway, but there was no sign of her whatsoever. "Sam!"

Frantic, confused, and scared-fucking-shitless, I went to the one person I believed could fix just about anything. Antonio double-blinked as I, suddenly, appeared directly in front of him on the veranda. "Sam…I can't feel her."

He stiffened in his seat. "How can you not feel her?"

"I don't know. But our connection…it's not like it *broke*. It's just like she's not on the other end of it anymore. Like she fell off the face of the Earth or something. I can't sense her at all – not what she's feeling, not where she is."

He shot to his feet, looking almost as anxious as I was. "Did you feel anything from her just before this happened? Fear?"

"There was a little anxiety, but before I even had a chance to *think* about acting, she was gone. Just like that." I clicked my fingers.

"Have you been to your apartment?"

So distracted by the panic circulating through me, I hadn't even realised that Wes was behind me until I heard his voice. I spun around to face him. "She's not there."

Pacing, Antonio asked, "Were there any signs of a struggle?"

"No. The front door was wide open, but that's all."

Wes placed a supportive hand on my shoulder. "You do understand what this might mean, don't you, Jared?"

Yes, I did know, but I wasn't going down that path. "There's no way. There's no way that she's dead. I'd know it."

"But you said she's not on the other end of your connection anymore," he said gently.

"That doesn't mean she's dead."

"Not much else could break it so abruptly."

I growled, pulling away from him. "Well what else *could* break it so abruptly? Because she's not dead!"

"Jared—"

"She's not! I'd know it, I'd feel it – connection or no connection, I'd feel it if she died!" And I was one hundred percent sure of that. No, she wasn't dead. And the second that the connection snapped back into place, I'd go to her.

Haste footsteps had us all looking to our left. If there was one person I hadn't expected to see, it was this guy – at least not yet, anyway. He looked absolutely livid.

(Sam)

Feeling like I'd just been spat out of a vacuum or something, I triple-blinked. When my eyes came back into focus, I instantly stiffened. Who wouldn't if they found themselves in a strange place with five strange vampires? My instinct was to conjure my whip, ready to defend myself if need be. That was when I realised that I couldn't move.

"No need to be alarmed, Samantha," a tall Pagori with black hair assured me. "We mean you no harm. If you allow us to explain, you will see that we speak the truth. My brother is going to unfreeze you now. I am trusting that you will not attempt to attack anyone. If you do, he will be forced to freeze you again, for our safety."

Experimenting, I tried crossing my legs. It worked. "Where am I?"

"What's the last thing you remember?"

As I spoke, I wasn't so much answering him as I was trying to figure things out for myself. "I was on my way back from the shop, heading for my flat...I knew a vampire was up there...Was that you?"

Looking oddly pleased with my answer, he replied, "No. I suspect the vampire in there was the one who attacked you. My name is Quinn. My brother here is Wyatt. The vampires around you work for us."

"I was attacked? Let's start from the beginning. How the bloody hell did I get here, and why am I here at all?"

The brothers exchanged an odd look before Quinn flashed me a bright smile. "I'm afraid that your memories will be a little shaky for a while. The process of bringing someone out of a comatose state can have that effect."

"Say again?"

"You were comatose until just now. I am guessing that the vampire responsible had been waiting for your Sire at the flat and was surprised by your entrance – it would seem that he upset the wrong people."

Victor had a terrible habit of doing that. "Are you one of those 'wrong people'?"

He appeared truly offended. "No, Samantha. Definitely not. We were strong allies of your Sire."

Well then I definitely didn't like these people. I had an urge to get up and pace around. Having five Pagori vampires standing over me wasn't making me feel relaxed, but perhaps the best thing to do would be to act as though I was at least open to trusting them. The last thing I wanted was to get frozen again.

"We heard about the plan to attack him, went to the flat to warn him, but unfortunately we were too late to help him. We found you and brought you here so that we could—"

"Wait a minute. Victor's dead? Then why am I not in agony? They say if a vampire's blood-link with their Sire is broken, the pain's excruciating."

"Perhaps it is because you were comatose at the time."

Oh this was bloody unreal. Attacked in my own flat. Surely I'd remember something like that. But as I tried to reach for Victor through our blood-link, I realised that the link had been severed. He had to be dead.

"I brought you here and one of my vampires used his gift to awaken you. How do you feel?"

He seemed truly interested...in a very paternal way. I didn't like it. "Confused."

"The confusion will wear off soon."

"Right. Well, as much as I appreciate your help and stuff, I should head home now so—"

"It would be an extremely bad idea for you to return to the flat, Samantha. The person who attacked you and your Sire could be waiting there."

"I'll take my chances, thanks." I moved to stand, and every person in the room tensed. What was with these people?

"Please, Samantha. I failed to protect your Sire, but I do not wish to fail you. I want only to protect you."

"Yeah?" I said doubtfully. Maybe I shouldn't be so suspicious, but there was something about this bloke that I didn't like. If these people truly had any wish to help me, it wasn't out of the kindness of their hearts. Crossing my arms over my chest, I suddenly became aware of something. I was wearing silk. Looking down, I studied the silky black robe, briefly noticing the white lacy underwear beneath it. "Whose clothes are these?"

If I wasn't mistaken, Quinn seemed a little stuck for words. Like a kid having to think fast on his feet because mummy had caught him out on a lie. "They're not yours?"

"No." I would never in my life have the money to afford this kind of stuff.

"You said you had been shopping, so perhaps these are new purchases and you were trying them on when the attacker struck," suggested Wyatt.

"But that makes no sense. Not just because the shop I went to only sells food and booze. But because I knew *there* was a strange vampire in the flat. The last thing I would have done is model new clothes while there was an intruder. And what are these things on my nails? Crystals?"

"I'm sure this will all make sense to you soon."

I kind of got the feeling that he was very wrong about that. There was something else that was bugging me. "Why do I feel...different?"

Wyatt's eyes lit up. "In what way do you feel different?"

My eyes widened at the sight of the silvery-blue wisps on my fingers. "And why is energy clinging to me like that?"

"We were wondering the same thing. Maybe the vampire did something to you during the attack."

But that didn't make sense, because I felt stronger, more powerful. Not that I had any intention of telling these people that. I didn't trust them as far as I could throw them, even if they had pulled me out of a coma.

A hissing sound distracted me from my thoughts. I looked around to find a large reptile tank that contained one hell of a huge snake. A python. Its black eyes regarded me, and suddenly I was thinking of another set of black eyes. The image of a brilliant blue snake flashed in my mind. "I have a snake." No, no, I didn't. I almost laughed at the absurdity of that statement. Of course I didn't have one, why would I ever—

The python hissed again, and another, similar image flashed before me; this time the same blue snake was curled up on a sofa...A sofa that I recognised, yet didn't. It certainly wasn't from my flat.

Maybe these blokes had slipped something in my drink.

"You have a snake?" said Quinn.

I meant to say no, but the word wouldn't come out of my mouth. It felt unnatural to deny ever having owned one, even though I had no recollection of ever having bought a snake.

As if Wyatt sensed my confusion, he said, "The disorientation is normal. Do you need to feed?"

I wasn't about to accept anything from these people who had obviously been giving me drugs or something. I shook my head. Involuntarily, I found my gaze moving back to the reptile tank. As I looked at the python, an image again flickered in front of my eyes. This time, it was the same snake as before, yet its colouring was different...Red. It was wrapped around me, hissing at...at...And then the memory was gone, and I couldn't reach for it.

But it couldn't be a memory, could it? None of that could be real. So why was I seeing these things? Why did I feel...*more* than before? And why did I feel restless – like there was something important I was supposed to do, someone important I was supposed to see?

That wasn't the only thing that I could feel. Strangely, I felt a mood besides my own. Not like when I sensed Victor's mood, no, not that type of connection. But I could feel echoes of irritation and apprehension that were not coming from me. Nor were they coming from a person. More like an animal.

"I would recommend that you stay here with us," said Quinn. "We can keep you safe and can help you avenge the death of your Sire."

Like I cared about that! If I ever met the vampire who killed him, I'd shake his hand.

"Yes," agreed Wyatt. "We can also help you find out why energy seems to be magnetised to you, and why you feel 'different', as you described it."

Quinn nodded. "It is what Victor would want."

"Besides, do you really want to be alone, Samantha?"

Once more, the damn python hissed. Like a trigger, the sound sent various pictures shooting through my mind: a blue snake twined around my arm, a red snake striking at a faceless person, a piebald snake tattoo on my arm, a black snake slithering from my arm to another arm. This arm was male, sprinkled with chestnut hairs.

More images now: the same arm holding me close, strong male hands cradling my face, thumbs brushing tears from my eyes.

Sensations rolled through me: hands knotting in my hair and tugging, fingers probing and sinking inside me, thumbs sending electric shards of pleasure/pain through me.

Another hiss stole me from my memories. Yes, memories. They were memories. "I have a snake," I said with utter surety this time. Again, I saw a flash of that snake on a crescent sofa...*my* sofa. "I have an apartment." An apartment with soft beige carpets, white walls, a glossy-cream kitchenette, and a queen-sized bed covered in rosy-pink satin sheets who I shared with—

"I have a fiancé." It was only then that I looked up, only then that I saw the horror and dread on the faces of the five vampires around me. "I have a fiancé, and his name is Jared."

Suddenly, with the force of a slap, everything came flooding back to me. *Oh the little bastards!*

CHAPTER SEVENTEEN

(Sam)

In under a second, my whip was in my hand and I'd cracked it at Quinn, slicing through his shirt and chest. Knowing Wyatt would attempt to freeze me, I remoulded my whip into a shield, wrapping it around me.

I almost jumped out of my bloody skin when Jared appeared beside me. Instinctively, I pushed the shield outward to encompass him as well.

He crushed me to him, kissing me hard. "I couldn't feel you. I've never been so fucking scared in my life."

"Blake took my memories of you."

Jared's eyes slammed on the person in question. "Oh did he now?"

"You could teleport you and Samantha away, Jared, but we would find her again," vowed Quinn. "She is ours." He couldn't have said a worse thing.

Jared's voice was deadly. "That's where you're wrong. She's mine. And neither of us is going anywhere until all five of you are dead."

Wyatt laughed. "Do you think that we are the only vampires here? I appreciate that you both are very powerful, but you are not a match for sixty Pagori vampires who have special gifts of their own."

Jared's smug smile had me instantly intrigued. "That would be a good point…if most of them weren't dead."

Confusion splattered across Wyatt's face. "What are you talking about?"

At that moment, he got his answer as several vampires barged into the room – all of whom I recognised: Sebastian, five of his men, Reuben, and Salem. I hadn't been expecting that.

Reuben shot straight to the brothers, momentarily touching their shoulders. That easily, their powers were weakened. Sebastian, his men, and Salem took out Blake and the other two vampires, leaving them nothing but ashes.

Still not willing to trust that they didn't have the ability to harm Jared, I didn't lower the shield as he and I walked to where the two brothers were now being held to the wall. *When did Sebastian get here?* I asked Jared.

He returned to The Hollow not long ago; said that he'd located the brothers and that they had you. I gathered the squad and we came here with Sebastian and his guys, and infiltrated the place. We'd been halfway through killing the vampires outside and in the rear of the house when I felt you.

Wyatt stopped struggling when he looked at me. "Quinn…her eyes."

Similarly, Quinn stilled. "They glow silver. Mercury. Beautiful."

I jiggled my head. "I tend to think of it as a bad side effect. But now that we have you, you're going to fix that for me."

Does Sebastian know what they did to me?

Yeah, I told him — I know we can trust him. But the others have no idea.

Obviously understanding that it was important that very few people knew about my new 'hybrid' status, Sebastian turned to his men. "Go and see if the others need any assistance." As his men did as ordered, Sebastian turned to Salem and Reuben. "Perhaps it would be a good idea for you to check on the rest of your squad."

When Salem and Reuben both looked to me, I nodded.

Only once they were gone did I speak to the brothers. "Now it's time to put right what you did."

"As your vampire has weakened our gifts, we cannot," said Quinn.

I shrugged. "That's fine. We'll just keep you in a containment cell at The Hollow while we wait for the effect of Reuben's gift to wear off."

"I could not reverse the changes even if I wanted to."

Jared shook his head. "If you did it, you can reverse it."

"I could try, but I would not be able to completely reverse them."

Narrowing his eyes, Jared demanded, "What does that mean?"

"It means that she would be somewhere between a Sventé, and what she is now." Quinn gazed at me curiously. "Would you really want to change, Samantha? Would you really want to go back to being a Sventé?"

"I was perfectly happy as I was," I told him.

"Perhaps you were. But wouldn't you prefer to have all this power, to know that you can protect Jared and your squad much better by staying as you are?"

Jared growled. "By being as she is, she'll always be in danger."

Wyatt looked at me with something akin to reverence. "She is not dangerous, she is unique." He sounded like a regular scientist talking about his subject.

"We're getting nowhere with this," I grumbled to Jared.

"So you can't reverse it?" Jared asked them.

"We could try," replied Wyatt. "Are you prepared to take the risks?"

Jared answered without missing a beat. "No." Without moving his eyes from them, he spoke to me. "Sam, could you go with Sebastian to see the squad, let them know you're safe. They've been worried about you."

"Jared—"

"I warned these fuckers that I would find and destroy them."

"Jared—"

Finally, he looked at me. "I need this."

Yes, he really did, I realised. In doing what they had done, in putting me through pain, they had left him feeling helpless, powerless, and unable to help and protect the one person he most wanted to protect. And by having me teleported to them, they had put him through all those feelings once again. He had a score to settle. Just like Jude had needed to destroy Orrin to ease the rage and pain, he needed this now. And he needed to do it alone, just as she had.

I could have quite rightly pointed out that it was *me* who had been the true victim, and that I had some rage of my own, but I was willing to give him this. Besides, there was another score that needed settling, and I wanted to be the one to settle it. If I let him have the brothers, I could claim the right to punish Magda as *I* saw fit.

Giving him a nod, I left the room with Sebastian. But no matter how far away I got, I could still hear the screams.

(Jared)

I couldn't stop staring at her. Didn't want to. Not simply because of how beautiful she was, but because I'd never appreciated the sight of her as much as I did at that moment. I could see that it was annoying her, and I was pretty sure that she was going to hit me with her pillow soon if I didn't stop. But after spending what felt like hours wondering if I'd ever see her again, I didn't want to take my eyes off her. I wanted, needed, to drink in the sight of her.

Although coming inside her had felt like letting go of a lot of the stark fear I'd felt, it hadn't been enough to reassure myself that she was back, here with me, and absolutely fine. The fact was, I had never had anything 'good' before, and I was petrified of losing what I never thought existed. Tonight had given me a tiny taste of what that would be like. Hell.

"Stop staring at me or I'll poke you in the eyes."

I smiled, running my hand through her hair. "Can't help it. When Sebastian took me to the house where they were keeping you, it took everything I had not to charge inside. Even though I knew it was best that I didn't risk exposing our presence to the brothers, all I wanted was to get to you."

"You did."

"How did you get your memories back?"

"I remembered Dexter first," she admitted, which made me frown. I still had a love/hate relationship with that damn serpent. "They had a snake, and it was making me have flashbacks of Dexter, and then that led to me having flashbacks of the apartment, and of you."

"So each memory triggered another?"

"Yeah, sort of."

"Is there any damage? I mean, do you have any blank spots, like some of the memories are still repressed?"

"I don't think so. Antonio said that Ryder can take a look for me, if I like. I'll think about it. Right now, all I'm bothered about is getting some sleep so that I'm awake for our ceremony."

"You're feeling up to having it tomorrow?" I scrutinised her face. "You have to be tired."

"The ceremony is not being postponed – deal with it." There was no room for negotiation in her tone, which made me smile.

"As long as you're sure, that's fine with me. What's *not* fine with me is that Magda's still alive." I hadn't known she was responsible for Sam's disappearance until an hour ago.

"She's in one of the containment cells. I want her alive when we Bind, Jared. You know this."

"And then?"

"Then I kill her."

"Good." I would have insisted on having the honour if Sam hadn't pointed out that I'd got to kill the brothers. I was pretty sure she'd planned it that way, though. Tricky bitch. Seeing that dawn was approaching, I groaned. "I have to go now, don't I?"

"Yep."

I snuggled closer to her. "I don't want to." It sounded a little petulant, but I didn't care.

"I'm not going to disappear again. Orrin's dead. The brothers are dead. Magda and Brook are locked up. I'll be fine."

"Are you pissed that the brothers couldn't reverse the changes?"

"Yes, and no." At my confused look, she explained, "Yes, because I don't want to always be worrying that someone will find out about me. And no, because it's nice to be able to wrestle you in bed. When you were stronger and faster than me, it didn't work so well."

Yeah, that was definitely a perk. But no perk could outweigh the huge problem that this would make her a target if the news somehow got out. People would come for her, wanting to either kill her or breed her. In any case, only one thing would happen – I'd burn shit down. I'd go to war if I had to, and I'd have every right to, because I'd be Bound to her.

"Don't think I don't know that you're lying there planning deaths."

"What can I say? I have weird hobbies."

She just shook her head at me, smiling. "Another benefit of being more powerful is that vampires are no longer fretting over whether I can protect them. I would never have let you step down from Heir."

"And I would never have Bound myself to anyone else. You're mine, I'm yours, and that's it." I cuddled her closer, kissing her hair.

"I have an idea. Why don't we give each other our Binding gifts now? It'll lift the mood, and I'm impatient to do it anyway. It was annoying that I couldn't spend money on you, but I figure you might like this."

THE BITE THAT BINDS

Whatever I was expecting, it wasn't for her to retrieve an A4 sized brown envelope from behind her bedside cabinet. Confused yet excited, I tore the seal open and pulled out a sheet of paper. I instantly laughed when I saw the heading.

PRENUPTIAL AGREEMENT

This agreement is made on this ____ day of _____, 200__, by and between Samantha Parker (herein referred to as "The Boss") and Jared Michaels (herein referred to as "Slave in All Things").

Both parties acknowledge that they have read and understand this agreement, and that they have not been subjected to any form of coercion, duress, or pressure – by orgasms, or otherwise.

The parties hereby agree as follows:

1. It is necessary for there to be a 100 mile radius between them and any ex-partners. Should this condition be violated, violence and death may be the result.
2. There will always be equal control of all remote controls presently used, and any that may be acquired in the future
3. "The Boss" will courteously fake orgasms if and when necessary
4. At all times, "Slave in All Things" will not tease "The Boss" endlessly with his tongue and fingers during foreplay
5. If "The Boss" discusses their sex life with others, she will always state that "Slave in All Things" has the stamina of a Trojan and an impressively sized dick
6. In the event that "Slave in All Things" needs to burp, fart, or spit, he will do this in a separate room from "The Boss"
7. Both parties acknowledge that it is important for "The Boss" to continue giving oral sex on a regular basis. Should she violate this condition, "Slave in All Things" has the right to tie her up and tease her mercilessly

8. "The Boss" understands that "Slave in All Things" will only *pretend* to listen to her if he is using his X-Box or laptop computer
9. "Slave in All Things" accepts that "The Boss" is always right, he is always at fault, and that it is not necessary for her to make sense during arguments
10. Both parties agree that "Slave in All Things" has the right to be protective and possessive, but he must not take this to extreme levels
11. "Slave in All Things" will always put the toilet seat down after use, and use freshening spray if necessary
12. Should either party ogle or flirt with another, violent scenes that some may find disturbing will ultimately follow

Signed and dated this _____ day of _____ 20_____.

_____

Slave in All Thing's Signature

_____

The Boss's Signature

Laughing, I kissed her hard. I certainly hadn't been expecting that, and I had to admit that I loved it. She knew my sense of humour well enough to know that I would. "Very creative. I'm holding you to those conditions, especially the seventh one, just so you know."

"I haven't signed it yet."

"You will." I gave her another hard kiss. "Right, now for my gift to you." In vampire speed, I retrieved the folder I'd kept hidden in the living area, and returned to the bed. "Here."

Taking the folder with an intrigued expression, she opened it. Just as I'd expected, the intrigue turned to confusion. "I don't get it," she admitted as she flicked through the printed sheets of different places around the world.

Smiling, I explained, "Well, like you, I was pissed that I couldn't spend money on you, because I wanted to take you on a honeymoon-kind of thing. I know that's not a tradition for vampires, but I still wanted to do it. Unfortunately, there wasn't a way around it unless I was prepared to break the rule of spending money – which would have made you mad at me. I don't like it when you're mad at me. I like it when you kiss me and do stuff for me and to me. So, instead, I made a plan of the places we could go to, places I knew you wanted to visit."

"A plan? Sneaky way to do it."

"First London, so I can see where you grew up, then Rome, Morocco, Rhodes, Egypt, and finally, California, so you can see where I grew up. What do you think?"

Her eyes lit up with excitement – just as I'd anticipated. It was sad to think that she had never once had a vacation in her entire life. "I think we should skip our after party and just go straight on this trip."

I laughed. "No, we're going to enjoy the entire night and celebrate it in this bed afterwards. Then we'll have a brief sleep and go. And *then* I won't have to share you for six weeks." I took that mouth like I owned it, because I did, and because I needed to know that she accepted that. As if she sensed that, she went pliant for me the way she only ever did when I kissed her neck.

Pulling back, she licked her bottom lip – which made me chase after that mouth. Chuckling, she placed a hand on my chest to stop me. "You need to go. Fletcher isn't going to let me sleep until dusk. He'll be too eager to get me up and start getting me ready, so I need what sleep I can get."

I was about to say that my staying there wouldn't stop her from sleeping, but of course it would, because I'd have trouble leaving her alone. Releasing a long-suffering sigh, I dragged myself out of bed and gathered my clothes.

"Where will you be getting ready for the ceremony?"

"My old apartment. My suit and the stuff I need are already there, waiting." Ready to leave, I hesitated. "Call Dexter and let him lie in bed with you."

"Why would I do that?"

"It'll make me feel better."

She rolled her eyes. "I'll be fine."

"Just do it, you stubborn bitch." Smiling at the irritation on her face, I quickly smacked a kiss on her lips and teleported out of there – I wasn't stupid.

CHAPTER EIGHTEEN

(Sam)

I'd had absolutely no idea about the pre-nuptial rituals for Binding ceremonies until Fletcher turned up at my apartment with half a dozen female Kejas. First I'd been covered in exotic-smelling oils and massaged from head to toe. Then there had been a spicy wrap, which I hadn't been very fond of. Thirdly there had been a milk bath, which I had to admit I'd quite liked. And then my hands and feet had been painted with a strange, glistening ink; the intricate knot and vine patterns perfectly complimented my Swarovski Manicure and Pedicure.

While waiting for the weird paint to dry – which hadn't taken long – I sat very still as my hair was slightly curled and then put into some kind of elaborate hairdo, leaving tendrils hanging here and there. I wasn't a very patient person, so I got kind of restless. At least I hadn't had to continue to sit there as they applied make-up. If the natural allure that came with vampirism hadn't cancelled out the need for it, my new Keja allure would have.

Following all that, I was helped into lacy, raunchy underwear that Fletcher had chosen. The bloke knew no boundaries! Lastly, my dress and shoes were carefully slipped on and fastened.

"Go on, have a look," urged Fletcher, giving me a gentle shove toward the mirror.

Hesitant – I wasn't sure why, maybe it was all the anticipation – I walked toward the mirror. My reflection startled the living shit out of me. It wasn't that I didn't look like me. I did. But I'd never really thought of myself as girly. Never been one of those kids who dressed up like a princess or played 'weddings'. As such, I'd never seen myself look elegant and 'voguish' as Fletcher kept saying.

"I am a genius," declared Fletcher.

"No humility in you, is there."

"Radiant and elegant, but also sexy without being distasteful. Happy?"

"I will be when it's time to go."

"Then you'll be delighted to hear that they're ready when you are," announced Norm as he entered. He smiled affectionately. "Oh look at you!"

"Gorgeous, isn't she," said Fletcher.

Norm kissed my cheek. "You look beautiful, sweetheart." His eyes twinkled as he added, "Jared looks hot as hell, by the way." That made me more eager to see him.

Fletcher offered me his arm. "Ready?"

Taking a deep breath, I threaded my arm through his and allowed him to lead me out of the bedroom. The female Kejas all showered me with compliments – all of which made me uncomfortable as I simply wasn't used to them – and wished me good luck. I was going to need it if I had any hope of not tripping in these high-heeled shoes.

Somehow I managed to make it down the stairs without breaking my neck – that might have been a lot to do with having Fletcher on one side of me and Norm on the other. I got a bit of a shock when I stepped out of my apartment building to find all the residents of The Hollow gathered around, smiling. Although most of them wouldn't be at the ceremony itself, they would be attending the after party.

Feeling awkward about all the attention, I merely waved and returned their smiles as I walked through the path between the hordes. When we finally made it through the front door of Antonio's mansion, we found him and his guards waiting. Vampires didn't do the whole 'giving the bride away' thing, but for him to escort me to Jared would be a symbol that he approved of, and blessed, the Binding. He gave me a fatherly smile. "Sam, you look—"

"Don't do it. The compliments are making me uncomfortable." He didn't look surprised by my words. I kissed Fletcher on the cheek. "Thanks for everything, you camp sod."

Fletcher laughed delightedly. "You're welcome, luv. Now go make him faint."

Winking at me, Norm followed Fletcher as they hurried down the hallway.

Antonio sighed, shaking his head. "You look almost as edgy as Jared. I will say to you what I have been saying to him for the past few hours. Relax. This is your Binding. Enjoy it."

"All right Yoda, enough with the wise words; let's do this."

Arm in arm, we walked down the hallway and took a right turn when we reached the open doors that led to the bat pool. As we stepped out into the warm night, I gasped. A trail of pink and red rose petals, bordered with tiki torches, marked the walkway to the floral arch on the beach up ahead. Standing there with the Prelate — who was basically a vampire minister — was Jared looking striking, enticing, and absolutely edible in a white open-necked shirt and a tan linen suit.

On either side of the walkway, the guests rose from the chairs that had been adorned in white ruffled covers and aqua bows. All of the guests – even Moaning Marcia – smiled. I could hear all the whispered compliments even from here, and was glad when soft music began to play and drown them out.

When Antonio and I came to the fringe of the beach, I removed my high-heeled shoes and kicked them aside. They wouldn't get me very far on sand. I was so focused on Jared that I almost didn't notice the huge object near the walkway. Realising what it was, I gaped. "The Tower of London." The seven-foot high sand sculpture was so unbelievably detailed, it was absolutely amazing.

"I thought you might like to have a bit of 'home' at your ceremony." Antonio swept a hand, gesturing for me to look around.

When I did, I gasped again. Dotted around the walkway and bordering the chairs were several sand sculptures of London monuments. Westminster Abbey, Buckingham Palace, Big Ben, The London Eye, the 02 Arena, the Royal Albert Hall, Globe Theatre, St. Paul's Cathedral, and the Eros Statue.

"A friend of mine has an affinity to sand," Antonio told me. "He is very difficult to track down, as he is very much a loner. But eventually I managed to find him and I had him create these especially for you. Think of them as my Binding gift to you."

Surprising him a little, I hugged him. He might be a big, bad, powerful vampire, but he was all squishy on the inside. "Thank you. I love them."

Locking eyes with Jared, I began to cover the distance left between us. On the way, I caught sight of my squad. They each gave me a beaming grin, and then opened their jackets. Pinned to each of their shirts was a sign that said 'Run'. Squashing my amused smile, I rolled my eyes at their immaturity. Of course Jared hadn't missed their little joke and he shot them all a playful scowl that they appeared to find hilarious.

With each step I took toward him, the knot in my stomach went tighter and tighter. Not with dread, but with excitement. It was the same excitement that I could sense in him. Finally reaching him, I placed my hand in the one he offered me, accepting Antonio's peck on the cheek. The powerful Keja went to sit between Luther and Evan on the front row. My very-soon-to-be-brother-in-law gave me a wink, while Luther gave me a respectful nod.

Turning my attention back to Jared again, I smiled one of those idiotic Barbie-like smiles. I seriously couldn't stop smiling, and the more I tried to drop it, the wider it got.

You look absolutely stunning, Jared told me.

Ah, bless him. I knew he wasn't great with compliments. *You look absolutely edible.*

His grin widened. Ready, we then turned to face the Prelate. Hearing a series of laughs behind us, I swerved around, curious. Fletcher, shaking with laughter, pointed at Jared. It was only then that I realised a piece of paper had been stuck to his back that said 'Help Me'. No prizes for guessing who was responsible for that – particularly since all ten of them were looking everywhere but at me, even as they laughed.

Snatching it from his blazer, I gestured for Evan to grab it. He quickly came forward and took it, fighting to shrink his smile. It didn't work. Fighting my own smile, I turned back to the Prelate.

I'll get the assholes back for that. Jared sounded close to laughing himself.

Just then, the Prelate – who didn't look impressed – began to speak. Not that I understood a word. What I'd learned from Luther in advance was that the entire thing would be spoken in Latin. Basically, the Prelate said a ritual speech before the vows. Apparently, the general gist was that our death as a human was not the end for us, as vampires, but the beginning of something new; that to find someone to spend our immortal lives with was a special thing that should not be overlooked or taken for granted, but welcomed and valued above all else. It was sort of sweet, actually.

THE BITE THAT BINDS

And the great thing about Binding ceremonies – well, great for people like me who didn't like cheesy stuff – was that you didn't have to recite a string of vows. After the Prelate asked in Latin if you agreed to love, protect, treasure, comfort, support, laugh with, and forsake all others, in good times and in bad, you simply answered, "ita vero", which was Latin's roundabout way of saying 'yes'.

So Jared and I remained quiet as the Prelate spoke. Despite not understanding him, I was quite enjoying listening to the flow of Latin. When he gestured for Jared and me to join hands, we did as Luther had previously instructed; we joined our palms together and then spread our fingers so that we could thread them through each other's. Rather than close our fingers, we kept them pointing upwards, so that we had created a 'V'.

Finally, he then began addressing Jared, who responded, "ita vero".

Well thank bloody God for that. I wasn't too proud to say that I'd still had my worries that he might back out.

As if he'd sensed that, he said, *Never*.

When it came time for me to respond to the Prelate, I said, "ita vero". I could have been mistaken, but it looked like Jared breathed a sigh of relief.

Only the fact that the Prelate was holding our wrists in place stopped me from wrapping my arms around Jared when his mouth met mine, giving me a drugging kiss followed by a sharp bite to my bottom lip. He took only one sip of blood before pulling back, giving me a chance to return the bite and take a sip of his own blood.

If the Prelate hadn't still been holding our hands in place, I most likely would have backed away, on guard, when a breeze suddenly began to build around us.

It's okay, it's supposed to happen.

It would have been nice if Luther had mentioned this part. Trusting Jared, I remained still and quashed my anxiety. As if that cleared the mental pathway, the psychic connection suddenly snapped into place. I'd expected it to be similar to the link I'd had with my Sire; for Jared to be a small presence in the back of my mind. But it wasn't like that at all. It was almost like I now had an extra sense, and that sense was totally focused on Jared – on his mood, his welfare, his whereabouts, his emotions, hell, even his vitals.

Pulling me from my musings, heat suddenly spread along my third finger. I had to resist the urge to snatch my hand back at the sensation of someone scraping at the base of my finger with a sharp nail. Then, where a wedding ring might have been, was a black, intricate, beautiful, and almost Celtic-like knot around my finger. The exact same one circled Jared's ring finger. Touching mine, I realised that although it was much like a tattoo, it was also bumpy. Like brail.

Knots are different for each couple, Jared told me. *Yours won't match anyone's but mine, and vice versa.*

Now I understood why Luther hadn't told me. He'd known I'd find this kind of nice, and he'd wanted me to have the surprise. Happily accepting Jared's kiss, I said, *I love it.*

Good, because it will never come off, never fade, never alter in any way.

As the Prelate then made some sort of gesture, the guests rose from their seats and clapped. Oh. It was over.

"And now for the feast," announced Antonio.

(Jared)

The Binding feast was taking place in the grand garden of Antonio's mansion. The numerous tables circled the space that had been designated to be the 'dance floor'. Seated with Sam and I on what was the main table were Antonio, Evan, Luther, Sebastian, Wes, and Lena. Although the garden had been decorated beautifully with torches, candles, butterfly lights, and a huge banner, I was too distracted by Sam to truly appreciate any of it.

She was absolutely enchanting, and that was nothing to do with her new Keja allure. It was because she was the most amazing creature ever. I'd felt connected to her before, but now I was linked to her on a whole other level. This new sense I had was totally attuned to her and only her. I couldn't just feel her emotions, I could feel *her* – her heartbeat, her general mood, her thirst level, her energy level, and – best of all – I'd always know exactly where she was. No one could steal and hide her from me again. Not ever.

When Antonio slowly rose from his chair, champagne flute in hand, all the chattering stopped. "Firstly, I would like to thank you all for coming and celebrating this glorious night with us. I am sure you will all agree with me that the ceremony was beautiful. I felt honoured to be there. These two people are incredibly special in many ways. Both are independent, strong-willed, inspiring characters who I, just like many others here at The Hollow, have grown extremely fond of. And so, I was more than happy to bless their joining. I would ask you all to raise your glasses."

As they all did, Antonio looked at us. "To Jared and Sam…May you enrich each other's lives and find happiness everlasting." After everyone had sipped some of the champagne flavoured NST from their glasses, he added, "I hope you all enjoy the upcoming feast, but before it begins, I wish to hand you over to Evan."

Oh, great. When my brother stood wearing one of his smirks, I quietly groaned. So did Sam.

"As it is tradition that a friend of the couple gives a little speech, I thought I'd say a few words." Turning to us, he flashed us a huge grin. "Sam, I have to say you look beautiful. And Jared…well, you look all right, I guess." Punk.

Evan included all the guests as he continued. "As most of you know, Sam and Jared didn't get off to a great start. But a lot of duels and whippings later, here they are…still fighting. But I suppose that means that this big step will suit them, because I've always thought that Binding was a bit like a war – both sides think they're right, and neither wants to back down…the only difference is that you're sleeping with the enemy."

Rowan thought that was hilarious. Marcia shot her life-partner a dirty look.

"Despite all the duelling, I truly believe that Sam is perfect for Jared. She has a number of qualities that I could list, but what I really love about her is that she makes my brother smile. Not a lot of people can do that. On that thought" – he looked at me, then – "Jared, you're a lucky bastard. Sam, take pity on him, he's only eleven."

I tried not to smile, but unfortunately it didn't work, particularly since Sam was laughing.

"It's no secret that Jared is popular with the females, just as it's no secret that he once enjoyed that. But as it's clear that he's utterly devoted to Sam, I think it would be a good idea if those of you who have a key to his apartment now hand it over."

I gawked as practically every female rose and came to the main table to place a key in the glass bowl that Evan was holding up. I could feel that Sam was irritated, but when Fletcher skipped over and put a key in the bowl, she realised that Evan was just pissing around and had obviously handed out keys earlier. Laughing, she discretely flipped Evan the finger. I scowled at the jerk.

Once everyone was seated again, Evan smiled at us. "I don't think I'm in the best position to give either of you any advice since I haven't yet Bound myself to anyone, but just think of it as a football game: there'll be a lot of shouting, balls are going to get manhandled, and there'll be some hard tackles…but if you keep at it and try real hard, there'll also be smiles and a whole lot of scoring." Nodding, he then sat again on the seat beside mine as everyone clapped.

"I could hit you for the key stunt," I told him. He just laughed.

And so the lavish feast began. Rum-flavoured NSTs were passed around as course after course was served – all of which were delicious – while the same band from the yacht played a variety of songs that covered all genres. I had to agree with Sam; Fletcher had most likely chosen the music once again. Most people got up to dance. Chico and Jude danced together a few times, which drew eyes. Sam got up dancing several times but would sit her ass back down the second a ballad started – still not a fan of slow dancing. She was therefore grateful that Binding ceremonies didn't include a 'first dance' like weddings did.

Dancing not far from her were my brother and one of Bran's consorts – or 'pretend' consorts – Alora. As usual for whenever he was close, the redhead slightly resembled a flighty deer. I literally had no idea what her problem was. I'd seen the way she looked at him, seen the deadly looks she had shot any females who went near him. It took a lot to not go over there and ask what had crawled up her ass and died.

The moment the song ended, she scampered. I couldn't help chuckling. Nor could Evan, who then made his way to me.

"Not so smooth anymore, are you?" I joked.

"Or maybe I'm too smooth and it's making her flustered."

"Have you told her about Luther's vision; that she was in it with you?"

He shook his head. "That would spook her out and send her running."

"She looks close to running anyway."

"She has her reasons."

"And you're not going to tell me what they are," I quickly realised.

"Another time," he promised. "This is *your* Binding. This is about *you* and that stunning woman over there who David is drooling over."

Yeah, I'd noticed that, and I had every intention of whisking her away any second now. I knew from experience that Binding celebrations could go on past dawn and I wanted some time alone with her.

I squeezed my way through the crowds to where she was dancing with David and tapped him on the shoulder. I didn't have to say a word; he instantly handed her over to me, congratulating us once more.

Pulling her close, I kissed her softly. "Ready to leave yet?"

Smiling, she arched a brow. "Anxious to get me out of this dress?"

"Actually, I'm totally fine with you leaving it on while I bury myself inside you." I'd been imagining doing that all night long. "Come on, let's go. I want you all to myself."

"But we'll miss all the fireworks."

"I'll make you come so hard you'll see plenty of fireworks."

"Cocky bastard. Okay, let me just tell—"

"No, trust me, you don't want to tell anyone." I began leading her to one of the darkened corners.

"Why?"

"Because it's tradition for the guests to then line up for the newly Bound couple to shake their hand."

"That's a bad thing?"

"Yes, because all the guys will kiss you, and all the women will kiss me; it's an age-old thing that, dumb as it is, people still do – it's supposed to get the blood running." The only thing it would do was piss me off and make me contemplate who to kill first.

Her smile fell. "You're right, then; I don't want to tell anyone. Let's just sneak away. But first…there's a little someone I'd like to see."

I didn't need to ask who she was talking about. "We can do that tomorrow."

"You want her gone, don't you? If we do this now, you won't have to spend one more second worrying about her. We can start our life as a Bonded couple without there being any loose ends that need tying up. She'll be gone from our lives for good. Then we can concentrate on enjoying this night."

Well, when she put it like that..."Okay, let's go."

"Wait, where's Evan?"

I frowned. "Evan?"

"He's still linked to her, remember. We need Chico to use his darts to put him unconscious for a while. That should help him skip the pain."

Nodding, I led her to where Evan stood, laughing with a dark-haired Keja female – and being scowled at by Alora for it, who was sat with Bran not far away. "Magda," was all I needed to say for him to understand.

"Sorry to ask you to leave the party early," said Sam, "but we'd like to get this part over with."

Evan held up his hand, smiling. "Hey, it's okay. I want her dead as much as you both do. I want my link to her gone for good. That's better than any party could be."

"One of Chico's darts will put you unconscious until it's over."

Evan kissed Sam on the cheek, still smiling. "Make it painful." He then patted me on the back and headed for Chico.

Taking Sam's hands, I teleported us to the main door of the containment cells beneath the large mansion. One of the guards slid open the door's small window, saw it was us, and opened the door wide. Having exchanged nods with him, Sam and I followed Magda's scent as we walked down the row of cells – all of which were constructed of unbreakable glass thanks to one of the vampires within the legion who had an affinity to glass and could shape and manipulate it.

Some of the cells were empty, and some contained weary looking vampires who clearly knew this was the end for them. Eventually we reached Magda's cell. She was curled up on the floor, shaking, panting, sweating, and moaning. Brook was in the neighbouring cell, also huddled on the ground as Magda's pain tormented him through their link.

Obviously having sensed us, she opened her eyes.

Sam smiled pleasantly. "Hurts like fuck, doesn't it?"

"Fuck you, bitch," hissed Magda, glaring at Sam with utter hatred in her bloodshot eyes.

"I'd like to call you the same thing, but you don't have warmth and character."

Magda's eyes shot to me and there was a plea for mercy in them. Was she for real? When I snorted, she slid her gaze back to Sam, curling her upper lip. "He still cares for me."

Sam cocked her head. "Not getting tired of this?"

"He'll always care for me. He still feels linked to me."

"No he doesn't, silly." The mock pity on Sam's face almost made me laugh. She held up her hand, admiring the knot on her finger. Magda's eyes honed in on it, and her face quickly twisted into a hideous scowl. "I did warn you that you'd lose the long-term fight, Magda. All you had to do was let it go. That would have been the fair thing to do for Jared, considering you owe him big time. And you would have escaped this agony that you're in now. Such a silly girl."

Magda growled. "Just you remember he was mine first. He loved me first. *I'm* the one who made him."

"Yes, you did make him. And as much as I'm grateful to have him, it seems that I actually have enough goodness in me to wish that you hadn't taken his human life from him. Jared and Evan – they both deserved to live long happy, human lives. And Magda, you deserve to die. That's right, I'm going to kill you. I'm going to kill you, and no one will fucking care. But on a lighter note, you won't have to endure that pain much longer. You should thank me for putting you out of your misery. Ordinarily I wouldn't put a dog down."

"Jared," she moaned. "How can you let her do this to me!"

"Very easily, actually. As if it's not enough that you Turned my brother against his will, you toyed with me and betrayed me and manipulated me into letting you Turn me. Worse than all of that, not only did you put the woman I love through a serious amount of pain, you later kidnapped her and handed her over to those fuckers. Why you're expecting any mercy is beyond me."

Magda's expression quickly turned cold. "Then I hope you both rot in hell."

"But that would mean meeting you again. I'd rather not."

Sam stepped forward at the same time as she conjured a large energy beam and began twirling it around like it was a baton. "A small part of me is going to miss you. You know how dear you are to me." She held it up, ready to aim. "Prepare to become a believer."

And then she threw the beam, which buried itself into Magda's stomach. She screamed and shook and writhed before eventually bursting into ashes.

I turned to Sam. "Feel better?"

Her shoulders relaxed. "Yes." Her gaze then went to a screaming Brook, who was clearly feeling the effects of his link with Magda being severed.

"I'll take care of this one." Not particularly because I felt the need to put him out of his misery, but because the little bastard had played a part in taking Sam from me. That wasn't something I could forgive. So I raised my hand and watched in satisfaction as the electricity streaming out of my fingertips made his body spasm and shake until, finally, he was ashes.

Sam exhaled heavily. "I think we both got closure, didn't we?"

I nodded. Now that everyone who had hurt her and tried to steal her from me was dead, it was like a saddle of anxiety and fear had been lifted from my shoulders. I could breathe properly again, and suddenly the air seemed fresher. I didn't have to worry that she would suddenly fold over in pain or lose control of her gifts or have an attack of bloodlust. It was over; my mind didn't need to have room for anything other than how much I would enjoy claiming her tonight. "*Now* can we go home?"

When she nodded, I took her hand and teleported her to our apartment. Standing in our bedroom, we both gasped at the sight of the rose petals on the bed and the large bottles of champagne-flavoured NSTs on the bedside table. There was even a tray of strawberries and nibbles. Presumably, Fletcher had arranged for someone to bring them up for us.

I brushed my lips against Sam's as I freed her hair from the pins, wanting to scrunch it in my hands. "I don't know about you, but I'm not hungry for *that* kind of food."

In answer, she fused her lips to mine. I opened for her, like I knew she wanted me to. Her tongue swept inside, stroking mine, and sending that familiar fire through us both. I shrugged off my blazer as she tackled the buttons of my shirt. Halfway through the unbuttoning, she impatiently yanked it open and whipped it off me. Raking her nails down my chest, she sucked hard on my tongue. Little witch.

Giving in to the need to take control, to take what was mine, I made the kiss my own. Quickly, it became raw, primal, and hungry. Our psychic link made it all even more intense. I *felt* as her heartbeat sped up, *felt* as her thirst level increased, *felt* as arousal zoomed through her. I growled into her mouth, needing her more in that moment than I ever had before.

She cried out as I suddenly freed her mouth and bit down hard at the crook of her neck. Her hand held my head in place as I drank from her, drowning in the syrupy punch to her blood. I hadn't had the chance to take all that much, however, because I was abruptly shoved onto the bed. And shoved *hard* so that I was lying on the bed with only the bottom half of my legs hanging off it. Not that I found that a problem.

Kneeling above me, she leaned over and brought her mouth down hard on mine as her hands took care of my zipper. "Stay."

Like I was going to move when I knew what was coming. Anything she ever did to me felt amazing purely because it was her, but damn she was good at this.

Keeping her eyes locked with mine, she slid down the bed until her mouth was level with my cock — which, of course, was standing at attention, and had been all night. Propping myself up on my elbows, I watched – totally entranced – as she ran her tongue from base to tip, licking up the drop of pre-come from the head. She retraced her path but didn't stop at the base. Instead, her tongue continued downwards. Then she was licking and sucking on my balls, making me wait for what I wanted most…because she was a wicked minx like that.

Then she went back to licking my cock, swirling her tongue around the head and occasionally grazing it lightly with her teeth. Impatient, I bucked a little, hinting at her to stop teasing me. I thought she might ignore me since I always teased her, but apparently she was prepared to take pity on me. Tilting her head back, she sucked the surrounding energy into her mouth and exhaled a small flame of fire, heating her mouth the way I liked it. And then she swallowed half of me. *Son of a bitch.*

I knotted a hand in her hair. "Just like that, baby. God, I love your mouth." Harder and harder she sucked, taking more and more of me. "That's it, suck me deep."

She ran her tongue along the underside each time, sometimes pausing to dance her tongue around me. It was almost frightening that she knew every little thing I liked, knew exactly what buttons to push and just where all those buttons were.

And now her mouth was fully impaled on my cock. Christ. The picture she made right there like that was too much. I was going to come and I knew it. Seemingly so did Sam, because she gently bit the head of my cock. The effect of her Sventé saliva combined with the hard suction of her mouth made me feel like my entire cock would explode. "Shit, shit, shit, shit, Sam." Unable to help it, I started lifting my hips and fucking her mouth. Groaning, I came seconds later, loving that she swallowed every single drop.

Although it felt as though she'd wrung every bit of energy from me, I wasn't about to lie back while I recovered. No, she deserved a reward for that.

(Sam)

I was kind of surprised to suddenly find myself on my back while Jared scooped my breasts out of my dress. But I wasn't about to complain. A gasp flew out of me as he latched on to one of my nipples, sucking and tugging on it with his teeth. I ran my fingers through his hair, moaning as he pretty much tortured my breasts, constantly switching his mouth from one to the other.

I arched into his hand as it snaked down my stomach and reached to grab the end of my dress. Still focused on my nipples, he bunched the dress up around my upper thighs. Then he placed his hand on the inside of my knee and began skimming upwards. A millisecond later, he froze. Knowing why, I smiled. Almost instantly, he was standing upright, shoving the dress further up, and gazing down at the white stockings and suspenders. Seeing the scorching heat in his eyes, I was glad that Fletcher had talked me into wearing them.

"I have a dilemma," he announced in a deep, throaty voice, swallowing hard.

Confused, I lifted a brow. "Yeah? What's that?"

"Well, I want that thong out of my way, but I don't want to take off the suspenders." He placed his hands on the inside of my thighs and skimmed his way along the silk until he found skin. He sighed. "There's only one thing for it. I'm going to have to tear it off."

Before I could protest, the thong was in two pieces on the carpet. And his tongue was flicking my clit. To tell the truth, I hated this as much as I loved it. The thing with Jared was that he was a bloody expert at teasing me until I couldn't talk, and as much as all the sensations always felt amazing, I didn't like to wait long to have him inside me. By the almost casual way he was toying with my clit, I suspected he'd be there for a while.

I was right. It could have been over an hour later that I was *still* writhing on the bed, practically shaking with the need to come, as his tongue licked and marked and fucked me. Oh that wasn't all. He'd bit the inside of my thigh, electrocuted my g-spot, and occasionally fucked me with his fingers. But not once had he let me come, and now I needed more than his tongue and fingers. Several times I'd attempted to shove his head away, but each attempt had been unsuccessful — he'd known in advance that I'd struggle, and he'd prepared himself for it.

"Jared, I really can't take anymore." Not that I hadn't already told him this. Multiple times, in fact.

"I like tasting you."

I pulled hard on his hair, trying once again to dislodge him. No success. "I want to be fucked!"

"I know."

A swirl of his tongue inside me made me gasp. That was it, I'd had enough. I literally pummelled his back with my fists. He actually laughed.

"You want to be fucked that bad, baby?"

"Yes." That had come out sounding almost animalistic.

He forced a long-suffering sigh. "Oh all right." The cheeky little shit.

Finding himself abruptly on his back on the bed with me kneeling above him, he double-blinked in surprise. A wide smile spread across his face, and he looked way too smug for my liking. When I curled my hand tight around his dick, that smug smile melted away and became a look of pure heat. He grunted as I pumped him, teasing him. But although it would be satisfying to put him through similar suffering, I needed to come too badly.

Positioning myself above his cock, I began to sink down on him. I moaned at the feeling of being stretched and filled, at the familiar burn. I could feel Jared's tension, his need, his thirst, and how he was relishing every sensation as I continued to lower myself on him. When I'd finally taken every inch, I took a second to simply enjoy and revel in that full feeling.

Jared's eyes were smouldering when they gazed up at me, but there was also something akin to awe there. I swivelled my hips, and he groaned through his teeth.

"Shit, baby."

I did it again, and that seemed to have been too much for him. His hands landed on my hips, and then he was slamming me down on him while repeatedly bucking his hips, punching his cock in and out of me. I tried prying his hands away, wanting to ride him, but he shook his head.

"You wanted to be fucked, baby. Now you're going to get fucked."

And then I was on my back again. This time, my legs were hooked over his shoulders and his upper body was curled over mine as he ruthlessly rammed in and out of me. The position meant his thrusts were deliciously deep – which was what he wanted, I could sense. He wanted to be as deep inside me as he could possibly go, wanted to come deeper inside me than he ever had before.

So close to climaxing, I was literally clawing at his back. "Jared, I'm going to come."

"I know, baby. Do it. I want to feel it. I want to watch you come."

Seconds later, a devastating climax crashed into me and a scream erupted from my throat. Rearing up, I bit into the crook of his neck.

"Fuck." Holding himself deep, he exploded inside me, groaning my name. As if to ring out every bit of his come, he rocked a few times before finally lowering my legs and slumping. Still shaking with the reverberations, we tipped onto our sides.

When I could finally open my eyes, I found Jared gazing admiringly at the knot on my finger. I took his right hand and examined his matching brail-like tattoo.

Jared smiled. "Cool, isn't it?"

I shivered when he lightly touched the knot, surprised by the small tingling sensation. "And it'll never fade?"

"No. No matter what, it stays."

Those words should have comforted me, shouldn't they? I should have found the 'no matter what' reassuring. Instead, I found myself thinking about the downside of that.

His words were gentle. "Hey, what's wrong?"

"You'll just tell me I'm being daft."

"You probably are." He merely chuckled when I slapped his arm. "No, seriously, tell me."

Admit a fear? Not my style. But this was the person who I was Bound to, and that made things different, didn't it? "It scares me that if you ever stopped loving me, or if you felt something for someone else, I'd literally be able to feel it."

He looked at me as if he did, in fact, think I was daft. "Seriously, baby, how could you think that either of those things would ever happen? Is it because I don't tell you I love you often? It's not because I don't."

I was about to say no, but he didn't give me a chance.

"It is that, isn't it? Sam, I know I'm not good at giving compliments and telling you what I'm feeling and stuff, but—"

"No, it's okay," I insisted. "You don't have to shower me with pretty words. I don't even like them."

"Tough, you're about to hear some. I'll tell you what you are to me." He kissed along my neck as he spoke. "You're strong. Talented. Determined. Wilful. Gorgeous. Intelligent. Tenacious. Capable. A good friend. A good mentor. A good leader. You have the biggest heart. And you're mine – whether you like it or not. My crazy, stubborn, homicidal bitch."

I could tell that he meant every word, which left me totally mystified. "You really see me like that? I mean, the latter part I fully agree with. But all the other stuff…You really think that?"

He looked at me wearing an incredulous expression. "Wait a minute, I've just pushed past my difficulty with giving compliments, and you don't even believe me? Oh the irony."

"It's not that I think you're lying," I chuckled. "I'm just surprised that that's how you see me."

"Well that's *exactly* how I see you." He brushed my lips with his. "I love every inch of you. It's why I get angry with you when you're hurt and I threaten to strap you to the bed – unfortunately, you like that, so the punishment isn't a success."

"It's not like I get hurt on purpose."

Hazel eyes pierced mine. "Doesn't matter. I need you to be safe, and well, and here with me. Always."

I nodded. "Always."

"No matter what."

"No matter what."

THE BITE THAT BINDS

ACKNOWLEDGMENTS

As always, a massive thank you to my husband for all the supports he gives me and for taking over with the kids sometimes so that I can lock myself away for a little while. Of course it's not long until they come knocking on the door, but fair play to him.

Big thanks to Ruby José for the fabulous cover she did for both 'The Bite That Binds' and its prequel, 'Here Be Sexist Vampires'. Ruby, you are so unbelievably talented and I truly appreciate what you've done. I'm literally floored by how you were able to create exactly what's in my head like that.

I wish to also thank Andrea Ashby, my wonderful Beta reader, for being the extra eye I so very much need. I really appreciate all the time you put into helping me, Andrea, and I adore you for it.

And finally, a huge thanks to all my readers for both buying and taking the time to read my book. Your support has been amazing. The positive response I received for 'Here Be Sexist Vampires' made it possible for me to make this into a series, so thank you so much for that!

If for any reason you would like to contact me, whether it's about the book or you're considering self-publishing and have any questions, please feel free to e-mail me at suzanne_e_wright@live.co.uk.

Website: www.suzannewright.co.uk
Blog: www.suzannewrightsblog.blogspot.co.uk
Twitter: @suz_wright

ABOUT THE AUTHOR

Suzanne Wright lives in England with her husband, two children and her bulldog. When she's not spending time with her family, she's writing, reading, or doing her version of housework - sweeping the house with a look.

TITLES BY SUZANNE WRIGHT:

Here Be Sexist Vampires
The Bite That Binds

⊰⊱

Feral Sins: The Phoenix Pack Series, Book One
Wicked Cravings: The Phoenix Pack Series, Book Two

⊰⊱

From Rags

Printed in Great Britain
by Amazon